Also by Erin Cornia

The Chicago Series

If It Can't Be Us
The Most Perfect Wrong
A Love That Broke Us (Duet Book 1)
Duet Book 2 – Coming November 2025

*To all the widows who have had
to face the immense challenge
of rebuilding and embracing
life after the loss of their
partners. This book is
dedicated to your
strength and
resilience.*

If It Can't Be Us

A Novel

Erin Cornia

Prologue

VIVIAN

January 21

18 Months Prior

"It's been good seeing you, too."

Ugh! Gag me.

I meet him halfway and give him an awkward side hug. I had almost avoided having to talk to Creepy the entire night, but as luck would have it, I bumped into him at the food and beverage table filling up my water. Seriously, I wish he wasn't here. Creepy, aka Sean, is my best friend Sarah's cousin. I don't understand *why* she invited him; they've never even been close. I guess having your cousin as your next-door neighbor your whole life warrants an invitation. Sean's a year older than Sarah and me. In high school, he'd stare at my chest and flirt with me non-stop, despite knowing I had a boyfriend. He was like a fly that wouldn't go away, always lingering and too touchy. After I caught him pervertedly staring at me earlier, he crept his way over to talk to me, and found a way to touch me again. *Ugh.* I shake him off. I'm not drunk enough for this. Actually, I'm not drunk at all—I'm probably the only sober person here.

I look around and notice almost everyone is on the dance floor. Realizing it's getting late, I check my watch. It's 10:30. If we leave soon, we can be home by 11:30. The music is too loud, and my feet hurt. I'm ready to go. Tonight has been a lot of fun celebrating Sarah's twenty-eighth birthday, and there's nobody in this world I'd rather celebrate than her. God, thirteen years of her by my side, inseparable since we were teenagers, is something worth celebrating! But damn, after a long and busy work week, I'm exhausted. I can't resist kicking off my shoes to give my feet a rest.

Determined to leave the party as soon as possible, I scan the room for the best-looking guy. After a few minutes of searching, I spot him in a dark corner, talking to a couple of friends, laughing. He exudes swagger in his cream suit with a navy-blue shirt, a brown belt, and brown shoes.

Damn. He looks really good.

His medium-brown hair is perfectly styled with a short fade and hard part. I love a good head of hair, and I imagine myself running my fingers through that thick crop. The thought makes me smile. He takes a sip from his whiskey glass, and glances in my direction.

Busted.

Our eyes lock. I slowly and seductively run my tongue over my upper lip. He nods and mouths something that looks like "oh yeah". I smile and laugh. His green eyes stay locked on me as he raises an eyebrow and mouths something else, which I can't quite make out but am certain is naughty. A half-smile creeps onto his lips. I pull my long, dark waves forward over my shoulders, slip my shoes back on, and make my way across the room towards him. As I approach, he leaves his circle of friends to meet me halfway.

He takes my hand, smiling, and kisses me on the cheek.

"Hello gorgeous. Where have you been?"

"Hey, you… I've been stuck talking to creepy Sean." I make a pouty face. "Where were *you* when I needed you to save me?"

"Shit, I'm sorry. I got caught up with the guys, reminiscing."

"It's okay… I survived."

He leans forward and whispers in my ear, "I can't wait to take you home and get you out of this dress."

Shameless flirt

The dress was a last-minute find on ASOS, one of the cheapest cocktail dresses I've ever bought. After scrolling online for an hour, I found it on sale with free shipping, and it fit perfectly when it arrived. It's a rosy-lavender mini dress, with spaghetti straps and a plunging neckline that accentuates my swelling breasts, giving me the confidence boost I need. I am definitely catching his eye—and everyone else's.

I cock an eyebrow and scrunch up my face. "Oh, I bet!" I place my hand on my slightly bulging stomach and rub it seductively. "Is this sexy bod doing it for you?" I playfully shimmy my breasts at him.

Laughing, he wraps his arm around me and pulls me close. "You bet it is. You know I've got a thing for pregnant women, babe," he says with a wink, leaning in to give me a quick kiss. With a more serious tone, he stares into my eyes and adds, "You always look incredible, Viv. Pregnancy looks good on you. You're sexy as hell."

God, he is the best.

This is why I love Ben. There has never been a dull moment with him in thirteen years.

Ben and I met in high school when I was a sophomore and he was a junior. I had just moved from Chicago to Park City, Utah, a charming and affluent mountain town, and didn't know anyone. I was pissed at my parents for moving us across the country, but on my first day, I met Sarah in my algebra class. She introduced me to her friends at lunch, including Ben.

We crushed on each other during that first month, and within eight weeks of moving, I had my first *and* last boyfriend. I broke up with him once in college for eleven weeks after a serious lapse in judgement on my part. A brief fling with someone I met on campus (don't ask) made me realize how stupid I had been, and I called Ben, ready to get him back. Fortunately, he felt the same way, but hadn't had the balls to call me. We knew we couldn't live without each other and got married four years ago. Now, I'm almost seven months pregnant with our first baby, a girl.

Last month, I finally got past the "Are you pregnant… or do you just love donuts?" stage. My belly has firmed up and rounded out. I'm still pretty small, but I look pregnant, and my boobs have never been so big. Seriously, they're massive. Ben's loving them! I feel great, but exhaustion is real when you are growing another human inside you. Hence, the tapping out early tonight.

I look at Ben. "Would you hate it if we left now? I'm exhausted."

"Of course not, babe. You're the DD, so that makes you the boss."

"I'm probably the boss whether I'm the DD or not," I say teasingly.

"Accurate," he says. "We have a long drive anyway. Let's make our rounds to everyone and then head home." He kisses me on the forehead and grabs my hand.

We circle the grand venue Sarah's fiancé rented in downtown Salt Lake City. I don't get why anyone needs such a lavish space for a twenty-eighth birthday, but I'm happy to be here celebrating Sarah. She's found a great man—Ryan, a successful plastic surgeon who's twelve years older than her. Though we don't see them often due to our busy schedules and living in different cities, I like him. He's charming, has a great laugh, and swept Sarah off her feet. She moved into his home down in the valley six months ago, and they're getting married in May.

We make our way around the room, saying goodbye to a few friends, Sarah's parents, and Ryan, saving Sarah for last.

I find her on the dance floor, "getting low" to Flo Rida. I call out for her and she comes running over, and I embrace my very drunken friend with the biggest hug I can muster.

"Happy Birthday to the best friend I could ever ask for," I say with a cheesy grin, simultaneously trying to hold back the unexpected tears springing to my eyes.

Sigh… Pregnancy hormones.

"Thank you so much for coming! I'm excited for our lunch next week!" It's loud in here, but Sarah's voice is three notches louder than necessary.

I'm taking Sarah to lunch on Tuesday for her actual birthday.

"Me too," I say. "I'll call you tomorrow, and we can decide where to go, so I can make a resy."

"Sounds great. Drive safe and text me when you get home."

"I will," I agree. We always text each other when we get home from driving through the canyon. I'm surprised she remembered to say something in her tipsy state.

"Happy Birthday, Sarah," Ben says, hugging her.

"Thanks, Ben. Thank you both for coming. You guys are the best!" She stumbles backward and almost falls. "Whoa, Ben, are you okay?"

Ben stifles a laugh. "Yeah, Sarah… I'm good."

She is sloshed.

"Viv." She points to me and then to Ben. "Keep an eye on Ben, he's really drunk. He took birthday shots with me all night!" She's practically shouting now.

Ben looks at me with his hands up. "Guilty. I did take birthday shots with her, but not all night. I only had two."

I laugh, looping my arm around Ben's.

"Alright, friend, I'll keep an eye on him. Wouldn't want Ben getting too frisky with me." I joke, elbowing him softly in the ribs and giving Sarah a wink. Ben shoots me a mischievous glance. "See you later, Sarah!"

After one final hug, Ben and I grab our coats and stroll towards the door, laughing together. I press the elevator button.

Ben struggles to contain his amusement. "She fell backward…and then asked if I was ok," he manages between bursts of laughter.

I join him, unsure if I'm laughing at Sarah's mishap or Ben's inability to gain composure. Our laughter echoes the hallway as we wait for the elevator. We attempt to calm ourselves, taking deep breaths, but a single glance reignites our laughter. I cross my legs and crouch down, overwhelmed with the urge to pee.

"Oh my God, please stop," I manage between tears. "I might pee." The elevator doors slide open. We stumble inside, pressing the P1 button for the parking garage.

"No, seriously," I gasp, "I'm pregnant. If you keep making me laugh like this, I'll definitely pee myself."

We rein in our laughter by the time we get to the garage, but as we near the car, the urgency grows.

"You know what, babe? I'm going to run back upstairs to pee. I don't think I can hold it another thirty minutes."

"I bet you wish you had a penis right now," Ben quips, thinking he's hilarious.

"Yeah, for so many reasons," I reply. "However, I'm not sure that I'd use it in a parking garage, even if I had one. I'll hurry!" I say, turning on my heel.

"It's ok, babe. I'll go back up with you."

We make our way back upstairs and locate the restroom before returning to the car. I glance at my watch… almost 11:15.

Thirty more minutes until I can sleep.

Ben and I discuss the evening as we enter Parley's Canyon. He recounts a story told by his friend Greg, which provokes laughter from me. I tell him about my encounter with creepy Sean.

"Why does he always have to touch me?" I say, annoyed just thinking about it.

Ben reaches toward me. "Hmm, let me think," he says, his hand sliding up my thigh. "I wonder why he would want to touch you." His graze sends a shiver down my spine.

Smiling, I squirm in my seat, gripping the steering wheel a little tighter. A mix of excitement and frustration courses through me, but I keep my eyes on the road.

"Stop that," I say teasingly.

"Stop what?" He continues, gliding his hand farther up my leg until he slips a finger under my panty line, causing me to inhale sharply. A tingling sensation ignites between my thighs, making my pulse quicken. My breath hitches, and a wave of desire tugs at my concentration.

"Not now, babe," I plead, conscious of the dark canyon road ahead. "I promise we can have fun when we get home." Reluctantly, he withdraws his hand, and I exhale in relief, trying to steady my racing heart.

"Have you given more thought to baby names?" I ask, shifting the conversation to regain focus. We should've just taken an Uber or booked a hotel room downtown. Driving through this canyon at night terrifies me, even though I'm sober. It's dangerous. Even on clear nights when the road conditions are good and the weather is nice—no snow, rain, or ice—like tonight, the darkness and the winding roads still make my heart race.

"I have," he replies. "I'm leaning toward Evie."

"Do you not like Eva?"

"I do, but Evie just feels right."

"But I prefer Eva!"

"We might have to settle this with rock, paper, scissors."

"No way are we deciding like that!"

"Should we let our moms decide?"

"Ew. Absolutely not!"

Ben leans forward and turns on my 2012 playlist (senior year), cranking up the volume. A Gotye song starts playing. Ben grabs his air guitar, and I take the microphone. "You can get addicted..." We sing out together as Ben strums his air guitar. I glance his way and can't help but giggle. He returns my gaze with my favorite grin of his—the one that captured my heart.

Ten minutes out from Park City, we're in the middle of a full-blown jam session, belting out the song at the top of our lungs. While laughing and shout-singing, I notice a car approaching us quickly, swerving all over the road.

"Ben!" I scramble to switch lanes, desperate to put distance between us and the out-of-control car. My plea for help is lost over Ben's oblivious singing. "Now you're just somebody that I..." His singing is abruptly cut off as our car is violently jolted. I scream, the sound merging with the screech of metal on metal. Darkness envelops me as the impact throws me against my seatbelt.

I blink. Each movement sending waves of pain through my body. A piercing ringing in my ears deafens my senses. I hear sirens in the distance, and spiraling lights create a haze around me. I try to call out Ben's name, but my voice fails me. The silence in the car is suffocating. Crushed against the airbag, every inch of my body aches. With great effort, I manage to twist my neck to where Ben sat, and panic consumes me.

"Ben," my voice emerges as a hoarse whisper, cracking with desperation. "Ben." Tears blur my vision as I repeat his name, but there's no response. Blood and glass coincide, and as I gaze at my injured stomach, sobs overtake me, uncontrollable and insufferable. Somehow, amidst the confusion, I know that I am the only living soul in this car.

I start hyperventilating. "I can't breathe."

My raspy voice repeats, "I can't breathe. I can't breathe. I can't breathe."

I hear voices.

"Ma'am, I need you to stay calm."

I can't breathe.

My eyes are closed… I think.

"Rolled," I hear them say. *"Drunk Driver. Didn't make it. Pregnant. The baby didn't make it…your husband didn't make it."*

I can't breathe. Someone is telling me to hold on.

I can't breathe.

"Do you want to hold her?"

I can't breathe. I want to scream. I want to die.

I can't breathe. I can't breathe. I can't breathe.

Chapter 1

VIVIAN

July

18 Months Later

I can't breathe.

My body jolts upright as I gasp for breath, clutching my chest. Slowly, awareness returns and I recognize my room. I tap my chest in an attempt to slow my breathing.

"Shit." I exhale shakily.

My heart is pounding, and my shirt is soaked from sweat. I can't believe this is happening again. Despite having frequent nightmares after the accident, I haven't had any for months now.

I reluctantly get out of bed and pad across my bedroom to the bathroom, turning on the light. I face myself in the mirror. Flashes of the accident blur in my mind, overwhelming me with grief. I lace my fingers behind my head, taking slow breaths, exhaling as if I'm pushing air through a straw to calm down. My reflection muddles as tears fill my eyes and softly stream down my face.

Pleading, I whisper to myself, "Not again. Not fucking again."

I scramble to turn on the faucet, splashing cold water on my face as a moan of sorrow escapes my mouth. Giving up, I back against the wall and slide down, letting the tears soak my face. I hug my knees to my chest and sob. Images of Ben's smiling face and our beautiful baby girl…Evie, torture me, keeping me from going back to bed.

I cry until the sobs fade into quiet, my body too drained to produce any more tears. Unsure if I've been sitting on the floor for minutes or hours, I force myself to stand. Splashing water on my face once more, I dry my eyes and wander aimlessly around the house. I find myself an hour later in a spare bedroom closet, flipping through my high-school yearbook from junior year.

To the girl who turned my ordinary life into something incredible. You make every day worth living. I can't wait to make more memories with you.

I Love You,

-Ben-

I smile. I remember this day like it was yesterday. It's the day that I lost my virginity. The last day of junior year for me, and senior year for Ben. I had just turned seventeen four days earlier, and we had been dating for almost two years. Released early from school, we packed into Ben's Jeep with the top down, along with three other friends, and headed to Ben's house to *pre-party.* Our pre-party consisted of going to Cold Stone, taking it back to Ben's and sitting around. We ate our ice cream, goofed off, laughed, and talked about our future.

There were five of us—Sarah, Greg, Jason, Ben and me. We were all good kids from good families, and none of us had ever had alcohol before. Our friend Chloe was hosting a graduation party that night at her parents' estate, a ski ranch tucked in the mountains. Ben and I had talked about having sex. I knew that he kept a box of condoms in his nightstand for when we were ready, but I hadn't been. He was patient, and never pressured me.

Chloe's house was full of chaos. Her parents were away on business, and it was packed. Kids from down in the valley had even come up. There was alcohol… a lot of alcohol. We had two groups of good friends that merged into one larger group in our high school. Chloe and a handful of others were part of one group, and the five of us were part of the other.

Chloe's group was always pushing boundaries and exploring, often reck-lessly with drugs, sex, and alcohol.

The five of us made a boisterous entrance and went straight to the kitchen, saying hi to people on the way. Hip-hop was blasting throughout the house from the speakers in the ceiling. I wore a black fitted dress that was "too short," according to my mom.

Ben and Greg grabbed beers from the ice bucket.

"What are you doing?" I asked.

"We're having a beer. It's graduation day. Relax, babe," Ben said, cracking open his can.

"We just wanna try one, Vivian," Greg added.

"Do you guys want one?" Chloe chimed in and handed one to me, Sarah and Jason. We all looked at each other, knowing it was wrong; we reluctantly opened them. Ben made a toast, and we all clinked our glasses and drank. I spit mine out immediately. Sarah made a sour face but man-aged to swallow. The boys, of course, all acted cool. Ben and I made our way to a couch in one of the many living rooms. Placing his arm around my shoulders he leaned back and sipped his beer.

I giggled. "You feel so cool right now."

"Only because I'm sitting with you." He patted my knee and let his hand rest there, caressing my bare thigh. His fingertips traced a slow, de-liberate path, stirring a fire within me that grew hotter with every touch. My heart raced as I looked at him, overwhelmed by the intensity of my love and the urgent desire to be close. I couldn't wait another minute to have him. With butterflies in my stomach, I whispered in his ear, "I think I'm ready."

He gazed into my eyes and just said, "Okay. Let's get out of here."

He sat his half-drunk beer on the console table as we walked out, hold-ing hands, practically running to the Jeep. We drove to his house because his parents were more lenient about us being alone in his room. We raced up the stairs and shut the door behind us. Panting, we stared at each other, waiting for the other to make a move. A giggle slipped out of me, and I clasped my hand to my mouth to stifle it. He slowly removed my hand, cupping it with both of his hands, and gently brought it to his lips.

"I'm sorry. I must be nervous." I searched his eyes for security.

"I'm nervous too… We don't have to do this tonight, Viv."

"I want to."

"How about we watch a movie for a bit? It might take the pressure off. We can see where things go."

"Okay, but I get to pick the movie."

"Deal." He led me to his bed where I leaned against him as he wrapped his arms around me.

"Rom-com, action or drama?"

Without hesitation, he replied, "Rom-com."

We decided to watch *Easy A*. The irony was not lost on us, considering the movie's plot is about a girl who lies about losing her virginity.

Laughing, Ben stroked my hair, pressing gentle kisses on my head, neck, and shoulders. Ultimately, I gave in to the nervous sensations in my body and turned to meet his lips. We kissed for a long time while our hands explored each other, lost in the excitement of it all. Things happened so naturally. When it was time, Ben reached for a condom, and with nervous laughter, I helped roll it on. He positioned himself in between my legs and looked so sweetly into my eyes.

"I've heard this can hurt for you… the first time." His voice sounded so sweet and sincere.

"I know," I replied.

He gently inched his way in and I gasped, gritting my teeth. He paused, checking to see if I was okay. I nodded, and he continued, moving his body back and forth, his speed increasing as the heat and urgency built between us.

When we were finished, Ben lay on his back as I caressed his abdomen. I'll never forget the cheesy grin he had on his face, like he had just hung the fucking moon.

"God, I *love* you, Vivian Stone."

I looked up at him adoringly. He was mine.

"I love you too, Ben Walker."

I set the yearbook aside and pick up the stack of high school dance photos. I've never entirely understood how looking at these memories doesn't upset me further. Instead, it calms me down. Even though I ache for him to be here with me, I'm able to appreciate the times we had together.

I make it back to bed sometime around three in the morning. Sleep comes quickly, thank God, as my head hit the pillow, getting much needed rest before my workday tomorrow.

* * * * *   * * * * *

I'm in my office going over my notes for tomorrow's meeting when I get a text.

Sarah: Hey, Ryan is having a guys night tonight. You wanna come over? Get some much-needed girl time?

Vivian: Ugh! I wish, I have a date with Bentley.

Sarah: That's great! You must like him… Didn't you just go out a few days ago?

Vivian: Yeah… I do. He's cute. He seems nice enough.

Sarah: Cute and nice enough? Come on, Viv, that doesn't sound like a guy who's pulling on your heartstrings. That's it? Cute and nice?

Vivian: No…

Vivian: I'm attracted to him and he's fun. We have good conversations. So far it's been pretty easy… and he's a great kisser. I guess I'm just in my head—this will be our fifth date.

Sarah: You worried he expects you to sleep with him?

Vivian: Yeah… our date on Tuesday was short and sweet. I had to get home early to get some work done and he kissed me on the doorstep… I could tell he wanted to come in. Idk. The last time he ended up coming inside, we took it pretty far—I told you about that… I told him I wanted to take things slow—now I'm afraid he will think things have been slow enough.

Sarah: Do you want to sleep with him?

Vivian: Ugh. I don't know, friend. I've enjoyed our make-outs, and we definitely have a physical connection… I just feel like it's too soon… in every way.

Sarah: Well, just be you, hun. Try to be open and vulnerable, but at the end of the day if it's not the time, it's not the time.

Vivian: I know… thanks!

Sarah: You're welcome babe. Just have fun either way! I'll see you tomorrow morning
for our Saturday walk and coffee, right?

Vivian: Yes of course, can't wait!

Sarah sends two kissy-face emojis.

Shit.

I only have twenty minutes until I'm expected on-site at a home to meet my boss. Closing my laptop, I grab my things and rush out the door.

My boss is my father-in-law, Seth Walker. I have always had a great relationship with Ben's parents, Seth and Jane. Seth started a custom home building company in his late twenties and quickly rose to success. Walker Homes now operates in seventeen states and is consistently ranked among the top ten custom home builders in Utah.

Currently, I am finishing a big project for the Parade of Homes in Park City. I was honored that Seth trusted me enough to not only design the architecture for the home but also to collaborate with my sister-in-law on the interior design. Seth has employed both of his children: Melissa, an interior designer, works extensively in the model homes and with clients, and Ben was a very successful realtor. His dad helped him make his first million by the time he was twenty-four, when he put him in charge of selling a massive condominium complex.

I meet Seth and Melissa at the home and we walk through, critiquing the space and taking notes as we go. Melissa and I still have some last-minute finishing touches to polish up the home and bring it all together, but overall, it's almost ready for the showcase, which starts in three weeks. The home is absolutely stunning. It's a two-story open floor plan tucked up on the side of a mountain, with vaulted ceilings lined with wooden beams. The entire back wall of the main living space opens up to the outdoors and a glorious pool that overlooks the entire valley. It has a contemporary yet homey feel, and the art that Melissa picked is sensational. Seth seems overjoyed with our work, and I couldn't be more proud.

"How are you doing?" Melissa asks as we walk to our cars after Seth has left.

"I'm doing okay." I force a smile. "I have good days and bad days, like everyone else."

"You seeing anyone?"

I love Melissa, but I don't want to talk about my dating life with her. It feels weird, and the guilt eats at me. I know she means well, so I say as little as possible to appease her.

"A little. Nothing serious."

She stops walking and turns toward me. "You know Ben would want you to be happy, right?"

"Yes. I know that," I say quietly.

If I had a dollar for every time someone tells me that…

It doesn't matter how many times I hear it—it doesn't magically make me feel better.

Melissa smiles and gives me a hug. "I love you."

"I love you too."

We say goodbye and head our separate ways.

* * * * *   * * * * *

Somehow, Bentley and I make it into my bedroom, lips locked. He swiftly pulls my shirt over my head and lays me down on the bed, his hand gliding to my breasts. "Damn, you have great tits," he says between heated kisses as he rolls a nipple between his forefinger and thumb.

Thanks, Ben paid for them.

A moan escapes my lips as the rising heat in my veins gives way to the butterflies in my stomach. I trace a hand slowly down his abdomen while he kisses my neck and breathes into my ear. "I want you, Vivian." His hand trails from my breast down my abdomen. My heart starts pounding as he works the button on my pants.

Shit. Ben.

I'm racked with guilt as my brain takes over my body. Feeling as if I've lost complete control, I grab his hand while a panicked "NO" escapes my mouth.

Bentley stops abruptly. "What's the matter?"

Is that… disappointment in his voice?

"I'm sorry," I stammer. "I think I need to take things slower."

"Slower? Jesus, it's been a month."

"I know," I say, my voice wavering. "I'm not ready yet."

"You can't be serious. You're just gonna leave me like this? Will you at least finish me off?"

Is he serious?

Offended, I unwillingly scowl, "Um… no, I don't think I'd be comfortable with that."

He grumbles a "fuck this" under his breath and abruptly stands up, aggressively putting his shirt back on.

"Are you *mad* at me?" I push myself off the bed to level the playing field while grabbing my shirt as well.

He doesn't say anything as he walks out of my bedroom down the hall to find his shoes. "Let's just say this isn't going to work, Vivian."

"Okay, wow! Are you serious? You're mad because I won't have sex with you?"

What. A. Dick.

"Look, Vivian." He fumbles for words. "You're super hot, and I've been more than patient, but I've taken you out five times!" He isn't shouting, but his voice is definitely elevated as he slips his second shoe on.

"Oh, and that means you're entitled to have sex with me?" I meet his tone while crossing my arms. I'm angry. No… I'm seething!

"Whatever, Vivian, I'm not wasting any more time on you." He reaches for the door.

"Good! Go, and don't let the door hit you on the way out!" I practically shout as I slam the door behind him.

What in the actual fuck?

I slip into my sandals and wait for his car to drive off before stumbling outside, desperate for fresh air. I inhale deeply.

Bentley is a dick. I hastily walk down the driveway and head automatically toward Sarah's house.

At least I know now. Better to find out what an asshat he is before wasting any more time on him. Even better that I didn't sleep with him.

The truth is, I've only ever slept with two people: Ben, obviously, and a guy named Chris, who I dated briefly in college while Ben and I had broken up. I wasn't intoxicated, but I was tipsy, and he knew he was taking advantage of me. I wouldn't have done it if I'd been sober. I was still so in love with Ben. My heart broke when I woke up in Chris's bed the next morning, both of us naked. Nausea overwhelmed me.

Ben had been understanding. Of course, he was furious with Chris, but he told me that, as jealous as he was, it was good that I got it out of my system and needed that time to be free and explore. I'll never know what I did to deserve someone like him.

Dating, swiping right and left, getting physical with new people—this was all so new to me. I never imagined this being part of my life. I waited seven months after Ben passed before I went on my first date. I wasn't really ready, but felt like I needed to try. On that first date, I cried so hard the poor guy didn't know what to do with me. He was very respectful, kind, and brought me home. I remember he gave me a hug and told me to call a counselor.

I laugh to myself at the memory.

I waited another three months before I tried again. Having had almost a full year to grieve and plenty of ongoing therapy, I agreed to go on a date with a guy a friend at work had set me up with. That one had been uncomfortably awkward from the moment I met him for dinner. I was withdrawn, trying to discover who I was without Ben. I thought ten months would be enough time to figure it out, but that date had bombed as well.

I continued to date, needing to practice being uncomfortable. Each date got a little easier as I found bits and pieces of myself again. I got better at flirting and was laughing more frequently. They were all one-time dates, so they never went anywhere physically besides an occasional brief kiss on the doorstep.

Five months ago, I picked up the pace and made it a goal to go on one date each weekend. A few led to multiple dates, but they all ended the same way: me, panicking about the possibility of having sex with someone who isn't Ben, or someone who isn't Ben trying to have sex with me.

I reach Sarah's house, but the lights are off. I glance at my watch—it's 11:50. I didn't realize it was so late. Turning around, I head back to my house, admiring the adorable homes on my street. The night is perfectly warm, and the crickets are out—my favorite. After the accident, I moved to Sugarhouse, an eclectic neighborhood surrounded by walkable bars and restaurants. At the time, I had work projects in the southern suburbs of Salt Lake City and couldn't bear driving through the canyon. Panic attacks would force me to pull over, so I just moved. I Airbnb our home in Park City. It's a beautiful house that I designed and built with Walker Homes. Seth gave it to us at cost as a wedding gift, and even put a large down payment on it.

Being close to Sarah and Ryan has not only been the greatest thing for my healing but fun as well. They include me in Sunday dinners and constantly introduce me to new people. I have felt so much love and support from them.

I try to process what happened tonight as much as I can before turning off the lights and heading to bed.

Bentley... *Ugh. Fuck him!*

* * * * *  * * * * *

I wait for Sarah on the porch. As she approaches my driveway, I cut across the lawn to meet her, prepared to crush her spirit. She is grinning at me.

"Tell me everything!" she exclaims. Her eyes filled with hope.

I raise an eyebrow, giving her a look that clearly asks, "Are you sure you want to know?"

"Oh no, that bad?"

"Worse," I say, as I begin recounting what happened with Bentley.

We round the corner to the coffee shop, a block from my house.

"Are you joking?" she says, her voice resonating with disbelief.

"I wish I was joking, what's wrong with me, friend?"

"What do you mean, 'What's wrong with you?' What's wrong with Bentley? That's the real question. He's an ass, Viv. Only a shitty person could respond to what happened last night the way he did. You dodged a bullet, babe."

It's my turn to order. I ask for two grande lattes with extra foam.

"I know. I really do know that, and thank God I'm not wasting any more time on him."

We step aside to wait for our lattes.

"I hope he wakes up this morning with balls so blue, he looks like a Smurf."

Her comment pulls a smile from me. "I doubt that," I scoff. "He probably jerked off on the car ride home. Didn't seem like the kind of guy who could last very long… if you get my drift."

We grab our lattes when my name is called and start walking toward Sugarhouse Park.

"Could you imagine if you had slept with him? He would have spilled his load in ten seconds, and you'd be lying there thinking, 'I held out all this time for that?' No, that's not acceptable. When you find someone you're ready to go all the way with…" She grabs my hand and looks at me intently. "And you will find someone," she says fervently. "Fireworks are going to explode from pleasure. You'll lie there afterward, knowing that Ben would be happy for you, and you will be so grateful you didn't waste any more energy on Bentley or any other douchebag."

I meet my friend's eyes as we approach the park, trying not to cry.

"Thank you." I squeeze her hand. "Thank you for that." Sarah always knows how to lighten the mood and lift my spirits.

The conversation shifts to more uplifting topics: work, Ryan, our families. As we complete our loop—1.4 miles—I stop her.

"I need to talk to you about something."

"Anything," she says.

"I've been thinking about something… for about a month now. I didn't want to talk to you about it until I knew it was a possibility. This whole experience with Bentley is solidifying my feelings, but I need to know your opinion," I say wearily.

She shakes her head, coaxing me to continue. "Go on, the suspense is killing me."

"What are your thoughts on me moving… back to Chicago?"

"What?" Her voice is filled with sadness.

"I don't know. I just…" I stutter. "I can't be here anymore. I feel like I'm suffocating all the time. Everything reminds me of Ben. I thought moving down here would help, and it did, at first… but every time I drive that canyon, every time I go to Park City for work, or hell, go anywhere… Ben is everywhere! I have memories of him all over—Salt Lake City, too. I feel like I can't move forward with these constant reminders of him. Not to mention that there is a new mother on every *fucking* corner in this city, reminding me that I am not! Every day, I feel like I'm struggling to breathe." I don't bother trying to stop the tears.

"Friend," Sarah says, wiping the tears from my cheeks with her thumbs. "You don't need my approval to make this decision. You need to do what feels right for you. And if this is what feels right…" She pauses. "As much as I'd miss you, I would be so happy for you to try something new."

"But I need to know what you think, Sarah."

"Why? I support you. Period."

"Because you're a therapist. I value your opinion."

"But I'm not your therapist, I'm your friend."

"My best friend! And a therapist… Come on, pretend I'm a client of yours. What would you tell me?"

She looks at me thoughtfully. "It's a big decision, and I understand why you feel like moving away might help you heal. I'm sure you have weighed the pros and cons. My only advice would be to make sure you are moving for the right reasons. Do you know why you want to move to Chicago? Or are you simply trying to run away from the hard?"

"Ouch." I say, scrunching up my face. I pause, letting her words sink in before continuing. "I'm not entirely sure. When I first considered moving, it was definitely about running away." I exhale slowly, glancing off to the side as if searching for the right words. "But the more I've pursued it, the more it feels right. Everything seems to be aligning perfectly, like this is the path I should take." I shift my weight from one foot to the other. "I talked to Seth about it, and he said I could transfer to the Chicago office. They have a lot of work there, and are always in need of design architects." I can't help but smile slightly. "He even offered to buy a place as an investment property. We found a gorgeous condo right on the river. He'll pay to furnish it, but I get to pick everything out and can live there for free for one year as a work expense."

I stop for a moment, gazing at the mountains in the distance before turning back to Sarah. "I hate winter, and from what I remember as a teenager, Chicago is brutally cold for months, but…" I shrug, letting out a soft sigh. "I'll be right on the river, and it will be an adventure! I'm still not sure if I'm not entirely running away, but when I think about it…" My voice trails off, and as I say it out loud, the weight of my decision seems to lift, as if speaking it into existence and having Sarah's support is making it all feel right. "I'm excited, and I'll get to spend time with my friend Kara. I'm sad to leave friends and family, but worst-case scenario, it's only a year."

Kara is my childhood friend. She lived on the same street as me growing up. I've visited her every year since I was fifteen.

"I think it sounds like a great opportunity."

"Really?"

"Really."

I sigh with relief, drying my eyes, and Sarah hugs me. "When do you think you will move?"

"Mid-August. After the Parade of Homes."

"No, that's too soon!" Sarah laugh-cries. "You have to let me throw you a big going-away party. I'll rent a cool space, maybe at the country club, and we'll invite everyone." She's ecstatic.

"You don't need to convince me… you had me at 'party.'" Sarah lives to throw a party, and I don't doubt that she'll throw me the best damn party of the year.

Chapter 2

LEO

Saturday, August 19

1 Month Later

I awoke this morning with a pounding headache and someone's hand around my cock, the consequences of last night's indulgences. I search my memory for the name of the woman warming my bed.

Christy? Christina? Christine?

Shit. I don't remember. Waking up aroused is nothing new, it happens every day. Waking up to someone tending to my arousal? I'm going to savor this.

Chrissy! That's it.

A groan rumbles deep in my throat.

"Don't stop," I say with a groggy morning voice.

She murmurs in my ear, "Good morning, Leo," as she glides her hand up my chest. "Last night was fun."

Last night *was* fun. I crack an eye open and check the time on my phone. It's almost 9 AM.

"Shit." I sit up quickly and hop out of bed. "You've got to go," I say, pulling on some joggers over my bare ass and stiffie while tossing her clothes toward her.

She stands up quickly, alarmed, and starts getting dressed. "Can't get rid of me fast enough, huh?" she mumbles.

"That's not it, Chrissy." *That's exactly it.* "I have a meeting in thirty minutes." *No, I don't.*

Lies are easier than truths in this scenario. Saves everybody unnecessary feelings. I find her bra under the bed and pass it to her. She catches it and slips her arms through the straps.

"But… it's a Saturday?" she says, confused.

"Yes, and some people work on Saturdays."

I really need to start picking women for more than just their looks. Chrissy is good-looking, sure. Probably looked even better last night after a few drinks, but still, she's hot, and we tangled in the sheets for hours.

"I'm calling an Uber for you. Type your address in," I say, handing her my phone. She rolls her eyes, standing in her bra and underwear, and types it in before chucking the phone back to me, not caring if I catch it or not.

"You might be the hottest asshole I've ever slept with," she says begrudgingly.

I scoff. "You weren't complaining last night, love."

I nudge her down the stairs before she even has her dress completely pulled down. I race behind, simultaneously helping her with her zipper.

She glares at me.

"Would you like a coffee while you wait?" I ask, trying to make up for my behavior.

"Yes please." She softens. "I would appreciate that."

Damn. She looks sad. I hate being the reason a woman feels that way. When I'm with women, I strive to pleasure them and love making them feel desired. I make her a cappuccino and hand it to her in a to-go cup.

"I apologize for rushing you out so quickly. You're beautiful, and I had a great time last night."

"It's fine. At least you were a good lay," she says with a smirk. "That accent of yours is hot."

I chuckle inwardly. Being British in America definitely has its perks. "Your ride's here, love."

I walk her to the door of my townhouse and open it for her. The morning sun filters through the skyscrapers, casting long shadows on the riverwalk.

She turns on the doorstep. "Thanks," she says, "I had a great time last night."

As she's speaking, I notice a gorgeous woman a few houses down, running along the sidewalk.

"I had a great time too." I give her a brief hug out of courtesy, mainly so I can get a better look at the runner.

As Chrissy heads down the sidewalk, passing the row of townhouses, to where her Uber is waiting, the runner glances over at me and her eyes linger longer than normal. She looks forward as she passes my house, and I watch her go by, unconsciously waving to Chrissy as she walks away, while checking out this girl's ass. She has a great ass. I'm standing there shirtless, my joggers hanging way too low around my hips, when she looks back for a double take. I smile and let that soak in. When she realizes I caught her looking, she abruptly turns her head forward.

I'm about to follow her when she stops running and rounds into my neighbor's yard. The townhouse that's been vacant for three months. The for-sale sign went down a few weeks ago. I walk down my front pathway and watch her go inside.

Holy shit.

She lives next door.

My new neighbor is a complete smoke show, and we've both been caught ogling each other. I stand there, stunned. This is awkward. For the first time in a long time, I don't know how to proceed with a woman. I obviously need to do the neighborly thing and introduce myself, but being caught half-dressed with my one-night stand as a first impression… I'm at a loss. I want to meet her, but I figure it's best to let this blow over first.

I walk back inside, feeling slightly guilty for kicking Chrissy out this morning. But I have certain protocols that I follow, and not allowing women to stay past 9 AM is one of them. I'm not a total jerk, I swear. I never bring women home if they've had too much to drink, and I'm always upfront about only looking for a casual shag—never promising more than a one-night stand or even a phone number. I figure grown-ass women can make their own decisions. Trust me, I've had my fair share of rejections. It's not for everyone.

Still, I foresee a potential challenge. My new neighbor is fucking hot, and I don't sleep with women I know, especially ones who live next door, but I definitely want to know her.

I leave for London tomorrow on business, so figuring out if she's worth the trouble is a future problem for when I get back on Thursday.

* * * * * * * * * *

Friday, August 25, 6:30 PM

1 Week Later

I gather my laptop and other belongings, placing them into my backpack, then I survey the room one last time, ensuring everything is prepared for Tuesday. Satisfied, I text Noah.

Leo: Hey mate, I'll be there in about 40 minutes.

Noah: I got you. The usual?

Leo: Make it an old fashioned tonight.

Noah: Consider it done.

I arrived home from London late last night. Exhausted and jet-lagged from the quick trip, I'm going to need something a hell of a lot stronger than a bloody beer. I tuck my phone into my pocket, loop my arms into my backpack and walk to my car. It'll be a fifteen to twenty-minute drive home from the university on a Friday night, followed by a ten-minute walk to Craft's Pub and Kitchen. I can practically taste the mouth-watering steak I'm planning to order.

My trip to London had been a last-minute decision. With it being my last week off before fall semester, I almost didn't go. It had proven to be time well spent. Not only was I able to wrap up some important business deals with my father, I spent some much-needed time with my brother Andrew.

"Ah fuck," I groan to myself. Sirens flash, indicating an accident up ahead. The traffic is horrendous. I check for new routes on my maps, searching for a shorter ETA. If I turn on to Lake Street up ahead, I can avoid the majority of the traffic.

It takes me twenty-five minutes to get home. Leaving me fifteen minutes to shower, get presentable and walk to Craft's. I'll be a few minutes late, give or take.

I rush inside, shower, and dress quickly. It's too warm for a jacket, so I throw on a fitted white tee under a blue shirt-jacket and pair it with grey denim. I quickly style my hair, throw some shoes on and run out the door.

I go to Craft's Kitchen almost every Friday after my last lecture of the day. A few years ago, I partnered with my friend Michael to open the restaurant. He's a well-known chef and his cooking style is farm-to-table. All the food is fresh, local, and delicious. He didn't have the funds to open the restaurant by himself, so I offered to help him out by becoming a silent partner. I didn't—*and still don't*—know shit about cooking or restaurants, but I had the capital and his best interest at heart. Four years later and Craft's Pub and Kitchen is thriving, and remains one of the hottest restaurants in Chicago for the second year in a row.

I arrive at Craft's at 7:20. There are loads of people waiting outside. I maneuver my way through the throng to where a young, cheerful hostess greets me.

"Good evening, Mr. Weston," she says. Noah has a seat reserved for you at the bar." With a smile, she gestures toward the far end of the restaurant.

"Thanks Lilly." I wink at her while beelining toward the bar, where I can see my drink waiting for me, as well as a petite, dark-haired woman occupying the seat next to mine. There is a vacant seat next to her. I assume her date will be joining her soon or has gone to the restroom.

Approaching the bar, I catch Noah's eye. He sets down the drink he is making and shouts out, "Leo!"

"Noah!" I bellow and reach my arm across the bar to meet his in a firm handshake.

"How are you, man?" He grips my hand and slaps me on the shoulder.

"I'm good, mate. Thanks for snagging a seat for me."

"No problem. Let me know when you need me." He pounds the countertop twice with his fist, picks up a drink shaker and starts rattling it.

Chapter 3

VIVIAN

Friday, August 25, 6:00 PM

I've been unpacking and organizing all week, with online orders and furniture deliveries arriving non-stop. My hair, a messy ponytail on top of my head, has pieces falling down at the nape and stragglers hanging in my face. I'm sweaty, gross, and covered in box residue. I walk over to the thermostat and crank up the AC, wondering why I didn't do that hours ago.

I take a moment to look around my new place. Things are coming together. My new home is gorgeous, freshly remodeled, and right on the river. It's a four-story townhouse with a rooftop deck to die for. The sunrise over the river is spectacular! My front door faces south toward the water, and my morning runs are incredibly convenient—I'm just steps away from the Riverwalk.

The move happened quickly. I barely had time to order the essentials before I arrived. I stayed in a hotel for the first few days until I had bedroom furniture and basic kitchenware. Most of the gym equipment arrived today, and I've hired people to assemble it early next week.

The Parade of Homes went better than I could have imagined. It was a huge success, and my father-in-law mentioned he might even buy the house Melissa and I worked on together as another investment property.

I'm wearing a loose pajama set with matching shorts and a tank, and I've just realized I forgot to put a bra on this morning. Not that it matters because I don't have saggy boobs—I have implants, a perfect large B, small C on a good day. Ben always said they were the perfect handful. But freeboobing in a loose shirt makes me feel more sweaty and undone. Right now, I just feel gross from unpacking all day. I need a shower and to get out of the house. I decide to get ready and treat myself to a nice dinner. It'll be good for me to explore the city.

While showering, my mind wanders to the embarrassing encounter with my new neighbor a week ago. *God, he was so hot!* I had come straight inside from my run and immediately texted Sarah about him. I keep replaying it as I wash my hair. I'd turned around for what I intended to be a quick glance at his glorious body, but ended up gaping at him for a few seconds too long.

Oh Lordy, his body.

Wow.

I didn't know eight-packs existed in real life—I've only seen them on Instagram. His joggers had been riding so low that if they had slipped any further, he would have exposed the goods. I can't get the sexy V shape of his muscles, prominently pointing down to his package, out of my mind.

God! He caught me staring at him! I was practically drooling, like I was in junior high again, watching my crush in Geography class. I groan in frustration, rolling my eyes, and roughly tugging at my hair while I rinse the conditioner out.

Ugh. How do I play this out?

It's been a week, and I haven't seen him since. I pray it won't be awkward when I do. I know I'll have to meet him at some point, but I hope that the more time passes, the more it will be forgotten.

I choose a cream, sleeveless, bodysuit with a plunging V-neckline and pair it with high-waisted, loose black leather shorts. The outfit is perfect for a date with myself. Since it's going to be warm tonight, I grab my black heeled leather strappy sandals from Jimmy Choo. I switch my hair part daily and settle on barely off-center, finishing with soft waves. I chopped my hair two weeks before the move and am still getting used to it; my once long locks now brush my collarbone. Anything would have been an improvement from how I looked forty-five minutes ago, but as I stare into the full-length mirror in my bedroom, I decide that I look pretty damn good.

I walk back into my closet, reach for my black YSL bag, and stock it with my essentials for the evening. I turn to my jewelry drawer and clasp two simple gold necklaces around my neck. One has a small V for my name that falls to the center of my cleavage, drawing attention to the ladies—never a bad thing—and the other is a plain gold chain that sits two inches above it. I complete my look with a ring I had made with the ashes of Ben and Evie. It's a double-banded gold ring with an opal-like stone in the center. It's dainty, beautiful, and I wear it every day. As I slip it onto my middle finger, my eyes linger on my wedding ring. I removed it a few months ago when I started dating more frequently. It's simple; a gold band from Tiffany's.

Absentmindedly, I start to rub my thumb over its smooth surface, my mind drifting back to when Ben had planned to ask me to marry him. I'd made it clear that I didn't want any jewels or diamonds. I'm not flashy with my jewelry and love simple pieces, so while he'd had the money to buy me a big gaudy ring, I hadn't wanted one. My stomach rumbles, pulling me back to reality.

It's 6:45, and I'm *starved.* With it being a Friday night, I know there will be long wait times. I check the mirror once more and, feeling confident, I head out for the night. There's a restaurant around the corner that my friend, Kara, told me about. It has rave reviews, and after looking at the menu, I've been anxious to check it out. I step outside and breathe deeply, taking in my new surroundings for the next year.

It's a beautiful summer night, and the temperature is perfect. My Maps app says it will be a ten-minute walk from my house—a walk I'm looking forward to after being cooped up all day. I step outside, the warm breeze brushing against my skin, and start my stroll. Luckily, these heels happen to be one of the more comfortable pairs I own.

Holy shit. The restaurant is packed. I had anticipated that I would need a reservation, but with it being the last minute, I didn't attempt to make one. I squeeze through the crowd to the hostess and pray they can fit me in.

The hostess looks up and smiles. "Good evening, do you have a reservation?"

I shake my head. "Do you have open seating at the bar?" I ask hopefully.

"We do." She nods and points behind her. "The bar is behind me and to your left, toward the back. You should be able to get a seat within fifteen-twenty minutes."

"Great. Thank you."

"My pleasure. Our cocktail waitress is Ellie," she points toward a tall blonde girl. "She can open a tab for you anytime, if you'd like something while you wait."

"Thank you."

I navigate through the bustling restaurant, the clinking of glasses, laughter, and the hum of conversations filling the air. The ambient noise is a mix of soft jazz playing in the background and the occasional shout from the kitchen. It's the perfect place to lose myself in the crowd and enjoy a night out.

I walk toward the back of the bar, taking in the sleek lines and meticulous modern decor. The lighting is dim and moody, casting a soft glow in just the right places. I can't help but appreciate the aesthetic harmony of the space.

At the bar, I eyeball people's plates to see if anyone looks close to leaving. An older gentleman has a credit card in hand, waiting for his check. I flag down Ellie and order myself a glass of Sauvignon Blanc. I really shouldn't drink on an empty stomach—I'm a lightweight—but it will help pass the time.

After ten minutes, the gentleman gets ready to leave. I'm hovering, ready to dart for the seat. As he stands, the bartender throws a reserved sign down on the countertop, at the now empty seat that I have been waiting for.

What. The. Hell!

Frustrated, I glance at the couple next to the now reserved seat. They look as if they could be leaving soon. Hopeful, I wait patiently and Ellie brings me my drink. Ten more minutes, a full glass of wine, and a buzz tingling through me, I'm finally able to sit.

A drink menu is placed in front of me at the same moment an old fashioned is set down at the empty seat next to me; the invisible customer getting phenomenal service.

"Good evening, miss. My name's Noah. I'll be taking care of you tonight. Are you dining with us or just having drinks?"

"I'll be dining." He places a food menu next to the drink menu. I order a charcuterie board and browse over the menu.

"LEO!" the bartender shouts over to someone, startling me. A man approaches and takes his hand, greeting him with a British accent. I glance to my right and freeze; my heart starts to pound. *Shit.* I'm ninety-nine percent sure it's my neighbor. My oh-so-hot, good-looking neighbor, who apparently has a British accent that is sexy as hell! I listen to the two of them speak. My *God*, his voice is incredible. I didn't think he could get any hotter, but this, *this* makes him hotter. Seriously, I could listen to his voice all day. I'd let him read me bedtime stories. My mind races, trying to figure out how to navigate this encounter without losing my cool.

He settles into his seat and rolls up his shirt sleeves, revealing a sleeve of tattoos on one arm and a Rolex watch on the wrist closest to me. I try to be subtle as I take in his masculine features. His dark brown hair isn't long, but it's not short either; it's just the right length to run one's fingers through, with a soft natural wave that gives it a polished, messy look. It reminds me of a shorter version of Bradley Cooper's hair in *The Hangover*. His short, well-kept beard, more like a long scruff, frames his face perfectly, and his white shirt looks crisp next to his tanned skin. Suddenly aware of my presence, he glances over, then turns to look at me.

He furrows his brows. "You're my new neighbor?"

It's a question.

I give him a confused look. "I'm not sure," I say, deciding to diffuse the awkwardness with humor. The only way out is through, right? "I'm having a hard time placing you with your clothes on," I add nonchalantly, sipping my wine.

He chuckles, and two deep dimples peek through his beard, making me drool all the more. "Do you need me to remove my shirt? I believe you stared long enough to be able to recall every detail."

Jackass… but also, drool.

"Ha!" I scoff. "If I remember correctly, you were staring first," I challenge playfully.

He looks at me, holding my gaze, and nods, amused. "Well played." He holds out his hand. "Leo Weston."

I take his hand and shake it firmly, displaying confidence that I'm trying ever so hard to achieve.

"Vivian Walker."

"Well, Vivian Walker, it's a pleasure to finally meet you."

"Likewise," I say, grinning at him. "So…" I casually turn toward him and slightly lean against the bar. "Who do you have to bang to get reserved seating and a drink awaiting your arrival?"

"I know the chef." He sips his drink, then looks at me with curiosity. "Are people still saying 'bang'?" He smothers a laugh.

The dimples again. God, I love the dimples.

"Oh, I do." Unsure if he realizes we're quoting one of my all-time favorite movies, *Crazy, Stupid, Love*, I can't help but laugh.

He nods toward the empty seat next to me. "Are you waiting for someone?"

"Nope… It's just me tonight," I say, smiling as I lean back in my chair, feeling oddly confident and flirtatious. "Sometimes, a girl just needs to take herself out."

He swallows as his eyes meet mine. "Lucky for me," he says, holding my gaze as the corners of his mouth lift into a playful smirk.

Beautiful.

This man is fucking beautiful.

"Guess we'll see how lucky you get after a few more drinks," I respond with a wink, taking another sip of my wine.

My heart races as I realize how bold that sounded. Did I really just say that? Well, no turning back now. I just have to own it.

Noah interrupts to take our orders.

"I'll have the short rib," I say, handing him my menu.

"I'll take the ribeye, medium rare… and another one of these." He picks up his glass and swirls it, the ice cubes clinking. Noah nods and walks away.

"So." I drum my fingers on the countertop. "You're British," I say matter-of-factly.

"Am I?" he says skeptically, placing his hand on his chest. "Well done, Walker, that is quite the observation. I'm impressed." Laughing, he slowly claps his hands together.

"Shut up." Embarrassed, I playfully nudge him with my elbow. I pause for a moment, noticing the way he called me by my last name. "Okay then, Leo, tell me something about yourself."

There is an unnaturally long pause before he says, "Care to make it interesting?"

I hesitate. "Sure… What do you have in mind?"

"Will you excuse me for a few minutes?"

"Of course." I raise my eyebrows, wondering what he is about to do.

He walks off, leaving me alone. I pick at the charcuterie board, inwardly smiling. Tonight just might be fun. This may be the perfect start to my new life in a new city.

After several minutes, he reappears with a stack of cash.

"What's all that for?"

"This is the game, Walker. We each get ten questions," he says, handing me ten one-dollar bills. "You can only answer with one sentence, and you can't ask a question that the other has already asked." He grabs two fifty-dollar bills. "These," he says as he hands them to me, "are for passing. Only two passes are allowed." He then hands me a twenty-dollar bill, two ten-dollar bills, and two five-dollar bills. "These can be used for half-truths, to ask for more details about a question, or to ask a question that's already been asked. You can raise the stakes or trump the other person with more money. Whoever runs out of money first loses, and the winner keeps the pot."

I'm amused. "Okay, two things: one—what is a half-truth?"

"A half-truth can be used anytime, but… say you run out of twenties and want to pass, you can say 'half-truth' and give a vague response that is part of the truth but not the whole truth."

I nod. "Alright, second—isn't this more exciting for me? This is all your money." I laugh. "What's in it for you?"

"What's in it for me? The chance to get to know you better through a friendly betting match, which I happen to love! Plus, I'm competitive by nature. I love winning, whether there is money on the line or not. I'll go first." He places a one-dollar bill between us with a confident grin. The seat next to me is now occupied, but Leo sits at the end of the bar, leaning casually with his elbow on the counter, a glint of challenge in his eyes. There is ample room for us to play.

"Where did you move from?" he asks, raising an eyebrow.

"Salt Lake City."

"Utah? Beautiful state. I've been there a few times for the Sundance Film Festival and skiing." He takes a sip of his old fashioned. "You're up, Walker." He tips his glass my way.

I haven't been called by my last name since high school. I don't know why, but I find it endearing.

I place a dollar on top of his. "Are you from London?"

"Are you sure you want to ask that? What if I say no? Then you've wasted a question, and you still won't know where I'm from."

"Okay, I see your point." Cautiously, I rephrase, "Where in the U.K. are you from?"

"London," he says, his eyes shining with amusement. "My turn." Another dollar goes into the 'pot'.

Noah comes over with our food.

"Thanks, mate," Leo says.

"You two need anything?" Noah asks.

Leo looks at me in question.

I shake my head. "I'm good. This looks incredible."

With a nod, Leo gives Noah a look that says, *I'll let you know if I need you.* He turns back to me as I take a bite.

I let out a moan. "Oh my God, this is so good."

His expression turns serious. "Do you need some privacy?" He says it all British-like, *priv-uh-see.*

"Yes. As a matter of fact, I may need to get a room for me and this short rib."

He laughs and continues, adding to the pile of money. "What do you do for work?"

I swallow and sip my wine. "I'm an architect." His eyes widen as he lifts his brows in surprise. I'm accustomed to that response, working in a predominantly male industry.

My turn. I place my dollar in the center. "Same question."

"You have to add one of your tens or twenties to ask the same question."

I groan and place a ten in the middle.

"I'm a psychology professor at the University of Illinois."

"Okay," I say, placing another ten in the middle and giving him the same look he gave me. "I need to know more about that. Explain." I'm shocked by his answer.

"Do you want to be more specific about what you want me to explain, so you don't waste any more of your money?" he offers.

"Okay… let me think." I cross my arms and lean back. "I'm surprised. I wasn't expecting you to say that. I don't know, how often do you teach? Do you do anything else in that line of work? You know… just… explain."

"You're cute when you're flustered, Walker." He grins at me. "This coming semester, I will have a lighter load than I'm used to. I have lectures three days a week and one on Monday afternoons. On Wednesdays, I see clients at my private practice."

"That can't be all," I say, narrowing my eyes. "I feel like there's more you're not telling me. Are you giving me a half-truth?"

"Why do you assume I'm telling a half-truth?"

Because I wasn't born yesterday.

"No reason." I pause. "You don't do anything else?"

Leo emanates wealth. I grew up in Park City, practically a playground for the rich… so I know wealth. For one, my father-in-law is ungodly wealthy.

Leo's dressed in expensive clothing, wears a Rolex watch, and lives in a multi-million dollar townhouse on the Riverwalk in Chicago. Psychology professor… doesn't add up.

"You didn't ask that. You asked about my psychology profession. Is that another question?"

I raise my eyebrow. "I don't know, *Leo*, is *that* another question?"

"Touché," he chuckles, signaling to Noah by looping his finger around in the air for another round of drinks. I'm already pretty buzzed, but the food is soaking up the alcohol, and I'm drinking slowly. One more round should be fine.

His playful demeanor is infectious, and I find myself more intrigued by him with every passing minute.

"Fine. I'll give you this one for free, but no more! I also dabble in some real estate and business ventures."

"Dabble?" I echo, my curiosity piqued. "That sounds like more than just a side hustle."

He leans in slightly, lowering his voice as if sharing a secret. "Let's just say I have a few projects in London and here in Chicago. It keeps me busy when I'm not teaching or seeing clients."

I nod slowly, processing. "So, you're not just a psychology professor. You're a businessman too."

"Something like that," he replies with a twinkle in his eye. "Now, no more freebies. It's my turn," he states, placing his dollar in the pile. "Do you have any siblings?"

"Nope. Only child." I place my dollar on the countertop. "What's your favorite holiday?"

"Easy. New Year's."

I give him a look. No one picks New Year's. Literally, no one!

"What's your favorite drink?"

"Easy," I say. "Coffee."

I ponder my next question as Noah sets our drinks down. "Have you ever been married?" I ask.

"Never. Favorite TV show?" he asks.

"*Schitt's Creek!*" I blurt out without even thinking.

Leo chuckles, "Are you channeling your inner Alexis right now?"

I laugh and shake my head, but then my expression softens. "Have you ever had your heart broken?" I ask, looking at him intently.

He turns somber and breathes out slowly. "Yes, definitely yes."

Shit just got serious.

"This question doesn't count, but did you just make this game up?" I ask.

His face lights up, and I can't help but stare at him. His face is fucking incredible, and that tousled hair of his screams sexy bedroom perfection. He locks eyes with me, his dark brown gaze intense, and a slow, knowing smile tugs at the corner of his mouth.

"No. We used to play this in high school. But instead of betting money, we would bet articles of clothing. A reinvented strip poker, if you will." His mouth parts into a full smile, showcasing his perfectly straight, white teeth. "I'd be happy to switch the stakes at any time if you'd like," he adds.

"I bet you would." In the most seductive way possible, I lean forward and whisper, "It's a good thing I'm wearing underwear."

His eyes slowly gaze over my body and land on my chest. A slow, mischievous grin spreads over his face, and he whispers back, "But I see that you are down one bra," and winks.

A wave of heat washes over my entire body.

Holy shit.

I'm extremely turned on.

The glance.

The whisper.

The British accent.

The dimples.

The wink.

I cross my legs, shifting uncomfortably in my seat. I haven't felt any-thing remotely close to this in a long time.

Leo's playful teasing brings a wave of nostalgia that feels strangely comforting. It reminds me of the way Ben used to joke around, making every interaction light and fun, no matter the situation. For a brief moment, the memory of Ben's laughter and our playful banter washes over me, bringing both a smile and a pang of loss. I push the thought aside, focusing on the present and the intriguing man in front of me.

Just because I find Leo attractive doesn't mean I loved Ben any less. Ben was everything to me, and his memory still holds a place in my heart. It's okay to feel something new, I tell myself.

I excuse myself to the bathroom. My thoughts about Ben and the dull ache between my thighs are distracting… I can't think straight. *Jesus Christ*, I'm so turned on—I don't know if I can handle this.

Chapter 4

LEO

Vivian excused herself to use the restroom, and you better believe I watched her walk away. I haven't had this much fun with a woman, without it involving sex, in a long time. I have plenty of female friends, and I thoroughly enjoy their company. But I've never experienced the thrill of flirting, the fun of light banter, and genuine laughter with someone I'm attracted to, without it leading to sex. I'm in uncharted waters.

I have attractive female friends too. One of my best friends is my colleague, Meredith, who is extraordinarily beautiful. She modeled in her teens and early twenties before coming out, and decided to pursue her passion for psychology. We work in the same therapy office: I specialize in couples therapy—go figure—and she focuses on substance abuse and trauma. Once, when she was single, I jokingly asked her how much money it would take for her to sleep with me, and she responded with, "One million dollars." I was tempted to see if she'd follow through, but she later told me no amount of money would tempt her because she would rather not inflate my ego. That's what I love about her. She's brutally honest, hilarious, and fun. Plus, there's never any sexual tension because she's not interested in men, and now she's married. It's easy.

Vivian returns, sliding gracefully into her seat with a smile that could light up the entire room.

"Whose turn is it?" she asks.

"I believe it's my turn." Pondering, I rub my chin. "I've got to make it good—you're getting low on cash, Walker." Calling her by her last name doesn't come naturally, but I force myself to do it to keep things platonic and friendly. I cannot sleep with this woman.

I glance at her, a crooked smile spreading across my face. I can't believe I'm about to ask this. "What's your favorite sex position?"

She scowls. "I'm not answering that."

I lean back with a grin. "You'd better pay up."

Reluctantly, she adds a fifty-dollar bill to the pile.

"You've got to step your game up, Walker."

She rests her chin on her fist and purses her lips, furrowing her brows. She looks up for inspiration.

"Okay, I've got it." She's confident that she is going to stump me. "Why is an attractive man like yourself, who is infinitely charming, still single?" A satisfied smirk follows her question.

"Well, that's easy. Because I choose to be. You'll have to do better than that if you want to win. I'm an open book."

Frustrated, she glances at her dwindling pile of cash. "Ugh! You're infuriating!" She puts a five into the pile. "Please explain."

I contemplate how to explain without seeming like a total dick. "I choose to be single because I like being single. I like my space, my freedom, and my independence. I don't want to get married, I don't want to be in a relationship, and I don't date… anyone. I have plenty of people in my life whom I care about and love, and I've never found it difficult to find a woman to satisfy my sexual needs, so I don't need a relationship when it may ultimately fuck things up." I study her face for a reaction. At first, I see disappointment, but after a few moments, a look of vindication crosses her face. She stares deep into my eyes, baring my soul.

"Ahhhh," she says, amused, nodding her head insightfully. "So, even a therapist can be emotionally fucked up, just like the rest of us." She looks as if she just won the fucking Nobel Prize. "Your turn," she says with a sly smile.

If only she knew the half of it. My mind drifts briefly to my childhood, when two police officers stood at the front door talking to Dad.

I quickly refocus on the present. I'm stunned but determined to keep my A-game. "Wow. The guns are coming out. But I'm still winning." I continue with the topic of sex, hoping she might give in this time. "When was the last time you had sex?" I'm ready to play hardball.

"Pass." She puts her last fifty into the pile, only one twenty, one five, and four ones remain. I trump it by covering it with one of my tens.

"Trumped. You have to tell at least a half-truth, and you have to add your remaining five to the pile for giving a half-truth," I declare, triumphantly.

"Fuck that. You're totally making up rules."

"The rules were clearly stated at the beginning of the game."

She counters, "I think I should be able to keep the five if you're trumping it."

"No, that's not how gambling works. If you want to stay in the game, you have to match the bet to continue. Otherwise, you fold and forfeit the game."

"But if we were really gambling, then to trump my bet, you would have to match it with your fifty, since that's what I used to pass." Damn, she's cute even when she argues.

"Fine." I remove my ten and replace it with a fifty. "I'm willing to forfeit a pass if it means you answering this question."

She hesitantly adds her last five to the growing pile in the middle. "A half-truth?" she asks, one eyebrow raised.

"A half-truth," I solidify.

"I'm practically a born-again virgin." She leans back, folding her arms.

"What the fuck does that mean?" I throw down a ten.

"It means, it's been a while," she says with a snarky retort, a playful glint in her eyes.

"C'mon, you could fuck *any* guy in this restaurant, and you're telling me it's been so long that you're practically a born-again virgin?"

"That's right."

"I don't believe you. How long is a long time?"

"Oh, is that another question?" She gestures toward the 'pot'.

I slap my last ten-dollar bill down. "Lay it all out, Walker."

She looks up, calculating how long it's been, ticking off her fingers. "Nineteen months." She sighs out a long breath.

Un-fucking-believable. I'm shocked. Vivian is gorgeous, funny, charismatic, and just down-right cool.

"That comes as quite a shock to me," I say honestly.

"Yeah… it does for me too."

I lower my voice, giving her a teasing look. "Are you saving yourself for marriage?"

"No. It just is what it is…" Vivian shifts her weight, giving me a pointed look, her voice becoming lighter. "Moving on! It's my turn." She goes easy on me. "What makes you tick?"

"Hmmm. What makes me tick? Probably people not being vulnerable or honest with themselves or others. How many tattoos do you have?" I know she has at least one, I can see it on her arm, but I want to know what else she might be hiding.

"I have three."

I still have plenty of cash in my pile compared to hers. I put a five down. "What are they?" I ask, hoping the question is vague enough that she'll answer with what they are and where they are.

"I have this one for Utah." She points to a UT on the inside of her forearm. "A floral piece on my hip, and two butterflies on my left shoulder."

I peek behind her to look at the tattoo on her shoulder. It's two monarchs–one slightly smaller and flying just above the other. It's bloody cool. Damn, I want to ask if it means anything but need to hold on to my remaining cash.

"I like it." I cock a brow, giving her a mischievous grin. "Will you show me the one on your hip?" I know she won't, but I can't help myself. Just thinking about that part of her body turns me on.

A shy smile creeps onto her face. "Maybe some other time," is all she says. She puts down her dollar, only two left. "Have you ever been in love?"

"Yes." I answer truthfully. "Yes, I've been in love."

She's trying to figure me out, as I am with her.

We are both done with our food, and our drinks are almost empty. I have two one-dollar bills left, better make them count.

"Why did you move to Chicago?" I ask.

I can sense her hesitation, her smile faltering. She wants to pass but can't, and if she half-truths, she's close to losing.

She slowly exhales. "To move on," she says finally.

Alright, I can work with that. I practically read people for a living, but I need a bit more to paint a clear picture. I put down my last five, leaving her vulnerable.

"Explain. Move on from what?" I know it's invasive, but she can still half-truth or fold.

"If I place my twenty for a half-truth, do I lose?"

"I'd say you're in until you're forced to fold."

While placing the twenty in the pile, the last remaining cash aside from two one-dollar bills, she scrunches her face. "I'm not sure what to say."

"Say the half-truth," I offer.

"Okay… I guess I moved here to work through some stuff, you know, dealing with PTSD. You're the therapist, piece it together."

I raise an eyebrow, trying to maintain my composure.

Whoa.

Shit.

PTSD.

That's heavy.

I study her for a moment, noticing the way she's fidgeting slightly and avoiding eye contact. People don't just drop that casually unless it's a coping mechanism. Defense. Deflection. I take a deep breath, feeling a mix of curiosity and concern.

She breathes and attempts to smile. "My turn again," she says, without giving me a chance to respond.

Noah interrupts, removing the empty plates. "Do you want another round?"

I can definitely go another round, but she shakes her head. "No, just the check, please."

"Put hers on my tab, Noah."

"You don't need to do that. It's not a date."

"It's nothing," I say. "I have genuinely enjoyed your company. Plus, I get a discount."

"You got it, boss," Noah says as he walks away.

"Wait," she says, confused. "Boss?"

"Oh… right. Did I forget to mention that I co-own this place?"

She looks like she's piecing something together in her mind.

"I guess, technically speaking, if one were looking for someone to"— I make air quotes—"'*bang*' for special treatment… it would be me." I flash her a victorious grin and take one last swig of what's left of my drink.

"Very clever, *Boss*," she says laughing, tapping her wine glass. Damn, she is witty, I'll give her that. She puts a *game on* look on her face and proceeds.

"Alright, Mister"—she makes air quotes—"*I don't date,* just how many women have you slept with?" She thinks she's got me.

Laughing, I reply, "Shit. The hell if I know."

"That's not an answer!"

Meeting her stare, I shrug. "A lot," I say. "Too many to keep count, nor would I want to. Are we satisfied?"

"Not really," she replies coolly.

"Are you jealous, Walker?"

"No, I'm not jealous. God!" She's flustered and I find it extremely sexy. "I'm just trying to gather information about you, and you're being vague."

"Well, I can't give you a number because I genuinely don't know, but if you need a ballpark figure to satisfy this curiosity of yours, then I can say it's definitely well into the hundreds. Which hundreds, though? That, I couldn't tell you. Does that help?"

Her eyes go wide. "Yes, it does." There's no judgment on her face, thank God. Instead, she looks surprised, maybe even amused? I'm not sure.

"Alright," I say, rubbing my hands together. "It's my last question. Are you ready? I'm determined to win."

"I was born ready," she says smugly, crossing her arms and legs. "Bring it."

I place down my last one-dollar bill along with my last twenty and say, "You're intelligent, witty, and fucking *gorgeous*. Why are *you* still single?"

She hesitates. "I appreciate you saying that. It's really kind of you. Wow," she breathes out, her eyes widening. "You don't make it easy, do you?" She leans forward, unwavering, staring me down. Christ, her eyes are captivating.

I meet her gaze, searching those beautiful, rich green eyes with intensity. I'm struck by them. I don't want to look away. They suddenly become misty; she blinks and breaks our gaze, looking away.

"I fold," she says somberly, and kicks back the last third of her wine in one large gulp.

FUCK.

She shut down. I pushed her too hard. Scrambling for something to say to make it better, make a joke… anything, she straightens, rolls her shoulders back, and extends her hand for a handshake. "Nicely played. You drive a hard bargain… *Boss*," she says confidently, a sly half-smile creeping up one side of her mouth.

Impressed with her ability to gain composure, I take her hand, shaking it firmly. "You were a worthy opponent," I reply with a grin. "I enjoyed every minute of it, love."

"I did too," she says sweetly. "Thank you for that. I haven't laughed this much in a while. You're a lot of fun, and… I'm really glad we ran into each other."

"Me too. You were quite the surprise tonight. I didn't expect to have this much fun with my neighbor." I playfully elbow her. "My last neighbors were in their seventies, and while they were good for a friendly sidewalk chat, they didn't quite bring the same excitement to the table. They also didn't approve of me bringing *strangers* to and from the home."

"Hold on." She puts her hand up in a stop sign. They would say stuff to you about you bringing women home?"

"Oh yeah, Gary would come over, knock on the door,"—I mime a knocking motion with my fist—"and he'd say"—I alter my voice to sound like him—"'Brenda and I don't appreciate you bringing strange women into the neighborhood. You're putting us and our grandchildren in danger. You don't know these women and what their true intentions are.'" I switch back to my normal voice. "Um… yeah, I do, mate. They just want a good shag."

She laughs. "No. You're not serious!"

"Dead serious."

"Well, I guess I'm a big step-up in the neighbor department."

I let my eyes slowly wander down her magnificent body and back up again, meeting hers with a charming and playful grin. "You most definitely are."

She bites her bottom lip and then bursts out laughing. "God, you are such a flirt!" she says, giving my arm a playful shove. We laugh together for a few moments, and I take her in. She is stunning—the epitome of sex appeal. Her chocolate brown hair—similar to mine—just brushes her shoulders, drawing my eyes to her delicate frame. Her smooth olive skin has a summer tan, making me wonder if she has tan lines, and her eyes are like nothing I've ever seen: a deep, bright green. Her full lips draw my gaze, and I imagine what they would feel like against mine. And that smile, it's contagious. She's petite yet fit, with muscles and curves in all the right places. And her tits are fantastic. Our eyes meet, and I feel an electric current run through my veins. I shrug it off as just the attraction I have for her.

She raises her water glass, her wine glass now empty. "I think this calls for a toast, *Boss*."

I pick up my glass. "And what are we toasting to?"

"To being friends."

"Are we friends?"

"Are we not?" she asks, scowling. "Are you one of those men who believes that men and women can't be friends because secretly one of them will want to be more than friends?"

"No, Walker, I'd say we're officially friends. And while I *can* say I'll never want to be more than that, I'll always want to have a go with you," I say, laughing out loud at her shocked reaction.

"Oh, come on, we're all adults here. Let's be honest with each other. I find you incredibly attractive, and I believe you feel the same about me. But you're practically celibate, and I'm apparently a man-whore… We can't be anything but friends," I continue, raising my glass again. "So, cheers to being friends."

She blushes and slowly raises her glass to meet mine, a slow smile spreading across her face. "Cheers," she says coolly.

I notice the time as I glance at my watch, reluctantly realizing that the evening needs to be wrapped up. "Shit. I've got to go. It's poker night with the guys. If you're going home, I'd love to walk you?"

Not only do I want to spend more time with her, there's a part of me that wants to make sure she gets home safe. It's not just about being a gentleman; there's something about her that makes me want to protect her. Maybe it's the vulnerability I sense beneath her confident exterior.

"Yes, I'd like that. Don't we still need the check?"

"Nah, Noah will write what I owe in a logbook." I slap a one-hundred-dollar bill down on the counter and scoot it toward Noah.

Vivian stands up, watching me amusedly as I gather my winnings.

We leave Craft's. Walking side by side toward Water Street, she looks at me, "So… who was the girl?"

I give a confused look, knowing exactly who she means.

"The woman, coming out of your house last weekend," she says.

"Ah, that woman. Let's see… her name was Chrissy. She had blonde hair, a great ass, and gave amazing head."

"Oh God! Never mind, I don't want to know!" she exclaims, shaking her head.

"What? It was my birthday! I went out for a celebratory night with my friends, met an attractive woman, and brought a birthday present home for myself," I say laughing. "The real question, Walker, is why *you* don't have men coming out of your house."

"Yeah, that conversation is not happening." She pauses. "How old did you turn?"

"Thirty-five. How old are you?"

"Twenty-nine."

"Hey," I say, nudging her, "do you see that guy over there?" I point up ahead. "He's glanced your way twice. Do you want me to snag him for you? Get you a good shag?"

She scoffs, "Okay, Leo, I get it. I need to get laid. I'm well aware. Let's leave this topic here for at least a few days." She's firm, but not angry. We walk comfortably in silence as we approach the line of townhouses.

"I'm sorry," I say as we near her townhouse, "if my questions were too invasive. I hope I didn't offend; I just really like winning." I flash her a smile.

"I'm not offended. You played fairly. My problems are my problems. The discomfort is… good for me, it forces me to grow."

We stop at her door. "Spoken like a therapist," I say, admiring her insight. "Could we swap numbers?" She nods and gives me her number. I send her a text that says *Leo Weston aka Boss*.

Smiling, she reaches for the handle. "I had a really great time, Leo. This was good for me. I'll see you around?"

"Definitely. Friends, remember?" I say with a wink as I back away and turn toward my house.

Chapter 5

VIVIAN

I close the door behind me, and immediately grab my phone to text Sarah.

Vivian: OMG Sarah I just had dinner with my super hot neighbor!!!

I add three red, hot, sweating-emoji faces.

I'm giddy with excitement as I see Sarah's message turn to *read,* and dots appear, showing that she is typing.

Sarah: OMG! Shut up!!! How did this happen? I need all the deets… NOW!

Vivian: Totally random. Ran into him at a restaurant. My GOD, he's super cool and fun. I had a great time!

Sarah: That's fucking fantastic, Viv! What's he like?

Vivian: He's a psychology professor and a therapist like you. He's funny, witty, flirty, and did I mention he's sooo fucking HOT? #beavertingles lol. Oh! Annnnnnd he's British. His voice…. #hotdamn

Sarah: Hahaha beaver tings!

Sarah: STFU! British? NEED a pic ASAP. Are you going to see him again?

Vivian: I mean, he lives next door so I'm sure I'll see him around. Idk… it wasn't a date or anything… just had fun getting to know each other. It was flirty but friendly. I laughed so much! I haven't laughed that much since… well, since.

Sarah: Hell yes! Glad you had a great time. Can I call you tomorrow or Sunday and we'll chat more? Sooooooo stoked for you!

She sends a *Schitt's Creek* GIF of an excited David, which makes me laugh.

I'm exhausted. I like her last message and head upstairs to get ready for bed, my evening playing on repeat in my head. I can't help but think about Leo. He's definitely a man of mystery, and I feel excited to slowly uncover more about him. Psychologist, business owner, funny, British, extremely handsome, wealthy, and doesn't date, which is unfortunate for me. He may be the most intriguing person I've ever met, and I'm pretty sure we just friend-zoned each other.

Lying in bed, I replay him looking me up and down, whispering in my ear about me being down one bra, even the memory turns me on. I had been so aroused, I had to excuse myself to regain composure. I toss and turn, thinking about his smile, voice, dimples, laugh, his muscles, the V-shape…

"Ugh!" Frustrated from not being able to fall asleep, I rummage through my nightstand for my vibrator. My fingers finally grasp it, and I feel a sense of relief wash over me. Settling back into bed, I prepare to find some much-needed release.

I think of Leo's smile.

His dimples.

His laugh.

His muscles.

The V-shape.

His sexy voice.

My body tingles with anticipation, and I can't help but whisper, "Oh my God, yes," as the waves of pleasure take over, leaving me breathless and satisfied. I lie there, catching my breath, a mix of satisfaction and amusement washing over me.

Yep, I just got off to my new neighbor.

What is my life?

* * * * *   * * * * *

Three Days Later

I love my new office. It's bigger than my old one in Utah and has a wall of windows overlooking the city, flooding the space with natural light. It's right off Michigan Avenue, just a ten-minute walk from my house. I came in a few times last week to get oriented, set up my office, and let my boss bring me up to speed. I've only met a handful of people, but so far, everyone has been incredibly welcoming.

I have my first official meeting with a prospective client in fifteen minutes.

I haven't had much time to think of Leo today, but the weekend was brutal. I kept hoping he'd text me. The constant thinking about it makes me feel like I'm in middle school. The worst part is that I'm reacting as if I'm actually dating him, and he hasn't called, when in fact, that is not what it is at all. I shake my head and take a deep breath. I don't have time to think about this now.

My phone rings, and I see it's the receptionist. "Hi Carrie," I say, pressing the button to connect the line through the intercom.

"Hi Vivian, your ten o'clock is here."

"I'll be right out."

I bring my clients back to my office, a couple in their mid-thirties, Matt and Jessica Marioni. The meeting goes well. We go over their vision, goals, budget, and timeline. They are very likable, and I'm excited to start drafting up some plans for them.

Finishing up early, I realize I don't have another meeting for an hour, so I walk across the street to get food and bring it back to my office. I'm halfway through my steak bowl when I get a text message. My heart skips a beat.

Leo: Hey Walker, are you free for lunch tomorrow? You know, as friends…

There it is. The proof of friendship. My last name and an invite, specifying strictly friendship. I guess I don't give a shit because I check my work calendar and respond immediately.

Vivian: Hey you, I'll make you a deal…

Leo: I'm listening. What's the catch?

Vivian: Lunch for 3 questions. You answer them all, and you pick the place to eat, and I pay. If you pass on a question, then I pick and you pay.

Leo: Damn. I was hoping articles of clothing would be on the line… Loser sends nudes?

Vivian: Ha. Ha. Ha. NOPE.

Leo: Ah c'mon, Walker. Make a guys dreams come true. We WILL play that version one day. Ask your questions.

Vivian: What kind of therapy do you practice?

Leo: Marriage and Couples, mostly. I can hear your laughter from here, Walker. The irony is not lost on me. I'm a bloody good therapist though.

Vivian: #DEAD

Vivian: I thought you were going to say you were a sex therapist… you're so good at that.

Leo: Why thank you, I think I'm rather good at it myself. I can show you sometime if you'd like.

I let out a laugh, shaking my head at his audacity.

Vivian: OMG, you know what I mean.

Leo: Right… Second question.

Vivian: How many siblings do you have?

Leo: Are you trying to lose? :-)

The dots appear, telling me that he is typing, then they go away. A few minutes later, they reappear.

Leo: Two

That's odd. I expected him to elaborate, maybe tell me if they're brothers or sisters, or how old they are. But he didn't.

Vivian: Are you close with your parents?

Leo: No more family questions.

Leo: Not over text.

Leo: Ask another.

Vivian: Alright, I'll take the win for the pass. And since I've already won—what's your favorite movie?

Leo: It's a tie between "Wedding Crashers" and "Remember the Titans."

Vivian: Those are complete opposite kinds of movies. Both great though. I'll only have about an hour tomorrow. I'll look at some options around my work and let you know where. Can you do 12:30?

Leo: I'll be awaiting your text. Have a good one, Walker.

I debate whether to 'like' his text or not, and decide against it, giving myself the upper hand.

The rest of my meetings go well, and I arrive home around six. Starved, I make myself some dinner, call my mom for a quick catch-up, and then head to my little home gym for a workout. As I lift weights, Eminem's voice blasts in my ears from one of my carefully curated workout playlists. My mind drifts back to Leo, the anticipation of our lunch tomorrow lingering, making it difficult to focus.

I start thinking about what to wear. The navy dress with buttons that I can undo lower for a little cleavage, or the black pencil skirt and blouse that make my ass look great? I sigh, realizing how distracted I am. Clearly, I'm not focused on my workout.

* * * * *   * * * * *

The Next Day

I see Leo approaching as I wait outside a True Food Kitchen near my work. I'd suggested he look over the menu beforehand so we could order as soon as we sat down. He flashes me a grin that makes my heart skip a beat.

"There she is," he says, coming in for a hug.

"No smart-ass greeting? You're losing your touch," I joke, soaking in the feel of his hug.

"I come tail between my legs today. I've accepted defeat, and I'm paying for lunch."

The hostess seats us at an outdoor table. The weather is perfect today. It's hot, but with the shade and ceiling fans, it's pleasant.

"As it should be," I say. "Are you working today?"

"I had a class from eight to ten this morning, but I have the rest of the day off. Tuesdays are my short days. Today was the first day of the fall semester."

"How'd it go?"

"It went well. Classes are all rather similar each year, and I've been doing this long enough that it doesn't really create any anxiety or stress for me. I like my job."

"That's great. What made you decide to go into psychology?"

"Good question." He leans back, folding one arm and rubbing his chin with the other, deep in thought. "I've always been fascinated by what makes people who they are—individual differences, perception, what makes them tick, what they value, how they're influenced, and how these factors shape personality and character. My own introspection as a young man drove me to pursue psychology, where I could delve into the complexities of the human mind." He shifts forward in his chair. "Not just to understand others, but to help them understand themselves."

As he talks, his eyes light up with enthusiasm, and I find myself leaning in, captivated by his explanation.

"Not just a pretty face, I see," I say with a smile, unable to hide my genuine admiration.

He smirks. "Well, I had to develop some other skills, Walker. A pretty face only gets you so far."

"You're very clever, I'll give you that."

"What about you? What made you become an architect?"

"Hmm, let's see." I hesitate, unsure how to respond without bringing Ben into the picture. I decide to tell the truth, but not the whole truth…a half-truth. "When I was younger, I dreamed of becoming a famous artist, with my art displayed in fancy exhibits and celebrities lining up to buy it." I laugh. "But a boyfriend in high school, whose dad owned a home-building company, suggested architecture. He told me I could still be creative and have a secure career, and keep drawing and painting as a hobby."

I don't tell him that my boss is the same 'said' boyfriend's dad and that the company I work for shares my last name.

"And do you still draw and paint as a hobby?"

"Yeah, I do," I say, nodding. "When I have spare time."

The waitress comes over, and I study Leo as he gives his order. He's so rugged and handsome. I'm a bit stunned by how much I actually like his personality.

The waitress leaves, and he turns his attention back to me.

"What do you like to paint and draw?"

"I love landscape painting, mostly with watercolors, but I use oil paints as well. When it comes to drawing, I enjoy sketching faces. Capturing different emotions on paper gives me a feeling of fulfillment that I can't quite describe. Is that weird?"

He shakes his head, and I continue, "I turned my rooftop room into my own little art studio."

"I'd love to see it sometime."

The thought of him coming over gives me butterflies. "You're welcome anytime."

A mischievous grin spreads across his face, the one he often wears when he's being devious. It makes his dimple stand out more than any other smile he has. "Anytime?" He cocks an eyebrow. "You know, sometimes the evenings get a little lonely. I might need someone to keep me company." He holds my stare, maintaining composure, waiting for my reaction.

I break. I can't help myself. Laughter explodes from me, and I playfully toss my napkin at him. "You really are such a flirt, you know that?"

He grins, leaning in closer. "Only with you."

Our food arrives, and I realize I only have thirty minutes until I need to be back at the office.

Smiling, he starts stabbing and cutting at his steak.

"Do you have any other businesses aside from the restaurant?" I ask.

He swallows, nodding his head, and takes a drink of his water. "Yes, I own a martial arts studio in London with my brother, Andrew. We have good managers, and Andrew oversees it. I have less stake in it since I'm not heavily involved. I also co-own multiple commercial real estate properties in London with my dad and a handful here in Chicago." He says all this like it's no big deal.

"Okay, so by 'dabble', what you really meant was you basically have an empire and are wealthy as fuck?"

"My dad's the one that's wealthy as fuck. He has more money than God."

"Was being a trust fund baby hard for you?" I ask teasingly. "Is this why you have relationship issues?"

He scoffs. "Here she comes with her claws out. I do love when you get feisty. I don't have relationship issues. I just love my life the way it is. And no, it wasn't difficult being a trust fund baby. Having money makes it wildly easier to make more money." He winks and adds with a grin, "Jealous?"

He has a way of flustering me. Just when I think I've one-upped him, he dishes it back ten-fold.

"Maybe a little." I cross my arms.

It's the truth. I am jealous—jealous that he can approach life so effortlessly and sleep with whomever he pleases without it being anything but a second thought.

"I was joking," he states.

"I'm not," I say seriously.

A moment of silence passes as we each take a bite.

"Martial arts? That's random," I say, steering the conversation back. "How'd you get into that?"

"Andrew and I got into jiujitsu in our teenage years and instantly fell in love with it. I found it incredibly grounding; it always helped me achieve mental clarity and focus. It's excellent for decompressing after a stressful week, and the rigorous training keeps me in shape too."

"Oh yeah, your, um…" I shift in my seat for added dramatics. "Sorry," I scowl and shake my head in mock frustration. "I'm just imagining you again without half your clothes, and… I'm having trouble gathering my thoughts. It all makes sense now, how you're in such great shape." I give him an *I'm a badass* grin.

He leans forward. "You're walking a very dangerous line," he says softly, his eyes scanning me up and down as if he's ready to pounce. I'm not sure if I don't want him to.

There it is again. Goddammit. I'm turned on. I feel a pulsing between my thighs, my stomach fluttering with anticipation, and my breath catching.

I clear my throat, searching for something to say. "You said you have two siblings: your brother, Andrew, and who else?"

The waitress arrives with the check, and he glances at his watch. "Don't you have to get back to work?"

I check my watch. "Shit. I do."

"I've got this. You can go if you need to."

"You sure?"

"I'm sure." He stands to say goodbye and gives me a hug. "Let's do this again, yeah?"

"Yeah. Let's. Thank you for lunch." I walk away, feeling unsettled. Just when I think I'm getting close to understanding Leo, something throws me off. He seems to avoid the topic of his family, yet he did mention his brother today, and even his dad, briefly. It's frustrating, but it also leaves me wanting to get to know him.

* * * * * * * * * *

Friday, September 23

One Month Later

I'm in my home office. A satisfied smile spreads across my face as I step back to admire the blueprints scattered across the table. Each line and detail seems to fall perfectly into place, reflecting the Marionis' vision. I can't help but feel a surge of pride at the thought of presenting this to them on Monday.

Just as I'm contemplating adding more windows to the sitting room to maximize natural light, I'm interrupted by the unmistakable sounds of sex coming from Leo's house—something I'm becoming accustomed to. The rhythmic moans and occasional thuds make it impossible to focus.

"Ugh!" I groan, absentmindedly banging against the shared wall, knowing it will just provoke him.

Sure as shit, he responds with a purposeful fist bang, and it infuriates me even more.

Am I jealous? Yeah, probably. Do I wish I was having wild, spontaneous sex that wakes the neighbors? Most definitely.

I put my AirPods in and turn on one of my playlists, drowning out the noise. It's a typical Friday night, and it's not unusual for Leo to bring someone back to his house either Friday or Saturday. It's not every weekend, but over the past month, this has happened at least three times. Who knows if there are more that I don't hear. I don't ask about it. I'm not sure if I want to know.

I work for another hour before I tire and turn in for the night. I'm restless, tossing, and turning for at least an hour before sleep finally claims me.

* * * * *   * * * * *

Leo has his arms wrapped around my waist, staring into my eyes. He takes a hand and tucks a piece of hair behind my ear. I moisten my lips and stare at his mouth. He leans forward slowly, savoring every moment before our lips touch. He meets them with anticipation and longing. I return the kiss with passion and fervor. We're now in my bed, naked and passionately making love. His hands wander up and down my body, then slowly move down, down, down... My body arches in anticipation...

Abruptly, I wake up. I blink, a pulse of desire deep in my core. "Agh!" I moan into my pillow, sexually frustrated. Did I just have a wet dream? No, this was a cruel dream—a sex dream involving my next-door neighbor, leaving me needing and wanting. I tap on my phone. 5:15 AM. My alarm is set for six, and I see no point in trying to go back to sleep. I debate getting out my vibrator, but I get up instead. I put on my Lululemon yoga pants and sports bra, and walk up to my rooftop patio to do my yoga. The mornings have become chilly, but I find them invigorating.

The door to my patio faces the river. It's the first thing I see as I step into the brisk early morning darkness. It's so beautiful and serene up here.

This is definitely my favorite place to be, and I'm dreading the day it's too cold to enjoy coming up here, which will be soon. My patio is shaped like a U. On the left side, I have an outdoor dining table. In the center, just outside the door, there's a patio swing that faces the river. On the right, I have an outdoor sectional with a chaise and a lounge chair that faces Leo's patio, and behind that a small room that I turned into an art studio.

I lay my yoga mat out in the center of my patio in front of my swing. Grabbing my iPad, I turn to my Peloton app and scroll to a slow flow class. I set it on a little side table and begin. Facing Leo's patio, the memories of last night and the dream this morning plague my mind.

Getting to know Leo over the past month has been a lot of fun. He's becoming a good friend. We've shared a meal at least once a week, all while texting almost every day. We ask questions all week long via text, and I've become pretty comfortable with him in the little time that I've known him. He loves to give me shit, and I rather enjoy dishing it back to him. He makes me laugh, and out of everyone I've met here, he is my favorite person to hang out with.

I've been spending Saturday nights with Kara over the past month. She has introduced me to some of her friends and keeps insisting that I let her line me up with some of the guys she knows. I've been hesitant to agree because I feel like I'm in such a great place right now. These past six weeks have been all about getting to know myself as a single woman in a new city. I don't want to do anything to screw up my mojo.

I haven't told Leo about Ben yet. I think part of me loves that I'm not broken, widowed Vivian in Leo's eyes. I avoid certain topics and don't share many stories from my past. He's been surprisingly open with me, and I've learned so many fun things about him. He came to Chicago at twenty-two after earning his bachelor's in London, went on to the University of Illinois for his PhD, and started teaching there right after. He met his best friend Michael, the chef, through a mutual friend in college, and they lived together for three years in their mid-twenties. Classic rock and rap are his favorite genres of music, and he's just as obsessive as I am about staying in shape, working out every day. We've even run together the past two Saturday mornings.

"Focus," I tell myself. I turn my attention to my breathing, realizing I've been doing a flow for ten-minutes on autopilot. I'm in downward dog, my eyes closed with my ass in the air. Inhale. Exhale.

"You know, this might be the first time I've wished I lived on the opposite side. The view looks pretty tempting." Leo's voice echoes onto my rooftop, startling me.

"Gah, Leo! You scared the shit out of me." I proceed to do my vinyasa. "Careful what you wish for. You might end up getting a view you can't handle." I say, as I slither into an upward facing dog, giving him a full shot of my cleavage.

I catch his eyes glancing down.

"What, you didn't get your fill last night?" I say sarcastically.

He bites the side of his bottom lip and grins, turning his head like he's been caught with his hand in the cookie jar. His dimples creep into his cheeks, and it's the sexiest thing while being incredibly cute at the same time. Ben had dimples too. It's one of the things that made him so adorable in high school. As he grew older, he became more masculine, but Ben never had facial hair. Something about the dimples on Leo gives him a boyish charm underneath all his manliness.

"Alright, Walker, you caught me. Let me have it."

I grin. "So how was she?" I ask as I move into warrior two. "The whole goddamn neighborhood could hear you last night."

"I'm sensing a bit of resentment this morning. Is it that time of the month?" He smacks his lips between his teeth, trying to suppress a smile.

"Oh no, you did not just say that!" I playfully give him the death look.

He lifts his arms, feigning innocence. "Did you hear anything in particular that you liked? Because if you did… you know we can always give it a go."

That's it, my focus is gone. "Don't be a jackass!" I say, laughing and giving up on my yoga altogether. "What are you doing up so early?"

"I'm always up this early. What about you? You don't usually get up until six."

"How do you know what time I get up in the mornings?" I ask, astonished.

"I see you leave to run some mornings, which by the way is another topic in itself. You shouldn't be out that early when it's dark, running alone."

I wave him off. "It's fine. I carry a Birdie."

"What the hell is a Birdie?"

"It's a little device that sounds an ear-piercing alarm if I'm in trouble. It can also dispatch 911 and send my location to emergency contacts. Sarah gave it to me a few years ago when I started running alone."

He doesn't look convinced. "You should start coming with me to jiu-jitsu to learn some self-defense tactics."

"Isn't it like… mostly men there? I don't want to be the only girl, that's intimidating."

"You strike me as the type who can hold her own with a bunch of men. In fact, I think you thrive in that environment."

"Why do you say that?" I ask, walking to where our patios meet, separated by a brick wall.

"Because you're a flirt by nature."

Placing my fingers on my chest, I give him a look of shock. "Me? A flirt? Whatever do you mean?" Dropping my playful facade, I let my arm fall to my side. "Why don't you just teach me a few things?" I say, my voice steady and sincere. "I'm sure you can give me some pointers to keep me safe. I don't want to go to a martial arts place. Ain't *nobody* got time for that."

He ponders. "I could do that sometime."

The thought of grappling with him sends a wave of excitement through me, an electric anticipation I can't quite shake. I imagine his body close to mine, the intensity of it all.

He extends an arm, offering me his hand. "Have coffee with me?" he says sweetly, smiling. He can be so damn charming when he wants to be.

I grab his hand and climb over the wall that separates our patios.

Chapter 6

LEO

Wednesday, October 11

Six Weeks Later

"Is it rude of me to reschedule to a later date?" Vivian looks up at me from her kitchen table, her eyes searching for reassurance.

"If you don't want to go on the date, then don't go," I say, trying to keep my tone gentle but firm. "But if you're just going to keep rescheduling because you're putting it off, then just cancel the damn thing. Don't string him or Kara along. Why'd you tell Kara you'd go out with him if you don't want to?"

I stand, clearing our plates to take to the kitchen sink. We're at her house, having just finished dinner after a long day of work for both of us.

"I don't know. I have a hard time telling people no sometimes. It makes me feel guilty."

I nod. "Yeah… guilt can be tough. Do you think it ties back to something from your past?" I ask, as I scrape the dishes and place them in the dishwasher.

This is my second time over here this week. Vivian is a great cook, and we've realized how impractical it is to be cooking for one person or to each be picking up dinner when one of us can grab dinner or cook for both.

She studies me quietly, contemplating. "I've never really analyzed it. Guilt is just… part of me, I guess. Always wanting to do right by people. I've always been this way."

"There's nothing wrong with being kind, but sometimes setting boundaries is also important," I remark, stacking the plates neatly. "You've known Kara a long time; you should be able to tell her your feelings."

"Right." She pauses. "But it's hard to backtrack once you've committed, you know?"

"Are you not allowed to change your mind?" I ask, taking a seat across from her.

She considers this, drumming her fingers on the table. "Yeah, I guess you're right. I should be able to tell her that I don't want to go. But I won't." She shrugs. "Maybe it'll be fine. Maybe he'll be really hot, and funny, and nice. *Maybe…* he'll be everything I could ever want, and our connection will be so crazy good that come Sunday, I'll no longer be a born-again virgin. And then you can stop being so concerned about me getting laid." She laughs at her own joke.

I chuckle, rolling my eyes at her. "I hope for your sake that is exactly what happens!"

"That's right. Let's manifest that shit! Up top!" She calls out, putting her hand up for a high five, and I meet it with mine.

All I know is, whoever does end up in Vivian's bed someday… is a lucky motherfucker.

She's in a playful mood, so I decide to tease her while we're on this topic. "So why haven't you had sex in so long? Still hung up on an old flame?"

She gives me a playful glare. "Nope. That's not on the table for discussion tonight."

I press on, teasing gently. "C'mon, at least tell me something about this guy who has you so hung up that you've completely closed yourself off to sex. You're practically celibate." I prod, grinning.

She opens her mouth to say something and then closes it, looking down. Her silence intrigues me, and I lean in slightly.

Staring at the top of her forehead, I ask, "Was he that big of a dick?" I know I'm close to getting her to share just a tiny morsel, but also close to her shutting down and pushing me out.

"He wasn't a dick," she says, surprising me. She sighs. "He was someone that I loved… someone I loved so deeply, I don't know if that kind of love comes along more than once in a lifetime. Sometimes I think it's pointless to even try to find it again." She pauses and then adds somberly, "I'm not ready to talk to you about it, but please trust me that when I am, I will. You can stop psychoanalyzing me now."

I consider that for a few moments and search her face and body language for clues. There is no malice or anger, discounting the possibility of an affair or abuse, which leads me to believe that something sad or really tragic might have occurred. And that makes me really fucking sad.

"You're right, I'm sorry," I say. "I respect that. I won't mention it again."

"It's okay," she says, forcing a smile. "I appreciate your concern over whether I get laid." She laughs softly.

Damn, she's so good at putting hard things aside and not letting them ruin her mood. It's one of the things I like about her so much. She never stays sour. I smile back at her.

"But also, Leo, I'm not closed off to sex. For me, sex has always been special and meaningful. I feel it's something that should be shared with someone you care about. I know not everyone feels that way, and I don't judge anyone who feels differently. It's just all I've ever known. It's about what feels right for me." She pauses, searching my face for a reaction. "I guess what I'm trying to say is that I need it to be with someone I have a connection with. It doesn't have to be love, just someone I like and trust. And until I find that, I'm okay waiting."

I nod, appreciating her honesty. "I get that. Everyone has their own way of looking at things. What matters is that you're true to yourself."

Watching her open up about something so personal, I can't help but admire her. It's rare to find someone who holds onto their values so strongly. It makes me think about how different we are, and yet, how much I enjoy being around her.

She smiles, relief evident in her eyes. "Thanks, Leo. That means a lot. And until then, I've got an excellent shower head and many vibrators to keep me company." Her eyes widen playfully as she raises her eyebrows in a daring challenge.

I laugh, surprised by her candor. "Good for you, Walker." I give her a nod of approval, "I'm glad you've got a backup plan."

God, that's fucking hot.

Vivian gets up to refill her water.

"Oh, hey, I forgot to ask you," I say, following her to the counter, and sliding into a stool. "I'm making reservations tomorrow at The Red Door for Michael's birthday, the weekend after next. Do you want to come? It's a bloody cool speakeasy, just a small gathering. I'd love to introduce you to some of my friends."

"What day?"

"Saturday the 21st."

She picks up her phone to check her calendar. "Yeah, I can make that work. You sure I should go? I don't know anyone, and it seems like an intimate gathering."

"Yes, I promise you're more than welcome. It's something I've planned anyway. I know the owner, so he's reserving a table for us. I want you to come. Don't worry, it'll be fun."

"Okay, I'll plan on it."

* * * * *   * * * * *

Two Days Later

I roll over, my breathing ragged. My *guest*, Amanda, heads to the bathroom to clean up.

My phone dings with a text. It's late, almost midnight. I pick it up. It's Vivian.

Vivian: Are we on for our run in the morning?
Leo: Yes, planning on it.

Vivian: 6:30?

Leo: Do you mind going a little later? I'm "entertaining" this evening. Don't know when my guest is leaving, but I can for sure make 8:30 work.

She sends an eye-roll emoji.

Vivian: Fine. I'll see you at 8:30. Don't be late or I'll leave your ass.

Leo: I wouldn't dream of it, Walker. Go to bed, you're up past your bedtime.

I send a winking emoji at the end of the text.

She doesn't respond.

Amanda comes back to the bed, and I take my turn in the bathroom. We end up going again around one in the morning, and she leaves sometime between two and three. I close my eyes and get as much sleep as possible before my alarm wakes me at eight.

* * * * * * * * * *

"You're like Ryan Gosling's character in *Crazy, Stupid, Love,*" she says between breaths.

"What?" I ask, catching my breath as we slow to a walk, my sweat cooling my body against the cold October air.

We've been running three and a half miles together on Saturdays, running the first three before walking the last half-mile. We just hit our three-mile mark.

"Ryan Gosling's character," she repeats. "You know, Jacob, the hot guy from the bar, whose goal in life is to find beautiful women to take home and bang. That's why I use the word bang, by the way. I love that movie. That's you. Tell me you've seen it!"

"Yes, I know the movie," I laugh, remembering it well. I'd forgotten about the bang scene. "I'm not like him." I wipe sweat from my brow and push my dripping wet hair back, away from my forehead. "If I recall, he teaches an old man how to get pussy, and I don't do that." Laughing, I dodge her as she moves to lightly shove me.

It's easy to joke around with her, but there's something more there. I've never felt this comfortable with anyone so quickly. Every Saturday run, every dinner, it all feels like it's filling a void I didn't even know was there.

"Just when I think you can't shock me, you always manage," she says, gaping at me.

"Doesn't Jacob end up falling for a girl he meets at the bar? That's definitely not me either. Never going to be."

She just shakes her head, smiling as if she doesn't believe me.

She's such a cool chick. We've become good friends over the past two months, and I've loved having a cool neighbor to hang out with. Much cooler than fucking Gary and Brenda. I laugh to myself… apparently out loud.

"What?" she asks.

"Oh, I don't know. I was just thinking."

"About?"

"How interesting life is." We walk a moment in silence.

"You gonna leave me with that cliffhanger? Come on, tell me your thoughts."

"It's nothing." We stop in front of my house. "I'm just glad you moved in, Walker. I like hanging out with you." I nudge her shoulder.

"Ahhhhh… it *does* have feelings!" she says, nudging me back.

"Alright, alright, that's enough sap for one day," I say, giving her a sweaty hug.

"Gross. You're so sweaty. Get off!" She pushes against me, laughing.

"So, you going on that date tonight?"

She rolls her eyes and groans. "Ugh, yes."

"Didn't have the balls to cancel?"

"No, I didn't, and I'm *dreading* it!"

"Well, you better practice saying 'no', for when he tries to get into your pants," I joke, but I'm one hundred percent serious.

"Okay, first, it's a first date. I don't expect that will be happening. Second, not everyone is as big of a perv as you, making it their life's goal to get laid by every woman they come in contact with."

I roll my eyes at her. "Oh, Walker, you truly haven't dated much since you've been single, have you? They may not all make it known on the first date that they want to get laid, but trust me, they do. *Especially* if they're on a date with you."

I mean every word I say to her. She's too gorgeous for her own good, and too sweet to know it.

"Ahh. Are you trying to tell me you think I'm pretty?" she says with a playful, snarky tone, framing her face with her hands.

"I'm serious! You need to be able to stand up for yourself. Guys can be pricks, and you're too nice. Tell me that you can stand your ground."

"Whoa. Okay. Chill, Leo. I appreciate your *big brother* concern for me, truly, I do… but this isn't my first rodeo. It's just dinner. And Kara has vouched for him; I doubt she would set me up with a total douchebag. Plus, I'll have my Birdie!"

I can't help being protective. I'd hate for her to be taken advantage of with her kind heart.

"Alright, you promise you'll be safe, yeah?" I raise an eyebrow in question.

"Cross my heart," she says, drawing an X across her heart with her fingertip.

"Alright, bring it in." I drag her reluctant self toward me, pressing as much sweat as I can against her while embracing her fully.

"God, this is so gross," she says, but doesn't pull away. Instead, she rests her cheek against my wet shirt and wraps her arms around my back.

Her body feels amazing pressed up against mine. I've always known she was in shape, but feeling her like this, so close, it's a different story. She's fit, curvy, and just… perfect. I shift slightly as I feel myself bulging against her hip, and I curse under my breath. Not now.

"Thanks for caring." She looks up. "Means a lot to me."

And goddamn, my stomach does a flip when her eyes lock onto mine.

I clear my throat. "Of course. I care about you. You're a good friend." I let go and back up a step. "Have fun tonight, Walker. I'll see you soon."

I walk inside, thinking that if I didn't know myself better, I might actually believe I was jealous of the bloke she's going on a date with.

Chapter 7

VIVIAN

"All I'm saying is that when someone has a mom that's hot as hell, they should come with a disclaimer."

His name is Nate, and he just finished telling a story from his early twenties about a blind date gone wrong. He had gone to pick her up, but when the door opened, he mistook her mother for his date because she was so attractive and youthful.

I laugh, looking across the dinner table at him. He chose a Mediterranean tapas-style restaurant, which I love, but find challenging for a first date. Deciding on dishes to share without knowing each other's preferences can be tricky. "I totally get that," I say, nodding. "My mom is a bombshell. She's a Pilates instructor, and has a rocking body. All the guys in high school wanted to hang at my house because my mom was a MILF."

He's cute, I tell myself. Not in an obvious way, but in a boy-next-door kind of way. His hair is blond with a high fade and a crew cut. He has beautiful blue eyes that light up when he laughs. He has a nice smile and a decent build. I'm not usually attracted to blonde guys, but I find myself drawn to him more and more as the evening goes on. Yes, he is definitely a good-looking human. I am pleasantly surprised to be having a good time. Nate is funny. He tells engaging stories, and I find myself laughing at them. He isn't as witty as Ben or Leo, or as good-looking, but that isn't a fair scale to go off for anyone.

Stop.

I'll never find anyone if I keep comparing men to Ben or Leo. I have to look at people with a fresh set of eyes.

The conversation has flowed easily tonight. Nate works in tech, but honestly, whenever someone mentions a tech job, I half-tune out because I know I won't understand it anyway. If I were certain there'd be future dates, I might be more inclined to grasp what he does for a living. But that's third-date material.

I glance at the tip line as he signs for the check. Good. He's not a shitty tipper. A bad tipper can be improved over time, but I can't stand a consistently poor tipper. To me, it says a lot about someone's character.

Everything about Nate looks good on paper so far. I guess I shouldn't expect less—Kara did set us up after all. She knows me, and she wouldn't waste my time with someone who isn't worth getting to know. The physical attraction is there, but I'm not sure if there's a connection yet.

We exit the restaurant, his hand on the small of my back, which doesn't bother me. I take that as a good sign.

"Do you live close?" he asks. "If you do, I could walk you home instead of you taking an Uber… unless you think it's too cold," he quickly adds.

Smiling, I realize he wants to spend more time with me. It is cold, but my blazer does a good job of keeping me warm.

I was careful with my outfit selection tonight, wanting to feel sexy without turning it on too much. I never want to overdo it on the first date, just in case we don't vibe.

I chose a black bralette under a fitted, sheer long-sleeve black shirt, tucked into dark fitted jeans, and black thigh-high boots. I polished the look with a black blazer and a black Gucci belt—a perfect outfit for fall.

"Yeah, I'm pretty close. Probably fifteen minutes. I'd love to walk," I say, feeling self-assured.

I ask him about his family, and he proceeds to explain his very large, very blended family.

"Oh my gosh, five sisters in a six-year span?" I ask, shocked. Two sisters from his dad and three from his stepmom, two of them being twins. "That's a whole lot of hormones."

"Let's just say things were never dull," he says, chuckling.

We're halfway to my house when he slows his walk to look at me hesitantly. What is that expression? Worry? Concern?

Oh, shit.

Sympathy.

All of a sudden, I know what's coming.

"So," he stammers, searching for the right words. "I hope you don't mind, but Kara told me about your situation." He seems unsure of himself.

"Oh? She did?" I look at him inquisitively. *Alright, dumbass, let's do this.*

"Yeah. She told me about your, um… your husband. And I, uh… I just wanted to make sure you were in the right mindset to be dating," he stammers. "Because I really like you. But I don't want to waste my time getting to know you if you're not emotionally ready for a relationship."

And there it is. His flaw. He completely lacks emotional intelligence.

Are people really this fucking clueless?

I try to think of some way to respond that isn't snarky.

I lost my daughter too, did you also want to talk about that? No? That's uncomfortable for you?

Fuck. I'm so angry with Kara right now. How could she? But then I think, how could she not? There's no way you set someone up with a young widow without divulging some of that sensitive information. You'd have to give them a forewarning, make sure they could handle it. Though I can't blame her, I'm pissed.

I feel betrayed.

This is *my* story to tell, when I am ready. My hell, I haven't even told Leo yet.

"Are you okay?" I hear him say over my shock. "I'm sorry if that was…"

I cut him off. "Stop." I turn my body toward him, my hand in a stop sign position, unsure what to do next.

He stares at me, confused.

"I'm sorry, Nate. You're a nice guy, but I'm not comfortable talking to you about this. Nor do I have to. I'll walk myself the rest of the way. Thank you for dinner; I had a nice time."

Leaving him stunned, I turn on my heel and take long strides to get the hell away from him and the discomfort as quickly as possible.

I'm devastated. For the first time, I think about myself through the eyes of my friends, and it makes me feel so small. I know they love and care for me, but they all treat me the same. They scamper around as if I'm fragile, afraid that I might break. My eyes get misty, and I fight the urge to cry or be offended.

All I can do is learn from this mistake and move forward. No more blind dates set up by friends.

* * * * *   * * * * *

Sunday - The Next Day

I end the call and reach for my hair dryer, feeling relieved. My mom is one of my best friends, and I tell her everything. We talk at least once a week, usually on Sundays. I know her opinions can be biased, but she is a wise woman whose advice has never led me astray. Talking to her was just what I needed after my date last night. I feel better.

She and my dad just got back from visiting my mom's family in Spain, so I had to catch her up on the past few weeks. She always asks about Leo. My mom is obsessed with him and keeps telling me to be patient because this is how her and my dad's relationship started. I mostly roll my eyes at that one. It's definitely not the same. My dad wasn't sleeping with the entirety of Boston while he was at Harvard when they met, and she wasn't a born-again virgin widow. See? Very different scenarios.

I look at the time on my phone. Shit. I accidentally slept in, and then my mom called. I talked to her with wet hair while standing in my bathrobe. Now I only have fifteen minutes until I meet Leo out front for brunch.

I love our coffee and brunch dates the most. I look forward to my coffee in the mornings more than anything, and I love breakfast food. Between that and Leo's company, it's an absolutely perfect start to my day.

Exhaling my burdens, I tip my head upside down and power dry my hair. At 8:55, I throw on some leggings, a cropped sweatshirt, and sneakers. My hair is straight today, a rare occurrence, and I didn't have time for much makeup. Just a swipe of mascara and a touch of lip gloss, but that's okay; I don't usually wear much anyway. As long as my lashes are done, I feel good. I race out the door, determined to beat Leo, but he's already there, waiting for me.

He looks at his watch, then eyes me, lifting a brow. "You sleep in, Walker?"

"I'm two minutes late!" I exclaim, meeting him with an embrace that makes my toes curl.

"Ah, I'm just giving you shit." He puts his hand on my head and ruffles my hair.

Fucker.

"Your hair is different," he says.

"Yeah, I didn't have time to curl it."

He shrugs. "I like it this way too."

"Thanks," I say, glancing his way with a smile.

"Wildberry?" he asks.

"Yes!"

"Which one? I mapped them both, and they each say a seventeen-minute walk."

"Let's go to the one that's north. I have a pickup order at Nordstrom. I'd love to swing by on the way home and grab it if you don't mind," I say as we near the end of our row of townhouses.

"North it is." He places his hand on the small of my back, and gestures to the right at the end of our street.

Wildberry is a pancake house and café that serves something for every palate. Their food always tastes fresh, and I love their skillets! My mouth is watering just thinking about them.

"I didn't hear any sexual escapades last night," I say, giving him a playful nudge. "Date night with your hand?"

He cocks an eyebrow. "Hey, at least I didn't have to wear a condom."

Smartass.

"How do you always do that?" I ask.

He furrows his brows. "How do I do what?"

"The comebacks. You're so quick and witty."

"Is that a compliment I hear?" He grins. "I'm flattered. Truly." He places his hand over his heart in gratitude, as if he just won a Grammy.

As we walk together, the conversation flows easily. It's as if we've known each other forever. While waiting for a walk signal, I breathe in the fresh air as it cools my cheeks. It's a beautiful morning. There's a chill in the air, but the sun is on full display, warming the skin on my face. I look around and up at Leo. He's tall, with the sun catching the angles of his face just right, making him look even more attractive than usual. I feel happy, and I welcome it.

As we approach Wildberry, the delicious aroma of pancakes and coffee wafts through the air.

"Oh, I almost forgot to ask," Leo says, resting his hand on my shoulder, "how was your date last night? Normally, I'd ask if you got laid, but since it's you, did you manage to run any bases?" he teases, as if we're teenagers.

We are bombarded with chaos as he opens the door for me. There's going to be a decent wait judging by the number of people here. We walk to the hostess desk and put our name on the list. Twenty to thirty minutes, that's not so bad. We find a bench outside to sit while we wait.

"So? How was it?" he asks, his hands bracing his thighs as he looks at me.

"Um… it was good… it was fine. No bases ran, wasn't feeling it."

Dumbfounded, he stares at me. "That's your answer?"

"Do you need me to repeat it again?" I ask sarcastically.

"You baffle me, Walker. That's all you're gonna give me?" He lifts his hand in an exasperated, questioning gesture. "Jesus, no bases ran? Not even a kiss? You play a hard game."

I glare at him. "What do you want me to say? That it was going great, I liked him a lot, then he asked me about something personal that he shouldn't have known about?" I ask irritably, my voice sharp as the memory stirs fresh anger within me.

"For fuck's sake. Yes! Be real with me. Now we're getting somewhere." He shakes his head. "What do you mean he asked you about something personal?"

I glance down, sighing. "Kara told him some… personal stuff. Things about me and my life that are mine to tell." I look up at him. "And mine alone."

"About your past relationship, or whatever it is that you won't talk about?"

I nod.

"And he had the audacity to ask you about it?"

"Ha. Yeah," I scoff. "And then I basically told him to fuck off and left him standing alone." I laugh softly to myself, still shocked by my own actions.

"Well, that's un-fucking-believable. Are you alright?"

I search his face, scanning his eyes for any hint of insincerity or pity, but all I see is genuine concern and respect. Keeping eye contact, my voice is barely audible. "I'm good," it comes out as a whisper. "Thanks, Leo." He doesn't break eye contact, and I feel… seen. Why is it so easy with him?

"Hey," he whispers, swiping a piece of wind-blown hair out of my face. "That was fucked up of him. And good for you, for standing your ground. You should be proud of yourself. Yeah?"

The corners of my mouth tug upward into a small smile. "You're right… I should be." It's all I can think to say, my thoughts scattering under the intensity of his gaze.

Despite this growing connection, Leo still shuts me out when it comes to any questions regarding his family. I feel like we have a mutual understanding. We both have something we aren't necessarily hiding, but aren't completely truthful about either. And I think we just know that when the time is right, and we feel ready, we will share it with each other.

* * * * * * * * * *

Saturday, October 21

The Following Weekend

I told Leo I'd meet him at The Red Door for Michael's birthday get-to-gether. He had a business dinner and was going to have to go straight from there to the speakeasy. I intentionally arrive twenty minutes late to avoid the chance of being there before him.

I'm standing outside the door, gathering all of my confidence as if it's something tangible, something I can hold in my hands. I'm incredibly nervous and uncertain as to why. I'm good with people… but these are Leo's people, and I want to make a good impression. I survey my outfit one last time in the reflection of the door. I have on a black sweater tucked into a warm taupe wool mini skirt, paired with black suede knee-high boots, showing off my legs. My hair is softly waved and parted down the middle.

I take a deep inhale, exhaling slowly as I enter the code that Leo gave me. Apparently, this place changes the entrance code daily, ensuring only those with a reservation can enter. The lock clicks, and I open the door, greeted by a hostess in a black flapper dress with a jeweled bandeau on her head. She is young and stunningly beautiful.

"Hi, what's the name on the reservation?"

"It's under Leo Weston," I say.

"Your party is this way," she says, gesturing for me to follow her. It's a decent-sized room for a speakeasy. Longer than it is wide, I take in the ambiance. It's early 1920s, the bartenders all dressed accordingly; the men in long-sleeve button-up shirts, buttoned vests, and newsboy hats or fedoras—many of them with mustaches that fit the time period—and the women in flapper dresses and bandeaus. It has a very *Peaky Blinders* feel. As she leads me to the back of the room, I spot Leo and give him a wave.

"Walker!" he shouts as he stands to meet me. "You made it!" Giving me a quick kiss on the cheek, he turns to his friends for introductions. "Everyone, this is my neighbor and friend, Vivian. Vivian, this is Michael, his wife Stella, Meredith, and Adam." I shake everyone's hands as he announces their names.

Our little corner is furnished with different styles of leather-back chairs, a leather sofa, and two round coffee tables. Meredith, who looks like a runway model, is sitting on the sofa, next to where Leo was, and the other three are in chairs. Meredith is the kind of stunning that makes you question your own confidence. If I didn't know she was happily married to her wife, I'd probably feel a pang of insecurity at the mere thought of any chance with Leo. She is that beautiful. Leo gestures for Meredith to scoot down to make space for me on the sofa.

"Let's get you a drink before you sit, love," Leo says, taking my arm and guiding me to the bar. "We have a waitress, but I don't bloody know where she is."

We inch our way to the bar, and Leo flags down one of the bartenders.

"Hey man, what can I get you?"

"Hey mate," Leo says to the bartender, then turns to me. "What are you drinking tonight?" He studies me so intently that I feel he's trying to memorize my face.

"I'll have a Manhattan."

"She'll have a Manhattan," he tells the bartender without taking his eyes off me. I look away, admiring the bartenders and their 1920s attire, but I can feel his eyes boring into me, making my palms sweaty.

"This place is really cool," I tell him, turning back to face him. "Do you own this place too?" I tease.

He laughs. "No, not yet anyway. I'm working on it." He winks at me, and I realize his accent is heavier tonight. I've noticed this a few times now. When he drinks, it's like all of his London upbringing comes out.

"Let's go get you acquainted with the gang." He starts to leave the bar but pauses, turning back to me with a mischievous smile. "By the way, Walker, you look fucking sexy tonight."

I feel a flush of warmth as he turns back around and heads towards our table. I follow, drink in hand and my confidence bolstered by his comment. *Goddamn him!*

He has a way of simultaneously making me feel nervous and comfortable, which doesn't make any sense.

"Vivian, you've got to come! This year it's going to be a casino-themed party with cocktail attire. Everyone goes all out, it'll be so fun. Right, Leo? Tell her she has to come!" Meredith insists as she looks toward Leo. She has just invited me to her big New Year's Eve party.

"Yes, Meredith's parties are epic. We can go together if you'd like," he says, placing his hand on my thigh, *my bare thigh,* giving it a little squeeze. It's friendly, but it sends a wave of heat between my legs.

What. The. Hell.

I'm two Manhattans in, and I am *feeling* it. I don't drink liquor very often, so I'm a lightweight when I do. Leo's hand remains on my thigh, his thumb now moving back and forth, caressing my thigh, no longer just friendly.

We are friends. We are friends. We are friends. I tell myself over and over.

Oh my God, I haven't been touched in so long. It's doing things to my body way too easily. Why is his hand still there? I look around at the group. Everyone is engaged in some form of conversation. I look at Leo as he sips his whiskey, and come to the conclusion that he must be drunk, which would explain the hand. I stare at it, willing it to move, unsure if I want it to move up my thigh or for him to remove it. I try to calm my breathing and act normal, everything is fine. He just doesn't realize his hand is still there.

I'm panicking inside. I'm so turned on and confused, and my inhibitions are starting to numb. I put my cocktail down and switch to water.

Chapter 8

LEO

My hand is on Vivian's smooth, *bare* thigh, and I can't seem to make myself remove it. I don't know what's come over me tonight. I can't take my eyes off her. The urge to keep my hand on her leg is overwhelming. If we were alone, I'd be tempted to graze it along her thigh, sliding it up to discover what's underneath that skirt that's been driving me crazy. The thought sends a rush of heat through me, and an image of us in the bar bathroom flashes in my mind. Just then, she places her hand on top of mine, gently removing it as she reaches for her water. Well, that settles it then.

Dammit. I'm going to pay for this tomorrow if I don't reel it in. Vivian is my friend, and I've made that very clear. I like her too much to do anything stupid to fuck it up. But keeping my feelings in check is proving harder than I thought.

"So, what kind of therapy do you specialize in?" I hear Vivian ask Meredith.

"I mostly see clients with substance abuse and trauma, and also specialize in EMDR, have you heard of that?" She responds as Vivian nods her head.

I knew they would like each other. The two women that I like the most in my life getting along fills me with gratification.

The conversation shifts to drunk stories, and Michael and I have our fair share, having gone through our twenties together.

Laughter erupts as we take turns sharing stories about each other. Meredith recounts the time I got so drunk I peed on her wall in the hallway and ended up sleeping next to it.

I share one about Michael waking up on the front lawn of an Airbnb in his underwear after a night out in Vegas.

Adam tells us that he slept with the maid of honor at his brother's wedding.

It's Stella that goes in for the kill.

"A few years ago, we went to Mexico—me, Michael, and Leo—for spring break. We went out for a night on the town. The nightclubs in Mexico are totally insane," she says.

I know where this is going.

"We're all on the dance floor, and all of a sudden, we can't find Leo. We're looking everywhere on the floor." She starts to giggle. "We didn't think to look up. We find Leo in a giant birdcage, elevated above the dance floor with one of the dancers. He's lost his shirt and is dancing like a drunken fool!"

Vivian bursts out laughing.

"That's not all," Stella continues. "The next morning, we wake up and can't find Leo anywhere! And I mean anywhere. We call his phone—it goes straight to voicemail. We knock on his door—no answer. We end up having to get a key to open his door. He's not there. At this point, we're starting to get a little nervous, but we think, *Leo's a big boy and can fend for himself. He's fine.* Well, noon comes around and still no Leo. Now we are actually worried. We go to the front desk to possibly file a missing person report, or whatever you do in Mexico, and as we're approaching the front desk, he's being escorted into the lobby by two police officers. He has no shirt, and is wearing someone else's sweatpants that look like they came from the streets." Everyone laughs.

"I'm lucky I wasn't arrested that night," I say, more to Vivian than anyone. "I was found sleeping on the beach in my underwear."

"Shut up!" Vivian shouts in shock, slapping my knee and grinning at me with her bloody beautiful smile.

"It's true," I reply, forcing a smile. As everyone laughs at the story, I can't help but feel a twinge of pain. It was one of the lower moments of my life. I'd had plenty of drunken moments as a teenager and young adult, but I got my shit together before I earned my PhD. But five years ago, the memory of that childhood torment was fresh, gnawing at the edges of my mind.

I find myself searching Vivian's eyes. There's a spark of joy in them from her laughter, but beyond that, a flood of calm washes over me as I look deeper, a respite from the grueling past that lingers in my thoughts.

"What about you, Vivian?" Stella asks.

"Oh, I don't have anything very crazy to tell. Just peeing on a curb in a back alley, trying to sleep on a dance floor at a club, you know… the usual. If anything crazier has happened, I was too drunk to know about it," she replies, her confidence radiating, and I find myself more and more attracted to her. She's funny, attractive, athletic, and loyal… she's the whole package.

The night starts to wind down. I pick up the bill, placing my credit card into the fold. Meredith and Vivian insist on splitting it with me, adding their credit cards as well.

Vivian and I walk home together, side by side, recounting the evening. She loved all my friends, but can't stop talking about Meredith. It makes me happy. As we walk, the cool night air wraps around us, and our laughter echoes softly in the quiet streets.

We walk down the long row of townhouses and stop in front of mine.

"Thanks for coming tonight, Walker. My friends loved you!" I take both of her hands in mine and kiss her knuckles, making her giggle.

"What are you… like pretending to be a fuckin' gentleman tonight?" She is buzzed for sure but stopped drinking well before I did.

"Well, we were just in the 1920s, love, and I wanted to kiss my lady's hands," I spout off, realizing that I'm more drunk than I thought.

"The fuck? Kiss my lady's hands? That's not the 1920s! How drunk are you?" She loses control of her laughter, doubling over and clutching her sides.

I keep trying to form a sentence, but can't between the fits of laughter and my drunken state. The more I try, the funnier it seems, and we both end up laughing uncontrollably on the sidewalk.

She suddenly sobers, a haunted look crossing her face, as if she's seen a ghost.

"What's wrong?" I ask, trying to calm myself while taking deep breaths.

"Nothing. I, um…" She shakes her head back and forth, scowling, "I just had a flashback, a déjà vu type of thing, you know what I mean?"

I search her eyes, still holding her hands, feeling a surge of lust. "Jesus, Walker… you're stunning," I say, suddenly dropping her hands, aware of my escalating thoughts and body's response. "I should go now, before I do something we'll both regret. See you tomorrow," I say, turning to walk inside—cock hard—leaving her stunned on the sidewalk.

As I close the door behind me, I lean against it, breathing heavily. This is becoming a pattern, walking away from her, only to end up finishing myself off later. It's either that or face the consequences of blue balls. Dammit. What is she doing to me? The intensity of my feelings for her is overwhelming, and I know I need to get a grip before things get out of hand.

What the hell was that? I'm going to owe her an apology tomorrow. My hand goes to my forehead, pressing hard as I groan, remembering all the things I did tonight. I completely crossed a line.

I stumble into the dark kitchen, ramming my thigh into the countertop. "Shit!" I make my way to the fridge and manage to whip up a concoction of coconut water and egg yolks, my hangover cure. The taste is vile, but I chug it down and head upstairs to my bedroom, shaking my head in disbelief.

I told her she was fucking sexy.

I put my hand on her thigh.

I stroked her thigh with my thumb.

I thought about what it would be like to fuck her at the bar.

I stared. All night long, I stared at her.

And I just told her I needed to go before I did something we'd regret.

I stare at my ceiling, feeling the weight of my mistakes settle in. *Shit. I'm a bloody idiot.*

* * * * *  * * * * *

Wednesday, October 25

Four Days Later

"There you are." I hear Meredith's voice echo through the break room. "I looked in your office, and you weren't there. How have I not seen you yet today?"

"Hey, Mer," I say, standing to meet her as she crosses the break room for a hug. "Busy day today. How are ya?"

"I'm good, how are you?" she asks, giving me a squeeze.

"I'm great. I've got one more session, and then I'll wrap things up for today," I say, sitting down and taking a bite of my steak. I purchased an indoor steak griller a few months back for the break room because I hate microwaved food—it tastes like shit. The aroma of freshly grilled steak fills the room, adding a touch of comfort to the hectic day.

Wednesdays are my therapy days, and I have one more couple that comes in at six.

The break room is homey, carpeted with two round tables and chairs. There's a kitchenette area with a small fridge and microwave, a couch and coffee table, and large windows that let in plenty of natural light. It's a cozy space that provides a much-needed respite.

Meredith takes a seat, crossing her legs casually. "So... Vivian is sweet..." She pauses, watching me as I eat. "I like her a lot."

"Yeah, she's great. I knew you'd like each other."

She continues to watch me, her eyes twinkling with curiosity. "And she's smart, and beautiful, and cool, and fun..."

I drop my fork. "Stop. I know what you're doing."

"What? What did I say?" she asks, giving me an innocent look and smiling sweetly.

My eyes narrow and my jaw tightens slightly. "I know you, Meredith. It's not about what you're saying, it's about what you're not saying; so just fuckin' say it."

She rolls her eyes. "Come on, Leo, you're not fooling anyone. You couldn't keep your eyes off her the entire night."

"Oh, bloody hell. She's my friend. We see each other a lot; she lives right next door…" I take a swig of my water. "And yes, Vivian is gorgeous. I'm not in denial about that. There, you done?"

"You sure about that? Because it looked like you were gonna pounce a few times there, Tiger."

"May I ask what your point is?" My patience is wearing thin.

"My point is, the way you were looking at her wasn't just about her being beautiful, Leo. Hell, it's no secret you can fuck a beautiful girl. You were looking at her with admiration. Different than I've ever seen you look at someone before."

"I admire you," I say, taking another bite. "Does that mean I wanna fuck you, Mer?" I smirk.

"Just be careful… For her sake. I know you. You're stubborn…" She pauses, drumming her fingers on the table, her eyes watching me with intent. Like a goddamn therapist.

I stay silent. I'm not giving her the satisfaction right now.

She continues, "However, if you *do* ever stop being such a stubborn ass, she's great, and I approve." She smiles as she stands and strides toward the door.

"Thanks for your concern, Meredith!" I yell, while flipping her the bird.

Christ. Sometimes I hate how insightful she is. She reads people better than a bestselling novel. Having therapists as friends is one thing, but having Meredith, who specializes in substance abuse, is another. She deals with professional bullshitters all day, so there's no point in ever trying to bullshit her.

Shit—was I that transparent with Vivian?

Chapter 9

VIVIAN

Thursday, November 2

I hate today.

It's the worst.

It's harder than all the other days. Harder than Christmas. Harder than Ben's birthday. Harder than Thanksgiving.

There is only one day that's worse than today, and that's January 21, the day of the accident.

But today is my wedding anniversary. The day Ben and I chose to declare our love. The day hundreds of people came to celebrate our union after seven years of being together. The day we committed to each other for the rest of our lives; Ben's being cut short decades too soon. Today represents all the hopes and dreams that I once had: the family we were going to raise together—*three kids*, the trip to Paris before my 30th birthday, and Japan for Ben's. The second home we wanted to buy in Maui. Growing old and still drinking our morning coffee together, maybe with more silence as we sat, but a comfortable silence. Today is a punch in the face to my reality. A *fuck you* to Vivian Walker and her dreams… to Ben's dreams. Today would have been six years married.

I took the day off, and I have zero expectations for today. My only hope is that it's slightly less hard than it was last year. I'll take one percent easier. Last year was gruesome. The entire day was spent in anguish. While I'm still feeling that pain, some days more than others, I am starting to notice more and more sprinkles of joy between the hard days.

I lie in bed staring at the ceiling fan, watching it go around and around as the clicking sound from the pull chain wobbles back and forth. It's 9:00, and I have no intention of getting out of bed for at least another few hours, except to get food, water and to pee.

I scroll Netflix for something to watch that will take my mind off the day.

Working Moms, nothing with moms.

Dead to Me, dead husband, no thanks.

Schitt's Creek, mine and Ben's favorite show… makes me miss him, but maybe.

I switch to Apple TV.

Ted Lasso, ah, another one of our favorites to watch together. A feel-good show that Ben and I loved. I realize season three dropped earlier this year, and I haven't seen it. This might just do the trick. Keep it light, keep it happy and nostalgic.

I go to episode one and prepare to settle in to this fabulous bed for the day. I walk into the bathroom, wash my face, brush my teeth, and pee.

In the kitchen, I grab some hard-boiled eggs and sprinkle some salt and pepper on a plate. I refuse to cook today. I open the fridge and grab a sparkling Topo Chico. With my arms loaded, I make my way to the stairs and then turn right back around. If I plan to stay put for a while, I'll need more than this. I craft my own little charcuterie with cheese, salami, grapes, and nuts, before gathering my goodies and heading to the bedroom.

Am I getting dressed today? Nope!

Bra? Hell no.

I prop a handful of pillows up all around me, making myself a throne, and settle in. I push play and sigh… *Ben, this show's for you.* Today will be a long day.

It's 4:30, I'm on episode seven when I get a text from Leo.

Leo: Hey Walker, just finished class—going to grab food on the way home. Do you want anything?

I can read it on my home screen, so I don't swipe up to open the message. This way it won't say *read,* and he won't think I ignored him. I turn my phone off. No distractions today. This day is all about Ben.

I do feel bad about not responding, but I can make it up to him. I've only seen Leo twice since Michael's birthday get-together. It's been a busy week and a half for both of us. The morning after the speakeasy, he showed up at my door unannounced, bearing lattes and pastries to apologize. What can I say? The man knows the way to a woman's heart. He said he was sorry if his behavior had been inappropriate or if he crossed a line, essentially blaming it on the alcohol.

I appreciate the gesture, I really do, and I understand where he's coming from, but his apology left me feeling more confused. Honestly, it chaps my ass that he can't just admit he might feel something more for me. I don't believe his behavior was based on sex alone. Leo can and *does* have any woman he wants. I felt him there all night, staring at me, engaging with me, touching me. Oh my, the touching. A knot forms in my stomach every time I think about his hand on my thigh. But then again, we did agree to be friends, and my feelings are a *me* problem, not a *him* problem.

Sigh... Back to Ben.

Later, I plan to take my photo album from our wedding, yearbooks, and a few other things that remind me of Ben up to the rooftop patio and have myself a little nostalgia sob party. I'll also write Ben a letter. My therapist said it's good to have something to do every year to honor and remember him. This is what I did last year, so I plan to do it again this year, and every year after.

* * * * *   * * * * *

Episode nine. I am loving this season, but I have cried so many times. I wasn't ready for that yet—I had planned for a good cry tonight—but no expectations today, so I'll allow it. Gosh, this show is so good. How can one episode make you feel so many emotions at once?

I drag myself out of bed and brave the mirror in the bathroom. "Ha!" I laugh out loud. I look a mess! My hair looks like a toddler's after a rough night in the crib, like the crazy cat lady who hasn't seen or spoken to anyone since '86. I splash my splotchy red face with cold water, pat it dry, and brush my hair, twisting it into a clip at the back. I change into some warmer comfy clothes: joggers and a matching half-zip pullover.

In the kitchen, I stand at the fridge like a zombie, scanning its contents aimlessly, trying to find something for dinner that doesn't need to be cooked. I end up with plain yogurt in my hand. I add some honey and fresh berries. Now, the big question is: to wine or not to wine. Eh, what the hell? This day isn't about being 100%. I grab a bottle of wine, a glass, and a warm blanket off the couch and trudge up the three flights of stairs to the rooftop patio. I set up my area of nostalgia around my sectional: wine glass and bottle on the table. Then I go back inside to get a space heater, my photo album, and a notepad and pen.

Pleased that I got a few steps in today, I finally get settled. It's cold tonight… probably low fifties. I have an incredible view of the city lights reflecting off the river. I wrap up in my blanket, the space heater close by, pour myself a glass of wine, grab my photo album, and let myself feel all the things.

The anger.

The hurt.

The sadness.

The ache.

The guilt.

The fear.

And then… I let the tears come.

Chapter 10

LEO

I get home from work just before 7:00. It's been a bloody long day, and I haven't heard from Vivian. She left my text message unread, and when I've tried to call, it goes straight to voicemail. This isn't like her, and I'm starting to worry. She's usually prompt with her replies, even when she's busy. I drop my stuff in the entryway, rush up the stairs to the second floor, and head outside to the front of the house. I scan her townhouse for any sign of her. Lights are on on every floor, including the rooftop.

That's where she is.

She wouldn't have the patio light on if she wasn't up there. She loves her patio and spends loads of her free time there. It's bloody cold, though. I go back inside, run up to my bedroom, and change into joggers and a T-shirt. I grab a heavy jacket and put it on as I run up the next two flights of stairs. Light from her patio spills onto mine as I step outside. Sure enough, there she is, sitting cross-legged with a fuzzy blanket wrapped around her. A space heater hums and oscillates a few feet away. There's music playing softly in the background. She has a large book on her lap, a glass of wine in one hand, and a tissue in the other. I look at the rather large pile of tissues next to her, and my heart lurches. She's sad, and I debate whether to leave her alone or interrupt her at such a vulnerable time. I choose the latter.

Walking quietly to the wall that divides us, I ponder what to say. Her sudden movement suggests she senses my presence but doesn't look up. I watch her for a few moments. She's beautiful. Even now, with her hair pulled back and her makeup-free face red and blotchy from what must have been hours of crying, she's still so beautiful. She tucks a loose strand of hair that's been blown by the breeze behind her ear, and I hear her sniffle.

I'm frozen. Despite all my years as a therapist, I'm rooted to the spot, unable to find the words to convey that I want to be here for her. I clear my throat so that I don't startle her. "Are you alright, Walker?" I say wearily. I silently scold myself—stupid thing to say, clearly she's not alright.

She nods, sets her tissue down, and wipes both sides of her face with the backs of her hands. She looks up and tries to smile. "Yep, all good," she replies. She inhales and exhales deeply as she stares up at the dark sky.

I proceed with caution. "May I join you?" I ask, ready to be turned away. I know better than anyone that you can't make someone talk if they don't want to.

She surprises me by nodding her head and allowing a soft, "Yeah, that's fine," to slip from her lips. She gathers all her tissues, crumples them into a ball, stuffs them behind a cushion on the other side of her, and pats the now open seat next to her.

I hop the wall and carefully approach, taking a seat next to her. "What are you looking at?" I ask, placing my hand on her shoulder blade and gently rubbing her back.

She responds by setting the book—which I'm now realizing is a photo album—on my lap and taking a large gulp from her wine glass.

She looks at me, waiting for me to say something first, but I don't. Years of training have prepared me for this moment, and I won't fuck it up. Now is the time to listen—to shut up, listen, ask a few questions when necessary, and listen more. I meet her gaze as she struggles to maintain eye contact. Her eyes wander to the side, down, and then back up to mine. I give her a small smile, letting her know she can trust me and that I'm here for her.

After a minute or two of silence, with me maintaining eye contact, she whispers, "I'm ready to talk to you."

A surge of pride washes over me as I realize she trusts me with this moment. I break our gaze and curiously look down at the photo album. They're wedding photos… her wedding. She looks gorgeous in a beautiful and elaborate wedding dress, her face radiating pure joy. I flip the page to find a picture of her and who I assume to have been her husband. He's handsome, and in this picture, they're laughing as they cut their wedding cake.

I turn my head to look at her; her eyes are down, toward the photos. "You were married?" I ask. She manages a slow nod. I flip through a few more pages. She looks so happy in these pictures. I come across a family photo. "Is this your mum and dad?"

"Yeah," she whispers, leaning in slightly for a better look.

It's obvious that the couple are her parents. Her mum is an older version of Vivian, with the same stunning beauty, and her dad is a handsome fellow with specks of gray in his hair and beard. They both have the same dark hair, but her mum's features are darker. I see that Vivian gets her green eyes from her dad, and her complexion and features from her mum.

"I see where you get your natural beauty from," I say, trying to lighten her spirits.

A small smile forms on her lips. "Thanks," she says, shrugging. "My mom's from Spain. She and my dad met while she was visiting a friend in Boston. He was going to Harvard Law School, and they met at a campus party her friend had brought her to. They were friends first, long-distance for two years, each taking turns visiting the other. Then realized they were in love, and she moved in with him. They got married shortly after, so she could get citizenship."

Flipping through a few more pages, I let the silence build. I'm comfortable in it, and I want her to come to me. I don't want to push. After minutes pass, and I've looked through the entire album, I close the book. "You look really happy here," I say. "What happened?"

She looks up at me briefly, and I see that her eyes are glistening. Her lips press into a tight line, and she blinks rapidly before looking away. She cups a hand to her mouth as she swallows audibly. A tiny cry escapes her mouth, and it's too much for me. My heart tears from my chest as I reach for her hand. She grips it, holding it as if she is hanging from the edge of a cliff and if she lets go, she may plummet to her death.

"He died." She takes a deep breath in and slowly exhales.

Holy shit.

I wait for her to continue.

"In a car accident." She sets her wine glass down and stares into the abyss. "I was driving us home from Sarah's birthday party. We were going up the canyon... back up to Park City. We were singing and laughing." She pauses to breathe, to hold her composure. "I saw the driver in my rear-view mirror, but there wasn't anything I could do. He was going so fast and swerving all over the road. He was drunk... and he hit us. Drove his car just right... right into us, into Ben." Her shoulders start shaking as she drops my hand and hugs her knees to her chest, resting her forehead between her knees.

I absentmindedly rub her back, sensing that there is more. She eventually looks up, finding her blank stare again. She sniffles. "I was pregnant," she says. "Seven months... I named her Evie."

I feel a lump in my throat, and my eyes blur as I struggle to maintain my own composure. *Fuck.* This is heavy, and I wish there was something I could do or say to take away all of this pain from her.

"They had to do an emergency C-section." She swallows, her voice wavering. "For so long I wondered why... why was I the only one who survived? What did I do to deserve to live? What did *Ben* do to deserve to die? He was the best person I ever knew..." She pauses, her fingers tightening around the edges of the blanket. "In the stillness of the car, moments after the accident, I knew he was dead. I *knew* he was dead. I knew that I was the only one still alive. That was the worst moment of my life. Ben and the other driver were killed on impact, and Evie, shortly after. I was so scared, Leo." Her voice quivers again. "I've played that night over and over in my head. What could I have done differently? If only I hadn't gone back upstairs to pee, if only we'd left five minutes earlier, if only we'd taken an Uber. So many 'ifs'."

My own emotions get the best of me. I can't rid the lump from my throat, and I wipe a tear from my face as I stare in admiration at her.

"I'm so sorry for your loss, Vivian," I say, my voice cracking.

She lets out a sound that's something between a laugh and a cry. Sullenly, she looks forward and says, "Do you know that's the first time you've ever called me Vivian?" The corner of her mouth lifts, revealing a small smile.

"Is it?" I ask, "Do you want me to say something or just be a listener right now?"

She laughs at that. "You and Sarah are so alike," she says. "I just want you to be you… be my friend. Don't be my therapist, but know that what you say matters to me. I know that whatever you say comes from the education and experience that you've had."

I nod in understanding and wait for her to continue.

"This is why I'm fucked up." She nods her head as if in agreement with herself. "This is why I'm stagnant… why I can't move forward." She looks up at me briefly. "It's why I haven't been intimate with anyone," she admits, swiftly moving back into her trance. "Every time I get close to anything happening… you know… downstairs…" She shakes her head. "Panic consumes me, I just… freak out, and then the guilt… GOD, the guilt is so heavy, it just… weighs on me. But it's not having sex that makes me feel guilty. No. It's the fact that Ben doesn't get to live, and I do. The fact that I get to move forward, and he doesn't."

She pauses, her eyes glistening with fresh tears. "The worst guilt comes when I feel angry that he left me. God, I'm so fucking *mad* that I have to go through life without him. What kind of person is angry at someone for dying?"

She looks at me, "And it's crazy because at the same time, I feel like I won the lottery to have loved such a wonderful person. But then it feels like God has a magnifying glass and is torturing me—like a bully, slowly burning ants alive."

I gently squeeze her hand, trying to offer some comfort. The mix of grief, guilt, and rage is palpable, and my heart aches for her.

"Why does my life get to go on as if nothing has happened and his doesn't? Why do I get another chance to fall in love when Ben can't?" She shudders, sobbing now. "I can't shake the feeling that if I have sex with someone else, it'll be like I'm officially letting him go." Tears stream down her face. I wrap my arm around her and give her a squeeze.

"I don't want to let him go. I want to move forward, but I don't want to forget him. How do I share something like that with someone who isn't Ben? Something that connects you so deeply to someone... how do I do that?"

She dabs at her eyes with a tissue. "I've only been with Ben and one other person, which was a drunken mistake," she says, gripping her head with her hands and slowly sliding them down her face as she groans. "It's not even about being horny or the orgasm, you know? My vibrator can give me an orgasm. It's about the connection. About *connecting* with someone like that. I don't want or need mindless sex; I want what I had with Ben. I miss that connection so much. I miss him. I *fucking* miss him. I can't..." She doesn't finish. She drops her head back on the sofa, unable to continue, looking up for inspiration.

I sit quietly and squeeze her hand, letting her know I'm here for her. So many things are running through my mind, puzzle pieces coming together, everything about her falling into place. *God, she's only been with two people!* The way she values sex as such an intimate bond, almost sacred... it's admirable. And I guess it would be if you've only ever shared that with someone you loved. Christ, what does she think about me? I've only attached emotions to sex with one person, and that completely backfired. Since then, I've vowed to never attach sex to feelings, to only allow it to be something fun, a playful means to an end. I almost envy her, but then I remind myself that this is *precisely* why I don't ever want to fucking fall in love. Your life can't be blown to pieces if you don't have someone to lose. You can't disappoint anyone. No one can leave you, cheat on you, or die. It's my coping mechanism for sure, and as a therapist, I've stared myself down in that mirror plenty of times, but I don't *want* to fix it, and I don't *want* to change. Love is not in the cards for me.

We sit in comfortable silence for a few moments while I gather my thoughts.

"You know you can have both, Vivian." I let go of her hand as she looks into my eyes.

"What do you mean?" she asks.

"Moving forward doesn't mean you have to forget Ben. You can hold on to his memory while allowing yourself to embrace new relationships. You deserve to have both, and it's completely possible. It's also completely normal to feel what you are feeling. There is no timeline with death, Viv. Some people move on by sleeping with anything that moves, while others take years to get to the point of trusting another with intimacy. There is nothing wrong with you, and you are not fucked up. You are perfectly imperfect in this fucked-up journey of healing."

A small laugh escapes her.

"I promise! There's nothing abnormal about this, and I'm truly sorry if I've been the cause of any of your pain. I never would have joked about it if I'd known." I wrap my arms around her, bringing her close as she rests her head on my chest. Her arms wrap tightly around me, and I feel her fingers grip my jacket. She nods her head as if she believes me and sobs quietly.

We sit there holding each other for what feels like an eternity.

She eventually loosens her grip and looks up at me. "Thank you, Leo," she whispers, a small smile forming on her lips.

"Hey," I say, wiping a tear from her cheek, "That's what friends do." I gently place a kiss on her forehead and give her another squeeze. As I release her, she sighs heavily, removes the clip from her hair, and lies on her side, placing her head in my lap and curling her feet up into a fetal position. I stroke her hair gently, feeling the weight of her trust in this moment. The night air is cool, but the warmth between us is palpable, a silent promise that she's not alone in this.

"Will you tell me something?"

"What do you want to know?" I ask, my voice deep and quiet as I mindlessly toy with my fingers in her hair.

"Anything… something real… something that makes me feel less broken. You know, I envy you."

"You envy me?" I say, surprised. She turns onto her back so that she can look at me, her knees bent and feet planted on the sofa.

"Yeah… you just have your shit together. You go through life as if it's *easy.* You're always so calm and collected… and confident. Tell me something, anything, big or small, that makes you human." She looks at me with so much depth, searching my eyes. The raw human emotion in her eyes, from having bared her soul to me moments ago, compels me to give her something in return.

I don't really want to go into the details of my past, not just because I don't want to talk about it, but because I don't want to overshadow her night of remembering Ben. I form a small smile and let a chuckle escape.

"Oh, Walker," I say, shaking my head. "I'm just as fucked up as everyone else. Isn't that what you predicted the first night we met?" I flash her a full grin. Tonight, I'll give her a half-truth.

Chapter 11

VIVIAN

I lie there, my head resting on Leo's lap, searching his face for any sign of humanity. I've just bared my soul to him, leaving myself exposed and raw with emotion. My face, I can only imagine, is a wretched mess—puffed and blotchy from crying. His hands gently tangle in my hair, and though there's nothing sexual about this moment, it's the most intimate I've been with anyone since Ben. I swallow back the lump in my throat, terrified of the emotions brewing inside me, ready to spill over again at any moment. Leo smiles softly, a quiet laugh escaping his lips as he reassures me that he's just as human as the rest of us. Then his expression turns somber, his gaze fixed on the shimmering lights reflected in the river. He looks like he's reaching for a distant memory, unsure if he really wants to find it.

The suspense is killing me. Part of me yearns for him to share something so horrific that it makes my problems seem insignificant by comparison. Yet, another part of me hopes his life is perfect because I wouldn't wish this kind of pain on anyone, especially someone I care about.

He sighs, swallows, and stares straight ahead. "Every woman that I've ever loved has either left me, cheated… or died." His face remains emotionless, his voice almost monotone. He doesn't break his stare, barely even blinks. My heart skips a beat, or possibly stops beating altogether. His words hang heavy in the air, weaving a tapestry of sorrow and betrayal that I can't fathom.

Without thinking, I hear myself whisper, "What?"

He looks down at me then, emotion threatening to surface. He swallows it down, blinks a few times, and then goes back to staring at the river.

"I had a twin sister… Chloe." Her name brings a fleeting smile to his lips. "God, she was great. She was my best friend. She was diagnosed with leukemia when she was twelve. Fought hard for over a year—enduring all the chemo, the pain, the tears, and the suffering. I sat with her through it all, holding her hand every minute. She beat it. After eighteen months, she beat it. That was one of the best days of my life, when they looked at her and told her the cancer was gone." He pauses, trying to regain his composure. He clears his throat and continues, "Three years later, it came back… with a vengeance. She was always so positive, so happy… she had so much faith in her ability to get better. She was so strong." He tries to smile as he looks at me. "You remind me of her sometimes. Your strength and ability to stay positive, even when I know you're fighting a battle of your own.

"Anyway… she died six months later. The cancer ultimately won. When you tell me that you wonder why it was Ben and not you, trust me when I say I empathize completely. Chloe was the good one. She was kind and honest, had integrity, and followed all the rules. I was a mess—a rebellious teenager, getting into trouble and fighting anyone who would fight me, verbally or physically."

I glance up at him, seeing the ghost of his past in his eyes. It's hard to reconcile this image with the composed man I know. My heart aches for the boy he once was, lost and angry.

"Chloe didn't deserve to die… they never do, the ones who are taken from us. They never deserve it."

I don't know what to say, and I get a glimpse of what people must feel when they find out about my situation. There is nothing you can say to make it better. I do know, however, what not to say. Abruptly sitting up, I turn my body to face him. "I'm sorry," I say. It's all I can say.

He looks at me, a faint smile tugging at the corners of his lips. "It's okay," he replies, giving me a slight nod. "It was a long time ago." His words are meant to reassure, but I can see the lingering pain in his eyes, a silent testament to the wounds that time hasn't fully healed.

I scoot my body over to the chaise section of the sofa and pat it, beckoning for him to join me. He slides over, extends his legs onto the chaise, and I settle my body against his and pull the blanket over us. For reasons unknown, I just want to hold him… or for him to hold me—I'm unsure. But I want to be close to him. I want to feel his chest rising and falling with each breath, to hear his heartbeat against my ear, and to feel his strength enveloping me… his muscles wrapped around my body, keeping me safe.

"Thank you for telling me about your sister," I say. I feel him nod above me, but he doesn't say anything.

We lie there in silence, staring into the night, holding each other, the deepest, darkest parts of ourselves exposed—two friends who finally have an inkling of understanding each other. The night is still around us, Florence and the Machine playing in the background, mingling with the gentle rustle of the blanket as Leo starts running his fingers up and down my back.

"Tell me something. Something I don't know about you." His voice is deep, and the vibration hums along the side of my face, resonating through my bones.

"Like what?" I ask, my voice soft, as I mechanically start to stroke my fingers along his chest, following the patterns he traces on my skin.

"Something fun or unique about you." He can't see the grin that spreads across my face as I think about something random to share.

"Hmmm… let me think." My hand lowers to his abdomen. God, these abs are made of steel, and I can feel the ripple of muscles through his shirt. The thought sends a tingling sensation through my body, but I strive to push it from my mind, because… you know, we're friends.

"I love music," I say. "Like, really love it. I think it can define any moment or feeling, and I have a playlist for everything. I have playlists for when I'm sad, for when I'm happy, for when it rains, when I run, when I lift weights, when I'm mad, for getting ready—I even have playlists for sex. And then I have playlists for each year and season. Each song can take me right back to where I was in that moment and why I put it on the playlist."

He chuckles, and I feel his abs compress and release. "What kind of music do you have on these playlists?"

"Oh gosh, everything. I had a friend tell me once that I have the most random mix of music he's ever seen. Everything from Tom Petty to Morgan Wallen to Jack Harlow. Literally, every genre."

"What's on the sex playlist?" he asks, his voice low, vibrating in his chest.

"Ha, wouldn't you like to know. That's the last thing I'm telling you. You'll start blasting my incredibly sexy playlist while you're *bangin'* hot chicks next door, and I'll be forced to listen." I shake my head. "No, no, that's not something I'm sharing with you," I tease. But as I say it, the thought of him with other women sends a rush of envy through my body, a feeling I've never experienced until now. I try to laugh it off, but the jealousy gnaws at me, unexpected and unsettling.

"Your turn," I say, "tell me something fun about you that I don't know."

"Okay. Let's see, I've watched *Friends* from start to finish at least a dozen times."

My brows knit together, "Really? I didn't pin you as a *Friends* kind of guy. I've only seen some of it, it wasn't as big for my generation."

"Yep. It was Chloe's favorite show. We binge-watched it over and over when she was sick, during her chemo treatments. After she died, I'd fall asleep to it every night. I did for years. Still do sometimes..." His hand lowers from my back to my side, then to my stomach. "Makes me feel like there's a part of her still here."

A wave of tenderness washes over me. The idea of him finding solace in something so simple, something so tied to his sister, tugs at my heart. It's strange how the things we cling to for comfort can become a lifeline. I press myself closer to him, wanting to offer some of the solace he's given me tonight.

I think of my own lifelines, the things I hold onto that remind me of Ben. Our high school yearbooks, *Easy A,* our shared love for *Ted Lasso.* Every time I watch an episode, I feel his presence, like he's sitting beside me, laughing at the same jokes.

His hand slips under my sweatshirt, and he delicately strokes the skin below my belly button. My breath catches, and I begin to crave his touches… *more,* I silently plead. *More.* Anticipation builds as he moves his fingers along my side, dragging them along each curve until his finger meets the side of my breast, where I am bare and braless. I suck in a breath, a fire building inside me. He pauses, seemingly surprised to find me without a bra, then slowly, softly traces the underside of my breast before working his way back down to the side of my waist. He splays his hand open and rests it there.

I can't think straight. His touch is electrifying, brewing butterflies in my stomach and stirring a desire I can barely contain. I inhale slowly, willing my heart to slow down so I can think of a question to ask him, anything to bring me back down to earth.

"You said you've been in love before?" I phrase it more as a question than a statement.

"Hmm," he responds, a noise reverberating from his chest instead of a word.

"Tell me about it," I say, deciding to play his little game. I slip my fingers partially under his shirt where it meets the waistband of his pants. He tenses, his muscles flexing as I tease him with my fingers. Brushing them ever so lightly over his chiseled abs, *Jesus.* I slow to appreciate the V along his hip, running the indent with my thumb. The heat of his skin beneath my fingers sends a rush through me. I can feel his heartbeat quicken, matching the rhythm of my own.

He relaxes slightly. "Not much to tell. I let myself fall in love, even had a ring. I was going to ask her to marry me. Then I found out she had been unfaithful… for a long time. She'd been cheating on me for over a year with multiple men. I don't know how I was so blind to it. I think I knew, I just didn't want to believe it—I was in denial."

"God, that's awful. I'm sorry."

"Yeah, well, apparently I wasn't cutting it. She needed a whole bloody team."

"Is that why you don't date?" I ask.

He chuckles quietly. "It's on the ever-growing list of reasons."

I continue with my strokes, running a finger along the inside of his waistband, triggering sudden movement from within his joggers. I smile to myself, pleased. He shifts, simultaneously removing his hand and pulling my sweatshirt down to cover my stomach. Grabbing my hand from inside his shirt, he intertwines his fingers with mine, putting them in a timeout from exploration. He holds my hand against his ribcage as if it's his lifeline, keeping him from doing the things I know he wants to do.

Damn.

But then I remember him saying that he would always want to have a go with me, but that we would never be more than friends. I scowl in frustration.

"Tell me something else," he says.

"Ask me a question," I offer.

"Just tell me something. Anything to get my mind somewhere else." His confession turns me on all the more.

"Okay, let's see… oh! I just booked a flight to Paris for April," I say. "It's on my list of things I want to do before I'm thirty. I haven't been yet, and since I turn thirty in June, I decided to treat myself to an early birthday present!" I'm really excited about this. I just booked the flight a few days ago after both my mom and Sarah encouraged me to do so. It was something I always planned to do with Ben, but with him not being here, I decided it was something that I could do for me anyway. The decision feels liberating, like a step towards reclaiming my life and dreams.

"You're going alone?"

"Going solo," I say, trying not to focus on Leo's thumb caressing my hand as I speak.

"Let me take you."

I give him a curious look, taken aback by his offer.

"C'mon, Paris is magical and meant to be shared with someone." He pauses, searching my eyes for a reaction. "We used to spend our summers there with our au pair. I speak French fluently, and I'd love to take you, show you the city the way it's truly meant to be seen. But I know it's something you and Ben had planned, and I understand if you'd rather do it on your own."

A travel buddy…

I could think of a worse travel buddy.

"You had an au pair growing up?" I ask.

"Out of all that, that's what you want to know? Yes, we had an au pair, my dad worked a lot and needed help."

"Where was your mom? Were they divorced?" I can't believe I don't know anything about his mom, but he's changed the subject almost every time I've asked about his family.

"My mum died when I was ten," he says, his tone flat.

"Oh, I'm sorry."

"Don't be. She was a shit mum."

His response shocks me, and I don't feel it's something I can press him on, so I answer his question about Paris.

"I'd love for you to come… to Paris. It's much more fun to sightsee with a friend."

"Can I plan it for you? Book the hotels and activities? Paris is incredible, and you've got to do it right."

I laugh. "Yes, you can plan it. As long as I get to see the Eiffel Tower, eat chocolate croissants, and drink way too much coffee, then I'm good."

We stay like this until the early hours of the morning, talking. At some point, I drift off to sleep and awaken to Leo nudging me around three in the morning.

"Shh. It's just me, it's getting cold, love. Let's go inside, get you to bed, yeah?"

He turns off the space heater and helps me gather all of my stuff to take inside. We walk down the three flights of stairs to the kitchen, setting the wine glass in the sink and the almost empty bottle of wine on the counter. Leo folds the blanket, setting it on the couch, and places my books on the coffee table. The house is quiet and dimly lit, creating an intimate atmosphere as we move around each other in comfortable silence.

I walk behind him to the door, the only light being under the cabinets, illuminating just enough to lead us through the living room and to the foyer. He turns to face me as he opens the door.

"Hey, Viv?" he asks. I love the way my name sounds on his lips.

"Yeah?"

"Thanks for letting me share this with you, for letting me in. I know that wasn't easy for you." He nudges my shoulder. "You're gonna be okay, Walker." He grins mischievously, deepening those damn dimples and making me laugh.

Damn him.

Chapter 12

LEO

Wednesday, November 22

Three Weeks Later

I blocked out my schedule for my usual evening appointments, taking my last client at 4 PM. I told Vivian I'd pick up dinner for both of us. With Thanksgiving tomorrow, we wanted to take advantage of the holiday and enjoy a weekend evening in the middle of the week. Our plan is to devour Thai food, watch movies, and have a drink. Drinking is something we usually reserve for weekends, Vivian even less than I do. I've made it a rule for the past decade: unless it's a holiday, or I'm on vacation, I only drink on weekends. It's one of the things that makes us click even more.

At 5:15, I text her.

Leo: Hey, I'm on my way. Do you want to order the Thai? We can DoorDash it?

Vivian: I'm on it.

Leo: ETA 20 minutes. FYI—Booked our hotel for Paris today. You're going to love it.

Vivian: Yesssss! Can't wait for you to show it to me.

My office is close enough to walk. It's cold, but not too cold for a ten-minute walk… yet. I pull my arms through my coat sleeves and head to the elevator.

The past few weeks have been a whirlwind. Vivian and I were already spending a lot of time together, but since that night on the rooftop, we've stepped up our efforts, making sure to see each other for at least a few minutes every day, whenever possible. She has become the kind of friend you wonder how you ever lived without.

That's the problem, though. We've become close. Really close. That night on the patio opened a door to physical exploration that I never should have touched. I've slept with *a lot* of beautiful women, but none compare to her. None have been nearly as cool, either. Every time I say goodbye to her, I ask myself what the hell I think I'm doing. I have no business spending this much time with her when I know what she's seeking is something I don't want. Period. I can't seem to help myself. It's selfish, I know. I'm feeding my ego every day, and it's a dangerous road I'm heading down.

I walk home on autopilot, lost in my thoughts, the city noises blending into the background like the white noise machine we use in the clinic hallways. I arrive home, retracing my steps without recalling a single detail of the walk, except for the vague sense of being surrounded by people.

After changing out of my work clothes, I head to Vivian's and let myself in. "Viv?" My voice echoes through the foyer.

"In the kitchen!"

I make my way through the living room, finding her removing lids and placing utensils into containers.

"Hey, perfect timing. The food just got here," she says, dropping everything to greet me with a hug. Wrapping her arms around my back and pressing her ear to my chest, she inhales deeply, almost like she's savoring my scent.

I respond with the same enthusiasm, my arms folding around her small frame. I resist the urge to bury my face in her hair or kiss the top of her head.

"How was your day?" she asks.

"It was good, busy but good. How about yours?" She releases me from her grip and goes back to prepping the food.

"Same. Really busy. I'm going to have to do some work in the morning before we go to Michael and Stella's. Construction started on two homes in the past three weeks, and we start another one next week. It'll be crazy busy, plus I might be working with another client starting next week." She gestures for me to grab a plate and start dishing up.

"Were you on sites today or at the office?"

"Both." She pauses. "I met with the general contractor today… Nick. I've met him multiple times, he's a nice guy." She stops, and I can tell she's debating whether to tell me something.

"And?" I ask.

"And what?"

"And… he's nice?" I ask, spooning a heap of rice onto my plate.

"Yeah… he's nice… and he asked me out," she says nonchalantly.

"Oh." *Oh!* "And what did you say?" I ask, watching her body language to gauge her feelings.

"I said yes. He's going to take me out on Saturday."

She looks happy about it, and something like jealousy sinks into the pit of my stomach. It's a foreign sensation, one I hardly recognize.

"And you're happy about this?" I ask warily, raising a brow.

"Yeah, I am." She responds too quickly, as if she didn't even have to think about it. She's actually excited about the prospect of going out with this guy… *Nick.*

"Well, that's great, Viv. I'm happy for you. I hope he's great and that you have fun." *Too much,* I think. An overly exaggerated response of excitement about her going out with some random guy.

We chat about life while we eat. Vivian tells me in more detail about her work and clients. I love watching her talk. She's so animated when telling stories, using her hands, and her laughter always warrants a laugh from me because it's so cute and genuine, like she can't help herself.

"Oh!" she exclaims, "you were going to tell me about Paris. You booked our room?"

"Yep. I booked us six nights at the Four Seasons. It's close to the Champs-Élysées, which has great shopping and food. It's a great place for getting around the city."

"Oooh. The Four Seasons? Seems a little extravagant, but I'm not complaining."

"Well, it is for your 30th, yeah? It's a big deal, you've got to exit your twenties with a bang."

"I knew you'd come in handy one day," she says, giving me a cheeky look. "I guess it pays off having a filthy-rich friend."

"At least I'm good for something, Walker." I lean back, crossing my arms and glaring at her, teasing her. I've realized I now use different names for her in different situations. When I'm joking or teasing, it's Walker. When we're just chatting, it's Viv. When things are more serious, it's Vivian.

"And what if I meet a charming, handsome Frenchman who sweeps me off my feet and wants to seduce me?" she asks dramatically, raising her hands in an exaggerated flourish before taking a bite of her curry. "Can I tell him you're my rich older brother? How would I bring him back to our room if you're there? We'll need to devise a plan, because I'm not going to deny myself the attentions of a man on my 30th birthday." She stares me down, waiting for my reaction with a mischievous glint in her eye.

"Hmm, let's see." I rub my chin thoughtfully. "You could be my escort—very *Pretty Woman* of you—or maybe you're dating my father for the money and I'm your soon-to-be brother after the nuptials. Those are both fun options. As for bringing men back to the room, we'll need a plan. Maybe we have a code word for needing the room for sex, because we know I'm going to need it."

She scowls at me. "Would you really pick someone up in France while you're there with me for *my* birthday?"

"Would *you*?"

"I think it's obvious based on my history what the odds are of that happening… And based on yours… well, we know the odds are definitely in your favor."

I clutch my chest. "You wound me. I can go a week without sex."

"Can you?" She cocks a brow. "I have yet to see it. What if you meet a gorgeous woman in Paris who's beautiful and chic? You'd turn that down?" she asks skeptically.

"I'd never ditch you, if that's what you're worried about," I say seriously, sensing she might actually believe I would. "But if anyone should be worried, it's me. You're stunning, and every man in Paris will be turning their heads, saying"—I attempt my best French accent—"'Who is this beautiful American woman? I must know her.'"

"Stop." She chuckles, "Okay, neither of us are getting laid in Paris."

"Well, I wouldn't necessarily say that… there's always the possibility of you and me getting drunk and having a bit of fun together." The words are barely out of my mouth before I regret them, a flicker of panic setting in.

Her eyes widen in surprise.

I stammer, searching for a way to undo what I just said. "I… I'm joking. Obviously, I don't really mean that. I even booked a room with two doubles." I don't know why I say *that*. The hotel doesn't have rooms with two doubles. They have suites with a king or two twins. There's no way in hell I'm sleeping in a twin bed, so I booked a king. There'll be ample space for both of us.

She laughs, "Are you planning to *roofie* me? Because that's how out of it I'd have to be for that to happen."

I give her a smug grin, rolling my eyes. "Three drinks is all it would take to get you into bed with me."

"Wow. You're feeling mighty confident about your seduction skills. Three drinks is not *that* many."

"Well, like you've said, based on *my* history, I am quite successful when it comes to seducing women. I'd have you *begging,* Walker."

"Pff," she scoffs. "I may not have as many conquests as you, but trust me, if I turned on my sultry side, *you'd* be the one begging." Her eyes narrow with playful challenge, a sly smile curving her lips. There's a confident gleam in her eye, and her voice drops to a seductive purr, making the air between us sizzle with tension.

I let out a mocking laugh. "Game on, Walker!"

She stares me down, folding her arms. "Game *fucking* on, Leo."

We hold our stare for a few seconds, both trying not to smile, before the tension breaks, and both start laughing. I'm not really sure what we just challenged each other to, but it's bound to be interesting.

"Oh God." Vivian's laughter subsides. "What movie do you want to watch?" she asks, shaking her head. "Action or comedy?"

"I'll watch either."

"Just pick one. I picked the last one."

"Okay, comedy then."

"*The Hangover* or *Wedding Crashers?*" she asks, clearly having thought about it, since they were right on the tip of her tongue.

"*The Hangover,* it's been a while since I've watched that."

"Done." She clears the dishes and takes them to the sink. She's wearing leggings… again. She's always in sexy Lululemon athleisurewear at home. Tonight, it's gray leggings that make her ass look ridiculously good. I almost hate it when she wears leggings. Every time she turns her back, I can't help but check her out. Her cropped sweatshirt reveals just enough of her toned stomach to get me thinking about what else is under it. Vivian has the sexiest abs—toned and defined but still feminine. This is exactly why I need her to put on some ugly, baggy clothes… although those would be fun to remove too.

I've got to get my shit together. The mere thought of her is making me hard. We pour ourselves some wine and settle on the couch—a camel-colored leather sectional. It's incredibly comfortable.

No big deal; we've watched dozens of movies here. But lately, Vivian has been scooting closer, practically snuggling up to me. And at the end of the day, I'm a guy, and it's tough not to want her this close.

Vivian sits on the chaise part of the U-shaped couch, stretching out comfortably. I sit on the opposite side, extending my legs as well.

"What are you doing over there?" she frowns. "Why don't you come over here so we can actually watch the movie *together,*" she says, patting the chaise.

God, Vivian, because I don't want a hard-on for the next two hours.

"I'll come over there if you'd like."

She hesitates, "Well, you don't *have* to," she says. She's being passive-aggressive, and my only move is to clearly go and sit by her, where she will be an absolute tease for the next two fucking hours.

Hesitantly, I walk to the chaise and sit next to her, folding my arms, giving her closed-off body language… *just friends* body language. We can sit here next to each other on the couch, no problem. We cannot intertwine, no body language suggesting we'll be getting physical at any point during the movie.

She doesn't seem bothered by my standoffish behavior. She sits next to me, her shoulder nestled into my arm, and extends her legs out long, crossing one over the other. She sets her arms on her lap. It's comfortable. It's appropriate. It's friendly. I'm hanging with my friend.

My gorgeous fucking friend.

* * * * * * * * * *

I try to focus my attention on the screen, where Alan just found a tiger in the bathroom. Vivian is laughing. We've been laughing together for a while, but now I'm no longer laughing. She just readjusted us, and all I can focus on is her body touching mine. She said she needed a new position to get comfortable, taking my arm and wrapping it around her shoulders so she could lay her head on the inside of my shoulder. Her knees are knocked together and leaning toward me.

Five minutes later, she shifts around. "Sorry, I can't get comfortable," she says, falling into the position of doom. Her body turns inward, tangling her legs with mine, and her arm now rests on my torso and chest. The problem with this position is that our hands do not stay idle; they start to wander… to explore… taking a little test drive on each other. She starts this time, the little game we seem to play more and more, where innocent touches become something more, testing the boundaries of our friendship.

She slowly starts drifting her fingers, softly at first, up and down my torso, tantalizing me as she splays her hand across my chest and caresses my pecks, like she's trying to feel the muscles. *Fucking tease.* She knows *exactly* what she's doing. Two can play this game.

She should know by now that when I play games, I like to win. And you better believe I plan to win this game. She will break first, giving in before I do. I don't even bother with over-the-clothes tickles; I go straight for the jugular and slide my hand under her cropped, loose sweatshirt. Wondering if I'll find a bra, I glide my fingers over her smooth stomach, feeling her inhale sharply, hoping to make her squirm a little, like I have been for the past three damn months. She matches my movements with equal intensity, proving she's just as determined to win. Her hand glides under my shirt, brushing the outline of muscles on my abdomen, dipping her fingers ever so slightly into the waistband of my pants, provoking, taunting me. I let her.

I'm fully hard now, my cock tight against my boxers, but I will not back down, and I will not lose. Suddenly, I'm back in time, playing chicken with my junior-high crush—a game of daring where neither of us wants to be the first to back down. Except this time, I'm not sure what the rules are or what the end game is, and I don't know if I care because I'm enjoying the game too much.

She shifts her body, scootching herself farther up mine and grinding her groin into me. My pulse quickens with the motion, and I slide my hand farther up her stomach, wondering if I'm really going to go in for the kill. Normally, I never wimp out or feel hesitant with women, but Vivian is different. For some reason, she makes me second-guess myself. I pull my hand to her side and up to the edge of her breast. She's wearing a bra, but it's smooth and feels practically naked. I trace the side of her boob, letting my fingers graze the top of her flesh. She takes a sharp breath and boldly moves to straddle me. She's being reckless, putting herself in this position. Is this what she meant by *game on*? Or is this her sultry side? Because if so, I am fucked.

My craving for her intensifies, like an alcoholic savoring a sip of whiskey. She slowly runs her fingers through my hair as she drops her forehead to mine and closes her eyes. She stills, breathing shallowly, and whispers, "Leo." I can practically feel my cock pulsating in my head, a pounding that makes me feel drunk, drunk on her. My hands move to her delicious ass, and I stare at her beautiful mouth, begging me to taste it. She went ninety; I'm supposed to go ten. Isn't that how this works?

I slide my hand to her thigh, guiding it up the curve of her body to her clavicle, grazing her neck as my thumb brushes her bottom lip. I caress her cheek, tucking her hair behind her ear as she bites her bottom lip seductively. "Damn you, Walker," I mutter, surrendering as months of pent-up desire surge through me, and I crush my lips to hers. I lose the game, but I feel like I've just won the goddamn lottery.

Her soft, supple lips against mine ignite every nerve in my body. I'm lost in the kiss, savoring every moment. My hands slide under her shirt, roaming the smooth skin of her back. I grip her hip and ass firmly, feeling the heat of her body against mine. My hands move up the curve of her body, exploring every inch. When my fingers brush the side of her bra, it takes all my willpower not to grab her tits, knowing that even this kiss is more than I should be doing—I've already crossed a line. We move in sync, as if we've done this a thousand times before, yet each kiss feels new and electrifying.

Her tongue dances with mine, exploring, teasing, as her nails gently rake through my hair. The world outside ceases to exist; it's just the two of us, wrapped in this intoxicating embrace. Each kiss grows more fervent, more desperate, as if we're trying to make up for lost time.

I trail kisses down her jawline to her neck, feeling her pulse under my lips. She lets out a soft moan, a sound that sends electricity down my spine and spurs me on. I return to her lips, capturing them again in a kiss that's both tender and demanding.

We break apart only for a brief moment to catch our breath, our foreheads resting together, eyes locked. Her breath mingles with mine, and for a moment, we stay like that, foreheads touching, sharing the same air. The desire in her gaze mirrors my own, and it's all I can do to keep from diving back in immediately. When our lips meet again, it's with a renewed intensity.

Time seems to blur as we kiss, minutes feeling like seconds. Her lips, her touch—it's all I can focus on, and I'm lost in it. It's not just a kiss; it's an unspoken confession of everything we've been holding back. But then, reality hits me like a freight train. *Shit.* This isn't just some random hookup—this is Vivian, my friend. The one person I can't afford to fuck up with. I'd never want to hurt her. She wants things like love and marriage—things I can't give her. This is a goddamn mess waiting to happen. I know I need to stop, but my body is screaming to keep going.

Summoning all my willpower, I drag myself back—my breath ragged, heart hammering. "Vivian, fuck… I'm sorry, we shouldn't be doing this," I manage, barely holding onto my self-control. "I got carried away."

I know I should have stopped sooner, but I couldn't. I try to get a grip, my cock's hard and my pulse is pounding. "Maybe we should talk about this," I say, but it comes out more like a breathless mess than the calm and collected conversation I'm aiming for. I can barely think straight with everything that just happened. "Figure out what we both want, set some boundaries… before we fuck this up."

She looks at me, a mix of surprise and disappointment in her eyes. Her expression stings—she didn't want to stop either. I reach up and gently trace her jaw with my thumb, our foreheads still close. The tension in the air is thick between us—both of us harboring a load of shit we're not saying.

"Fuck, as much as I want you, Vivian… you're too important to me."

She nods slowly. "You should probably go," she whispers, her voice trembling.

"Yeah… you're right." I hesitate, hating how this feels.

"Yeah," she manages, wiping at her cheek quickly. "Let's not talk about this right now, okay? We'll deal with it later."

I nod and stand, feeling like a teenager caught doing something I shouldn't. Everything feels off now, awkward as hell. We walk to the door, neither of us knowing what to say.

At the door, I turn to her. "You still want to drive with me tomorrow?"

She forces a smile and nods. "Yeah, I'll meet you in the parking garage at noon."

She hugs me quickly, a shadow of the warmth we usually share. "Goodnight, Viv."

"Goodnight. See you tomorrow."
I walk out, praying that we didn't just fuck everything up.

Chapter 13

VIVIAN

The Next Day—Thanksgiving

Confusion—that's what plagued my mind last night as I lay awake, my thoughts racing in a million different directions, replaying the evening. What was I thinking, playing with fire like that? Dangling our friendship by a thread. I got up early to work, knowing sleep wouldn't come anyway.

I've been sitting in my home office for hours, staring at blueprints, trying to focus but making no progress. The lines blur together as my mind drifts back to Leo and Ben. It's Thanksgiving today, my second one without Ben. Last year, I was a complete mess, barely getting through the day. This year, I'm not around family or my long-time friends, and though I've had more time to heal, I'm worried about handling the emotions, especially with my conflicted feelings and thoughts about last night. It's almost noon. I give up, leaving the blueprints on my desk to get ready for Michael and Stella's.

I head downstairs to the parking garage to meet Leo, my thoughts spinning. What do I say? How do I act? I don't want it to be awkward, but I can't ignore the tension from last night. I can't ignore the fact that I sat on Leo's lap, grinding against him while we made out—his tongue in my mouth, his hands tracing up and down my body. A knot tightens in my stomach just thinking about it.

God, I like him so much. He's my friend, and there's a connection and undeniable attraction between us. But deep down, I know we don't want the same things. Hell, was I really willing to risk everything on the slim chance that he might change his mind for me?

My thoughts linger on our brief make-out session. Wow. His lips, his hands on me, his body. He's an incredibly good kisser. I've made-out with a few guys over the past year, but those encounters ended in disappointment. The emotional connection wasn't there, or they lacked the patience I needed. Some moments were nice, but nothing compared to last night. I haven't felt such a mix of excitement, nerves, and attraction since high school with Ben—the feeling of newness and anticipation.

I know he enjoyed it—he was hard as hell—but I can't shake this feeling that it meant a lot more to me than it did to him. Maybe I'm just another one of his Saturday nights… except those usually end in sex for Leo. It might've just been kissing, but for me, it was everything. It felt so damn right, and I was so turned on, I didn't want to stop. That's a huge win for me. Why did he stop? Was he really afraid of ruining our friendship, or did he think I couldn't handle more? Or was it something else? Did he think I'd reject him, and that's why he pulled away before it went further?

"Hey, Viv." My thoughts are interrupted as I approach Leo's parking spot. I'll follow his lead. He's confident, mature, and I trust him to handle this normally. He embraces me with a hug, but doesn't linger too long. Short and sweet, *almost* like before.

We get into his BMW and head to Michael and Stella's in Evanston. We drive in awkward silence for a few minutes before Leo clears his throat. "It doesn't have to be awkward, Viv. We had a glass of wine, watched a movie, and made out for a bit. No big deal."

No big deal.

Easy for him to say. Now I know how he feels about it—just another make-out.

Leo glances over at me. "Do you want to talk about it?"

"Yeah, maybe later," I say, waving it off, trying to keep my voice steady. "I'm already nervous enough with this being my first Thanksgiving away from home. Let's just focus on getting through today. We can talk later, maybe on the way home tonight."

He nods, seeming to understand. "Yeah, of course. We'll talk later." He grabs my hand and gives it a reassuring squeeze. "I know you don't have your usual support system, but I hope you know that I'm here for you. It's not the same, I get that, but I'm here. If you need a break, just say the word. Do we need a code word for *'get me the hell out of here?'*" A smile spreads across his face.

I smile in return. I don't know how he does it, but he has a way of making everything better. For a brief moment, I really do feel like it's going to be okay. "Yes, we definitely need a code word. Should it be a Thanksgiving word or something completely random?"

"A Thanksgiving word is obviously less noticeable. You know, cranberries, gravy, stuffing... or maybe we go for a random, inappropriate word like titty, dildo, boner... or bang! I know you have a special attachment to bang."

I laugh. I can't help it. "Oh, it's definitely dildo!" I exclaim, keeping my tone as serious as possible. "I can't wait to find a way to slip 'dildo' into the conversation at dinner. *'Stella, can you please pass the gravy? By the way, I have an incredible new dildo I just bought on Amazon. I can send the link to anyone who's interested.'*"

Leo laughs and kisses the top of my hand. "We got this, love," he assures me, letting go of my hand and returning it to the steering wheel. And I believe him.

I change the subject, keeping it casual. "I feel bad not bringing anything for dinner."

"Don't worry about it. Michael's a top chef. He's got it covered. Your bottle of wine is more than enough."

We pull up to Michael and Stella's, the last to arrive. Their home is beautiful, a two-story with two front porches that wrap around either side. It's Michael, Stella, their two kids, Stella's parents, Meredith, and her wife, Piper, whom I haven't met yet. Stella welcomes us inside and introduces me to her parents and Piper in the kitchen.

The kitchen is a dream. Truly designed for a chef—a culinary haven with handcrafted cabinetry, Wolf appliances, and an extra-large island with quartz countertops and backsplash. It opens up to a spacious living room with ample windows for natural light and a two-story fireplace tiled all the way up. I admire the fine craftsmanship and design, finding myself wanting a tour of the rest of the house.

Soft background music plays, mingling with the sounds of kids playing nearby and the voices in the kitchen. It smells incredible, and I can't wait to try Michael's take on Thanksgiving dinner. The sounds and smells remind me of home. As I look around at the faces, some new and some familiar, I realize that today is going to be fine. *I'm* going to be fine.

We're all in the kitchen making small talk. I'm getting to know Piper, while Leo and Meredith are in a corner, deep in conversation. Stella is laughing with Michael as he oversees all the cooking that she is helping with. I instantly like Piper. I find myself laughing with her easily, as if we are old friends. It's fun to finally meet Meredith's other half, and I can see why they mesh so well.

After a couple of hours of socializing, appetizers, and drinks, we take our seats at the table, which has been elegantly decorated for the holiday. Our conversation is light and fun as we dish up our plates. I sit between Leo and Stella's mother. As I spoon cranberries onto my turkey, Leo leans over and whispers, "Do you need your dildo?" he asks teasingly, drawing a smile from me.

I lean my head close to his. "I mean, always," I retort, "but not right now." I pat his thigh, a silent thank you for checking in on me. A surge of emotion overcomes me, and I'm suddenly worried that I might cry. It's a mix of gratitude for him and the emptiness I'm trying to fill inside. I fight back the tears and breathe deeply, gaining control.

The rest of dinner is great. Stella's dad is hilarious and inappropriate in the best way. He tells funny stories and dirty jokes that make her mom blush with embarrassment. I really like these people.

After dinner, we all help clean up. I'm in the middle of washing dishes when Leo stands behind me, gripping my shoulders to take my place. He nods toward Meredith, who's sitting at the table with Stella. "I've got this, why don't you go have a chat and relax."

God, he really is great.

"You sure? I'm happy to finish."

"I insist. Go relax." He scoots me out of the way, and I can't help but think about what a great partner in life he would be, just like Ben was. I force that thought from my mind, as it's a moot point, and join Meredith and Stella. They immediately include me in their conversation about their December holiday plans. This is something I'm genuinely interested in, knowing I'm going to miss some of my favorite holiday activities and traditions this year, not being in Utah until later in December. Stella tells us that they take the kids every year to a light show and this year's will be at the botanical gardens. Meredith tells me about the Christkindlmarket downtown, which piques my interest. I love the one in Utah and have gone the past few years.

"You'll have to get Leo to take you. It's fun, and a great Christmas market! The spiced wine is to die for." Meredith lights up with excitement as she tells me about some vendors and different food creations there.

Stella turns to me, "Speaking of Leo, what's the deal with you two?" She asks as she nods to where Leo is doing the dishes.

"What do you mean?" I ask, feigning ignorance.

"Oh, come on. There's nothing going on between you two? You know, more than friends? It just seems like there's maybe… something more, you know?" I notice Meredith out of the corner of my eye, watching cautiously.

"You think?" I ask, scrunching my face. "No, we're just friends. I mean, we have a flirtatious relationship for sure… but just friends." I can tell my answer doesn't convince Meredith, but Stella seems to buy it.

"Ah, okay… damn. I had a bet going with Michael that you two were secretly more than friends. I swear, the way he looks at you, I've never seen him look at anyone like that… I've actually never seen him with any woman more than two or three times, except you, Mer, but you don't count." She laughs as she shrugs. "Guess I owe Michael a blowjob."

Meredith interjects, "Oh, come on, Stell. You know Leo—he never lets things go beyond friendship." Hearing Meredith confirm that reality makes my heart sink. I glance over at Leo, who is still at the sink, oblivious to our conversation. He looks sexy doing the dishes, and the weight of Meredith's words settle heavily on me. I force a smile as I nod along to their banter.

The rest of the night goes perfectly. After cleaning up dinner, we linger around the table, immersed in conversation and laughter. It feels like being with old friends, and I savor every moment of that easy, familiar comfort. As we ready to leave, I'm overwhelmed with a sense of peace and gratitude that I could spend a holiday I expected to be difficult, away from home, with genuine, caring people.

Leo and I grab our coats and say our goodbyes to everyone. As we walk toward the car, my heart begins to race.

I click my seatbelt into the buckle and find myself torn. Part of me wants so badly to talk to him, to set boundaries and define what we are to each other so that there is no more confusion and conflicting emotions. The other part of me wants him to pull me into the back seat and fuck me. I glance at Leo, wondering if he can sense the turmoil within me.

Leo pulls out into the road and we both start saying something at the same time, making us laugh.

"You go," he says.

"I was just going to say that I had a really great time. Thank you for inviting me to your Thanksgiving and for making this day not only bearable but enjoyable." My voice cracks. *Goddammit.* "You have no idea what this day has done for me, knowing that I can have some normalcy during a holiday. It's a huge stride for me." I look at him tenderly, "Seriously, Leo. Thank you so much for everything."

"Anytime. You know you're one of my closest friends. I'd do anything for you… I hope you know that."

I form a slight smile as I blink back the moisture pooling in my eyes. "I do. And I feel the same way. You're my very best friend here in Chicago, and after last night…." I pause, choking back the tears threatening to fall. "I don't want to lose your friendship." I guess I'm starting the uncomfortable conversation.

"Look… Viv, I know this is difficult. No one wants to have this kind of chat; it's uncomfortable and hard. If I didn't care about you so much, it wouldn't be worth having, but I do. I care about you… a lot. So I think it's crucial for us to talk about what happened last night."

I nod, knowing he's right.

He continues, "I'm very attracted to you, that's no secret. From the moment I saw you running past my house to now, my attraction has only grown stronger. And I doubt that will ever go away. You're an incredible woman, and goddamn, you can kiss!" He flashes a smirk. "I'd never want you to think I didn't enjoy last night. It was fucking incredible." He pauses briefly, earning a smile from me. "But I also know we want different things in life. And I respect you enough to admit I can't give you what you deserve. I don't want to stand in the way of your happiness or complicate your life in any way."

He stops talking and waits for me to respond, as if I know what the fuck to say to that. It feels like an impossible situation, and I find myself not wanting to deal with it, leaving the elephant in the room and tiptoeing around it—that might be easier.

He glances in my direction, silently urging me to speak.

I take a moment to gather my thoughts. "Thank you for being honest with me. I appreciate it. I'm obviously attracted to you too, and I value our friendship." I pause, choosing my words carefully. "I know you don't want a relationship. Last night wasn't about that. It was just lust, a moment with someone I'm attracted to and feel comfortable with—something I haven't felt in a long time. Honestly, I know we should set boundaries, and define our friendship, but I just don't want to. I like how things are. I have fun with you, I trust you, and I like our dynamic."

I take a deep breath, my voice steady but vulnerable. "Pushing the boundaries of our friendship last night had more to do with me than with you. Since Ben died, I've struggled with getting close to anyone. But with you, I felt safe enough to push past those walls, to see if I could move beyond the guilt and fear that's held me back. I'm sorry for crossing a line; I won't do it again. But I didn't do it with the intent of snagging a boyfriend… I'm not that naive."

I sigh deeply and lean my head back against the headrest, closing my eyes for a moment. "I just don't want things to change between us. I know that's taking the easy way out, avoiding the problem, but can we pretend this never happened and go back to how things were?" I open my eyes and look at him, hoping he understands and feels the same way.

Leo glances at me, his expression softening with understanding. We reach a red light, and the quiet sound of the car fills the space between us.

"Hey, I get it. I don't want things to change between us either. But pretending nothing happened isn't realistic. We both know the attraction is too strong to ignore."

The light turns green, and we continue driving. As the river comes into view, he pulls into the parking garage and parks the car. Leo turns to me, his eyes earnest. "I'm worried that if we keep sitting close and touching, even if it's just friendly, it'll be too hard to avoid crossing that line again. It's not about setting boundaries to define our friendship, it's about protecting it. We can't have any wandering hands. I care about you too much to risk messing this up."

"Noooo. I love the wandering hands," I say in a playful, whiny voice, not wanting to comply with these new rules.

Leo chuckles, "I do too, love. I do too." He reaches out, taking my hand in his. "Maybe we can find a middle ground. We don't have to let what happened define us, but we can acknowledge it and be mindful. We can let it be okay without pretending it never happened." He gives me a reassuring smile, his eyes filled with warmth. "What do you think?"

"You're right," I say softly. "We need to protect what we have."

Leo's grip on my hand tightens briefly before he lets go. "So, we'll keep it platonic. The flirtatious nudges and hugs are fine, but no more snuggling during movies, no wandering hands. We can keep the loving, friendly touches but nothing beyond that, to avoid temptation."

I smile, a mix of relief and sadness washing over me. "Agreed."

We both sit in silence for a moment, absorbing the new boundaries we've set. Then, with a deep breath, I open the car door. "Thanks again for today, and for talking this through."

He nods, his eyes soft. "Anytime. You know I'm always here for you."

We step out of the car and walk towards my back door, then turn to face each other.

"Goodnight, Leo," I say softly as I wrap my arms around him for a *friendly* hug.

"Goodnight," he replies, his voice warm and steady.

Chapter 14

LEO

Sunday, November 26

The light from my lamp barely reaches the corners of the sitting room as I sip my morning coffee. I'm on my sofa, facing the window with a view of the river. It's too cold now for mornings on the patio. As I scroll through my X feed, catching up on the news and random updates, I spot Vivian heading out for a morning run. I hate that she runs alone in the dark. It's early—5:30—a lot earlier than usual for her. I remember she had a date last night, and for reasons I can't quite pinpoint, I find myself needing to know how it went.

I run upstairs, quickly change into warm running clothes, and rush outside.

After eight minutes of running, I see her in the distance. I close the gap, calling her name. She doesn't turn around, and I know she has her AirPods in, blasting a playlist. I'm within feet of her, and she still doesn't turn when I call her name again. Finally, I catch up and tap her on the shoulder.

She whips around, yelling, "Holy shit," panic-stricken as she drops her phone and pulls apart her Birdie, sounding an ear-piercing alarm. Realizing it's me, she shoves me. "Jesus! What the FUCK, Leo!" She removes her AirPods, laces her hands behind her head, and paces back and forth, gasping for breath and trying to calm her nerves.

I pick up her phone and check for damage as I calmly approach, feeling terrible. "Viv, I'm so sorry. I didn't mean to scare you." The Birdie is still screeching, waking neighbors and drawing unwanted attention. Her eyes are frantic and wild as I reach for her hands, gripping them in mine. I pry the Birdie from her grip and reattach it to the hook on her running belt, silencing the alarm and leaving us with ringing ears and Vivian's sharp breaths.

"Hey. Hey," I say, searching her eyes. "Look at me." Her eyes slowly move to meet mine. "It's okay. It's just me. I'm so sorry, I didn't mean to scare you."

She clutches her chest, her voice shaking. "Jesus, you scared the shit out of me."

"I'm so sorry. You're okay, yeah?"

She nods. "I will be. Sorry, I just can't catch my breath." She laughs, "Shit, my heart is pounding."

I wrap my arms around her, squeezing gently to help her calm down. "I guess we know your Birdie works," I say with a chuckle, trying to soothe her. "That thing just woke the whole goddamn neighborhood."

Laughing, she pulls away from me and playfully nudges my chest. "Don't you *ever* do that again."

"I won't, I swear. What are you listening to anyway? Is it loud enough?" I joke. "You know, I really wish you'd learn some self-defense. An attacker could easily grab the Birdie from you and reconnect it like I did. And since there aren't many people around right now, it's not enough. Plus, your music is way too loud for you to be aware of your surroundings."

"Okay, Dad." She rolls her eyes. "I told you I'd let you teach me some things."

"Alright. Well, let's get that on the schedule. It's important. Can I run with you?"

"Yeah, of course. But I think I just want to walk for a minute. My heart rate just went high enough to replace a mile of running." Smiling, she turns to walk, and I follow suit, side by side.

"How was your date last night?" I ask coolly.

She looks at me with surprise and a hint of confusion. "You don't really want to know about my date, do you?"

"Of course I do. Friends talk about these things, don't they?"

"Yeah, I guess they do." She hesitates a moment, gathering her thoughts. "It just feels different now, talking about this with you." Keeping her gaze straight ahead, she continues, "But it was good. I actually had a lot of fun with him. He was nice and funny, our personalities clicked, and the conversation flowed easily…" I listen, taking in her words. "And… he's a good kisser," she adds, her tone laced with deliberate sharpness.

I raise an eyebrow, a teasing grin forming on my lips. "Oh, so you got on base then?"

She laughs softly, shrugging her shoulders. "Maybe, maybe not."

"I'm glad you had fun. You deserve that."

Damn it, why does this bother me so much?

"Did you book your flight home for Christmas yet?" I ask, hoping to shift the topic.

"I did. The flights dropped last week right before Thanksgiving, so I snatched up a ticket. I'm going home December seventeenth to the thirtieth. I'm excited to see my friends and my parents."

"That's great, so you'll be home for Mer's New Year's Eve party? You're planning to come still, yeah?"

"Yes, I'm planning to come. That's why I'm coming home on the thirtieth." She bends down to tie her shoe, a slight sigh escaping her lips. "I don't have anywhere else to go. Do you wanna run?" she asks, standing and looking down the Riverwalk, her breath visible in the chilly air.

"Yeah, we can run." We set a comfortable pace, running side by side. The cold bites at my face, and while I enjoy cooler temps for running, it's pushing my limits. I usually avoid running outdoors once the temperatures drop below the thirties, and it's probably mid-thirties right now.

We run in silence for a good half mile, the sounds of our breathing and feet pounding on the sidewalk blending with the city's hum. Each exhale forms a misty cloud before dissipating into the crisp morning air. It's Sunday, so we pass an occasional runner, but it's mostly quiet and still. The moon's reflection shimmers on the river, casting a light that contrasts with the city's distant murmur. It's peaceful, and one of my favorite ways to start a morning.

She breaks the silence. "When is the fall semester over?" Her concentration remains unbroken as she stares straight ahead.

"In a week and a half, December sixth."

"Wow. I didn't realize you got done so soon. That's great that you get the whole month of December off."

"It is great. I'm thinking of going to London the day after the semester ends, for a week. I was going to look at flights today. My brother and his wife just had their first baby a few days ago, so I'm officially an uncle." A smile spreads across my face at the thought. "I'm so happy for them. I want to go meet my new niece and see the two of them; it's been a few months since I've been back." I pause to catch my breath.

She looks at me with a smile that reaches her eyes. "Oh my gosh, you're an uncle! That's so exciting! Why didn't you tell me your brother was going to have a baby? I didn't even know he was married."

"It wasn't intentional, it just never came up."

We reach our halfway point and turn around, the city skyline looming ahead.

"Still… that's a big deal, a big thing in your life." She grabs ahold of my elbow and slows us to a walk. "Seriously, Leo. I tell you everything. Why don't you ever talk about your family or London?"

I gesture forward. "Let's keep running, this isn't the time to dive into that." I sprint forward, only to be pulled back and slowed by her.

"Come on, give me something. It's your home and what makes you— you. I want to know about your family, and your life growing up there."

I lace my fingers behind my head, taking a deep breath. "You know how it took you months to open up to me about Ben?"

She nods, her expression softening. "Yeah."

"Well, this is like that. I don't want to talk about it right now, so please respect that, and stop pushing." My voice is clipped, harsher than I intended. She's taken aback, her eyes widening in shock and hurt. I soften. "I'm sorry. I didn't mean for it to come out that way."

She's clearly upset, but nods in understanding. "Okay. Yeah, I get it, I'm sorry for pushing. I just want to understand you." Her voice is quiet, laced with sincerity and a hint of sadness.

"I know. And I love that about you." I give her a half smile. "C'mon, let's keep running."

We pick our pace back up. "What's her name? Your niece," she asks.

"Emma. Emma Jones Weston. My brother's wife's last name is Jones." I can't help but smile, thinking about my brother and his family. "I'll show you a picture of her when we get back. She's adorable and so tiny."

I glance at her, a surprised look on her face. "I didn't know you were so fond of babies." She playfully nudges me. "Look at you, having a soft side I didn't know about. Have you ever wanted kids of your own?" She's still prying… poking—albeit subtly, not about my family but families in general.

I let out an exhale. "It's not something I give much thought to, honestly. I wouldn't want a broken family, and my lifestyle doesn't really permit that, so I don't see how I would have kids." I say in between breaths. "I like kids well enough, and honestly, I haven't been around many babies, so I can't speak to that. But I'm excited for my brother and Nichole. If this little baby can bring them so much joy, then I know it will for me as well because I love my brother, and the things that make him happy make me happy too."

She laughs. "I don't know what to say right now. I've never seen this side of you."

"Well, I'm a complex man, Walker."

"Apparently." We run in silence for a few more minutes and slow to a walk as we reach our last half-mile.

"You do know how babies are made, right?" she jokes. "Because you are having a lot of sex with people that you really don't know well. What if you had a whoopsie? It's not like that couldn't happen."

I chuckle under my breath and stare up at the sky. "Oh my God. Are we really having this conversation? You worried about my safety habits with my sex life?" I give her a mischievous grin. "Trust me, I'm careful. I'm not looking to add '*dad*' to my list of titles anytime soon."

"That's great. But my question is, what IF you got someone pregnant? What would you do?"

I let out a deep breath, contemplating the seriousness of her question. "I would do the right thing, whatever that meant in the moment." I slow my walking pace slightly, glancing at the ground as I gather my thoughts. "I would support her in whatever way she needed. If she didn't want the baby, I'd respect her decision. If she wanted to keep the baby, I'd be there for both her and the child." I look up, meeting her eyes. "I'd struggle with not being involved in a child's life if I knew it was mine." I pause, searching her face to gauge her reaction.

"Okay, so let's just say, hypothetically, someone gets pregnant, the baby is yours, she wants to keep it, and she wants you to be in its life. Do you try to be a family? Live together and do the whole works?"

"God, you're so cheeky." I shake my head with a smirk. "No, I'm not going to force myself to try to fall in love with someone I didn't have those feelings for in the first place. That doesn't seem like a healthy way to go about life or build a family. I would focus on building a friendship with her and hope she's more than just a pretty face. We would raise the child amicably, co-parenting as best as we could."

"And you know she's pretty because?" she teases, giving me a hard time as usual. It's our thing—constantly giving each other shit.

"Because I don't bring home anyone who isn't attractive," I reply with a smirk.

"Oh my God," she says, rolling her eyes.

As we near my townhouse, she suddenly stops and looks at me with a soft smile and genuine admiration in her eyes.

"What's that look for?"

"You're a good guy, Leo. A genuinely good guy." She grins. "I don't understand the philosophy that guides your life, or your sexual shenanigans. Well, no, I do understand them; I just don't get why you reject the idea of anything more ever coming from them. But regardless, you are a great person. I'm lucky to know you."

I chuckle softly. "Oh, c'mon now, I'm tearing up... Come inside, let's have coffee."

"Ugh, I'm all gross and sweaty. I need to shower."

"You can wait to shower. I'm sweaty too. I've seen you at your worst, you know. Just come have coffee."

She sighs, "Fine."

We walk into my townhouse, the warm air intensifying the sweat on my skin. I remove my jacket and beanie, running my fingers through my damp hair. Vivian is already at the fridge, grabbing the milk. I watch her as she moves to the espresso machine, expertly pulling out the two porta-filters.

"Do you want a latte or a cappuccino?" she asks as she tamps the espresso.

"Cappuccino," I answer, admiring her ass as she works my espresso machine. I love watching her move comfortably around my kitchen, it's incredibly sexy. I sit at the counter and check flights for London on my phone, while she steams the milk.

I find a flight for December seventh that arrives the next day at 11 AM, and a return flight a week later. I'm selecting my first-class seats when Vivian slides my cappuccino toward me and unzips her jacket, revealing her incredibly toned body and great tits. She's wearing a matching green set that makes her eyes pop. Her top barely grazes the waistband of her leggings, teasing a bit of skin, and her tank pushes her tits up, placing her incredible rack right at eye level as she leans into the counter and sips her cappuccino.

She catches me staring and smirks. "You know, if you're going to stare, you could at least try to be a little less obvious."

I shake my head with a grin. "Well, Jesus, you take your jacket off and stand right in front of me. Where am I supposed to look?"

"I'm sorry. It's fucking hot, and I've gotta let the girls breathe." She grabs her cappuccino and walks around the counter to sit next to me. "What are you doing on your phone?"

"Booking a flight to London, which reminds me, I need your flight info so I can upgrade you to first class when I book my ticket to Paris."

"Who says I'm not already in first class?" she teases, placing her elbow on the counter and resting her chin in her hand as she looks at me.

"Are you?" I say, amused, meeting her gaze.

She laughs. "No. I did book business class, though. That's still good, right?"

"Yeah, it's better than economy, but it doesn't even compare to first class."

"Okay, I'll send you my flight info later. What will you do in London while you're there, aside from visiting your brother and his family?"

"I'll mostly spend time with Andrew, but I'll have some business meetings, see my dad, and hang out with my friend Brian. We like to hit the local pubs." I sip my coffee. "He's coming here for Christmas and New Year's, so I'll get to spend plenty of time with him."

"Oh? You've never mentioned him before. You have this whole secret life that I don't know about." She puts her hands up, innocently. "I'm not prying, by the way, just stating facts."

"It's not a secret. Brian comes every year for New Years, this will be the first time he's coming for Christmas. He's my longest childhood friend, and we went to university together… He's like a brother to me, you'll like him. What do *you* have planned for when you go back home?"

"I don't have a lot of set plans yet." She takes a sip of her cappuccino. "I'm taking my niece and nephew to Zoo Lights with Ben's sister, Melissa. We do that every year. It's just a girls' thing with the kids—get them hot cocoa, the whole deal." She sets her cup down and leans back in her chair. "Aside from that, I'll go to Ben's house on Christmas Eve. I don't know if that's weird, that I still do stuff with them, but they are my second family. I've known them since I was fifteen."

"I don't think that's weird at all.".

She sighs and runs a hand through her hair. "I'm staying with my parents because both my houses are rented out during that time. I'll spend Christmas Day with them, and of course, Sarah and I will see each other multiple times, but no specific plans yet." She smiles, thinking about it. "I'll be happy to go from this cold to Utah cold; it doesn't even compare."

I nod in agreement. "The Chicago cold is bloody brutal. It sounds like it's going to be a great trip. You'll have to send pics."

"I will for sure, and you too, from London. I've only been there once, and it was in high school. I don't remember as much as I'd like to."

"You'll have to come back with me sometime." I pause, remembering something. "Speaking of pictures, I forgot to show you a picture of Emma." I pull up the photos Andrew sent me and hand my phone to her. "Look how bloody beautiful she is."

She takes my phone, her beautiful smile spreading across her face. "Oh my God. She is so perfect." Her voice is a whisper, as if she's in a cathedral and doesn't want to disturb the peace. "Look how tiny she is!" She swipes through the photos, a sense of longing coming over her as she strokes the phone, trying to grasp my niece in her fingers. A pang of sadness hits her face, and I realize that one of her most painful memories just surfaced. It makes me feel like shit.

"God, Viv, I'm sorry. I didn't think about what these photos might do to you." I wrap my arm around her shoulder, giving a gentle squeeze as I lean in.

"Don't be sorry," she says, wiping a tear from her face. "It's not your fault. I'm so happy for your brother and Nichole."

"I know, but that was shitty of me. I can't imagine that kind of loss, losing someone that you created with the person you loved more than anyone else… and then losing them both."

"It's okay. I don't want people to not experience this joy just because I lost mine. She's beautiful, and I'm so excited for you to meet her. I want you to share the experience with me. Please don't hold back because of my past." She places her hand on my leg, "I can tell this means a lot to you."

"I will, I promise." Giving her another squeeze, I stand up. "Let's do something to get your mind off this. Want me to teach you some self-defense?"

"Yes, that would be great," she says, a smile taking over her face.

We move to the family room, and I teach her a few basics: strikes, blocks, how to escape a hair pull, a chokehold, and how to prevent being taken to the ground. We work on her technique, and I give her a few real-life scenarios and tips to be aware of her surroundings. She's a natural—already strong and physically fit, she just needs practice.

She goes home to shower and get some work done before returning later for dinner. After dinner, we make some popcorn on the stove and settle on the couch to watch the British version of *Love Island*. The show is a bloody mess, a psychological shitshow, but she loves it.

I have a large white sectional with two brown leather chairs opposite. We sit with the popcorn bowl between us and our feet up on the coffee table. There's a comfort in these moments with her, an effortless ease that feels like we're an old married couple.

"Nick asked me out again," she says casually, her eyes fixed on the TV. "We're having lunch on Tuesday."

"That's great," I reply, keeping my voice light.

Inside, a familiar knot tightens in my chest. What if she falls in love with the wanker? The thought of losing this closeness terrifies me.

Sometimes I wonder what it would be like to be with Vivian. I imagine us not just sharing a couch, but a life—laughing at inside jokes, supporting each other through everything, and having incredible sex.

God, sex with Vivian would be insanely good. Once you've had sex with someone you love, though, it becomes personal, intimate—something Vivian had with Ben, but then lost. The thought of being that close to her, in every way, is intoxicating. But the fear of loving her only to lose her is too strong.

I've lost too much already.

Chapter 15

VIVIAN

Tuesday, November 28

I walk through the kitchen area of the Marioni's home in Naperville, meticulously checking every detail. "The framing looks really good, Nick. I'm impressed with how you're keeping things on track despite the weather," I say, smiling despite the hard hat that's matting down my hair. Nick, on the other hand, looks rugged and handsome in his hard hat. Why do men always look so good—no, almost sexy—in construction attire?

The framing was just completed over the weekend, and I'm meeting Nick to review the site plans.

"Thanks, Vivian. I have to admit, it's a bit easier to stay motivated knowing you'll be stopping by," he says, winking at me.

I laugh. "Well, if that's all it takes to stay on schedule, I'll be stopping by multiple times a week. I hear the General Contractor's pretty cute too, added bonus for me." I clear my throat, shifting to a more serious tone. "I did notice a few things I wanted to go over with you. Can we check the plans in there?" I gesture toward the trailer. It's cold as balls out here, and the trailer will at least be slightly warmer.

"Sure thing," Nick says, giving an *'after you'* signal with his hand.

Shoving my hands into my coat pockets to keep them warm, we walk to the trailer. This is the only thing I hate about my job—on-site days when it's so cold that my nipples could cut glass.

I hate the cold.

The trailer has a large table in the middle with a couple of cheap folding chairs surrounding it. The site plans are spread out in the middle of the table, ready for review. Seeing my plans being brought to life always brings a smile to my face.

I remove my hard hat and tousle my hair, trying to regain a bit of volume.

We take a seat next to each other, and I flip through the sheets to find the correct floor plan I want to discuss. "Here in the living room," I say, pointing. "These windows need to be precisely aligned for the view we're aiming for. Everything looks good on the plans, but can we double-check the measurements on-site before the frames are finalized?"

"Definitely." He leans in slightly. "I'll make sure it's perfect."

"Thanks, Nick. I appreciate the attention to detail. It really makes a difference."

"Anything else you need, just let me know."

"Actually, I think that covers it for now. Ready for lunch?" We make eye contact. He hesitates for a moment before leaning in and kissing me. It's a soft, lingering kiss, gentle yet stimulating. His lips are warm, and as he pulls away, he softly tugs at my bottom lip, sending a delicious warmth spreading through me.

A grin spreads from cheek to cheek; I can't help it. "If this is our appetizer, I think I might need seconds. I'm not quite finished yet."

With a mischievous grin, he removes his hat and sets it on the table. In one smooth motion, his hand slides to the back of my neck, pulling me closer as his lips meet mine. The kiss is intense yet tender, and I find myself melting into it. His lips move expertly, sending goosebumps down my arms.

Just as I'm getting lost in the moment, a sudden realization hits me. I pull back and let out a breathless laugh. "Oh my God, Nick, we're making out at work! We can't do this here," I say, still grinning.

"You're right," he chuckles. "Got carried away. Let's go to lunch. I just need to speak to some of the crew briefly, and then we can go."

"I can head out now and get us a table. I'll meet you there?" I ask.

"That sounds great. I won't be too far behind you."

"Well, Nick," I say, extending my hand for a handshake, a playful smile tugging at my lips, hinting at our earlier indiscretion. "Thank you for all your hard work in keeping me satisfied, both in *and* out of work."

He chuckles and takes my hand, shaking it. "Always a pleasure. I aim to please, in *and* out of work."

I grab my hard hat and walk to the car, grinning. I immediately turn on my heated seats and crank the heat as I scroll through my playlists for the drive to lunch. On a cold, gray November day like today, I settle on an early 2000s mix, letting Green Day, Matchbox Twenty, and Red Hot Chili Peppers fill the car with nostalgia. It's a comfort playlist for days like this.

* * * * * * * * * *

Lunch with Nick went great. It was fun and easy, the kind of lunch where you lose track of time in conversation. We talked a lot about work, which made things effortless. We exchanged stories about our current projects and discovered more and more that we have similar interests.

Nick is kind, funny, and genuine. I'm really attracted to him. He has sandy blonde hair that's shorter and styled in a sleek, sophisticated manner, neatly trimmed on the sides with a bit of length on top. His chiseled features are accentuated by short stubble, adding a touch of ruggedness to his appearance. His green eyes are striking against his complexion. Nick's overall look exudes a blend of suave charm and refined masculinity. He's hard-working, dedicated to his job, and I enjoy working with him. There is an ease to our conversations, a natural flow that makes everything feel right.

I knew it was important to bring up the fact that I was a widow before we planned anything more for the future. I didn't want to go into full detail, as that usually leads to me getting emotional. Nick listened intently as I briefly mentioned Ben, explaining that I was a widow and wanted to take things slow, especially regarding sex. He was understanding, nodding and assuring me that he was okay with taking things at my pace.

By the end of the meal, we had agreed to another date this weekend. As I walk back to my car, I feel a mix of excitement and guilt. Nick is wonderful, and I like him a lot; he checks all the boxes. But the thought of Leo lingers at the back of my mind, more persistent than ever, and it ticks me off because I know it's wasted energy to think of Leo that way.

As I start my forty-minute drive home, I decide to call Sarah. I need her perspective.

She picks up on the third ring. "Hey, Viv, how are you?"

"I'm good, friend. How are you?"

Sarah laughs. "I'm good, but we can talk about me later. What's up? I can tell you need to bounce your thoughts off me."

"God, how can you tell that just by asking me how I am?"

"It's in your voice. I know you too well, friend."

"That's almost pathetic." I laugh. "Okay, so remember the guy, Nick, I told you about?"

"Yeah, you had a date this past weekend, right?"

"Yes, and it went well. Really well. I like him a lot. We have a lot in common, and he kissed me on the porch at the end of the night. It was fire!"

"That's great! So what's the problem?"

"Nothing. We made out for a couple of minutes in the site trailer before we went to lunch. Whoops."

Sarah laughs. "Okay, that's hot."

"Yeah, it was. Lunch was great too. I like him even more."

"But…" Sarah prompts.

"Ugh. I like him a lot, but Leo is still in the back of my mind, and I don't know what to do."

Sarah's quiet on the other end.

"We had a great day on Sunday."

"Wait, you and Nick or you and Leo?"

"Me and Leo. We had a great day hanging out, just being us. Kept it strictly platonic as we discussed, and it felt normal… It was great. But I brought up something about his family earlier in the day, and he completely shut down, almost got a little defensive, which is something I've never experienced with him. I just wish he would tell me about it, so I could understand."

"Because you think if he told you about it, that would make him want to be with you?" she asks doubtfully.

"Well, when you put it that way it sounds stupid and naive, but yeah, I guess that's what I hope for."

Sarah sighs. "Ah, God. I'm sorry that you are dealing with this. I know it's hard, especially since you've been seeking this kind of connection for so long. It's not stupid; it's totally normal to have those hopes."

"But…" I say. I know how this goes: listen, validate, then give the blunt honest truth.

"But if Leo *is* dealing with some sort of say, 'childhood trauma', which we don't know if he is, that could look like so many things. I'd really focus on this Nick guy and dating other people. Try to make some other connections. You can stay friends with Leo, and if he ever changes his mind and wants more, then maybe you can explore something beyond being friends. But if being just friends with Leo is too hard or makes it difficult for you to explore other possible relationships, if it were me, I'd put some space in the friendship for a while. I know you don't want to take a step back, but you could always give it a try, see how it goes."

It's my turn to be quiet now. "What if I can't do that?"

"I think that you can; you just don't want to, and that's okay. That's your decision to make."

I let out a sigh of frustration. "I just don't understand how someone with his kind of knowledge and career can be emotionally unavailable and fucked up."

"Unfortunately, trauma doesn't skip those with psychology degrees, especially if something happened as a child."

"Right. But then to go on and get a PhD in psychology? Why wouldn't he deal with it then? It makes no sense to me… I mean, he won't even talk about it," I say, baffled.

"Honestly, it'd be hard to become a therapist and not deal with your past shit. But that being said, there are many reasons people choose not to deal with trauma—psychologists included."

"Why would he choose that?"

"For so many reasons: control—something he can choose and be in charge of, avoiding reopening old wounds, a protective mechanism to stay guarded, emotional detachment—focusing on others' problems to avoid his own—and fear. Leo's fully aware of why he is the way he is. In my opinion, he's chosen this lifestyle because it protects him—it's a coping mechanism, and that's normal, even if it's not always healthy. I don't know if he'll change, but it has to be his choice. You can't make him. He's been this way for a long time, and with all his education and experience, it's definitely purposeful. Just be careful, babe, and I'm really sorry you're going through this."

"Well, shit. This sucks. You know, he once told me that all the women he had ever loved had either died, left him, or cheated… except that he loves Meredith, and she's still around."

"God, that's sad," she says. "I doubt that's completely accurate, but there's got to be some truth to it for him to say that. But remember, we are speculating here; there might not be anything going on with Leo. He may just be the way he is because he chooses it. What do you think you're going to do?"

"I don't know. I have to sit on this."

"Yeah, it's a tough call."

"Alright, enough about me. Thanks for listening and giving me sound advice. Tell me everything that's going on with you, and let's talk about plans for when I'm there."

Sarah catches me up on things with her and Ryan, and we shoot some ideas around for when I come to visit, making me all the more excited to go home.

I can't breathe.

My eyes fly open, and I gasp for air, sweat clinging to my skin. *Fuck.* Not again. I haven't had one of these nightmares since I moved. I deliberately take deep breaths to slow my racing heart. Squeezing my eyes tight, I try to think of anything but the car accident. I think of Leo. Since meeting him, I've felt lighter—he's helped ease the constant weight I carry. I know that when I'm stressed my nightmares surface. And with all these decisions looming and second-guessing every choice I make, my anxiety is creeping back in.

I get out of bed and pace around the house, trying to shake off the tension. After an hour of aimless wandering, I end up in my office. I might as well work if I'm going to be awake anyway. I sit down and focus on the Johnsons' blueprints—a new client I picked up about a month ago. They're building a large home in the northern suburbs of Chicago. I work until my eyes start to close, then drag myself back to bed, falling into a deep, dreamless sleep.

Chapter 16

LEO

Sunday, December 3

I jolt awake to the sound of my phone vibrating on the nightstand. Groggily, I reach for it and squint at the screen. A message from Vivian. It's 1:23 AM.

"What the hell?" I mutter, rubbing my eyes.

Vivian: Hey, are you asleep?

What do you think, Viv?

I consider putting my phone down, but it's not like her to text in the middle of the night.

Leo: I was… I'm not anymore, what's up?

Vivian: Sorry for waking you.

Vivian: I just need a distraction for a bit.

Leo: Everything okay?

Vivian: Yeah. Well, I will be… I had another nightmare. Third one this week. This one's hitting me hard, can't calm down… Must be stress.

Shit.

Vivian mentioned a few days ago that she has recurring nightmares. She said it had been a while since she'd had one, but they started again earlier this week, the first since she moved.

Leo: What do you need?

Vivian: Can I come over for a bit? Need to get my mind off things.

I feel a stir next to me and glance over to see Ashley looking at me.

"What are you doing?" she asks, half asleep.

"Sorry, love. A friend needs me. Are you okay if I sneak out? You can stay and sleep; I'll be back soon."

She nods and turns over.

Damn, I forgot Ashley was here. We've hooked up a few times over the past few years, running into each other at various events. She's a cool chick, looking for the same no-strings-attached arrangement as me. I trust her enough to leave her alone here for a bit.

I quickly text Vivian back before she decides to head over… that could get awkward.

Leo: I'll come to you. Be there in five, just need to throw some clothes on.

I add a winky face emoji.

Vivian: Thanks, just let yourself in.

I have Vivian's door code for the keypad lock, and she has mine. Quickly, I throw on some joggers and a fitted long-sleeve athletic shirt before heading downstairs.

I let myself into Vivian's place. The main floor is dark, so I head upstairs toward her bedroom on the fourth floor, where light spills into the hallway.

Her lamp casts a soft glow around the room. Vivian is sitting up, resting against a pile of pillows, knees pulled tightly to her chest. She stares blankly at the wall, her face a mask of emptiness, save for the tear stains that show she's been crying.

When she turns to look at me and offers a weak smile, I'm immediately by her side. Climbing into bed next to her, I pull her close, wrapping my arms around her in a bear hug and drawing her near.

"Do you want to talk about it? What do you need from me?" I hold her close and stroke her hair as she rests her head on my shoulder.

"I don't know." She sits up and looks at me. "Can you just stay with me for a bit? Be a distraction?"

God, I can think of a million distractions I'd love to give Vivian right now, but those are off the table. "Of course. I'll stay with you for a bit."

"We can put pillows between us if we have to." She pulls one of the pillows from behind her to create some space between us.

I grab the pillow midair and return it back behind her. "There's no need for that. Given the circumstances, we can blur the lines for one night. I'm here to comfort you, and that's what I intend to do."

"Really?" She says doubtfully, leaning back against the pillows. "I expected you to be a bit more of a pussy… you're normally such a rule follower." She looks up and smirks.

There she is.

She's just fuckin' with me, trying to laugh and take her mind off things.

My eyes widen in shock. "A pussy? Really, Viv?"

She lets out a soft laugh, and I'm overcome with the need to make her feel better. She needs me right now, so I push aside the fact that she looks sexy as hell in her tight little pajama top that's low-cut, her nipples faintly visible, and matching shorts that are so short her ass cheeks are practically hanging out. For the first time, I notice a larger floral hip tattoo peeking out from the side of her shorts. I want to see all of it, but right now, I have to be the friend she needs.

I relax, keeping one arm wrapped around her shoulder. "Talk to me. What's going on in that head of yours?"

She sits up to face me, crosses her legs and pulls a blanket into her lap, aware that her shorts would give me a full view if she didn't cover up. "Where did you end up going tonight?" she asks casually, picking at a fuzzy on the blanket.

"Meredith and Piper dragged me to a cocktail lounge for Piper's employee's birthday."

"And? Did you enjoy yourself?" She makes eye contact and forces a smile.

"I did. You know Mer and Piper, it's hard not to have fun with them. The birthday boy, Johnny, is the manager at the bar Piper owns. He practically runs the place. He does his job well and helps Piper out a lot. He's a good friend of hers."

"Well, that's great. I'm glad you had fun." She hesitates. "I'm surprised you weren't occupied when I texted you."

Ah, fuck. Now I feel obligated to tell her about Ashley, at home, warming my bed. "Actually… I do have company. She's at my house… in my bed."

She flinches. "You left a random person in your house to come over here?" she asks with concern.

"No," I say gently, "I do know her a bit. We've hooked up a few times before."

"I thought you didn't do revisits." Her voice is somewhat clipped.

"It's definitely not the norm. There have been a few women I've hooked up with multiple times, but not close together. I've maybe bumped into them months later, and we have another go at it. Ashley is Johnny's friend; we've occasionally been at the same functions, and then one thing leads to another…" I stop talking when I see the hurt in her eyes. "Let's not talk about my sex life. Didn't you have another date with what's-his-name tonight?" I ask, trying to change the subject.

"Don't be like that," she says so softly I can barely hear her. "You know his name is Nick."

I take a breath, knowing she's in an emotional state. "Sorry… How was your date with Nick?"

"It was good." She sighs and lays a pillow flat, lying on her side to face me, pushing her boobs together.

I follow suit, placing a pillow flat and resting my head on it to face her, willing myself to keep my gaze on her face, and not on her incredible tits that are inches away.

"Let's not talk about this… can we just be Leo and Viv right now?" she asks, her eyes focused on mine like laser beams.

I chuckle. "Do you want to fill me in on what that means?"

She lets out a sigh and laughs, shaking her head. "I don't know. Just talk to me," she whispers.

"Okay…" I think of what I can say to lighten her mood.

"You know that first day I saw you… when you were running by my house?" I ask.

"When you were half naked, standing by the door?" She grins. "How could I forget?"

"Do you want to know what I thought when I caught you checking me out?" I ask teasingly, and that does it.

She laughs—the most beautiful, genuine laugh—followed by her gorgeous smile that I love, as she playfully pushes my shoulder. "I don't quite remember it like that, but I'll bite. What did you think?" she asks, still smiling.

"I thought… that is the most *gorgeous* woman I have ever seen."

She scoffs in disbelief. "Okay," she says, rolling her eyes.

"And…" I continue, "I told myself, *I have to get to know her*. Because there was something special about you. You weren't just some ordinary hot girl. There was something about you that drew me in, and now, after months of getting to know you, I finally understand why."

I let the silence hang in the air.

"Well, don't keep me hanging… Why?" she nudges me on.

My eyes wander across her face, tracing every beautiful detail, until they lock onto her sparkling green eyes. There's an intensity in her gaze that captivates me. "Because you are the most incredible person I've ever met," I say, my voice sincere and unwavering.

Her eyes fill with moisture, and she blinks rapidly. She tries to turn onto her back to stare at the ceiling, hiding her tears, but I reach out, gently turning her face back towards me as a tear falls. I catch it with my thumb, brushing it away, feeling the softness of her skin.

"You don't have to hide from me," I say softly.

"Why are you so good to me?" she asks, her voice wavering.

"Because you deserve it."

"Thank you," she whispers.

We lie there, staring at each other in comfortable silence. It's a vulnerable position to be in with someone, but I'd never know that because with Vivian, this feels good. It feels right, being here with her. And yet, it terrifies the shit out of me.

"Why is it that every time I feel like I'm starting to heal and move forward, something happens to set me back? I haven't had this nightmare since before I moved, and now it's the third time this week."

"Healing from grief and trauma doesn't have an ending point, Viv. There's no finish line. It's a journey; you're going to have growth and healing, setbacks, good days, and bad days." I brush a strand of hair from her face. "Don't let this get you down. Stress and anxiety can bring on nightmares." My hand moves down to her cheek, gently caressing it. "Why don't you tell me about your nightmare?" I urge softly, lying close to her, our faces inches apart.

"It's always the same," she begins, her voice trembling. "A replay of that night. Sometimes the details change or things blur." She furrows her brows, as if she is concentrating on recreating the scene for me. "But the ending is always the same. Me, calling Ben's name as we get hit, the car spiraling out of control. I don't remember what we hit or if we flipped or how many times… just a wave of dizziness and confusion." She swallows hard, her voice barely a whisper. "And then it's just me. It's *deathly* quiet, except for this faint, piercing ringing in my ears. Then the sirens come, then the spiraling red lights. I struggle to breathe with the airbag crushing against me." Tears stream down her face. "I look over at Ben, and…" Her voice cracks. "God, when I saw his face, Leo…" She clasps a hand over her mouth. "That image of him… lifeless, bloody… it's seared into my mind." She shuts her eyes, shaking her head. "It was awful." She opens her eyes, and I find myself not wanting to blink, afraid my own tears will fall. "That's the last way I saw him. My last image of Ben, the love of my life, is him, mutilated, bloody, and lifeless." She cries out, "That's when the anxiety kicks in, the panic, the struggle for breath, and then I look down at my stomach and I know I lost our baby too." She looks at me, her eyes filled with anguish, and takes a few deep breaths. "God, I miss them!" She covers her face with both hands. "I miss them so much," she cries, her body shaking violently.

Without thinking, I reach out and pull her into my arms, holding her tightly. "I'm so sorry, Viv," I whisper into her hair, my voice thick with emotion. "You don't have to go through this alone. I'm here, always."

She buries her face in my chest, her sobs muffled against me. I stroke her hair gently, trying to offer what little comfort I can. "Let it out," I murmur. "I've got you."

Her cries gradually subside, leaving us in a quiet, intimate embrace. I can feel her heartbeat against mine, her breath slowing as she calms down. Slowly, she lifts her head, her eyes searching mine. Then, with hesitant vulnerability, she leans in and presses her lips to mine—a brief, tender kiss, more of a thank you than anything else, and it ends almost as quickly as it began.

Holy shit.

"Can you just hold me and stay until I fall asleep?" she asks softly, her voice raw but steady.

"Of course."

As she turns around, settling herself into the curve of my body, we find ourselves spooning. Normally, in an intimate position like this, I'd be turned on. But right now, all I feel is a fierce need to be here for her, to take away her pain.

I wrap my arms around her, holding her close as she nestles against me. "I'm not going anywhere," I whisper.

* * * * * * * * * *

I make my way back to my house around 5 AM. Ashley's still sleeping, and I desperately want her to be gone. I turn on the cold water for the shower and immerse myself.

The icy sting hits me, but I need it. I need the numbness, the clarity it brings. The water cascades over me, washing away the remnants of the night, but not the weight of her pain. Vivian's nightmares, the trauma and sadness in her eyes—it's all etched into my mind, haunting me more than I'd care to admit.

Under the relentless cold water, I feel my composure cracking. My chest tightens, a lump forming in my throat.

Tears threaten, but I hold them back. The freezing water mingles with the emotion buried deep inside me, and I let out a shuddering breath.

I brace myself against the shower wall, taking deep breaths. My mum's angry voice echoes in my mind, yelling at me for reasons I never understood. Lately, I've been wondering if there's more to my mum treating me like shit than I've let myself admit. Fuck, that's a mess I'll have to untangle someday.

I've done the work—hell, I had to unpack loads of shit in grad school. I've forgiven my mum, processed the trauma, come to terms with it. But the scars? They're still there.

The water keeps pouring over me, each drop a bitter reminder of my own loss and the pain I see in Vivian. I take another deep breath, exhaling slowly, finding a strange sense of release. It's fleeting, but it's enough. Enough to remind me why I keep my distance, why getting too close is dangerous. But also enough to show me that, despite everything, I care more than I should.

The water eventually feels tepid against my skin, and I step out, wiping my face, washing away any evidence of the few tears that I shed. I drag my hands through my hair, "Get it together," I mutter to myself. I glance at a framed picture on the wall, a quote I came across during jiujitsu as a teenager: "The obstacle is the way."—Marcus Aurelius. I repeat it silently, finding strength in the words, reminding myself that every challenge has made me who I am.

Chapter 17

VIVIAN

Wednesday, December 6

I fling my purse onto the sofa and collapse beside it. Exhaustion washes over me. This week at work has been a whirlwind of deadlines, new clients, and preparing for my upcoming trip to Utah. I'm eager for the getaway but determined to avoid working while I'm there, which means cramming extra hours into my days until I leave. No time to dwell on my fatigue, though, Nick is picking me up in an hour for a night out at a winter rooftop bar. He's been raving about the phenomenal chef and the incredible view of Millennium Park for days. Since weekend reservations are nearly impossible, I suggested we go tonight.

My phone dings with a text.

Leo: Fall semester officially over… Let's go celebrate?

I glance above his message at the last text I sent him this morning. I hadn't heard from him all day and had forgotten that today was his last day of the semester.

Vivian: I can't tonight… I have dinner reservations with Nick. Tried to text you this morning. Congrats on last day tho, yay! Rain check?

Leo: I leave tomorrow…

Vivian: I know! How about later tonight? I can text you when I get back… we'll have a celebratory toast.

Leo: Sure. Text me when you get back. Enjoy yourself, love.

Dammit. I really want to spend time with Leo before he leaves tomorrow, and I can't believe I forgot his last day of the fall semester. Right now, all I want is to slip into my pajamas, curl up on the couch, and watch TV. But I am excited to see Nick. I'm liking him more and more, and while I'm not ready to have sex with him yet, I love kissing him. I grab my purse and walk up the two flights of stairs to my bedroom and stare at the clothes in my closet. What to wear? I choose a black sweater dress and knee-high boots. It'll be cold, but we'll only be outside for a minute. I think we plan to Uber to the bar. I freshen up my hair and makeup and stock my cream Valentino tote with my essentials for the evening.

I have thirty minutes to spare, and I'm not about to waste any of them. I turn on *Love Island.* Leo is always nice enough to watch it with me because he knows I love the mindlessness of it.

Nick texts me that he's one minute away with the Uber. I grab my wool trench coat, throwing it on as I walk outside, lock up, and walk down the row of townhouses to the street.

As I slide into the Uber and put my seatbelt on, Nick surprises me with a soft kiss on my lips. "Hey, how was your day?" he says sweetly, laying a hand on my thigh. A smile slowly spreads across my face.

I could get used to this.

"It was great," I say, placing my hand on top of his and interlocking our fingers. "Busy, but great. How was yours?"

"A shitshow," he laughs, "but it's better now."

"Were you in the Naperville area today?" I ask.

"Do you mean—did I swing by the Marionis' to see how it's coming along?" He grins.

I laugh. "Yeah… that's exactly what I meant. So, did you?"

He nods. "I did. It's going great. I think you'd be pleased with the progress from last week."

We catch up on work stuff as we drive. There is an ease and comfort with Nick. I'm naturally a little flirtatious. Sarah once told me that I flirted with all men, including her husband, Ryan. She wasn't mad about it; she was simply pointing out that my communication language with men is flirtatious and that I should hone in on it for the dating world. Nick and I don't have the same playful banter that Leo and I share, but that's okay. We have our own thing going on.

We arrive and head up to the thirteenth floor, and holy shit, this place is cool. Nick looks at me and grins. He gets it. A good architectural space is like foreplay for me—it turns me on, and this place is making me all sorts of horny.

"Oh my God, Nick, this place is amazing."

He just laughs and gives his name to the hostess. As we follow her to our table, I am in awe of the design. The room is under a glass atrium, with one wall entirely made of windows and the opposite featuring one of the longest bars I have ever seen, stretching along the entire length of the room. Lights string across the glass ceiling, casting a warm glow that creates a cozy patio vibe. The design features elegant mid-century modern elements, with clean lines, organic curves, and a mix of wood and metal accents that add a touch of 1950s sophistication.

Once we're seated and have a chance to look at the menu, we order a charcuterie board because, well, I love a charcuterie. I stick with water since it's a weekday, and Nick orders an IPA on tap.

"Are you going to the company Christmas party?" Nick asks, his fingers idly tracing patterns on the edge of his glass. The casual question carries an undercurrent of curiosity that makes me pause.

"I'm not," I say, realizing that I'm actually bummed about it. It would have been fun to go with Nick. "I'll be in Utah. But I'll probably go to the work party there. Dang, I really wish we could have gone together. That would have been fun." I make a sad face.

"Oh, that does suck that you won't be here. The Walker Homes Christmas parties here are always a blast, and they do not skimp…"

"Oh, I know! I used to help plan them in Utah. Seth would give me the biggest budget, and I'd go all out. I freaking love him; he's so generous."

Our drinks arrive, and Nick has the most confused look on his face.

"Wait, you actually know Seth Walker? Like the owner of Walker Homes, Seth Walker? And you know him well enough that you love him?" His eyebrow raises higher and higher with each question.

"Oh my gosh, not like that!" I say, laughing. "He's my father-in-law—well, to my late husband. Did you not know that?" I ask, surprised, adjusting my napkin on my lap. "You do know my last name is Walker, right?"

He lets out a laugh. "Oh my hell. I did know that, but I never put two and two together. I guess I just thought it was a coincidence." We laugh together. "Geez, he must be rich as hell."

My eyes go big as I nod. "Oh yeah. He's very wealthy, but again, he's also a good man, and I love working for this company, knowing that. I've known him since I was fifteen." A soft smile of nostalgia creeps across my face.

Nick leans forward, resting his elbows on the table, and stares intently at me. "Ben must have been an incredible guy, Vivian, if what you say about his dad is true." His words are so sincere, so genuine, that I notice I'm not uncomfortable talking about Ben. I've always shifted the conversation on dates, not wanting to bring Ben up, but with Nick, it feels safe.

"He really was," I say, my voice soft. "Thank you for saying that, Nick."

Our charcuterie board arrives, and we order our entrées. I can't wait to dig in. Cheese might be the way to my heart… and coffee. I shift the conversation, as I don't want to dive into my life with Ben any more than we have.

* * * * * * * * * *

We wrap up dinner and call an Uber. As we slide into the back seat, the city lights flicker through the windows, casting a soft glow over us. The driver greets us briefly before focusing on the road ahead, leaving Nick and me in our private bubble.

Nick turns to me, his eyes searching mine with a playful intensity. Without a word, he leans in, his lips meeting mine in a tender kiss. The warmth of his mouth sends a thrill through my body, and I instinctively press closer to him. His hand finds its way to my thigh, grazing it gently and igniting a spark of excitement.

Despite the driver's presence just a few feet away, I can't help but lose myself in the moment. The thrill of being kissed so passionately in such a confined space makes my heart race. I am nervous, but that nervousness only heightens the exhilaration I feel.

Nick deepens the kiss, his hand moving in slow, deliberate circles on my thigh. I feel the heat of his touch as his fingers graze the hem of my dress, and I melt into him, savoring every second. His other hand cups my face, holding me close as if I might slip away.

I pull back slightly to catch my breath, a smile playing on my lips. "You know, the driver can see us," I whisper. Nick's eyes sparkle with a mischievous glint, a rebellious grin spreading across his face.

"Let him watch," he murmurs before kissing me again, more urgently this time. My heart pounds in my chest, the mixture of public and private, combined with my nervousness, making every touch and kiss feel electrifying.

As the car nears the townhouses, I feel a pang of disappointment. I don't want to stop kissing Nick, but I also know that things get complicated when men come inside. As we pull up to the curb, I'm debating whether to ask him to come in or not. Nick gives me one last, lingering kiss, his hand gently squeezing my thigh.

"We should do this more often," he says with a wink. "I'll walk you to your door." He asks the Uber driver if he can wait for him as we get out of the car.

Nick, always the gentleman, walks me to my door and kisses me goodnight with a respectful tenderness, leaving me breathless as I shut the door behind me.

I breathe out slowly, grinning in the darkness of my entryway. That was a lot of fun. I flip a light on and walk across my living room to my kitchen, tossing my coat and purse on the couch as I pass by. I notice the time—10:30 PM.

With a pang of guilt for sort of ditching Leo tonight, I swipe up on my phone to send him a text.

Vivian: Hey you… I'm home. Want me to come over?

Part of me hopes he's asleep because exhaustion is taking over and I work in the morning, but another part wants to see Leo, even if it's just for a few minutes before he leaves for the week.

I fill up a glass of water, turning off the lights behind me as I walk back into the living room to put my coat in the closet. Phone in hand, so I don't miss a text from Leo, I walk upstairs to ready myself for bed.

With my face washed, pajamas on, and eyes half-closed, I sink into the softness of my sheets and stare at my phone. 10:50… no response. The message is left on delivered. Maybe I can catch him in the morning. I lie on my back, staring at the ceiling, deep in thought.

I really like Nick, and while it may be old-school to enjoy just kissing someone, the benefit of waiting to have sex is that the build-up and anticipation is half the fun, making it all the more exciting when the time comes… *if* it comes, I remind myself. I can't help but have doubts that I'll revert to the same old pattern I've had with other guys.

I groan and flip over to my side, picking up my phone again. My message is still marked as delivered. Putting my phone down, I toss and turn, trying to get comfortable and quiet my mind—my fucking ego insisting on analyzing every detail and possibility, making it impossible to sleep.

Chapter 18

LEO

December 8

The taxi weaves through the familiar streets of London, the chill of the December air seeping through the windows. The fall semester ended two days ago, and the holiday break is a welcome respite from the constant demands of teaching. Leaving Chicago behind, I hope the change of scenery might clear my head. London always has a way of grounding me, even with the bittersweet memories it holds.

My thoughts drift back to Vivian, who came over early this morning to give me a quick hug before I left for the airport. I had hoped for more time with her, but her touch lingered with me. I had fallen asleep waiting for her text last night, missing the chance to see her before bed. Now, as the cityscape blurs past, all I can think about is how much I already miss her presence.

The taxi pulls up to Andrew's modern flat in Islington. I step out, the cold air biting at my skin. Andrew is at the door, grinning like a madman, with baby Emma bundled up in blankets and cradled in his arms.

"Leo!" Andrew calls out as I approach, meeting me halfway.

"Andrew, it's good to see you, mate," I reply. We greet each other with a brotherly side hug, patting each other's backs, careful to not squish my new baby niece. Emma is sleeping in Andrew's arms, and I can't help but smile as I look at her. "Oh my God. She's beautiful, Andrew."

Nichole greets me in the entryway with a warm hug, the smell of freshly brewed tea wafting through the air. Stepping inside, an odd sense of nostalgia washes over me. Seeing Andrew here, creating a family life of his own, fills me with pride.

"Can I hold her?" I ask Andrew.

"Of course, but Nichole is going to make you wash your hands first." He gestures to the kitchen as he flashes a grin at his wife.

Nichole gives Andrew a look. "Well don't say it like I'm insane for asking people to wash their hands. It's a normal request."

Andrew laughs and kisses her on the mouth. "I know, babe, I just like to give ya shit."

After washing my hands, we make our way to the living room and Andrew places Emma in my arms, taking great care to teach me how to hold her head and neck. Honestly, I don't know shit about babies, I've only ever held a couple of them in my entire life and was never around them growing up.

"She's so fucking tiny," I say in awe.

"Leo!" Nichole shouts, scolding me for my language.

"She's a baby, Nichole, she doesn't even know what fucking means," Andrew retorts. "She's always getting after me for the cussing in front of Emma... and we all know that she has the mouth of a sailor," he says, pointing to Nichole.

I laugh, "Sorry, Nichole, I'll try to filter around the baby."

I love spending time with Andrew and Nichole.

"There's a Liverpool–Chelsea game starting in an hour, do you want to watch?" Andrew asks.

"Fuck yes, I do!" I say enthusiastically, as Nichole gives me a glare, and I grimace. "Shit. I'm sorry, Nichole." Andrew and I both laugh. "But I do miss proper football."

Nichole brings in some tea, which is something that I don't miss. I'm definitely an American when it comes to my love for coffee. I sip on it anyway as we catch up on the past three months. Andrew is the only one in London that I talk to on a regular weekly basis. Naturally, he knows a bit about Vivian, but I've kept the details pretty vague; she's my cool, hot neighbor, who's become a good friend.

After an hour, Nichole takes Emma upstairs for them to both nap. Andrew and I sit in the living room, a couple of glasses of scotch between us, the soft glow of the fireplace casting shadows on the walls. The sound of a Chelsea match plays in the background, adding a familiar comfort to our conversation.

"It's good to have you here," Andrew says, breaking the comfortable silence.

"It's good to be here," I reply, taking a sip of my drink. "You've done well for yourself, Andrew. I'm proud of you. You've managed to escape dad's constant pressure of working in the family business, to do something that you love instead, while moving on, falling in love and building a life… a family. It's commendable brother." I lift my drink up, toasting his great efforts and accomplishments.

Andrew smiles, but there's a shadow in his eyes. "Thanks, mate. It hasn't been easy, you know that. But I've had to… for Nichole, for Emma." He pauses, then looks at me more intently. "You didn't escape dad's pressure but at least you escaped London."

I nod, watching the game out the corner of my eye.

"But what about you? Are you ever going to settle down?" Andrew asks cautiously.

Here we fucking go.

"For fuck's sake, I am settled, Andrew." I glare at him. "I have a great career, thriving businesses, a townhouse on the river, a fuck-ton of money, and friends I care about. I'm fulfilled." I'm not angry with him—I love my brother—but we have this conversation at least twice a year. I brace myself for what's next: a lecture about not dating, never getting married or having a family, and not understanding how meaningful life can be when shared with someone. It gets bloody old.

"But you won't let yourself be completely happy, mate. Why do you keep holding onto the past?" Andrew's eyes soften, taking the conversation in a direction I didn't see coming.

"What are you getting at?" I ask slowly.

"With Mum," he states. "You've never really let it go. You've never *wanted* to. It's almost like you enjoy the anger that you have for her."

I stare into my glass, swirling the amber liquid. "It's not that simple, Andrew. You know what we went through, how she was. It's not something you just shrug off."

Andrew leans forward, his voice softer but insistent. "We both lived it, Leo. She was tougher on you, I get that. But at some point, you have to move forward. You can't let the past run your life."

I let out a dry laugh. "You think I haven't tried? She didn't care about me the way she cared about you. She blamed me for her misery."

"Mate, you're a bloody psychology professor. You know better than anyone that she was sick. She was depressed, anxious, an alcoholic… She was out of her mind most days."

"I know that. I've spent years coming to terms with it. But forgiving her doesn't erase what she did."

Andrew places a hand on my shoulder. "I get it. But maybe it's time you stopped letting her mistakes define how you live."

I shoot him a look, and he raises his hands in defense. "Hold on—just hear me out."

I wait for him to continue digging this grave.

"I think you've convinced yourself that you don't deserve the kind of happiness I have, like you're somehow responsible for what happened to her. And it's bullshit. You've punished yourself for long enough. It's holding you back."

The fire crackles in the silence between us, occasionally interrupted by cheers from the television as Chelsea makes another advance. I stare blankly at the screen. "I fucking love my life, Andrew… But maybe you're right," I finally say, barely above a whisper. "I've always carried the blame, like I could've done something to change things."

Andrew's eyes cloud with sorrow. "You were a kid, mate. None of that was on you. You know that."

I scoff. "I know it logically, but it's hard to forget when those words come from your own mum." I take a heavy swig of my drink. "She said some fucked up things to me the night before she left."

We sit in silence as I swirl the scotch in front of me, the ice clinking in my glass. The cheers from the football match blur into the background. I can feel Andrew's eyes on me, his concern digging into me like a knife. I fucking hate that. I'm the older brother, the strong one, the one who holds it together, his protector. But I've carried this truth for twenty-five years, and now I've handed it to him like a burden he never asked for.

Andrew's face twists in anguish. "God, I had no idea. Why didn't you tell me?"

"Because I'm not a goddamn victim, Andrew. I never have been. But that's why I struggle to fully forgive her. She was ill, I get that, but what she did left scars. It's not about hating her—it's just something I can't fully let go of." I set my drink down a little harder than I intended. "Can we talk about something else now? I'm done rehashing this."

I turn the TV up and we watch the game in silence.

I pull my phone out to text Vivian because I know that talking to her will help my shitty mood.

I have an unread text from her. We'd been texting last night before I boarded my plane. This one was sent a couple of hours ago, probably when she woke up. I somehow missed it in the chaos of leaving the airport to come here.

Vivian: Hey, did you make it safely?

Leo: Yes. Got here a couple of hours ago. You at work? Sorry I didn't text, got wrapped up in family and catching up. Emma is beautiful… I'm embarrassed to admit she is only the third baby I've ever held. It's a pretty incredible feeling being an uncle and holding my niece for the first time.

I hope that my text doesn't stir too much emotion for her, talking about the baby.

Vivian: Ahhh! That is so sweet. Yes at work… Send me pics!

Leo: Will do. Can you find time to squeeze me into your busy schedule for when I come home? Maybe Friday the 15th? I'd love to take you out—catch up. Un less you already have plans…

> **Vivian:** OMG! You're around a baby for five whole minutes and now you want to take me on a date? Slow down, Leo. I'm not ready to jump into things. (Laughing face emoji)

She's so cheeky

> **Leo:** You're so insightful… I'm practically standing at the altar. Call it whatever you want. I'm taking you to the Christmas market. Mer told me you haven't been. It'll be a fun thing to do when I get back… I don't want Nick being scheduled over me.

I send it and immediately regret the comment about Nick, as the tone will probably come across as more of a jab than I intended. I don't want to seem jealous, either, but it's true—I don't want to be scheduled over like I was the night before.

> **Vivian:** God… I really am sorry. I spaced that we had talked about doing something the night before you left. I promise I won't forget. I have you scheduled into my calendar on the 15th. I'm all yours! I'll be very much looking forward to seeing you. (Kissy face emoji)

> **Leo:** Good. We can look for rings afterward.

I don't send any emojis, letting it hang in the air.

> **Vivian:** Ha. Ha. Ha. We have a comedian on our hands. I've got to get back to work. Text me later. :-)

* * * * *   * * * * *

I help Nichole clear the table and then possessively take Emma from Andrew. I can't get enough of her. I leave tomorrow morning, and I need to soak up the sweetness of this little girl.

Sitting at the table, I watch Nichole and Andrew move around the kitchen with a harmony that speaks of years of love and a comfortable ease. I look down at Emma; her eyes move back and forth watching my face, filled with wonder, and I'm overcome with an unfamiliar emotion.

I look back at Andrew and Nichole. Nichole is teasing him. He playfully swats her with the dish towel, she splashes water on him and laughs. He wraps her into him and gives her a kiss, and I realize it's the first time in my life that I'm envious of what my brother has. All these years of lectures about finding someone to share my life with, and finding true meaning to life hit me like a load of bricks.

I look back down at Emma and then imagine something bad happening to her, and a knot forms in my stomach. I bring her up to my chest and hold her tightly, shutting my eyes. No, No. I don't want this. It's like taking a gamble with high-risk stocks—you might hit the jackpot, but you could lose it all in a matter of minutes.

Chapter 19

VIVIAN

December 14

Vivian: Hey, I know it will be late when you get home, but will you please swing by, so I can give you a hug?

Leo: Sure thing, love. Probably be close to 11:00.

Vivian: I'll make sure I'm up.

God, I have missed him over this past week. I had another date with Nick this last weekend… well—two dates. We went out Friday night and then had lunch on Sunday. Things are going great with him. We have fun, and our chemistry is great. He's a fantastic kisser, too. It's still new, though, and I'm giving it time.

I'm on my couch, relaxed in my sweats, mindlessly watching television, and waiting for Leo. The seconds feel like hours as I wait for Leo's message. Finally, at 10:00, my phone dings.

Leo: Touchdown.

A rush of excitement floods through me. I heart the message, my thumb hovering over the screen for a moment before I snap out of it. Almost instantly, my phone dings again. This time, it's Nick.

Nick: I know this is last minute, but my friend gave me two tickets to the Bulls game tomorrow night. I'd love for you to come? It's at 7:00, we could grab dinner before.

Damn. The idea of a night out with Nick is tempting. Bulls game, good food, and his easygoing company? It sounds perfect. But Leo and I have plans for tomorrow, and I can't bail on him. More than that, I don't want to. Just the thought of seeing him makes my heart race.

Vivian: Ugh! I'm so sorry, Nick. That sounds like so much fun, but I have plans tomorrow night with my friend, Leo. I mentioned it Sunday… remember? Thank you so much for thinking of me, though. I hope you have a great time!

A pang of guilt hits as I press send. Nick's reply is almost immediate.

Nick: Oh yeah… I forgot you had plans with your guy friend. Okay, next time. Have fun.

I roll my eyes. Why are guys so fucking weird about women having guy friends? Nick had acted a little funny when I had told him I had plans on Friday with Leo. He didn't say anything, but it was obvious that it bothered him.

It doesn't matter, though. We aren't an official thing. As much as I like him, I won't stop being friends with Leo or dating someone else if they come along. I'm in an exploratory phase, and right now, Nick is first runner-up when it comes to dating, but I'm keeping my options open. Leo has always been there for me, and I'm not about to let that go just because it makes someone else uncomfortable.

I stretch out on the couch, glancing at the time again. Leo's probably grabbing his bags and heading home by now.

At 10:40, there's a knock on my door, and I jump off the couch, running to answer it. I swing the door open and practically leap into Leo's arms, wrapping my arms around his neck and squeezing him tightly.

He chuckles softly in my ear and tightens his arms around me. "Wow, this is quite the welcome home," he says, kissing my cheek before slowly loosening his grip on me.

I back up slightly, laughing. "Sorry… I just really missed you!"

"I was only gone a week," he replies, grinning.

"I know, but I could just feel the emptiness of your house next door. It felt lonely knowing you weren't right there. Plus, I've become so accustomed to listening to you *bang* women while I work in my office; it's almost like white noise now. I couldn't keep my focus in the silence." I flash him a teasing smile.

"I missed you too," he says with a playful smirk, his suitcase standing beside him on the porch.

"Well, thanks for swinging by. I'll let you get unpacked and settled. I imagine you're worn out after such a long day of travel."

He lets out a deep sigh. "I am. I'm actually excited to go to bed."

"Okay, so what time should I be ready tomorrow?"

"How about four? We can explore the Christmas market and then head to Craft's for dinner and drinks. Noah will save us a spot."

"That sounds amazing. I'll be ready."

"Okay. Goodnight, Viv."

"Night, Leo."

I close the door behind me. The soft glow from my modest Christmas tree and the flickering fireplace light the entryway with a warm, soothing ambiance.

As I turn off the lights and ascend the stairs, my heart races, and I struggle to steady my breath. The excitement I feel around Leo doesn't seem to wane; if anything, it intensifies with each encounter. His presence has a magnetic pull that I can't seem to escape.

As I settle into my sheets, I remind myself not to dwell on the future or let worries take over. I focus on living in the present—day by day, minute by minute—trusting myself and the process, and striving to savor each moment as it comes.

* * * * *   * * * * *

The next day

I stand in my closet, staring at the array of clothes before me. After trying on five different outfits and hating each one, I'm no closer to achieving the look I want. It's freezing outside, so I need to dress warmly. Even though it's not a real date, I'm treating it like one. It's Leo, so he's seen me at my worst and won't be fazed by whatever I choose. But I still want to look great because, well, it's Leo.

One of my get-ready playlists is blasting through my bedroom at full volume, Megan Thee Stallion's *Body* is pumping me up for the evening.

I yank off another outfit and let it fall to the floor, not bothering to hang it up since I have only fifteen minutes before I need to head out the door to meet Leo. Frustrated, and standing in my underwear—a strapless black lace bra and matching thong—with my full ass facing the open door, I hear Leo's voice.

"Viv?"

I turn around to see Leo standing in my bathroom, arms folded and grinning from ear to ear.

"What the hell, Leo?" I slam the door shut, then crack it open just enough to peek through. "What are you doing here, and why are you in my bathroom?"

He laughs, clearly amused and not sorry in the slightest. "I'm sorry. I texted you to let you know I was coming over early. I rang the doorbell, knocked, and even called your name all the way up to your room. If your music wasn't so damn loud, you might have heard me. I was just looking for you; it's not like I came into your bathroom to be creepy," he shouts, trying to be heard over the music.

It occurs to me that I can turn the music down with my watch, so I do. I close the door fully and speak loudly enough for him to hear while I quickly throw on an outfit that, I hope, will be right.

"So, you just assumed I'd be in the bathroom fully clothed, hanging out? God, it's a bathroom! You don't barge into someone's bathroom without permission."

"Well, if you'd looked at your phone or kept your music at a reasonable volume, this wouldn't have happened!" he retorts.

"You know I like my raunchy music to get me in the zone. I mean, technically, I'm playing it loudly for you. I want to make sure I bring my A-game, you know?"

I slide a pair of black leather leggings up over my hips and adjust them at my waist.

I hear him chuckle through the door. "How thoughtful of you… to think of me while in your underwear."

Oh, he did not just say that! "When I get out there, you're in so much trouble!" I call through the door as I slip on an off-the-shoulder emerald-green sweater and a pair of boots. Standing in front of the full-length mirror, I assess my look. This will do. The off-the-shoulder style adds just enough sex appeal while still being appropriate for our friendly outing, and the leggings showcase my ass perfectly. I grab a few pieces of jewelry and open the door.

"Will you help me with my necklaces?" I ask, hurrying over to my purses and grabbing my black YSL bag. Leo strides into my closet, a smug smile painted on his face. I offer him a tight-lipped smirk as I hand him two necklaces and turn so he can fasten them while I switch items between purses.

As I move my lip gloss and credit cards, Leo stands behind me, draping a necklace around my neck. I lift my hair to give him better access. His breath is warm and soft against my neck, sending a shiver down my arms.

When he finishes, he lightly grips my shoulders. "There. All done," he says, giving them a gentle squeeze, and then whispers in my ear, "By the way… you look really incredible in your underwear."

Holy shit. I think I just came.

I whirl around, stepping out of the vulnerable position, and give him a light pat on the chest, trying to shake off the intensity. "Thanks, friend," I say with a smile, pretending that his comment was perfectly normal. "Ready to go?" I ask, struggling to keep my voice steady when all I really want to do is jump his bones.

"I've been ready, Viv. That's why I'm here. Do you have your coat? It's bloody cold out."

"Ugh! Why do I live here?" I whine. "My coat's downstairs; I'll grab it on the way out. I just did my hair, but am I going to need a beanie? That does not go with my outfit."

"I think you'll be fine since it's still early and the sun is actually out. I've got an Uber that's three minutes away."

We rush downstairs, grab my coat, and step into the brisk December air.

* * * * * * * * * *

"Cheers, Viv." Leo raises his wine glass and waits for me to clink mine to his. The second bottle of wine is empty on the bar top at Craft's. Laughing, I lift my glass and tap it against his, stifling my laugh as I take a sip, trying not to spit my wine out.

I'm not even sure what we're laughing about. We've been laughing at everything all day. My cheeks actually ache from all the smiling.

"I shouldn't have any more. I'm already more drunk than I usually allow myself to get." I set my glass down and pick at the crumbs on our charcuterie board, desperate for something to soak up the alcohol.

"Nah, you're fine. You've been pacing yourself. It's been a long day."

"I know. But right now, I'm the perfect kind of drunk—just enough that everything is fun and funny, but not so much that I don't know what I'm doing," I say, pointing a fork at him as if giving a lecture.

Leo sucks in a breath through his teeth. "That is the perfect drunk. Why don't we finish these off, switch to water, and then walk home? By the time we get there, some of it will be burned off, and the cold will help sober us up."

"I'll drink half," I compromise.

"Deal," he replies with a wink.

We had so much fun at the Christkindlmarket. The whole experience was magical, with charming little shops that looked like Christmas cottages, phenomenal comfort food, and treats. Of course, the mulled wine was a highlight for us. We loved supporting that vendor. Despite the cold, the wine warmed us up as we walked side by side, my arm linked with Leo's, exploring each row of shops. Christmas lights glittered all around us, and festive music played in the background. It was a great time. I picked up some adorable ornaments for my bare tree at home, as well as gifts for Sarah, my mom, and Ben's mom.

It's almost nine, and I mentally tally the hours we've been out. "Technically, I've only had one drink per hour, which isn't all that terrible." Leo has had much more than I have, but he's also bigger and handles his alcohol much better than I do.

"That's not so bad at all. Should we pound this and get going?"

I grimace, "Ugh. I never want to pound anything, Leo—let alone wine."

"Ah, come on. We can get home and watch a movie."

"No," I say, pointing my fork at him again. "You promised you'd teach me more self-defense tonight." My fork is inches from his face.

He swats the fork away. "God, you're like a toddler with that thing. You're going to scratch my eyes out. I don't know, Viv, I might be too tired for self-defense. I'm still jet-lagged. You might be able to take me tonight."

I laugh, stick the fork in my mouth, and slowly pull it out, examining it, confused. There's no food on it, and suddenly, I'm acutely aware of how drunk I am. "Oh God," I say, laughing, "I didn't have any food on that." I let my face fall into my hand, my elbow resting on the bar.

Leo folds his arms and leans back, suppressing his laughter. "Dinner and a show," he says with a grin.

"Okay, get me out of here. I'm about to get borderline embarrassing," I say, pushing my wine glass away and chugging the water in front of me.

Leo's shoulders shake with laughter as he tries to contain himself. "My life must have been so dull before we met." He picks up my empty fork and moves it toward my mouth. "Here, why don't you have one more bite?" His laughter becomes uncontrollable as I smack my lips shut, and he tries to press the empty fork into my mouth. He eventually drops the fork, squeezes the bridge of his nose, and bows his head, laughing heartily.

I belt out my own giggles. "Fuck off," I say, playfully shoving him and wiping tears from my eyes.

Luckily, no one is next to us, and Leo is at the end of the bar, but we're starting to make a scene.

Leo gathers his wits. "We've got to get out of here before I end up kicking myself out. We'd deserve it." He slaps a hundred down for Noah, grabs our coats off the backs of our chairs, and links his arm with mine. Thank God because I need it for balance.

The bitter cold bites at my skin, like a cold plunge to the face, making me grateful for the alcohol. I know it would feel much colder if I were sober. The ten-minute walk takes us almost twenty because of my drunken state. By the time we reach our row of townhouses, I do feel a bit more sober—still drunk, but less so.

"Your house or mine?" I ask as we approach his townhouse.

"Yours, of course. You have more food in your fridge."

"True that. Though, apparently I'm like the Lost Boys from *Hook* tonight—pretending to have a feast and eating imaginary food," I say, sending a flood of giggles through me again.

Leo chuckles along with me. "God. What are we going to do with you?"

We walk through my front door. As I reach down to unzip my boots, I lose my balance trying to take one off. Leo's strong hands wrap around my waist, steadying me.

"You okay there, Walker?"

"Yes! I just lost my balance trying to get these damn boots off!" I yank on one, and it goes flying into the wall.

I give up, moving to the living room, where I plop down on the rug and lift the other foot in the air. "Can you help me?" I plead, making a pouting face.

Leo grins at me. "Oh, I rather enjoy watching you struggle."

"You know I could kick you in the dick right now, right?" I make a kicking motion toward him as he cups his junk.

"Don't you fucking dare," he chuckles, grabbing my foot to hold it steady. With one swift motion, he pulls off my boot while I try to trip him with my other leg. But he's too quick and not nearly as drunk as I am.

"Oh, you wanna do this, huh?" he asks, a playful glint in his eye.

"Bring it on, tough guy," I taunt back, wiggling my foot free from his grip.

He lunges, and I roll to the side, laughing as I scramble away. But he's faster, pinning me to the floor with ease. His hands grip my wrists, his body hovering just above mine, and I can feel the heat radiating off him.

"Got you," he murmurs, his breath warm against my ear.

For a moment, we're both still, our breaths mingling. The air between us shifts, becoming charged. His grip on my wrists loosens slightly, his thumbs brushing over my skin in a way that sends a chill down my spine.

"So, what do I do now, Sensei?" I whisper, my voice sounding breathless even to my own ears.

His eyes darken as they meet mine, the playful glint replaced by something more intense. He locks my wrists down and settles on top of me, wrapping his legs around my calves to pin them in place as well. I am completely and utterly helpless. "Now," he says, his voice low, "you use your hips and legs to push your attacker off balance."

I follow his instructions, pushing my pelvis up into his, but the closeness of his body makes it difficult to focus. I shift beneath him, attempting to push him off, but it only brings us closer together. The struggle makes me acutely aware of how vulnerable I am. I can feel his dick hardening against me, and the awareness sends a rush through me. *God*, the way he feels pressed against me, it's almost too much.

"Try pulling your arms straight down and jamming your elbows into my knees."

"Like this?" I murmur, my voice quivering as I quickly pull my arms down, releasing his grip. The thrill of getting it right, combined with his closeness, makes my heart race.

"Yeah," he breathes, his gaze dropping to my lips. "Just like that."

"Let's try it again," he says intensely, grabbing my wrists again and locking them to the floor above my head. His eyes lock onto mine, and the tension between us is palpable.

I can feel the warmth of his body as he leans closer, the heat simmering between us. My heart pounds in my ears, and my stomach does flips in anticipation. For a moment, time seems to freeze.

Before I can react, his lips are on mine, and all thoughts of self-defense evaporate. The kiss is hot and urgent, a clash of desire that had been simmering for far too long. He releases his grip on my wrists and cups a hand behind my neck, pulling me closer as he deepens the kiss. Instinctively, my arms wrap around his neck. I've wanted this for so damn long. The intensity of it all leaves me breathless, my mind struggling to catch up with my racing heart.

We're a tangle of limbs and heated kisses, his body pressing me into the floor. His lips trail down my neck, and I arch into him, feeling the hard length of him against my thigh. Every touch sends a jolt of electricity through me, making me crave more.

I manage to flip us over, straddling him, our positions reversed. His hands rest on my hips, and I can feel the tension in his grip, the barely restrained desire. I want to be the one in control, even if just for a moment.

"Teach me something else," I say, sliding off him but keeping close.

He stands, pulling me up with him, and then he presses me against the wall. His hands are locked around my wrists on either side of my head, pinning me in place. "You'll need to know how to defend yourself if you ever get pinned against a wall." His eyes are intense, boring into mine. The way he looks at me, like I'm the only person in the world, is intoxicating.

"What do I do?" I ask, my voice barely above a whisper.

His eyes are drunk with lust as he leans in closer. "Duck underneath, and rotate your arms inward to get out of my grip. Then use your elbow to clock me in the face," he murmurs, his voice low and rough.

"And what if I don't want to get away?" I say breathlessly, meeting his gaze head-on. I don't want to be anywhere but here, with him.

For a moment, the air between us is electric. Then his lips are on mine again, fierce and consuming. His hands slide under my shirt, pulling it over my head in one swift motion. I tug at his shirt, desperate to feel his skin against mine, to see him… touch him. His hands roam over my bare skin, memorizing every inch, his touch matching the heat of my own desire.

His lips trail down my neck, and I moan softly, arching into him. His hand cups my breast, his thumb brushing over my nipple through the thin fabric of my strapless bra, sending shivers of pleasure through me. He pulls my bra down, his mouth replacing his thumb, and I gasp at the sensation.

God, he's driving me crazy.

"Oh my God, Leo," I gasp. I never imagined it would feel this good.

I run my hands over his solid chest, tracing the hard lines of his muscles and chiseled abs, the V at his hips that disappears into his jeans. My fingers fumble with the button of his jeans, desperate to feel more of him. I've fantasized about this for months now.

"Christ, Vivian," he murmurs between kisses, "you have no idea what you do to me."

I gasp and breathe a hot moan into his ear. His words send a thrill through me, making me want him even more.

I am lost in his touch and consumed by desire. Nothing in my mind is screaming for me to stop; it just wants more... more.

His hands grab mine and sweep them above my head, pinning them to the wall. Locking both in one hand, the other trails possessively down my body, caressing and teasing. I try to release his grip, aching to touch him.

"I need to touch you," I say. The need is overwhelming, almost painful.

His lips curl into a wicked grin as he leans in closer, and I want to kiss those fucking dimples. "It's my turn, Walker."

The throbbing between my thighs intensifies, the warmth of wetness spreading and igniting every nerve in my body as he plays with my nipple. He slides his hand down to my ass, giving it a squeeze, and *my God,* I want to touch him.

His kiss becomes more demanding, and I'm uncertain if I'm drunk from the alcohol or him. The room spins, but all I can focus on is him.

We're lost in the moment, our bodies pressed together, the wall cool against my back. He releases his grip, and my hands move furiously over his body, worshiping his masculinity. My fingers thread through his hair as his hands find my waist, lifting me slightly so that my legs wrap around his hips. He grips my ass, the friction between us almost too much to bear.

I slither my hands back down to his pants and start working the zipper. Just as I'm about to reach in, he sets me down, grabs my hand and pulls away, his breathing ragged. He rests his forehead against mine, his eyes closed.

"Fuck," he murmurs, "we should stop." It sounds like he's trying to convince himself more than me.

I stand there gasping for breath, my arms wrapped around his neck and tangled in his hair. "Leo," I whisper.

He doesn't look up, his forehead resting against mine, eyes fixed on the rise and fall of my chest.

"Leo," I say a little louder.

He glances up, making eye contact.

"Leo, don't stop… please," I say with a desperation that I hate. But I can't help it; I need him.

His eyes burn into mine, and I can feel the passion that was just there a moment ago. "We can't. You're drunk, and I don't want you to get hurt."

"Leo," I whisper, my voice trembling but still strong. I feel so vulnerable, my boobs out on display, practically pleading with him. "Please, don't treat me like I'm going to break. I'm not that fragile, I'm not going to break." I whisper again, more raw this time, "I want this."

"Dammit!" he pounds his fist against the wall, the sound echoing through the room. "Viv," he says, his voice breaking as I see the turmoil in his eyes, the internal struggle he's fighting.

His eyes meet mine, filled with a mix of longing and something deeper, something painful. "It's not you I'm worried about breaking," he says, his voice rough. "You're so strong. I just don't know if I can be the one to give you what you need. And if I fail… if I lose you, I don't think I could take it."

Trembling, I stand as tall as I can and look him in the eyes. "Leo… either fuck me, or get the fuck out." I say boldly, gesturing toward the door.

He slowly backs away, running his hands through his hair. He's hurt; I know my words just hurt him. But so am I.

As he stumbles for words, picking his shirt off the ground and pulling it over his head, he finally speaks. "Viv, please. Don't do this. Don't kick me out, not like this," he implores, shaking his head, "Please," he pleads again, "let's talk first."

Narrowing my eyes, not daring to blink as moisture fills them, I scowl at him. "I can hardly *look* at you right now, let alone talk," I say, my voice slightly elevated. I pick up his coat, walk toward him, and shove it into his arms. "Now get out!" I shout, pointing to the door.

I don't bother getting dressed. I stand there, exposed and angry, having let my guard down. For a brief moment, I empathize with that douchebag Bentley. How humiliating it is to be denied when you've completely allowed yourself to be vulnerable. On second thought, no, this isn't like that at all because I *know* Leo wants this. I *know* he has wanted it for a long time, and he kissed *me!* This is about *him.* So I stand there, half naked and stripped down, arms folded and glaring at him, never losing eye contact. I refuse to let this be okay. I can't keep playing this cat-and-mouse game, not when it ends like this.

He sighs, his shoulders slumping as if carrying an unbearable weight. "Okay. I'll go." Sliding his arms into his coat, the fabric rustling softly in the silent room, he slowly walks toward the door. He looks back one last time, his eyes filled with regret, before opening it and stepping out into the cold night air.

I cry out in agony, shame, and embarrassment. I know he can still hear me, and I don't care. I begged him, pleaded with him to stay, to be with me, and he denied me. There was so much passion between us, so much chemistry; you can't fake that. I collapse onto the couch, tears streaming down my face as the reality of the situation hits me.

I sit in silence on the couch, the darkness enveloping me, tears streaming down my cheeks. My heart can't take this. I've been through too much already. This is it. The straw that breaks the camel's back. I wanted things to be normal after our first kiss, but this... there's no going back to normal after this. Leo's mouth and hands were all over me, and I wanted them there. If we try to go back to normal, this will keep happening again and again, and I can't take it.

The weight of what just happened presses down on me, the longing and rejection mingling with a deep, aching emptiness. I feel hollow, vulnerable, and exposed, a raw nerve laid bare.

I take a deep breath, wiping my tears. I'm not fucked up after all; I was ready to go all the way with him. I just hadn't met anyone I wanted to do that with until Leo.

But now, I have to protect myself.

Chapter 20

LEO

The next morning

"Leo." I hear Meredith's voice, muffled in the distance. I briefly open an eye, just enough to see a blurry outline of a person across the room, then close it again. My memory is a haze, flickering in and out of consciousness as fragmented visions flash through my mind.

"Where's mum?" seven-year-old Andrew cries, standing in the kitchen with his stuffed monkey and baby blanket.

"She's gone," I hear my ten-year-old self say, angrily.

"When is she coming home?"

"She's not coming home, stupid!" I yell, earning a glare from Chloe.

Her eyes well up with tears. "Don't yell at him, Leo. It's not his fault she's gone." Andrew starts crying as Chloe tries to console him, wrapping her arms around him and rubbing the top of his head. She whispers softly, "Shhh. It's alright. Leo's not mad at you, no one is mad at you."

Yes it is, I think. It's his fault, it's all of our fault. She didn't want us. She hated us. She hated being our mum.

"FUCK HER!" I scream, my first time using the F-word. "I fucking hate her!" The second time using it, my eyes fill with tears, threatening to drown my face. Needing to throw or break something, I pick up the closest thing to me, my Discman, that sits on the counter. I scream as I throw it

with all my might into the nearest wall, as if somehow this control over something will take the pain away, make it make sense.

The cops had left an hour prior. We drove her away... I drove her away.

"Leo... Leo..." Struggling to open my eyes, I see Meredith standing over me holding a glass. "I made you your hangover cure," she says patiently. She's blurry; I'm peeking through two tiny slits, trying to gather my whereabouts. "Hello... Leo." She nudges me. "Did you hear me?"

I clear my throat and rub my eyes. "No, I'm sorry. What? Am I at your house?"

"Sit up, Leo." I feel her tugging at me, trying to lift me. "Yes, you're at my house."

"I'm up..." I say groggily, the effort making my head throb even more. I reluctantly sit and open my eyes, straining to bring them into focus. "Fuuuuuck." My head is pounding. I feel like absolute shit. I take the glass uneasily from Meredith, unsure if I should be apologizing for something, as I can't remember a damn thing that happened last night after I left Vivian's.

Fuck... Vivian.

"Do I owe you an apology?" I ask wearily.

Meredith is tight-lipped. She glares at me like a mother about to scold her child. "No," she says finally, shaking her head. "No, you don't owe me an apology." There is a hint of laughter in her voice.

"What happened?" I pinch the bridge of my nose and squeeze my eyes shut. "Why am I on your couch?"

"Is there anything you want to talk about?" she asks, avoiding my question, and takes a seat next to me. "I know this time of year can bring certain memories back for you... that it can be hard."

"God, Meredith." I scowl at her. "No. I'm fine."

"Are you sure?" She looks at me as if she knows something I don't know. "There's nothing going on in there that's bothering you?" She gestures upward, toward my brain. "About your mom?" she offers.

"Why are you asking about my mum? You know that hasn't been an issue in years," I say, feeling paranoid as I vaguely recall the dream I was just having.

"Well, you were on the couch mumbling that you fucking hate her, and I know the only person you've ever hated is your mom… and Rachel… well, and maybe Brian for a bit too." She laughs softly. "So which one were you dreaming about?"

I run a hand through my hair, trying to shake off the lingering remnants of the dream. "I don't remember," I lie, not wanting to delve into it.

"Hmm. I don't believe you," she says.

"Ugh." I grip my face in my hand as if I can push the memory away. "I don't want to talk about it."

She scoots closer, practically on top of me, and pats my knee. "Too bad," she says, "because we're going to talk about it."

I sigh, the weight of the conversation pressing down on me. *Why does she always have to push? Can't she see I'm barely holding it together?*

My mum had left a week before Christmas. What kind of mum leaves her family right before Christmas? A very sick one, I know that now… but at ten years old?

She never wanted to be a mum. Hated the whole thing. We always had an au pair from France who practically raised us. We spent summers in Paris, my mum never wanting to be around us. She didn't even try to hide her distaste for us or my dad. She was an alcoholic, an addict, and she slept around.

It took years of therapy, and a lot of breaking it down in grad school, to realize it was never about me. It was her, plain and simple. She had all the money, freedom, and distractions in the world, and she was still miserable. She wanted Dad's attention, but he was barely there. When he was around, he was a good dad but a shitty husband—a workaholic with his own affairs.

I get it now, the dysfunction of it all, but when you're ten, rejection from your own mum cuts deep. It fucks with you in ways you never fully shake, no matter how much you analyze it.

Reluctantly, I respond, "It was my mum," I say somberly, my face permanently planted into the palm of my hand.

"What do you think's drumming up the past?" she asks, but I get the feeling she already has an idea of the answer, which irritates the living hell out of me.

"I don't know," I say honestly. "I have a feeling you might think that you do, though, yeah?"

A wicked grin spreads across her face. "Well, now that you've asked…" She pauses. "I think it has something to do with Vivian."

"And why do you think that?"

"Because you were a mess last night," she states, wide-eyed, her eyebrows raised. "You showed up here at midnight drunker than a skunk, Leo. Piper opened the door, and you came waltzing in here, rambling on about all sorts of things with Vivian… Vivian this and Vivian that, how you had fucked everything up. God knows what happened; you weren't making any sense, and every word slurred together. You went straight to the liquor cabinet and poured yourself a glass… a *glass* of tequila, which I was able to get out of your hands after you had drunk half of it." I grimace, and she continues. "You then proceeded to want to"—she makes air quotes—"'talk.' Luckily, I talked Piper into getting back to bed and letting me handle you. She had a staff meeting at 8 AM."

"God, I'm sorry. I'll apologize to Piper when I see her."

"Oh, I'm not done," she cuts me off. "I sat here with you while you rambled. An hour later, you puked in the kitchen sink."

I scrunch my face. "I did?"

She nods again.

"At least I didn't pee on the wall again… I didn't, right?" I ask hopefully.

"No, you didn't pee on the wall," she says, nudging me lightly. "I won't push you, but I think we should talk about it." She flashes me a playful grin. "You know I'll figure it out eventually, or worse, I'll try to guess what's going on and constantly bother you about it until I get close."

"*That,* I cannot deal with," I say, chuckling. "Okay," I hesitate, "but I don't know what I was talking about last night. The last thing I remember was leaving Vivian's house. Probably around 10:30. We'd had dinner and went to the Christmas market."

"You had dinner and went to the Christmas Market… that's it? Were you two drinking? How did you get annihilated in just ninety minutes?"

"Yeah, I had a couple of drinks with Viv."

"Well, if that's the last thing you remember, then you must have had more than a couple."

"Oh wait. It's coming back to me. I went to my house. Yeah. I went to my house and took some shots of whiskey, and then I went for a walk… I don't remember whether I was planning to come here or not. I may have stopped at a few bars along the way," I shake my head in utter disbelief. "I don't know, and then I guess I ended up here. I'm sorry for disrupting your night with Piper and for the inconvenience… and drinking your tequila… and for puking in the sink." I run my hands through my hair. "I'm really sorry."

"It's okay. I'm concerned more than anything. I haven't seen you that drunk since you were in your twenties."

"Well you didn't come to Mexico," I say laughing.

She laughs. "Seriously, I'm worried about you. This isn't like you. You're one of the most responsible drinkers I've ever met. I've only known you to get this drunk a handful of times. You weren't just drunk, you were plastered… and upset."

"I know. I didn't intentionally get smashed. Does that make it any better?"

She holds her thumb and index finger an inch away from each other, "A little," she says. "Can we unpack this? Why did you leave Vivian's and immediately take shots when you got to your house?"

"Ugh," I groan, "don't make me talk about it."

She's quiet for a moment. "You know you can talk to me," she puts her hand on my knee and gives it a small shake. "I'm your person, Leo. Your *in case of emergency* person, your friend, your therapist—well you don't actually pay for my words of wisdom… but I'm the person you tell your deepest darkest secrets to, that's me." She gives me a playful nudge. "Come on, what happened?"

I glance at her while sinking back into the sofa, my head resting on the back of the pillow, staring at the ceiling straight above. She knows me too well. She really is my person, has been for a long time. Mer and I met at University. We were in the same PhD program, and she's the only one who knows about my mum. Michael knows she died when I was ten, but Mer… she knows everything. I've never kept anything from her and honestly, there's no point trying. She's insightful as hell, and she'll eventually find out anyway.

"I don't know. Last night was… intense. We made-out. Things got heated, and I wanted it to go further, but I freaked out… I pulled away. I was scared of what it would mean, scared to care about her… of losing her, scared of fucking everything up."

She nods, listening intently. "And that's why you drank yourself into oblivion?"

"Yeah, I guess so. When I stopped, she was really upset with me. She told me to get the fuck out…" I groan, giving Meredith a sidelong glance.

She nods in understanding, urging me to go on.

"She didn't want to talk, said she could hardly look at me. I just… I didn't know how to handle it. Seeing her, wanting her, feeling out of control—not just emotionally, but physically, too. It was like my body had a mind of its own. God, I've spent the last thirteen years avoiding anything that could make me feel this way, it's been my coping mechanism, and now it's all backfiring."

I take a swig of the concoction Meredith made for me. My friend Brian and I discovered the hangover cure our first year in college, and I've shared it with all of my close friends since then.

I bring a hand up to the back of my neck and press hard against the base of my skull, releasing the tension that's pounding through my head. "Vivian shared some things about her past a few weeks ago. It's heavy stuff. She's a champ, though—doing everything right, taking every step to heal."

I pause, looking out the window as I gather my thoughts. "But she needs and wants connection, while I've spent my life avoiding that kind of connection. We're dealing with the exact opposite issues, fearing the exact opposite things. She's lost so much already, I would never want to add to her grief." I lean back, frustration bubbling up. "And I don't ever want to know how that feels again. Love has only ever brought me pain. I don't know if I even want to try."

I shake my head. "God, what do I do? I've never wanted a relationship to worry about, and I definitely don't want to get married. These days, you've got a 50/50 chance of it ending in divorce. In my practice, I see couples every day trying to patch up broken marriages, dealing with infidelity, resentment, and a complete lack of communication. Of that fifty percent, only a handful of them are truly happy. The odds are stacked against us all. I'm not a fool; I don't gamble with shitty odds unless I'm willing to lose it all."

Meredith looks at me with a mixture of sympathy and determination. "I get it. Your fears and concerns are valid, and I know where they're coming from. But as we grow, things that used to work for us can stop being effective. You know this. Coping mechanisms that kept us safe can become barriers. You've done the work before, but it doesn't mean it's over. It's about recognizing when it's time to revisit it—to go back and work through things as they evolve, as you evolve.

I shake my head adamantly. "No. I don't want to revisit that. That was brutal enough the first time." The conviction in my voice surprises even me, the words rushing out faster than I intended.

Meredith's eyes narrow, her keen insight already picking apart my defenses. "You know burying things doesn't make them go away."

Ignoring her, I glance around the cozy family room, the couch beneath me is comfortable, yet I feel anything but relaxed. "I've been fine all these years, happy even, doing what I've been doing. Revisiting it would only open old wounds. I'm fine with my barriers."

I can see Meredith wants to say something, but I forge ahead, needing to get it all out. "Plus, I've never wanted to be in a position where I could be a shitty boyfriend, or husband… or father." The last word catches in my throat, an ache I can't quite shake off. "The idea of fucking up someone else's life scares the hell out of me."

Meredith remains silent, her gaze unwavering. I swallow hard, forcing myself to meet her eyes. "Or worse, having everything to lose and watching it all fall apart." My heart races, the thought of Vivian creeping into my mind. "When something happens to a person you choose to share your life with, like Vivian, that's... It feels reckless to love someone that much... to put so much hope into one person."

She sighs, her eyes softening with understanding. "It's not reckless to love someone. It's human. And yes, there's risk, but there's also incredible reward. You can't live your life in fear of what might happen. Nothing worth having comes easy. And honestly, when I see you with Vivian, you're different. You're more relaxed, more yourself. You laugh more, and you seem genuinely happy. She brings out a side of you that I haven't seen in years. Don't let fear hold you back from what could be an incredible future."

I take a deep breath, feeling the weight of her words. "I've never felt stuck until now... Why would I want to change things when they have always worked out for me?"

She lifts a brow and purses her lips. "I think you know why."

"Look, I'll take what you're saying into account. But for now, I need to focus on repairing the trust I broke with Vivian last night. That's my priority."

She places her hand on my back and rubs it softly. "Okay," she says softly. "I'm not going to push you, but I'm here if you need anything." She gets a playful look in her eye, "Now... can we please talk about how you kissed Vivian?" She grins. "So... how was it?"

I can't help but smile. "It was... amazing." I lean back into the sofa, running a hand through my hair as a laugh escapes my lips. "Honestly, it felt like everything just clicked. Like for a moment, all the shit I've been carrying around didn't matter. I felt... free. She's fucking incredible." I look at Meredith, still grinning.

I leave Meredith's with no real clarification, only the desire to fix my friendship with Vivian. I pull out my phone to text her.

Leo: Viv… we need to talk. Can I come over?

I walk outside to get in my Uber, staring at the screen to see the status of my message turn to read as I fasten my seatbelt. The drive home is a blur, deep in thought and waiting for Vivian to text me back. It's almost noon, I know she's awake.

The Uber drops me off at the end of the street, and I run down the path of townhouses straight to Vivian's door and pound on it.

My phone dings.

Vivian: I'm packing for my trip tomorrow. I am not ready to see you or talk to you. I have a date tonight, and then I leave early in the morning. Please respect my space, I will contact you when I am ready to talk… and I don't know when that will be.

Jesus.

I have fucked things up more than I could have imagined. She just built a ten-foot wall, and there is nothing I can do but wait for her to come to me. "Ugh!" I groan in agony as I respond to her text.

Leo Viv, please… Don't leave for the holidays with things like this. Please let me tell you how sorry I am… how much your friendship means to me. Please…

Vivian: Well that's the problem, Leo. I don't know how to just be your friend anymore. So please let me figure out what it is that I want, and process everything that has happened. I will get back to you after I have a chance to think about things… when I am ready. I need to see my therapist in Utah. I want you to know that I care about you. I just need some space.

I stare at the screen, my heart sinking. She needs space, but at least she said she cares about me. Maybe there's still hope.

These next two weeks will feel like an eternity.

Chapter 21

VIVIAN

Christmas Day

I take a deep breath, savoring the smell of bacon, eggs, and waffles as I stand by the sink. My mom and I move in sync—she washes, I dry—our routine perfected over the years. Bing Crosby and Dean Martin play in the background, their Christmas classics filling me with nostalgia. A fire crackles in the family room, and the Christmas tree sparkles with lights and ornaments. The main floor feels cozy and festive, filled with the scent of breakfast and the warmth of holiday music. Dad is on the couch, scrolling through his X feed and managing the playlist. It's Christmas morning; we've just finished opening gifts and eating breakfast, all in our matching Christmas pajamas. My family is small, just the three of us, but the love we share is big.

A wave of emotion fills me as I remember Ben and me doing the dishes just two years ago. I washed while he dried, and I couldn't stop smiling that morning. He had surprised me with a planned trip to Paris for my 28th birthday in June, and I was over the moon. But Ben wasn't there the following summer, and the thought of going without him felt unbearable at the time.

My mom interrupts my thoughts. "Have you spoken to Leo yet?" she asks, her voice full of motherly concern.

I sigh. "No, not yet."

I tell my mom everything. I've been home, Utah home, for a little over a week now and leave in a few days. Despite the weight of sadness that plagues me between my memories of Ben and my confusion with Leo, I've had some great moments over the past week. I went skiing and snowshoeing with my mom and dad. Sarah and I went to the ChristkindlMarket in Salt Lake City and had breakfast at my favorite place in Park City, Five5eeds. I took my niece and nephew to the ice castles and Zoo Lights with Melissa. Last night, I spent the evening with the Walkers, where we went around the circle and shared our favorite memories of Ben. It was bittersweet but has become one of my favorite new traditions on Christmas Eve.

"Do you think today might be a good day to reach out?" She's prodding, but in that sneaky mom way.

"I don't know, Mom. I still don't know what to do or say. I've never been so conflicted before." I stare blankly at the snow falling through the large wall of glass in the family room.

"Well, maybe you just start with 'Merry Christmas,' just to let him know you're thinking of him. The rest will fall into place, I'm sure of it." I don't know how my mom does it, but she's one of the most positive people I know. She has this unwavering belief that what you put out comes back to you. I used to be that way too… until my life went to shit, and I lost everything in a matter of seconds.

"I can only imagine he's going crazy not having heard from you for this long."

Why? Why does she have to go there right now?

"You're probably right, Mom. And I'd say that it serves him right… I'm going crazy too."

"Vivian, honey, it's not a game. Have some faith. I believe things will work out if you trust the process." She stops washing and looks at me. "You should call him."

"I'm not calling him. I'm not ready for that. I'll send him a text today."

She smiles. Sometimes you just have to give your mom a small win.

I laugh softly. "Geez, Mom, when are you going to mind your own business?" I say jokingly.

She laughs. "Never. It's my job not to."

Grinning, I bump her with my shoulder, and she bumps me back.

* * * * * * * * * *

I sit on my bed, coffee in one hand and my phone in the other, staring at an open message to Leo. I've reread his last text to me, and mine to him, a dozen times, each time stirring a whirlwind of emotions inside me. My heart starts to pound.

Taking a deep breath, I start typing, my fingers shaky. I type, "Merry Christmas, I hope you have a great day."

I erase it and try again, typing out "Merry Christmas" again and stare at it. I'm stuck. There's almost too much to say, and I can't find the right words. Finally, I leave it as it is, passing the ball to him.

Vivian: Merry Christmas.

I anxiously wait as ten minutes go by, and Leo responds.

Leo: Merry Christmas, Viv. I miss you. Can I see you when you get home?

Damn. I gave him the ball, and he just passed it back. I have no team-mates to pass it to, and I'm unsure what to do with it. If I see him on Friday when I get home, I still have four full days to figure out what to say. I type out "sure" and then delete it. I need to sound confident.

Vivian: Yes.

Vivian: I land at 7:00 PM

Leo: Can I pick you up from the airport?

Vivian: No, I'll take the train. I don't love that setting for the talk we need to have.

Leo Okay. Can I come over at 8:30?

Vivian: Yeah, that works.

Leo: Okay. My friend is in town, but Mer can babysit him. I'll see you then. And Viv, have a great week. I'm excited to see you.

I drop my phone on the bed and shut my eyes, trying to hold back the tears that are unwillingly wringing their way out. He's excited to see me.

I don't know what I am.

December 30

The fifty-five-minute journey home on the train flies by in what feels like seconds as I anxiously rack my brain for the upcoming conversation with Leo. I still have no idea what I want to say. I'm going to have to rely on my mom's motto and trust my gut in the moment, hoping it won't backfire.

I walk into the empty, dark house and take all my stuff upstairs. I'm exhausted and would love nothing more than to fall into my bed and let sleep take me. I haven't slept well all week, my thoughts racing every night since I texted Leo. Shit. It's 8:15, which only allows me fifteen minutes to pull myself together.

I look like hell, and there really isn't enough time to do anything about it. I fix my ponytail, apply some deodorant, pat my cheeks with a little cream blush, and swipe on a natural pink lip gloss.

When Leo arrives, I open the door, gesturing for him to come in. My stomach twists in knots.

"Hey, Viv." Leo's lips curve into a soft smile as he steps inside.

"Hi," is all I say, matching his smile with effort.

Walking into the living room, I sit on the chaise and turn my body toward the rest of the sofa, so I can face him as he takes the cushion next to it.

"How was Utah?" he asks.

"It was good." I fidget with the throw pillows, trying to get comforta-ble. "Can we skip the semantics for now?" I ask, hoping it doesn't sound bitchy, but I can't do small talk until we've cleared the air.

"Sure. Whatever you want." He's being cautious, his eyes wary, and I feel on edge. He's never seen me like this; hell, I don't think I've ever seen myself like this. I'm usually easygoing, but I've built a fortress around myself, and I don't know where the door is.

There's an uncomfortable silence, a first for us.

"Okay… do you want me to go first?" he offers.

I only nod.

"Alright." He stumbles for words, his face filled with anguish. "Christ, Viv, I never meant for any of this to happen. I'm sorry. I've been a mess trying to figure out what the hell I want, and honestly, I'm still unsure. But I crossed a line. I got caught up in wanting more… physically, and I let it take over."

I'm stunned by his excuse, my face contorting in confusion. "You wanted more physically? Are you seriously going to blame what happened on your physical desires? God, that's such bullshit, and you know it." Wow. I can't believe how harsh I'm being. I'm surprised by my own bluntness.

Leo's eyes widen, and his expression shifts from sorrow to hurt. He looks down, swallowing hard, clearly taken aback by my words.

"Look, I'm sorry if that came out wrong," I say, my voice softening but firm. "But I need honesty from you."

"Don't be sorry. I deserve that. And if that's how you feel, it's how you feel."

"It's not about how I feel, it's about how *you* feel. And right now… it feels like you aren't being honest about that." I fixate on the pillow cushion I'm leaning against for a moment, rubbing the leather and tracing the seams, trying to figure out what to say next. Why won't he admit that he has feelings for me?

My hand stills so that I can focus on him. "I just don't see a clear path forward for us right now. It feels like we both want more… physically, but you keep holding back. Why is that?" I frown, feeling the weight of my own confusion. "What is it that's stopping you from wanting to be with me? I need to understand, but I can't unless you tell me."

He breaks eye contact with me for the first time tonight. "It's not that simple. I care about you a lot, but I think we need to stay friends. We just need more self-control."

"Self-control? Are you serious?" I sink back against the cushion as I rub my temples. "Come on. You say it's not that simple, but I know you care for me. And after what happened, there's no way you don't feel the same way I do. I was there, and…" I trail off, shaking my head in frustration. "You can deny it all you want, but I won't accept you saying it was just your physical desires taking over. Fuck that."

"Vivian, I…" He sighs, running a hand through his hair. "Of course I care about you, and I don't want to lose you. You're too important to me. There are parts of my life you don't understand."

"How can I? You never let me in completely. You keep everything so locked and guarded. God!" I throw my hands up in frustration, my voice rising. "It's exhausting."

"It's more complicated than that. There are things I just don't want to talk about." He pauses, rubbing the back of his neck before continuing. "Look, I know you want more—a real relationship, commitment. But that's just not me. It never has been. And sex… it means more to you than it does to me." He sighs, still not meeting my eyes. "I care about you, but this is just… not what I can give."

I scoff, letting it hang in the air. I take a deep breath and look him straight in the eye. "You can't keep running from your feelings." I feel my eyes getting misty. "They're going to catch up to you someday. You think we can just go back to being friends, but this physical affection will keep happening again and again… we can't ignore it."

"I don't want to ignore it. I'm just trying to protect us both. We can still be friends, feelings and all; we just need boundaries."

"Boundaries? God, are you serious? We've already tried that, and we've crossed so many lines." The discomfort is palpable as I shift in my seat. My body temperature rises, heat creeping up my neck, and I suddenly feel hot and stifled. "Maybe we need to take a step back, see less of each other for a while. Give ourselves space to figure this out."

His face tightens, and I can see the pain in his eyes. "I don't want that. I love being with you. I don't want to lose you in any capacity."

"I don't want to lose you either. But being around you and not being able to have more… it's hard for me. Our chemistry… the way we connect—it makes it even harder."

I watch his face for understanding. My heart aches with the possibility of distancing myself from him, but I know it's the only way to protect my sanity.

He clenches his jaw, the tension clear. "I don't want to step back. But I also don't want to keep hurting you."

"But you do keep hurting me… It's not something I want to do either. But I think it's the best way forward… at least for now. We can still be friends, just… with some space."

His shoulders sag, resignation setting in. "What does that even look like?" he asks, his fingertips pressing against his forehead.

"I don't know. Maybe we see each other once a week, just to catch up. Keep things light until it gets easier."

He sighs, smoothing his fingers across his forehead. "I guess that makes sense… Fuck. It'll be tough, though."

"I know," I say softly, biting back the ache in my chest. "But I think it's the only way we can make this work without losing each other completely."

"Fine, we'll try that." He rubs the back of his neck, clearly uneasy, then glances at me, hesitating. "Are you still going to Meredith's New Year's Eve party tomorrow night?"

I nod. "Yeah, I'll be there. I told Meredith I would be. I could use a distraction, anyway."

He offers a small, tentative smile. "Good. I'm glad you'll be there."

"Me too… How was your Christmas?"

"It was nice. Brian's in town, as you know, and we went to Meredith and Piper's like I usually do. It was good."

"That sounds great," I say, genuinely happy he had a good time.

"How was your trip to Utah?"

"It was good. A bit of a whirlwind, but it was nice to see everyone."

He nods again, looking like he wants to say more but thinks better of it. "Okay. Well, I should probably get going. See you tomorrow night?"

"Yeah, I'll see you tomorrow," I reply, my voice steady despite the swirl of emotions inside me.

I walk him to the door, and he gives me a hug goodbye. I can feel myself resisting, pulling away because what I really want is for him to take me into his arms and kiss me like he did before. As the door closes behind him, I let out a breath I didn't realize I was holding.

Chapter 22

LEO

December 31

Brian and I step out of the Uber at 8:55 PM. I'm wearing a navy suit, Brian a cream one. Meredith's party always has a cocktail dress code; she invites the people and pays for the food, while I rent the venue and cover the staff expenses. She used to host it at her house, but the parties grew bigger each year. It got so packed that you could hardly move, so I offered to pay for a larger space the next year, and she reluctantly agreed. This year, it's a casino-themed party, and it's on the ninety-tyninth floor of the Willis Tower.

"Are there going to be any good-looking women here tonight that you know of?" Brian asks, naturally. Brian is a serial dater, but he actually wants to settle down and get married someday, which makes him better than me, according to most.

"There always are, mate. It's a big party, usually about a hundred people. I've never had trouble finding someone to take home." As I say this, my mind drifts to Vivian. She'll be here this year, and I know she'll outshine them all. I'd offered her a ride with us, but she politely declined, making me wonder if she really does intend to stick to the boundaries we agreed on.

Brian knows I think Vivian is hot and a great friend—I've talked about her enough. But only Meredith knows about my deeper feelings for her and our mutual attraction.

We take the elevator up to the 99th floor, and as soon as the doors open, the sounds of chatter and music fill the air. The room is decked out like a high-end casino, complete with poker, blackjack, and craps tables, along with roulette wheels. I immediately look for Meredith to see if she needs help with anything, even though I've spent a small fortune ensuring there's plenty of staff to handle everything.

I find Meredith near the bar with Piper on one arm, and a drink in the other hand, talking to the bartender. She's in a sleek black dress, effortlessly commanding attention as always. We're right on time, with only about fifteen other people here. The majority will roll in within the hour, and the rest after that.

We make our way across the room. "Mer," I call out.

She turns around. "Leo! Brian! You made it!" She gives each of us a one-armed hug, carefully holding her drink to the side so she doesn't spill it.

"This turned out great. You've really outdone yourself." I grab her by the shoulders, grinning like a proud father.

"It's really great, Meredith," Brian chimes in.

"Ah, thanks, you guys! Honestly, I couldn't have done any of it without you, Leo. And Piper puts up with my crazy for all the weeks leading up to it."

Piper goes wide-eyed and grimaces, causing us all to laugh.

While we catch up on the week, I order a whiskey on the rocks for myself, and a Liquid Death water for Brian. Brian is somewhat of a situational alcoholic, so he doesn't consume much alcohol, and when he does, it's usually just one or two beers. His drinking became a problem when he was twenty-two after his dad, who was his role model and best friend, died suddenly of a heart attack. That loss sent Brian into a nine-month spiral of heavy drinking, alienating everyone around him. He went on another bender in his late twenties after his fiancée broke off their engagement, but since then, he's managed to keep his drinking under control.

At 9:15, Michael and Stella arrive and join us at a standing table to mingle. By 9:30, I still don't see Vivian and the party is in full swing, with glittering decorations and a sea of people filling the room. Laughter and chatter mix with the music, creating a vibrant, almost electric atmosphere. Streamers and stringed lights hang from the ceiling, and the faint smell of champagne and hors d'oeuvres lingers in the air.

I text her because yes, I am that pussy-whipped, even though I'm adamant that we stay just friends. Everything is better when Vivian is around. Plus, I want to normalize things as quickly as possible, get rid of any leftover tension.

Leo: Party can't start until you're here. What's your ETA?

She responds within two minutes.

Vivian: Slow your roll… I'm in an Uber, almost there.

I give her message a thumbs-up and realize just how anxious I am for her to arrive, mindlessly tapping my index finger on the table—a nervous tick.

Finally, fifteen minutes later, Vivian steps out of the elevator, and I practically have to scrape my jaw off the floor. She is drop-dead gorgeous—the sexiest I've ever seen her. I can't help but kick myself a little for being such a stubborn ass.

She's wearing a low-cut sequin mini dress. The front plunges in a deep V, almost down to her belly button, showing off the perfect curve of her tits—the same tits I rubbed, kissed and sucked on just a few weeks ago. It's sheer… and it's fucking with my head—I can't tell if it's skin or fabric, but it's going to drive me crazy all night. And her strappy heels make her long legs look sexy as hell. All I can think about is what's underneath— what color are her panties, is her pussy bare?

Fuck. I'm in deep shit tonight.

This friends thing is going to kill me. All I want is to close the distance between us and forget about all the reasons why I shouldn't.

I watch from across the room as she finds Piper, every guy she passes glancing at her, their eyes lingering a moment too long. The best part is that she doesn't even realize how beautiful she is. She doesn't flaunt it.

She and Piper start talking, and I watch as she laughs, her smile lighting up the room.

Vivian glances in my direction, her eyes locking on mine. She smiles and gives me a little wave. I gesture for her to come over, and she holds up her index finger, indicating she'll be over in a minute.

She and Piper make their way to the bar, and I watch as two different guys approach her. One is definitely not her type, but the other is a decent-looking guy. A wave of envy crashes over me as I watch her smile and flirt with him, placing her hand on his chest. Damn. I know what it's like to be on the receiving end of that hand and laugh, and I don't like that it's someone else. I can't wait any longer. I excuse myself from the table where Michael, Stella, and Brian are conversing and make a beeline to the bar before another guy can flirt with her.

"Hey, Viv," I say casually, interrupting her and Piper.

"Oh hey, you!" she says, offering me a side hug.

Hey you? A side hug?

She's never given me a side hug before; that's what you give your father or brother… or, shit, a friend. Well, fuck me. I guess this is what it's like to be Vivian's friend with her guard up.

"Have you been here long?" she asks, her voice cheerful.

"About an hour." I look her up and down and grin. "You look fucking incredible, by the way. You're turning heads as you walk through this room."

She smiles shyly. "Thanks. But there's only one head I care to turn in this room," she says unwaveringly, her green eyes locking with mine.

"Well, it's been turned, love," I respond, my voice low and sincere.

"You don't look so bad yourself," she says with a sly smile, patting my shoulder and then slowly running her hand down the length of my arm. "You clean up nice."

Brian approaches, a grin on his face. "Are you going to introduce me to your friend, Leo?"

I watch Vivian take Brian in, her eyes widening slightly. Smiling, she reaches out her hand. "Hi, I'm Vivian. I'm Leo's next-door neighbor," she says, giving me a playful nudge.

I know she's teasing, but God, I've been demoted to next-door neighbor? Here's the thing: it's a fair assumption that I'm an attractive guy, based on the way women respond to me. But Brian is also an attractive guy, and the last thing I want is these two hitting it off.

"Brian, this is Vivian, my *friend,*" I say, emphasizing the word friend and giving her a pointed look. "Viv, this is Brian, my longest childhood friend."

Brian takes her hand, his smile widening. "Pleasure to meet you, Vivian. I've heard a lot about you."

She returns his smile. "Have you?" she asks, giving me a questioning look. "Good things, I hope?"

"I'd have nothing but good things to say," I say with a wink.

Brian asks her a question, and before long, they're talking and laughing like old friends. I can feel a knot tightening in my stomach. I need to steer this conversation before it goes somewhere I can't control.

"So, Viv," I say, stepping a bit closer, "can I get you another drink?"

She gives me a playful, confused look, tilting her head slightly. "No, I'm good. I'm still working on this one." She lifts her glass, showing that it's still clearly half full.

"God, are they putting something in the water in London?" she says with a teasing smile, her eyes dancing between Brian and me. "How is it that the two of you are both this good-looking and friends since you were kids? I need to know where all the handsome guys from your old neighborhood are hiding because my dating calendar just opened up." She takes a sip of her drink, her eyes sparkling with mischief as she waits for my reaction.

What kind of game is she playing? Is she trying to make me jealous? If so, it's working. Every laugh, every flirtatious glance in Brian's direction feels like a jab.

Brian starts asking her about her job, and soon they're deep into a work conversation. I stand there, trying to keep my frustration in check. I can't help but notice how animated Vivian becomes when she talks about her work, her eyes lighting up and her hands gesturing passionately. She loves her job. I watch as she laughs and flirtatiously places a hand on Brian's arm, his eyes lighting up as she does.

Fuck this.

If she's trying to prove a point, she's making it loud and clear. I need to get a grip, but it's hard when all I can think about is pulling her away from this conversation and reminding her of the chemistry that we have… of her moan when I took her nipple into my mouth, the way she cried out my name and begged to touch me.

"Well hey, maybe we can go grab drinks before you leave town," I hear Vivian say, snapping me out of my thoughts and the memory of our intense physical interaction, which is making my cock hard.

"Oh, Brian's not much of a drinker," I blurt out before I can stop myself, immediately regretting inserting myself into their conversation.

Brian gives me a puzzled look, and I can feel my face heat up. "Sorry, mate, that came out wrong."

What the hell is wrong with me?

Brian just shakes his head, clearly frustrated with me, but he bounces back quickly. "I actually don't drink much, Vivian. But I'd like to take you out while I'm here, if you're interested." He shoots me a quick, understanding look, letting me know he's not holding a grudge.

"Of course, I'd go out with you. I'd love that. Find me later, and we'll talk more about it," she replies with a warm smile. Then, turning to me briefly, she adds, "I'm going to go find Meredith," before waving goodbye to us.

Brian and I spent most of the night at the craps table, watching the dice roll and cheering each other on. Brian's been on a hot streak, but I'm down more than I'd like to admit. I can't find Meredith, and I haven't seen Vivian. It's ten to midnight. Normally, by this time, I have an attractive woman on my arm, ready to kiss at midnight, while dazzling her with my charm before taking her home. This year, I'm frantic, searching for Meredith because I need her to talk me off a ledge. The ledge that is Vivian Walker.

I find Piper and she tells me Meredith is meeting her by the bar in a few minutes for a New Year's Eve kiss at midnight. I tell her to have Meredith find me afterward, not wanting to intrude on their moment.

Five minutes to midnight.

Where the hell is Vivian? I scour the crowd, the room now dimly lit by stringed patio lights across the ceiling. Normally, I'd be appreciating this ambiance, taking it all in, thinking about my last year and the new year ahead. Instead, I've turned into a crazed lunatic in need of meds; my drug of choice: Vivian.

Two minutes to midnight. Meredith's big countdown clock, with its large red numbers, is displayed prominently in the center of the wall.

My eyes catch sight of Vivian on the other side of the room… with Brian. A knot forms in the pit of my stomach as the clock hits forty-five seconds. I make my way across the room, weaving through the crowd.

Ten, nine, eight—I'm halfway to her. Seven, six, five—I'm close, but I won't make it through the crowd. Four, three, two, one—"Happy New Year!" echoes off the walls, but my eyes are glued to Vivian and Brian. They lean in, their movements slow and deliberate, as if in a scene playing out in slow motion. Their lips meet, and it feels like I've been punched in the balls. They separate briefly, eyes locked, before kissing again. Vivian's arms wrap around Brian's neck, his around her back.

Everything swirls around me, and I feel like I'm going to be sick.

Chapter 23

VIVIAN

January 6

One Week Later

New Year's Eve was fun. I felt Leo's eyes on me all night, a boost to my ego. Leo seemed torn—he says he just wants to be friends, but his actions say otherwise. The compliments, the lingering looks, the way he's always so attentive—it's confusing. While I enjoy it, I'm starting to realize it's holding me back from future potential. I need to focus on finding someone who is truly available, despite my mom's insistence that Leo will eventually come around.

Brian left early this morning. We had dinner two nights ago and ended up making out on my couch for over an hour. I thoroughly enjoyed it. Exactly what I need right now—fun, light, uncomplicated. Brian is smart, funny, and undeniably attractive. He reminds me a lot of Leo.

It's unlikely that anything serious is going to happen with Brian. I mean, he lives in London. We said we'd stay connected through texts and calls, but long-distance isn't easy. Besides, I don't know how Leo feels about it, or why I care how he feels about it.

I went over to Leo's place last night for dinner and to say goodbye to Brian. It felt… somewhat normal, or as normal as it can, considering everything that's happened.

Before I left last night, Leo asked if I wanted to come over in the morning for breakfast and coffee. Naturally, I said yes, though a part of me wonders if I'm falling back into the pattern of spending too much time with him.

I make my way over, wearing a matching Lululemon jogger and half-zip set in heather gray, my hair pulled back into a ponytail. I'm dressed entirely for comfort and warmth, with no intention of impressing him, keeping my priorities straight.

I let myself in because that's what we do most of the time, and I'm immediately hit with the aroma of breakfast sausage and eggs, which I freaking love.

"Hey!" I call out, walking into the kitchen. I spot Leo by the oven, cooking up a skillet. "It smells incredible in here."

He takes his eyes off the skillet long enough to greet me. "Hey, Viv, this will be ready in five."

"Do you want me to start the coffees?" I ask.

"Yeah, that'd be great!"

I head to the espresso machine, like I have dozens of times, to make two cappuccinos.

I get lost in thought as I steam the milk, mindlessly making our cappuccinos. I think about everything that's happened over the past month. Leo, Nick, now Brian. I went out with Nick the night before I went out with Brian. We also made out, but on the porch. I told him I wanted to slow things down a bit, that I need time to see and date other people. He must like me a lot; otherwise, I don't understand why he would agree to take things slower than we have already been.

I think about Ben. For reasons unknown, I imagine him hanging out with these guys. Would he like them? Would he vibe? It matters to me what I think he would think, as if his approval would validate my choices.

"Hey," Leo pulls me from my thoughts. "What's going on with you? You're in a twilight zone."

"Oh," I tuck some hair behind my ear, "I'm sorry, I'm lost in thought."

"What are you thinking about?"

"Oh, nothing… everything, I don't know." I scrunch my forehead, shaking my head and shrugging, as I hand him his cappuccino. "How did everything go this morning getting Brian off?"

He lifts a brow, "You mean sending him off?" he chuckles, "I think getting him off is more in your department."

My eyes widen. "Oh my God, I didn't even realize I said that." I laugh and take a sip of my coffee. "Mmm. This is my favorite part of the day," I say, smiling as I breathe in the rich aroma of my cup of joe. There really is nothing better than a cup of hot coffee on a bitter cold morning.

Leo hands me a plate of food—a sausage and egg skillet with sweet potato hash, avocado, and red onions. "Damn. You really know your way into a woman's heart," I say affectionately. I stand on one side of the kitchen island, facing the living room, watching the fire Leo lit crackle and dance, its warm glow flickering across the room. Leo sits across from me on a barstool.

"I don't know about that… I think I just know how much you love a skillet and coffee." He grins at me, and this feels… nice. It feels nice and normal, something I was worried we wouldn't get back to. There is definitely a layer of invisible caution tape surrounding us—don't be too flirty, don't touch—but overall, it feels normal.

"This is nice," I say, smiling, unable to help myself. I feel genuinely happy right now.

We catch up on some work talk. Leo fills me in on some real estate ventures he's pursuing, and I tell him about my projects.

After we finish eating, I take his plate and mine to the sink, rinse them off, and set them in the dishwasher.

"Viv," he says, prompting me to turn and look at him.

"Yeah?"

"I need to talk to you about something," he says hesitantly, and I can't read the look on his face.

"Okay…" I say slowly.

"It's about New Year's Eve."

I straighten up, standing across the counter from him. "What about it?" I ask, a feeling of dread washing over me.

Leo rubs the back of his neck. "Look, I saw you and Brian… kissing, and it really irked me."

I frown, bracing myself.

"That whole night had me feeling not myself. You came in, looking how you did," he gestures to me, "and all I could think about was how stupid I was for being… well, me, the way that I am. Then Brian came over, and you two seemed to hit it off. I thought, '*No, not Brian, anyone but Brian, flirt with anyone but him, kiss anyone but him,*' and then I saw you two kissing and, God, it sent me over the edge. I was pissed. I was jealous." He looks down, as if he knows what he's saying is ridiculous. Leo never struggles to make eye contact, but he's having a hard time now. "I know he lives in London, but I need to ask you not to continue any kind of relationship with him beyond friendship."

I'm stunned into silence. Part of me is happy because this is what I wanted—for him to be jealous, possibly realizing that he has deeper feelings for me than he lets on. The other part is filled with annoyance.

I clear my throat, setting my coffee down, and do my best to be mature about this situation. Looking directly at him, I say, "You, of all people, have no right to be upset or jealous when it comes to who I want to flirt with, date, or kiss." I shake my head, my voice growing firmer. "The audacity…" I stumble, trying to maintain my cool. "To ask me to only be friends with Brian, when I actually have a connection with him, well, that's some real nerve. You better have a damn good reason for that." I lean back, crossing my arms, trying to calm the storm of emotions brewing inside me.

"I do," he says calmly, "and it's not something I *want* to discuss with you, but I'm trying to open up here, to be honest with you. I want you to understand it."

He takes a deep breath, "Brian has been my best friend since I was six. We went through everything together. He was my person, and I was his. We were rebellious teenagers and did the dumbest shit together." A small laugh escapes his lips. "Then we went to university together, where I met Rachel." His index finger starts tapping the counter, something he does when he's nervous. "She was my girlfriend for three years. And the only girlfriend I've ever had." He folds his arms, but I notice he's still tapping his finger against his bicep.

"I loved her… Bought a ring for her, wanted to get married—possibly have a family with her one day." He swallows a few times, struggling to continue. "Around the same time, Brian's dad died of an unexpected heart attack. He and Brian were really close, best friends. His dad was even a second father-figure to me. It was a tough time."

He takes a sip of his cappuccino. I can tell how difficult this story is to talk about.

"Brian took to drinking, he spiraled quickly, became an alcoholic, unable to handle the situation and his emotions. He was drunk all the time." He stares at the counter now. "He'd steal money from me, lie about where he was going, you name it—all the behaviors that alcoholics exhibit, he had them. One day, I went over to his house because I couldn't get ahold of him, I was worried…" He trails off, going back and forth from looking at the counter to me, as the silence lingers. "I found him in his room… in bed… with Rachel."

Holy shit. My first thought is that I can't believe Brian would do that to him, and then I wonder how he could ever forgive him for that.

He continues, "They'd been sleeping together for three months. I kicked his ass. Literally, right there, I beat his naked ass up, something I regret to this day." He lifts a hand and shrugs. "I don't know… so when I saw the two of you kissing, it felt like history was about to repeat itself." He pauses, looking dead set into my eyes. "So when I say anyone but Brian, I mean *anyone* but Brian."

A heavy silence fills the kitchen, like a weight pressing down on my shoulders. I feel bad that he had to witness that, but I'm also irritated.

"Look, I'm sorry you saw us kissing. But you need to understand, I'm not your girlfriend—by *your* choice. I can see how it would bother you, given your history, but you don't get to control who I kiss or date." I steady my breath, looking directly at him. "It's unfair to ask me to limit my relationships because of your past, especially when you're not willing to date me yourself."

Leo remains silent for a moment, his focus on the counter. I watch as he processes my words, his brows scrunched in thought.

He nods slowly, "I get it. It's not fair for me to ask that of you. Brian's a different person now, but the past still haunts me. I love him like a brother, and I've forgiven him, but seeing you with him brought back all those old fears. It's not right for me to impose my baggage on you. I just want you to understand where I'm coming from."

"I understand. But it feels like you always let me in a little too late." I pause, collecting my thoughts. "Had I known this before, maybe I could have made different choices. But now, I like Brian. I have fun with him, and *he* wants to date me… even if it is long distance."

I take a deep breath. "You still won't talk about your family life with me, Leo. There are *so* many things you keep locked away. I can't keep waiting and wondering." My fingers absently search for split ends in my hair, a nervous habit. "I think I need some space from you to figure things out… actual space. Not like what we talked about last week. I need to date without feeling like I'm betraying you or treading on your past."

Leo's brow furrows with concern. "Viv… don't. Don't shut me out, again."

I shift uncomfortably, my fingers nervously picking at the strands of my hair. "I have to, Leo. At least for a bit." I sigh. "This morning has been great. I was truly starting to believe that we could figure this thing out— how to be friends while keeping it platonic. But I think our friendship was doomed from the start." I pause, meeting his gaze with a mix of sadness and resolve. "We don't stand a chance at being in each other's lives if you keep contradicting yourself and avoiding your inner demons." I press my hands against the counter, seeking some physical support as I gather my thoughts. The cool surface steadies me, grounding my emotions. "You say one thing and do the complete opposite. It's utterly exhausting, and I can't keep riding this emotional roller coaster. It's just not fair to me." I swallow hard, feeling the weight of my words hang heavily in the air between us.

Leo remains silent, his jaw clenched.

"It's simple. You either want me or you don't. You know where I stand, so why don't you figure out what the hell it is that you want." I feel tears threatening, but I blink them back. "Until then, I think we should take some time away from each other."

Leo swallows, his face unreadable. "Is there anything I can do to change your mind?"

I momentarily question my decision. Am I moving too fast? Reacting instead of finding a better resolution? No. If I want to defuse the situation, I need this space between us. "There's nothing you can do to change my mind."

Leo runs a hand through his hair, a familiar gesture when he's anxious or uncertain. "Okay. I understand," he begins quietly, his tone sincere. "I never want to cause you any unhappiness… Take all the time you need. I'll be here." He pauses, meeting my eyes with a hint of sadness. "Just… promise me we won't lose what we have in the process."

"I don't think I can promise anything, Leo." I'm afraid to say more for fear of losing control, and I've got to remain strong. "It's probably best if I go."

I start toward the door, Leo rising to follow. "You don't need to walk me out," I manage, my voice quivering. "Thank you for breakfast."

I close the door behind me, struggling to maintain composure. Once outside, I lose control completely. Sobbing uncontrollably, I make my way next door. The emptiness inside my house mirrors the void within me. Doubts flood my mind; did I just make a terrible mistake?

Chapter 24

LEO

February 14

Six Weeks Later

Valentine's Day. What a bloody stupid holiday. Do we really need a day to fake affection while reminding all the singles they're on their own? If you truly care about someone, be a good partner every damn day. Date them, kiss them, cuddle up—show love by speaking their love language daily. That's what I drill into my clients, albeit with more professional finesse. Today was a marathon of that, and it's always heavier on V-Day. People pile on expectations, only to end up disappointed by their partners. Maybe we should just scratch this day off the calendar altogether.

I've got a session with Mer in fifteen minutes. We've been at it for six weeks now, doing EMDR. This is our fourth session. Normally, I wouldn't mix therapy with friends, but I wouldn't trust this with anyone else. EMDR's a different beast; being friends matters less.

It's been tough, brutal even, confronting my past again—emotional turmoil that's painful to dredge up.

I want to do this for myself, for Andrew, for Chloe, but deep down, I know I'm doing this for Vivian. New Year's made me realize that I want her in my life, I need her… but I don't know how to step up. I'm unsure if that's truly what I want. Can I commit? Can I be a good partner? I don't even know if she'd accept me at this point—she won't see me.

"Leo," I hear Mer's voice echo down the hallway. I'm sitting in the break room. "I'm ready for you."

I walk down the familiar hallway to Meredith's office. It's strange to be on this side of therapy, the patient's chair instead of the therapist's.

"Have you spoken to Vivian yet?" Mer asks, her tone hopeful, fingers laced together in anticipation.

I shake my head as I enter the room. "No," I admit quietly. "She's still avoiding me. I texted her this morning, wishing her Happy Valentine's Day and letting her know I was thinking of her. She replied with a simple, 'Thanks, Leo'."

"That's it? That's all she gave you?" Meredith asks, sounding shocked.

I shrug. "It is what it is. She's been cordial. We text here and there. Occasionally, I see her coming in or out. I just miss her."

"I'm sorry," she says, wrapping her arms around me, and I reciprocate.

"It's alright." I reply, my tone somber.

"Okay," Meredith gestures toward her couch. "Are you ready to get started?"

"I guess as ready as I'll ever be," I mutter, sinking into the sofa and trying to find some comfort.

"Today, let's continue our work on processing your feelings about your mom, okay?" Meredith suggests gently.

I nod, familiar with the routine.

"I want you to think about a specific memory or image related to her that brings up strong emotions for you. Can you bring that to mind?" Meredith adopts her therapy voice, distinct from her usual tone. Our first session didn't go well because I kept laughing, never having heard it before.

I take a deep breath. "Okay, I'm thinking about the day the police came to our house. I was ten years old, and they were talking to my dad at the door." I pause, trying to relive it. "I had been hiding around the corner, listening to them."

"Good. Now, as you hold on to that memory, notice any physical sensations or emotions that come up for you. Rate the intensity of those feelings on a scale from zero to ten," Meredith says in a soothing tone.

With my eyes closed, I feel tension building. "It feels like a weight on my chest… maybe a seven out of ten."

"Now, as you recall that memory and those feelings, I want you to follow the flashing-light movements with your eyes. Keep track of any thoughts, feelings, or images that come up."

I nod once more, opening my eyes.

"Let's begin," she says professionally.

Meredith activates the light bar for bilateral stimulation, and I follow the flashing movements with my eyes—left, right, left, right.

"What are you noticing?" Meredith asks gently.

I take a few moments, choking down the emotion that bubbles in my throat before responding. "I'm feeling a lot of anger… resentment, hurt, confusion, and sadness. I never understood why she left… I blamed myself for so long. I don't understand why she even had all of us."

"Stay with that, Leo. Notice where you feel it in your body. Let it come up and then let it go. You're safe here." I hear emotion in Meredith's voice, a rare occurrence.

"I feel abandoned, alone. She left us because of me. She hated me, Mer. It's my fault that my siblings didn't have a mum." I choke out the words, tears streaming down my cheeks. I look away, pinching the bridge of my nose, squeezing my eyes shut.

"God, Mer. I fucking hate this."

"It's okay. It's just me. You don't have to be a hero with me."

"I have so much bloody hatred for her, but somehow I still miss the idea of her. I miss that I didn't have a mum, even though she was shit. It's so goddamn confusing."

"Okay. That's okay. Let those feelings come. You're processing it now, letting go of the pain that's held on to you. Keep following the movement."

I continue to track the movement of the light bar, waves of emotion crashing over me.

"Are you noticing anything else? Anything new?" Mer asks calmly.

"I have a knot forming in my stomach. I feel nauseous. I just… don't feel worthy of love, not from her, not from anyone. I was only ten and felt like a disappointment, like I failed my family. I couldn't keep Chloe alive… She needed her mum, and she wasn't there for her." I shake my head, overwhelmed with shame. "I didn't know how to help. I had to be everyone's everything. Andrew and Chloe's mum and dad."

"Okay, this is good. Let it out."

"Even my dad was shit. Sometimes he was good, when he was there, but he didn't even take time off when Chloe was on her deathbed. He just went to work. No wonder my mum hated him." The realization surprises me. I shake my head in disbelief. "I had no idea I blamed my father for so many things."

After thirty minutes of emotional torment and being vulnerable with Meredith, she turns off the light and takes a seat next to me.

"Hey," she says, nudging me softly with her elbow and meeting my gaze. "That was really fucking awesome of you. Great job." She wraps an arm around me. "Are you okay?"

I pull her into me. "Yeah, I'm okay. It was cathartic, but my pride is wounded." I playfully nudge her. "Don't ever tell anyone about this."

She scowls. "You know I would never! I'm offended you feel you have to remind me."

"I know. I know you wouldn't. You're a great friend, Meredith," I say, forcing a smile.

"I think you had some great self-discoveries today. How do you feel?"

I meet her gaze. "I feel… lighter."

She smiles. "Good. That's great. If only you'd done this ten years ago." She takes my hand and squeezes it, and I squeeze it back.

She starts to stand, but I stop her. "Mer, what do I do about Vivian?"

A sad smile spreads across her face, and she shakes her head. "I don't know," she whispers.

"I'm supposed to be taking her to Paris in two months, and I keep holding out on cancelling. I don't want to. I'm so mad at myself. I just want to be what she needs, and I wish being her friend could be enough for us both."

Meredith stares at me intently. "Why?" she says. "Why would you want that? To only be friends when the two of you could have so much more? God, you two could be so fucking great together."

I'm taken aback by Meredith challenging me, and she presses on.

"Sometimes, you have to take risks, Leo. I don't know what to tell you about Vivian, but be patient, keep doing the work for yourself." Smiling, Meredith pats my knee and gets up. "I'm kicking you out of my office now, so I can lock up and get home to my wife. You know, my person that I risked everything for."

"I get it." I chuckle softly. "I get it."

Chapter 25

VIVIAN

March 20

Five Weeks Later

"I'll walk you out," I offer, handing Nick his coffee in a to-go cup. His hair is a wild mess of bed-head, and he blinks groggily, trying to wake up fully, clearly not a morning person. It's endearing enough to make me laugh.

"Don't laugh at me," he teases, giving me a playful nudge as he heads towards the door, with me trailing behind.

"I'm not laughing at you," I protest, trying to stifle my laughter, "I'm laughing with you."

He scoffs, "I think you're the only one laughing, babe."

He opens the door and steps outside into the spring morning. It's sunny with blue skies, a welcome change from the recent gloomy weather. I follow him, craving the warmth of the sun on my face.

"God, it feels great out here!" I exclaim, closing my eyes and letting the sun's rays wash over me, feeling the heat on my skin.

"I'll call you tomorrow," Nick says, then turns to me with a mischievous grin. "Come here." He pulls me into his arms and kisses me, and I can't help but smile. I love kissing Nick, and wrap my arms around his neck, savoring the moment.

He finally pulls away, and I playfully pout, "Noooo, don't go."

He chuckles at my expression and leans back in, pressing his lips to mine.

We finally pull away, both of us breathless and smiling stupidly.

"I've got to go, my Uber is here," Nick gives me one last quick kiss and heads down the steps. My heart skips a beat as I notice Leo coming back from a run, his gaze fixed on us.

I force a smile, nodding my head and giving a little wave. This is awkward.

God, he looks good.

He pulls the bottom of his shirt up to wipe the sweat from his face, revealing all of his sexy, well-defined abdominal muscles that I once touched.

Oh, shit. He's coming over here.

"Hey, Viv," he says nonchalantly, wiping sweat from his brow with the back of his hand.

"Hey," I reply awkwardly, at a loss for words. I'm flustered by the sight of his abs and the exertion evident in his breath. I've never worried about my appearance in front of Leo before, but suddenly, I'm very aware that I'm fresh out of bed, having slept in late.

"Was that Nick?" Leo asks, though his tone suggests he already knows.

"Yeah, it was," I say casually, running my fingers through my tangled hair and taming flyaways.

"Looks like things are going well; you look happy," Leo remarks, smiling genuinely at me. I can't help but wonder what his angle is.

"Yeah, things are going really well."

I joined a widows' support group in January, and it's been incredibly helpful. I had something similar in Utah, and I realized I was missing that connection here with people who really get it. In the group, we joke about being part of the 'wid-hoe-ers club', where some of us dive into dating and sex after losing a partner.

"Well, since I've got you pinned for a minute, I've been meaning to text you... talk to you, if you'll let me," Leo says, looking slightly nervous.

I gesture for him to continue.

"Paris," he continues, stumbling over his words, "do you still want to go? I can cancel my flight if you want to go alone… or if you'd, um… rather take someone else. You're welcome to use all the things I booked. I can't get a refund anyway. I really want you to have the best time."

He's nervous. Leo Weston is nervous right now, and I can't help but laugh to myself.

"Who are you and what have you done with my friend?" I ask playfully.

Leo's famous grin, complete with deep-set dimples, spreads across his face. "Are we friends?" he asks, a hint of nostalgia in his voice, echoing our first night together.

"Are we not?" I ask, feeling a rush of emotion that surprises me. *My God, I've missed him.* "Are you one of those men who believe that men and women can't be friends because secretly one of them will want to be more than friends?"

Leo chuckles softly, shaking his head. "Turns out, that's more nuanced than I originally believed."

"And do you still want to have a go with me?" I tease lightly.

He laughs. "I respectfully decline answering that."

I fold my arms, a smile playing on my lips as I lock eyes with him. "Sure," I say confidently, "we'll go to Paris. What the hell, right?"

"We, as in you and me?" He raises an eyebrow skeptically.

I shrug nonchalantly. "Unless you're having second thoughts?"

"Oh, I always want to go to Paris." He takes a deliberate step up to be closer, bringing us eye to eye. "And I definitely want to go with you if you're sure. It's been ten weeks since we've talked, besides a few texts." His gaze pierces mine, and a sudden wave of nerves hits me. Did I just make a mistake agreeing to this? I feel my heart racing in my chest.

I shrug it off as nothing. "Yes, I'm sure. I'm in a good place right now. I'd love for you to come with me… as a friend."

Leo's lip curves up on one side, a half smile playing at the corners of his mouth. His eyes fixed on me, "As a friend," he agrees.

"Okay," I say softly.

"Okay," he mirrors. "Breakfast Sunday?"

I nod, a smirk sneaking onto my face. Well, damn him. He just snuck his way back into my life and I didn't even see it coming. We'll see how this goes, but right now, this feels good. Maybe, just maybe, things will be different this time.

Chapter 26

LEO

April 17

One Month Later

Being patient with Vivian has finally started to pay off. Over the past month, we've slowly rekindled our friendship. I've made a conscious effort not to be possessive of her time. We've only seen each other a few times during this period, and I've been careful to ensure our interactions remain entirely platonic and respectful of her relationship with Nick.

I haven't shared any details of our plans for Paris with her. I offered to tell her, but she chose to be surprised and said she's just along for the ride. All I provided was a packing list.

After a brief layover in New York, we're now boarding the Air France flight to Paris. Vivian pauses in front of our seats, 1A and 1B, and turns around to face me.

"This can't be right. It says these are our seats." Her face shows a mix of confusion and awe.

We flew first class from Chicago to New York, and Vivian has flown first class in the States before, but I decided to go all out and splurge on two of Air France's La Première cabins. These aren't your typical first-class seats. Each suite is a private cocoon of luxury with a fully flat bed, plush bedding, and privacy curtains. The cabin crew treats you like royalty, and the gourmet dining experience is like eating at a top-notch restaurant, complete with fine wines and impeccable service.

"These are our seats." I gesture toward them with a smile. "Take your pick, love. It's an early birthday present."

Her eyes widen with excitement. "Shut up! Are you joking? Is this for real?"

"No, I'm not joking. Now hurry and sit—we're holding up the line," I say, chuckling as she practically bounces into her seat.

I settle into the seat next to her, a seat divider separating us. She grabs my arm, her face alight with joy. "I've always wanted to sit in one of these seats. This must have cost a fortune. Really, it's too much… thank you." Her smile seems permanently fixed on her face.

It *did* cost a fortune—close to twenty grand for the two of us—but seeing that smile was worth every penny.

Our flight attendant comes by, and we order drinks because why not?

An hour into the flight, Vivian pulls a stack of books from her backpack. I watch as she rummages through sudoku, crossword puzzles, magazines, a novel, and a sketchbook.

She'll choose the magazine; she likes to wind down at night with mindless activities.

She pulls the magazine from the pile, returning the others to her backpack.

I grin. "You're so predictable," I say, laughing softly.

She furrows her brows. "Why do you say that?"

"I predicted you'd pick the magazine. It was an easy guess. If it were morning, you'd have chosen the sketchbook because that's when you're the most creative. The others would be for the afternoon, when you're most focused." I smirk. "I know you like the back of my hand."

She smacks her lips shut, trying to hide a smile.

"Do you think you're not predictable?" she scoffs. "I bet I know you better than you know me."

"How much?" I ask, intrigued by where this is going.

She shakes her head. "Not money. Clearly, you have plenty of that if you can justify buying these seats. It has to be something else."

"Okay… what then?"

She mulls it over for a moment.

"I've got it," she says, "whoever wins gets to, at any time, call in a favor for something they want."

"Okay, give me an example of what you mean so we're on the same page."

She grins wickedly. "Let's say it's three in the morning, and I really want a pastry. I can wake you up and say I'm calling in my favor, and then you"—she pokes my shoulder—"have to go and get it for me." Her smile widens, clearly pleased with her idea.

"Okay," I say, nodding in agreement. "So if it's eight in the morning, and I want to, say… take shots with you"—I glance her way as she grimaces—"of Jägermeister, you'd have to take a shot with me?" Her face reflects full disgust, and I laugh.

"You wouldn't," she says pointedly. "You know I hate that stuff with a passion."

"Oh, I would," I reply with a charming smile.

"Game on," she says, narrowing her eyes.

"So how do we determine who knows the other better?" I ask.

She purses her lips, deep in thought. "How about this?" She pulls out a notebook and a couple of pens. "Each of us takes turns asking the other a question about ourselves. We write down our answers on paper. After answering, we reveal our answers to each other. This way, there's no cheating or changing of minds. We'll each ask ten questions."

"You think I'd cheat?"

"I wouldn't put it past you. I know how much you like to win."

"As I plan to do, right now. You go first," I say smirking.

She googles *"questions to see how well you know someone"* and clicks on one of the search results, which brings up a list of questions. "We'll use this. We'll go down the list in order: I take number one, you take number two. No matter how easy the question is, we'll just take turns."

I nod in agreement.

"Okay, first question: What's my all-time favorite movie?" she asks, cursing under her breath because she knows it's an easy one. She writes her answer and looks at me expectantly.

"*Crazy, Stupid, Love*," I reply. "Way too easy."

"My turn," she says, handing me the phone.

"Next question: What's my middle name?" I ask.

She smiles smugly. "James," she says. "Easy peasy."

"These are too easy." I take her phone and scroll down the list. "You're on the easy questions. Look," I say, showing her the phone, "this list has harder questions. Let's use one of these instead."

She takes the phone back and looks at the new list. "Okay, first question here is... What's a show I can watch over and over again and never get tired of?" She sighs, "These are still too easy."

She writes her answer down, and I quickly respond, "Schitt's Creek."

She shows me her answer, and sure enough, I'm right. I glance at the list and ask, "Who's my favorite artist or band?" I write my answer down, curious to see if she knows this one.

"Post Malone," she says without skipping a beat. She's right, still too easy.

"Oh, this one's good. What's a job that I would hate?" she asks, knowing it could be literally anything. She writes her answer down.

I think about it—there are many jobs I know she would hate, but then I remember her freaking out while watching Saving Private Ryan. All the blood had her nauseous, and she couldn't continue watching.

I take a guess, "Something in the medical field. A nurse or a doctor?"

She frowns and flips her paper over. It reads '*a nurse.*'

I laugh loudly. "You are so fucked, Walker!" I playfully nudge her as she gapes at me.

"Have I ever broken a bone?" I ask, trying to recall if we've discussed this, as I write my answer.

"Yes, you've broken your arm and your collarbone," she says with a pleased smile.

I turn my answer over, and she's correct, again.

"Let me see this list. There have to be harder questions on here. Okay, new rule: we get to choose the questions. Someone has to start losing."

"Fine," she agrees, taking the phone back to find a question. She examines it, taking her sweet time.

"Today, Walker," I say jokingly.

She glares at me. "Calm down, I've got it. What would my parents say is my worst personality trait?"

I don't even let her finish writing before I say, "Too nice. You're way too bloody nice. A people pleaser."

She scrunches her nose in disgust and turns it over to reveal *people pleaser*.

I take the phone, determined to stump her now that I can select my own question.

"If I were a superhero, what superpower would I have?" I ask, writing down my answer.

"Teleportation?" she guesses, arching an eyebrow.

"Dammit." I turn my paper over. "How did you know that?"

"I didn't. It's just what I'd pick. It's obviously the best superpower," she says, laughing. She looks at the list and smirks. "What's the last thing I posted on Instagram?" She knows she's got me.

"Shit. Come on. You know I don't have Instagram."

"That's unfortunate for you," she says, unapologetically. "You fucking weirdo. Literally, the *only* person in the world without Instagram," she playfully shoves me, teasing.

I take a wild guess. "A picture of you and your family at Christmas?"

"Nope," she says, smiling.

"Prove it," I challenge.

She pulls up her Instagram account and shows me her page. Her last post was from a few weeks ago, featuring a group of friends at dinner.

"Are these your friends from your support group?" I ask, pointing to the picture.

"Yeah," she replies, starting to name each one as I look over her page. Her next post is from Christmas time, showing her with her family. Then there's one with several people I don't recognize. "Who are these people?" I ask.

"That's Ben's family," she says, and proceeds to tell me who they all are.

The next post is one of us—the night things got out of hand. I take the phone from her and scroll through multiple photos. There's a picture of us at the Christmas market, our glasses of wine together, and us at Craft's. I look further down her page, noticing there are so many pictures of us together. A pang of sadness hits me in the chest.

I look at her with remorse. "I'm sorry I fucked things up for a while." I swallow, "We can get back there, yeah?"

She smiles and takes the phone from me. "We're already on our way," she says, positioning the phone in front of us to take a picture. I smile, beyond happy to be here with her.

We continue to play until we've answered ten questions each, and she wins. She gloats, and we order drinks to celebrate her victory.

The plane is warm, and Vivian removes her jacket, revealing a very low-cut athletic tank top. Although I've been focused on rebuilding our friendship and enjoying our time together, the sight of her cleavage makes it challenging to ignore the attraction I've been trying to suppress. She opens her text messages and scrolls through a list of unread notifications. I notice names with a blue dot next to them: *Sarah, mom, Nick, Grant, Brian.*

Brian? Jesus.

She glances up and catches my reaction. "Relax. We're friends. You asked me to keep it friendly, and I have," she says with a calm smile.

"I didn't say anything," I reply coolly.

She gives me a tight-lipped look, noting the disapproval in my expression. "But I know what you're thinking. You don't have to say it out loud; your face shows it all. Didn't we just prove that I know you?" She relaxes, "We truly are just friends, I promise."

I nod. "You're allowed to be more… if that's what you want," I say, tapping my finger on the wall between us. The rhythm is more for my nerves than anything else.

She notices, her eyes flicking to my tapping finger, then back to me. She knows this isn't easy for me—letting go of control, choosing to be okay with what she decides, even if it twists me up inside. But I mean it. Her happiness matters more. She nods, and the gratitude in her eyes says it all.

We don't need more words; we understand each other.

* * * * * * * * * *

We make our way to the eighth floor of the Four Seasons, where our room is located. I hand Vivian the key. "You do the honors?"

She takes the key with a grin and opens the door. As she steps inside, her eyes widen. "Oh. My. God!" she exclaims as she walks over to the window. "Look at this view!"

I watch her take in the room with a sense of satisfaction. The suite is a stunning Premier King Room, remarkably spacious for Parisian stand-ards. The grand marble bathroom, the elegant coffee bar, and the king bed with its plush linens all exude luxury. A cozy sofa sits a few feet in front of the bed, facing a large television nestled among beautiful built-in cabi-nets. A chandelier hangs gracefully from the ceiling, and three floor-to-ceiling windows line one wall, flooding the room with natural light.

She walks around, exploring the suite, ooh-ing and aah-ing. She stops at the bed and frowns. "Hey," she looks at me, "you said there would be two beds."

I grimace. "Well, it looks like I was mistaken. It's fine, Viv. It's a big bed. I'm not going to bite or roofie you. Besides, I know you're with Nick. I'd never be disrespectful of that."

"Well actually," she hesitates, "never mind," she says, shaking her head. "So… what are we doing first?"

"God, I forget how energetic you are. Can't we take a quick nap? I'm exhausted."

"What? We are not napping! We're in Paris. You can nap at home or when you're dead. You know what I want?"

Vivian bounces onto the bed, flopping down on her stomach with a dramatic sigh, her feet kicking playfully in the air.

"I don't know, a Xanax?" I offer, grinning at her.

She rolls her eyes and props herself up on her elbows. "Okay, Grandpa, chill out. I want a coffee and a pastry from a café in Paris."

"A coffee and a pastry? God, you're so wired, if I didn't know you better, I'd think you'd done a line of coke on the plane." I raise an eyebrow, teasing.

"I'm not wired, I'm excited. There's a difference," she says, sitting up on the bed and crossing her arms.

"Okay, it's your trip; let's go get you what you want. Does this count as your favor?"

"Hell no! This is just you being nice because you're a good person," she says, poking me as we head out the door. "When do I get to see the Eiffel Tower?"

"Whenever you want. Today is wide open. I figured we'd just explore and chill a bit after the long flight."

"Really?" She gasps, her eyes wide with excitement.

I let out a laugh. "Yeah, really."

"Sounds great to me," she says, her smile lighting up the room. "Leo?"

"Yeah?"

"Thank you," she says, turning toward me as we wait for the elevator. "Thank you so much for this trip. And if I forget to tell you later, it was unforgettable."

We stare into each other's eyes until the elevator dings.

This trip might be harder than I expected, being here with her... as just a friend.

* * * * *   * * * * *

Three Days Later

The trip so far has been incredible, and Vivian is loving every minute of it. We've fallen back into our old routine as friends, keeping everything strictly platonic. Our sleeping arrangement has been fine, except Vivian seems to think sexy pajamas are perfectly appropriate. She comes to bed in matching sets, usually short shorts and a low-cut top. It doesn't matter whether they're tight, loose, soft, or silky—I'm turned on either way. I'm left falling asleep with my back turned, dick hard, and my mind scrambling to think of the most boring shit possible—taxes, traffic jams, real estate documents—anything to deflate my damn hard-on.

We've been to the Louvre, the Eiffel Tower, Notre Dame, and the Arc de Triomphe. We've shopped on the Champs-Élysées, gone on a bike tour, and dined at three different Michelin Star restaurants. Tomorrow, we have Versailles in the morning and tickets to the Moulin Rouge for the evening. It's been a packed trip and a lot of fun.

I'm waiting for her to come out of the bathroom. I have a surprise evening planned. We're going to an exclusive art exhibit I found online. The tickets were expensive and require black cocktail or formal attire. After that, I've arranged a private yacht cruise along the Seine, with a five-star chef for dinner tonight.

I wait patiently in my black suit, white shirt, and black tie. When I hear the lock click on the bathroom door, I turn to see her step out.

I'm momentarily speechless. Her New Year's Eve look had been jaw-dropping, but this—this is on another level.

God, I want to tear that dress off her. Just the thought of her lips on mine, her body pressed tight against me, her panties sliding down around her ankles—it's going to drive me crazy. I want to taste her, run my hands and mouth over every curve, claim every inch of her.

Jesus, get a grip, man.

She's with Nick.

I had my shot, and I blew it. I take a slow, calming breath. "Christ, Vivian," I whisper, "You look incredible. That dress…" I trail off, taking in every detail from top to bottom. "Fuck."

Am I seriously supposed to keep my hands to myself when she looks like that?

Her dress is strapless and black. The bottom's flowy and long, grazing the floor, while the top—I swear to God—looks like lingerie. It's tight and pushes her tits up, making it impossible to look away. The whole thing is sheer, her skin teasing through the lace patterns—solid fabric only covering her nipples. A high slit runs up her thigh, giving me a perfect view of those legs. It'd be so easy to push the fabric aside and tease her until she's begging for it—begging for me.

She smirks as she fastens her earrings and walks toward me. Placing a hand on my chest, she looks up at me with a calm, collected gaze. "Thank you. You look very handsome," she says, her voice steady and sincere.

I'm starting to understand the resentment she felt toward me months ago. She chased me for months, only for me to pull away. It feels like we've reversed roles. I've always wanted her, but now, now I truly want her, and she is unavailable. It kills me. I extend my arm for her to take, and she links it with hers, flashing a smile that makes me weak in the knees.

"You ready, Tiger?" she asks playfully, bumping her shoulder into mine.

"I'm ready," I say steadily, my voice low.

* * * * *  * * * * *

The exhibit was incredible, and Vivian turned heads everywhere she went. The art was unique and intriguing, and as an artist herself, Vivian truly appreciated it more than I did.

Having her on my arm, even as a friend, has been a blast. We've spent the evening laughing together; I love that she finds my jokes funny and that I can't help but laugh with her.

We just finished our dinner on our private yacht, which was beyond delicious. We have the elaborate dining room all to ourselves. I'd arranged for a playlist of some of Vivian's favorite music to play in the background, featuring some of her favorite British artists. The room is filled with flower arrangements and lit candles, creating a romantic atmosphere. It's a perfect setup, and I have to give myself props. If she were my girlfriend, I'd for sure be getting lucky tonight.

It's almost eight, and the Eiffel Tower should be lighting up soon.

"Do you want to go outside?" I ask.

"Yes, that sounds great."

I fill our wine glasses and we step outside. She grabs my elbow and links her arm with mine as we walk to the middle of the deck, standing by the railing. It's chilly, so I slip off my suit jacket and drape it around her, brushing her shoulders gently to warm her.

"Always the gentleman," she says sincerely, smiling. "It's beautiful out here."

We stand in silence watching the river, the city glowing behind it. Bands play along the steps by the river, and people dance. The river is calm and steady.

I glance at my watch. "Look over there," I say, pointing toward the Eiffel Tower.

Ten-seconds later, it lights up, sparkling as its reflection shimmers on the river.

"Wow," she whispers, placing her hand on her chest and toying with her necklace. "That's incredible," she adds, a soft laugh escaping her lips. She slips her hand into mine and gives it a squeeze. I squeeze it back, a small smile tugging at my lips. The quiet stretches on for several minutes, a comfortable silence, just like old times.

She takes a sip of her wine, and finally breaks the silence. "Do you think Ben knows I'm here?" she whispers, her voice tinged with a longing for reassurance.

"Sure he does," I reply. "Yeah, Viv, he knows."

She takes a deep, shaky breath. "I always imagined him being here with me the first time I saw the Eiffel Tower," she says, looking up at me. "I know we already saw it the other day, but seeing it like this, it's like experiencing it for the first time again."

I listen quietly, sipping my wine, sensing she needs this moment to work through her thoughts.

"I pictured us standing in awe, looking up at it, holding hands, taking it all in. This picturesque, magical moment, and then he would pull me in and kiss me, and we'd make out right there, not caring if people stopped to watch," she laughs, shaking her head. "Stupid dreams... I'm sorry," she says, glancing at me. "I didn't mean to talk about Ben right now." She turns her body close to mine. "I'm glad you're here, Leo." She places her hand on the side of my arm and gives it a slight rub.

There's a yearning in her eyes, whether for Ben, her dreams, or maybe for me—I can't tell, and at the moment, I don't care. I pull her close by the waist and press my lips to hers. I kiss her slowly, deliberately, and then pull away, locking eyes with her.

She gasps, "What was that for?" Her voice is soft.

"I just wanted you to have your perfect moment," I say, searching her eyes for any sign of upset. "I know I'm not Ben, and I know you're with Nick. I just wanted you to have your kiss in front of the Eiffel Tower, I didn't mean anything by it."

Vivian's eyes narrow, and her lips press into a thin line. She shakes her head, almost scowling, as if she's disappointed. "Don't say that," she says, her voice trembling slightly. "Don't say it doesn't mean anything."

I furrow my brows. "What do you mean?"

"I'm not with Nick, Leo," she takes our wine glasses and sets them on the ground, along with my jacket. "We aren't exclusive… and we haven't slept together, so please, don't downplay this moment when I want it to mean something so badly." She wraps her hands around my neck and pulls me to her, crushing her lips to mine. We kiss deeply, our tongues taunting one another.

She pulls back, staring into my eyes, waiting for my reaction. The gentle sway of the yacht on the Seine is nothing compared to the storm inside me. Vivian holds me close, her breath warm against the cool air as she whispers against my lips, "It's you, Leo. It's *been* you."

Her words send a shockwave through me, erasing any lingering doubts. I've been soaking in every detail of her appearance all night; I can't resist her anymore, and I don't want to. I kiss her again, hard—pouring all my emotions into this moment. She responds with equal fervor, her fingers tangling in my hair.

Pulling away again, her eyes search mine. "Hey," she says, taking a deep breath, "can I call in my favor?"

I look at her, confused.

"Will you please not stop this time?" she asks delicately, a smile slowly forming on her lips as her eyes lock onto mine. "It can be just this one time… just sex," she continues, her voice trembling slightly. "I won't expect anything more from you. Please… I trust you. Help me move forward."

Holy shit. This is it. Vivian's in a good place; she trusts me… wants me—and I've *never* wanted anything more. I feel the last of my resolve crumble.

"Vivian," I murmur, my voice a mix of desire and hesitation. "You really sure about this?" I pull her closer, eliminating the space between us. The warmth radiating from her body seeps into me, making my heart pound faster and harder.

She nods, her eyes unwavering. "Yes, I'm sure."

I reach out, my fingers gently brushing a stray piece of hair from her face, tucking it behind her ear. "I've wanted to do this for so long," I confess. My gaze drops to her lips for a fleeting moment before returning to her eyes.

"Then do it," she whispers. "Fuck me, Leo." Her voice is barely audible, but the challenge in her words is clear. Hearing her say those words ignites a raw need in me to please her.

I brush my lips over hers, savoring the moment. She whimpers as she parts her lips, a plea to give in to her desires.

My lips meet hers, slow at first, deep and sensuous, a tentative exploration. But the heat between us quickly builds, her hands finding their way to my chest.

We move in a heated frenzy, hands exploring, bodies pressing closer. I back her against the railing, kissing her neck, trailing down to the tantalizing neckline of her dress.

"You're so fucking sexy," I say huskily. She responds with a moan against my jawline as she trails kisses up to my ear. She nibbles and flicks her tongue, teasing the shit out of me. My cock is hard as a rock, and I grind it into her against the railing.

She gasps as I roam a hand over one of her tits, brushing my thumb over the smooth skin that spills above her dress.

"Let's go inside," I murmur against her skin, feeling her shiver.

"Okay," she gasps between kisses.

I grab her hand and lead her down the stairs. We stumble into the dining room, and I pause to look at her. The dress she wears is designed to drive any man wild, but on her, it's a weapon of mass seduction.

Our lips connect again, my hands wandering, exploring this body I've admired for so long. She arches into my touch, and I feel her hands working the buttons of my shirt. I loosen my tie, and finger the back of her dress, trying to figure out how to undo it, but it's a damn puzzle. "Fuck! How do I get this thing off?" I growl in frustration, making her laugh. I spin her around, pulling her close to me, my arm wrapping around her stomach as I kiss her neck.

I slide my hand up to her tits again, caressing her, moving my hand inside her corset top to stroke her nipple. She arches her back and lets her head fall onto my chest. My other hand travels down, sliding slowly through the layers of fabric until I find her skin. I stroke the inside of her thigh, and she moans softly.

Moving my hands to her back, I kiss every part of her neck and shoulders while fumbling with the tiny hooks on her dress, undoing them as quickly as I can. Hell, at this point, I'm ready to rip the damn thing off her. When the last hook snaps open, I grip the corset and pull it apart, letting the dress fall to the ground, leaving her in nothing but a black lace thong.

She turns to face me, and I take a moment to worship her with my eyes, letting them roam over every inch of her gorgeous body. I exhale. "God, you're fucking perfect," I say, the words slipping out like a reverent prayer.

Her eyes grow intense as she slides her hands up my abdomen, her touch sparking a fire in my veins. "Is that so?" she says, her voice soft and sensual. She pushes my shirt off, biting her bottom lip as her fingers drag down my torso, tracing each ridge of my abs. Her eyes follow the path of her touch as she takes her time mapping out my body. Her thumb dips into my waistband, and my breath becomes shallow, my heart pounding. She meets my gaze and smirks. "You're not so bad yourself."

I chuckle, the sound low and rough as I press her against the wall, my hands grasping her hips. "Not so bad, huh?" I lean in so my lips brush against her ear. "I want to make you feel things no one ever has—drive you crazy, fuck you until you're senseless with pleasure. You'll be begging for more."

She lets out a breathy laugh. "You talk a big game." She grips my cock over my pants. "I hope you can deliver."

I grip her ass, lifting her into the air as her legs wrap around me. "Is that a challenge?" I growl before claiming her mouth with mine.

"Yes," she whispers against my lips.

I groan and set her down, grabbing her hands and pulling them up above her head, our fingers intertwining. We stare wildly into each other's eyes, breathing hard. Grinning, I let out a soft laugh. "Fuck, Walker," I say, kissing her forehead as her gorgeous smile spreads across her lips.

Keeping her hands locked with one of mine, I slowly trail a finger down her arm to her collarbone, and let it continue down to her tits, where I circle her nipple with my thumb, relishing her quiet moans as she arches toward me. I splay my hand over her boob, gently caressing it before sliding it down to her navel. She watches me with an intensity that makes my heart race. My fingers stop at the top of her panty line, toying with the fabric. Her breath catches, held in anticipation. My hand brushes over the lace as I gently tease her, making soft strokes with my fingers over the thin wet fabric, eliciting a gasp from her.

She arches into me, begging me with her body. "Leo," she pleads, "more... God, stop torturing me."

"Are you sure?" I ask, my hand hovering above her pussy, waiting for final consent.

She nods, her eyes full of lust. "Yes. I'm sure. I want this... I want you."

I don't need any more encouragement. My fingers dip into her panties and slide between her folds. She's so wet and warm, it's intoxicating.

She gasps. "Kiss me."

Grinning wickedly, I whisper in her ear, "You're soaking wet, love." I plunge a long finger deep inside her and watch her lose control.

"Oh my God," she moans as her hips move into me and her head falls back. God, I love how she responds to me. The way her body trembles, the sounds she makes—it provokes me all the more.

I release her hands. Her mouth crushing into mine as her hands swiftly move to my pants, frantically working to get them off as quickly as she can. She yanks them down, and I step out of them in a hurry.

I pick her up and move to the sofa, gently laying her down, hovering over her. The soft fabric of the cushions presses against my knees as I lean in. Our mouths meet again and again, desperate and unyielding, her breath warm against my lips. The faint scent of her perfume mingles with the fresh night air coming through the open window, creating a heady mix that makes my pulse race even faster.

I trail frantic kisses along her jaw, neck, and collarbone, working my way down to her tits. Taking a nipple into my mouth, I flick it with my tongue. She moans loudly, her fingers weaving in my hair and gently tugging.

I hook my fingers under her panty line and tug. She lifts her hips, allowing me to slide them down her legs, then moves to pull off my boxer-briefs, sliding them over my ass until I spring free.

I settle between her legs, holding myself up on either side of her head. My blood burns with desire, a delicious fire I welcome. I pause, taking a moment to appreciate the woman beneath me before I devour her completely. "God, you're beautiful," I say hoarsely.

She grips the back of my neck, her eyes glistening. "So are you," she whispers. Her fingers glide down my chest, unhurried and teasing, until she grips my length in one smooth, deliberate stroke. A groan rumbles out of me, a mix of pleasure and shock at what her touch does to me. She continues to stroke me, the rapture rising like a wave in a hurricane.

No one—absolutely no one—has ever had the effect that Vivian Walker has on me.

Chapter 27

VIVIAN

I have died and gone to heaven. Leo hovers over me, his muscles taut. *Good God, he looks good naked.* Every inch of him is strong and defined. I can feel the tension in him, every muscle hard as he keeps himself just high enough to avoid crushing me.

He lowers himself, his gaze fixed on my mouth. Slowly, he brings his lips to mine. His tongue teases mine, each flick met with my own. His mouth is heaven, his body that of a god, and I feel like a queen as he worships every inch of me with his hands and mouth—touching, tasting, winding me up like strings in a quartet, ready for the performance of a lifetime.

A James Arthur song plays softly in the background, and this feels too good to be true. The perfect song, a yacht on the Seine in Paris, and Leo—it's like a movie, and we're the leads.

His fingers glide over my slickness, plunging in as his thumb circles my clit. The pleasure building fast and deep, my inner muscles clenching with each pump. "Right there… oh, yes," I gasp, barely able to catch my breath as I feel the orgasm start to rise within me. Waves of ecstasy flood my body, filling me with heat as I lose all control. My back arches hard, forcing my head back, a cry tearing from my throat as I shatter around him. My whole body writhes, toes curling tight, every nerve burning with ecstasy as I come undone.

"God, Leo… don't stop," I beg, my breaths short and shallow as I gasp through the euphoric sensations searing through my body. I shudder, my eyes practically rolling back, lost in the intensity as I climax.

His eyes are wild and gleam with satisfaction at how easily his touch made me come.

Cupping his balls in one hand, I gently knead them. He groans deep and low against my neck, continuing to kiss me. His dick is perfect—just the right length and girth. I continue to tease him with strokes and tickles, and as he loses more and more control, it deepens the pleasure surging through my veins.

He stands to get a condom from his pants pocket, rolling it on with practiced ease. He positions himself between my legs, and I arch into him, desperate for every inch of his perfect cock to fill me. "I want you inside me," I pant.

Despite the overwhelming excitement, a flicker of nervousness courses through me. This is the first time since Ben, and while nothing makes me want to stop, the reality of it hits me.

Sensing my hesitation, his lips brush against mine in a slow, lingering kiss that melts away my nerves.

I gently tug on his bottom lip with my teeth, and he loses control, possessively claiming my mouth. He pulls back slightly, his breath ragged, his eyes dark with a hunger that cuts the air from my lungs. "God, you drive me crazy," he says, his voice low and rough with need. He positions himself at my entrance, spreading my legs with his knees, pinning one against the sofa. I hold my breath, bracing myself as he dips his tip inside, just enough for me to feel him. He pulls out, rubbing his cock against my clit before pushing in again—teasing me—hovering on the edge of fully giving in, only to draw back, making my body ache for more.

He's torturing me, and it's maddening, like I'm being held hostage by my own pleasure, trapped in a cycle of anticipation and aching need. I can't take it anymore. "God, stop teasing me," I gasp, desperation seeping into every word. "Just give it to me already," I beg, just as he predicted I would.

His eyes flare with a dark satisfaction, his control slipping just enough to finally push deeper. He continues with slow, deliberate strokes—in and out—drawing it out until I'm trembling beneath him. Grasping the back of his neck, I pull him closer, craving his mouth, and he gives it to me. The fire inside me builds as he plunges into me wildly.

My legs wrap around his back, and something primal takes over us both as he thrusts furiously. Realizing there was no need to be nervous, I surrender completely to the overwhelming sensation of how fucking good this feels. He continues to move within me, our bodies synchronized in a rhythm that makes everything else fade away. His thrusts deepen, his pace steady and relentless, drawing out every ounce of gratification. A bolt of lightning rushes through my limbs; I shudder in response, crying out as I peak. He comes with me, his body quivering over mine as he groans against my mouth, our breaths rapid and hot.

I feel him release, and his body goes limp as he pulls out. He drops his head beside mine, chuckling and pressing tender kisses along my temple. "God, Vivian," he whispers, pulling back to gaze into my eyes. "That was… fuck. You're incredible." He searches my eyes, ensuring I'm okay. I'm overwhelmed with emotion as I realize that I just had sex with a man who isn't Ben, and I enjoyed it… immensely.

Tears spring to my eyes, and I bring my hands to my face to hide.

"Hey," he murmurs, stroking my face gently. "Are you okay?" He searches my eyes, checking that I'm okay. "It's okay, Viv. It's okay to feel all the things right now." He rolls over and spoons me from behind, taking my hands in his, lowering them to my chest, and kissing my cheek.

I nod because words will fail me right now. I hate that I'm about to cry. I feel vulnerable but also safe, knowing it's Leo. I know he under-stands the conflicting emotions inside me.

He kisses my forehead and strokes the hair around my face.

"I want to hold you, but we probably need to get cleaned up and dressed. We'll be docking soon," he says.

I nod. "Okay, let's get cleaned up."

I'm suddenly very aware that I'm in a dining room on a yacht that is not ours, on a couch that God knows who's been on, and hopefully not doing what we just did on it. The reality of our surroundings hits me hard.

"What if someone sees us?" I say, knowing the bathroom is at the other end of this large room.

He lets out a low laugh. "Don't worry. When you throw enough money at people, they'll do whatever you want. No one is going to come in, just be quick."

"I think I've underestimated how much money you actually have," I say, laughing.

He smirks a half smile, one dimple protruding deeper than the other. "And I'd be willing to spend every penny on you." He gives me one last kiss on the mouth, then moves to stand, pulling me up with him.

After cleaning up, I get dressed and stand in front of the bathroom mirror. I smooth my wild hair and can't help but wonder what's next. I told Leo this could be a one-time thing, that I didn't expect anything more from him, and now I'm worried I spoke too soon, not understanding how strong my feelings would be.

It feels different, like he might have changed, but I can't get my hopes up.

Leo takes my hand in his as we exit the yacht. It's late, and I'm exhausted, but I could stay up forever doing what we just did.

Once we're inside our hotel room, I'm not sure what to do. We made out the entire ride back. Leo touched and teased in the back seat, sparking a hope within me, and now that there's a flame, I don't want it to burn out.

I decide to act normal, as if we're just friends again. I'll let him take the lead on this and follow suit. I change into my pajamas, stepping out of the bathroom to hang my dress as I'm brushing my teeth. With my mouth full of toothpaste, I catch Leo's eye in the oversized, elegant mirror. He stands behind me, shirtless.

I gawk at him, not knowing if I'll ever get used to looking at his incredible body. He wraps his tattooed arm around my waist from behind and kisses my neck. "Hmm, you don't think we're going to bed already, do you?" His voice is low and gruff. He trails kisses to my shoulder and back up my neck as he slides his hands into the front of my shorts.

And… I'm drenched.

I spit the toothpaste and rinse, just in time for him to pull my shorts down and pick me up. I wrap my arms around his neck, laughing. A mischievous grin rests on his face as he walks me to the bed and lowers me, removing my panties at the same time. Hovering over me, his lips find mine, and I moan into his mouth.

He leans into my ear. "What do you want?" *God* the way he just asks that—with his sexy fucking voice—is almost enough to get me off.

"Just… more of you," I say, flustered and unable to think straight.

He removes my shirt and kisses my neck, and décolletage. Moving down my body, he presses delicate kisses on my breasts, down my torso to my thighs. I gasp as his fingers slide against my sensitive entrance, and I automatically open my legs in response while he continues kissing down my thigh to the curve of my knee. He makes his way back up, driving me crazy, my body responding uncontrollably, a steady beat drumming between my thighs.

His hand moves to trace the floral tattoo that starts at my hip bone and winds down to the side of my upper thigh. "This is sexy," he murmurs, his fingers following the delicate lines of the ink. He lays one last gentle peck on my hip bone and looks up.

I let out a whimper. "Don't stop," I plead. He gives me a wicked grin, splays his hands against my thighs, opening them even more, and buries his face between them.

Oh. My. God!

I'm a complete wreck of moans, whimpers, gasps, and cries. I bury my hands into his hair, gently tugging as he works his magic with his mouth. My body convulses in response to the flicking of his tongue and the plunging of his fingers. The anticipation builds and builds until pleasure runs through my veins, jolting my body in complete euphoria again and again.

When we've finished, I lie useless like a rag doll on the bed. He plants kisses all the way back up, kissing me tenderly on the mouth.

I move to touch him, desperate to make him feel what I just did, but he softly grabs my hands and shakes his head.

"No, love. I just wanted to pleasure you."

Is this real life?

He lies on his back and pulls me into him. "Come here," he says as I rest my head on his chest and wrap a leg over him. He traces his fingers along my back, and something about the simplicity of his words, his loving gesture, and the processing of all that just took place unravels me. I lose complete control as a wave of raw emotion crashes over me. Knowing I just overcame a giant obstacle in my journey of moving forward, I let my guard completely down, and begin to cry. I curl up to Leo, the tears flowing uncontrollably.

Leo tightens his hold on me, murmuring soothing words. "It's okay. Let it all out. I'm here."

The physical intimacy had been terrifying, but now, having let Leo break through that wall, I feel an overwhelming sense of peace washing over me—a release I've never experienced. I tighten my grip on him, feeling both physically and emotionally naked.

Leo strokes my back gently. "You're so strong. It's okay to let go."

I cry so hard and for so long that I begin to hyperventilate. I had thought I'd been dealing with my grief, but now, in Leo's arms, I realize that I haven't completely let myself be fully exposed. There has always been some sort of mask or facade on display, trying to be okay, especially the first year after Ben and Evie died. I was so busy planning the funeral, figuring out life insurance, getting to work, and trying not to cry every moment, that I never processed what had happened—I never fully grieved. I was numb.

I bury my head in his chest, not wanting him to see my ugly cry. "I thought I was okay," I choke out. "God, I've been holding so much of this pain inside me."

He kisses the top of my head. "You don't have to hold anything in. You're safe with me."

My body convulses as I let out a wail. Snot drips from my nose, and I wipe it away, mortified by the rawness of my emotions and my vulnerability. "Oh my God," I cry out.

Leo only holds me tighter. "You don't have to be strong all the time. It's okay to feel everything… to release it all," he whispers softly.

I've never cried like this before—these are tears of grief mixed with happiness, and it's so fucking confusing. It's a happy turmoil, a release from holding everything together.

"I'm sorry," I sob, my words barely audible between gasps. "I don't want to ruin this."

Leo's grip tightens reassuringly. "You're not ruining anything. This is part of healing. You'll have these bouts of emotional release probably many more times, and they can come out of nowhere. You'll always be healing, learning, and shifting as you move forward, holding on to Ben and your daughter while making space for new things, and people in your life. I'm here for you, always… I promise."

Having Leo as a witness in this unraveling makes me feel safe enough to finally feel all the things. The closeness and connection I have with him, and his presence provide a container where I can grieve differently, almost as if he can take some of the burden from me. I cry and cry, thinking that I will run out of tears, but I don't. It turns out you can't run out of tears—there's an infinite well of them. I cry until I exhaust myself, and finally, I fall asleep, utterly spent, but feeling a strange sense of peace.

* * * * * * * * * *

The next Morning

I awaken to the sound of the door clicking shut and a rustling. I pry my eyes open to find Leo walking towards the window with coffees and a paper bag in hand.

"What are you doing?" I ask groggily.

He turns to me, changing course, and walks to my side of the bed. He sits on the edge next to me, setting a coffee down on the nightstand. "Sorry… did I wake you?" he asks, reaching forward, gently pushing the hair out of my face before bending over to kiss me on the cheek. "How did you sleep?"

Well hell, I could get used to this.

I smile, remembering last night. "I slept well. How about you?"

"After last night?" He smirks, "Best sleep of my life." His hand strokes its way down my arm. Taking my hand in his, he squeezes it. "How are you feeling this morning?" he asks sincerely.

Squeezing back, I am very aware that I am still naked in the sheets, and I don't know where we stand. Leo's gaze doesn't falter; his concern is genuine, his care for me very real, but that doesn't change the fact that Leo doesn't do relationships, and that I told him one night would be fine. I broke down last night in a way that even Sarah hasn't seen. I fell asleep on him, naked and vulnerable, having exhausted myself with tears like a baby would with her mother.

As I look at Leo, a realization hits me, shaking me to my core. I love this man. I love him so much, and it's not because of last night. I've loved him for a long time, but I just connected with him in a way that I've only connected with Ben, and it scares the shit out of me.

I take a shaky breath, deciding honesty is best. "I feel better than I have in a long time," I say genuinely, pausing. "But I also don't know where we stand now," I add cautiously. "I know I said just one night, but last night…" I trail off as Leo interrupts me.

"Was fucking spectacular?" he asks, grinning.

I let out a soft, breathy laugh, the sound escaping involuntarily. Closing my eyes, I nod. "Yes." Opening my eyes, I search for Leo's. "Last night was spectacular," I confirm.

He's thoughtful for a minute. "Look, I've never done this, not for years anyway. It scares the hell out of me, I'm not going to lie. All I know is that you are the person I want to spend all of my free time with, you're my best friend… and after last night?" He lets out a slow exhale. "You're also now the only person I intend to *bang*," he says, grinning as he playfully nudges me.

I can't help but smile, the biggest grin spreading over my face in relief. He just might love me back. "You're my best friend too."

He bends over and kisses me, tugging on my bottom lip as he releases. "This coffee here is for you," he says, "and a *Pain Au Chocolat,* just how you like in the mornings."

"Thank you," I say, sitting up and bringing the sheet up with me. Grinning, I take a sip of coffee as Leo rises and walks to the window to pull the curtains open, letting sunlight flood into the room. Needing to use the restroom and brush my teeth, I wonder how I will get from point A to point B without having to walk naked across the room.

To hell with it.

I stand, dropping all the covers, and stride confidently to the bathroom, Leo's eyes fixed on me.

"Do you think we will get anything done today with you walking around like that?" he asks teasingly.

"I hope not," I say, and disappear into the bathroom to freshen up.

I emerge from the bathroom in a bathrobe. Leo is waiting for me, back against the wall, arms folded across his chest. His eyes are sharp and focused, his jaw clenched—a lion ready to pounce, and I'm his prey. And I am not mad about it.

I laugh. "Have you been waiting there this whole time?"

He nods, uncrosses one arm, and curls his index finger, motioning for me to come to him. I walk toward him, feeling the tension crackle between us. He pulls me close, his mouth meeting mine in a heated kiss. My robe slips off, and his clothes fall away. Moving to the bed, we lose ourselves in the moment... again.

Later, we lie in bed together, spooning. Leo traces gentle fingers along my side, his touch soothing and intimate. The room is quiet, save for our steady breathing—a silent testament to the connection we just shared.

"Tell me about your first time," I say, turning to look at him.

"Hmm?" he grunts, raising a brow.

"When did you lose your virginity?"

"I was sixteen." His voice is low and gruff. "Her name was Emily. We had math together. She was popular… and so was I," he chuckles. "She was a nice girl, everyone loved her, and she was really hot." His hand feathers across my chest, cupping my breast, his thumb stroking back and forth against my skin, making me crave more of him. "We were at a party, and I was pretty drunk because I was a shit at that age. We went into one of the back bedrooms and shagged. I don't remember many details, except that I enjoyed it," he laughs, "and that kicked off an even wilder streak for me—horny and reckless. What about you?"

"I was seventeen… barely, Ben and I were at a party as well." I smile, "he had opened a beer for the first time. When it was half drunk, I leaned over and told him I was ready. I loved him so much, it was just time, you know? We went back to his house, watched a movie and eventually did it. It was great… perfect, really. No regrets," I say, reaching upward for his lips.

Leo tightens his grip on me, bringing me close to him, his cock hard and pressing against me. My fingers trace the script inked across the top of one pec, the words blending seamlessly into his skin. It's sexy. "What does this tattoo say?" I ask, noticing the name Chloe at the end and assuming it's for his sister.

"Je t'aime pour toujours, Chloe," he murmurs, the words rolling off his tongue. "It means '*Love you forever, Chloe.*'"

"That's sweet," I say, admiring it with my fingers while also enjoying the feel of his muscles beneath my touch. God, his voice is always sexy, but the way he says it in French does something for me, low and smooth, like it's second nature.

I slowly explore his upper body with my hands, feeling the warmth of his skin on my fingertips as the sound of our breath fills the air.

"Leo," I say hesitantly, searching his eyes.

"Hmm?"

"Tell me about your mom," I whisper, knowing there is something buried deep inside him. My voice shakes, fearing he might shut me out.

His eyes close tightly, and I think I've lost him.

He opens them, and a comfortable discomfort hangs in the air.

He clears his throat. "My mum left us when I was ten," he says, his voice rough. "She was found a week later in a hotel room, dead." His eyes find mine. "She committed suicide. And the last thing she said to me was that I made her want to die." He takes a deep breath and exhales slowly, the hot air hitting the top of my forehead.

I blink multiple times, trying to keep tears from falling.

What the fuck?

"Oh my God." I shake my head, unable to comprehend it. The difference in our mothers, the contrast between my childhood and his—it's overwhelming. "I'm so sorry." It's all I can say.

"Don't, Viv. Don't say you're sorry. She was mentally ill, but I've never wanted to feel sorry for her. I've held on to this anger and resentment for twenty-five years. It fueled me for a long time, made me who I am today. But I'm starting to see that maybe it's time to let some of it go, even if it's bloody hard." He pauses, swallowing. "After you said you needed space, I realized I needed to deal with this, so I've been doing EMDR with Mer. But... I'm telling you this now—even though I'm working on it, I never want to talk about it again. Truly. You asked, and I'm trying to be open, but this is not a topic that brings joy to my life. You make me happy, and this thing is fucking evil. It has no place in our lives."

I scowl slightly, then soften. "Okay... I promise I won't bring it up again." I bring a hand to his cheek, saying "Thank you for telling me," and kiss him gently on the lips.

I'm overwhelmed, knowing he chose to face this for a chance to be with me—for us, wrapped in each other's arms, sharing breath, our body heat simmering.

"I'd say I'm sorry for pushing you away, but I'm not," I say earnestly. "If that's what brought us here, then I'm not sorry at all." I smooth my hand over his chest, "I think sex was bound to happen on this trip, and if I hadn't done what I did, and you hadn't gone to Meredith, things would have been a lot different right now."

"You're probably right," he pauses, raising his brows, "We'd be in some deep shit," he laughs, making me laugh too.

We spend a few minutes kissing, savoring each other, until Leo pulls back. "We should get ready for the day. We still have a lot to see and do in Paris."

I smile up at him, soaking in this core memory while making space for it in my heart. I'm learning to move forward, keeping Ben's memory alive within me at the same time, and it feels perfect right now.

The rest of our trip is pure bliss. We dive into the sights Paris has to offer, steal kisses in dimly lit alleyways, and get lost in each other's arms. Between the tangled sheets and city streets, we share stories and secrets, laugh our asses off, and create memories that blend the old with the new.

Chapter 28

LEO

Thursday, May 2

One week after Paris

"Enough about me. Let's talk about you now. How was Paris? I've been dying to hear all about it," Meredith says, taking a bite of shrimp from the platter we ordered and washing it down with a sip of Pinot Grigio.

I met Meredith at one of my favorite steakhouses in the city for dinner to catch up. We haven't had a chance to see each other or talk since I got back a week ago. Between lectures, catching up in the office, and spending every other waking moment with Vivian—doing it on every surface of her house—I haven't had a spare moment.

"It was good," I say, fighting the urge to smile like a besotted idiot. "It was great, actually." I say as casually as I can, grabbing a shrimp for myself and taking a bite.

"It was? That's great. Did Vivian enjoy the art gallery?"

"Yeah. She loved it." I beam. "It was really cool to watch an artist take in art, actually."

"And then you rented that yacht for the night?"

I nod as I chew my shrimp and swallow. "The yacht was incredible. You and Piper really need to get to Paris."

"We'll get there. It won't be the same type of trip that you take," she says, swirling the wine in her glass. "It must be nice to be filthy rich," she teases, the corners of her mouth turning up.

"It's fucking great, you should try it sometime," I joke back.

I've learned that the best way to handle comments about my money is to roll with them. Mer's one of the few people who never makes me feel weird about it, so I can joke along without feeling self-conscious. She knows she could ask for anything, anytime, and I'd give it to her in a heartbeat.

"Tell me more," she gestures.

"God, I don't even know where to start. Everything was great. We reconnected on the plane ride over, laughing and joking like we always do. We did a bike tour, the Louvre, Moulin Rouge, had fantastic food, the whole bit."

The server brings our entrées—mine, a tomahawk steak, and hers, a lobster tail.

"We went to the art gallery and then to the Seine River for the cruise. The yacht was exquisite, and the chef and dinner were incredible. Vivian looked…" I pause, letting out a slow exhale. "She looked stunning, absolutely beautiful. Um…" I clear my throat, my brows knitting together as my face flushes with heat.

"Oh my God," she lets out a knowing laugh, shaking her head.

I glare at her. "What?"

"Nothing. It's nothing," she says, smothering a laugh. "You're just acting weird, is all."

"What do you mean? I'm not acting weird."

"Yeah, you are." She smirks and raises a brow.

"What makes you think that?" I ask, knowing I've got whipped written all over my face.

Meredith leans back, folding her arms. "You two totally had sex in Paris, didn't you?" She's wide-eyed and grinning. "Probably on that goddamn boat." She takes a sip of her wine, "Oh, excuse me, I mean yacht." She points to herself. "I mean, even I would have fucked you on that yacht. Well played." She's grinning from ear to ear.

How does she always fucking know?

I swear to God the woman is psychic.

She waits patiently for me to comment as I sit, gaping at her.

"Yeah," I chuckle, "We had sex, okay?" I feel my face reddening as I reflect on all the sex we've had. "We've had a lot of sex. And it's been great. She's just… I don't know how to describe it. She's everything I didn't know I needed."

"Were you not going to tell me?"

"I was, I swear. But it's more fun this way," I admit.

Meredith's smile softens, her teasing replaced by genuine warmth. "I'm thrilled for you. You deserve this… you deserve her. I take it the EMDR sessions helped then? You're still seeing each other… this wasn't just a Paris fling?"

I sigh, unable to hide my smile. "Yes, we're still seeing each other. The EMDR definitely helped me let go of some of the shit that's been holding me back. It's been… incredible. And terrifying. But mostly in-credible."

"So what? Are you two a thing now?" she asks, a look of curiosity painted on her face.

I scrunch my face up in thought. "I don't know." The question rattles my nerves, and I quickly sip some water. "I don't know what we are; I don't want to define it. I just like whatever it is that we have." I give her a look of concern. "Is that fucked up of me?"

Meredith frowns, a look of worry crossing her face. She reaches across the table and squeezes my hand. "I don't know. I guess it depends on how Vivian feels about that… Just don't screw it up, okay? This is a good thing that you have." She gives me a half-smile and digs into her lobster tail.

We finish our dinner with lighter conversation, but the weight of my feelings for Vivian lingers in the back of my mind.

As we part ways, Meredith gives me one last knowing look. "Hey… just be honest with her. It's the best way to keep what you have." She gives me a hug, and I squeeze her tightly.

"I will, Mer. Thanks for everything."

Two Weeks Later

I wake up in Vivian's bed alone, having slept in. After pulling on boxers and joggers, I head downstairs and make a cappuccino with her espresso machine—the same machine I have at home. She ordered it after falling in love with mine. The rich aroma of the coffee fills the kitchen, grounding me in the familiar routine.

With my cappuccino in hand, I take the stairs to the rooftop and step outside. It's sunny, and though the morning air is cool, the sun's heat cuts through the chill. She's not here, but I see a light on in her art studio. I walk around the patio to the back where her studio is, the faint smell of paint growing stronger with each step. The door is open, and I slip inside quietly.

I find her sitting on her stool painting, her back to me, completely lost in her work. She has a picture displayed upright next to her canvas, showing what looks like a Utah mountain landscape: pine trees and a lake with snowcapped mountain peaks. Her painting is an exact replica of the picture, and she's adding small strokes of detail to the lake.

I prop myself against the door, one arm crossed and the other holding my coffee. Intrigued, I watch her work. She looks sexy in a black satin pajama set. The flowy shorts are short, and the top is revealing in the best possible way, with one of the thin straps hanging off her shoulder. Her hair is pulled into a clip, with strands brushing her shoulders. Her coffee sits next to her on an empty stool, a space heater is on in the corner, and music plays in the background.

Grinning, I clear my throat, not wanting to scare her but making enough noise for her to turn around.

She doesn't. "How long have you been there?" she asks without losing focus.

"A few minutes," I say, my eyes laser-focused on her back, as if she can feel them.

I cross the room, stopping just behind her. Brushing my fingers on her shoulder to avoid messing up her brush strokes, she stops. I grip her shoulders and press my lips on her neck. "Morning," I murmur into her ear, and she grins.

"Morning," she turns just enough to kiss my lips, letting it linger for a moment.

I stand behind her for a few minutes, planting soft kisses on her shoulders, kissing her butterfly tattoo, which I now know is for Ben and Evie.

I move toward the wall across from her and lean against it, so I can watch her face while she works. There is something extremely intimate about watching Vivian paint or draw. You can almost feel what she is working on from the intensity in her eyes and the emotions that show on her face. She pulls back to look at her work, tilting her head slightly and biting her bottom lip, her eyes scanning her painting before she dips her brush and continues.

The song changes and as its melody starts to play, a smile creeps over her face.

"What are you smiling about?" I ask. A smile spreading over my face as well.

A soft laugh escapes her lips. "You wanted to know what was on my sexy playlist," she says. "This song is on it."

I don't recognize the song, but its familiar, slow rhythm definitely has a sexy vibe. The music fills the studio.

"I was in the car with Ben one day when this song came on. Niall Horan sings it." She breaks focus for a moment to see if there is a flicker of recognition. *"Slow Hands?"* she asks. I shake my head. She furrows her brows in concentration and continues, "Anyway, I told Ben I thought this would be a great song to have sex to. After that, anytime he was in the mood, he'd blast this song throughout the house"—she glances up—"summoning me." She lets out a laugh. "So, let's just say I've had a lot of sex to this song… A lot."

"Have you?" I ask with a smirk, holding her gaze as I slowly close the gap between us. The chorus starts to play in the background, amplifying the pull between us.

"Yeah," she says softly, a smile playing on her lips.

I pull her up, wrapping my arms around her waist, and stare intently into her bright-green eyes. Her hands rest on my chest.

"Do you wish that Ben were here?" I ask—a fucked-up question, but I have to know.

"I always wish Ben were here," she says honestly, "but that doesn't take away from the fact that I want you here too."

I search her eyes, hoping she's not just saying what she thinks I want to hear.

"Leo," she whispers, her hands skimming down my bare chest as she leans in to give me a soft kiss, her lips brushing against mine. "Fuck me… Right here. Right now." Her eyes lock onto mine, bittersweet and filled with longing.

Fuck yes.

She doesn't need to tell me twice.

I slowly meet her lips with a hunger that I can't suppress, a craving that I can't get enough of. I slant my mouth to hers, my tongue stroking inside it.

Her fingers weave into my hair, fists clenching, as she softly moans into my mouth.

It starts slow—our kisses tentative, like a spark fanning a flame. But the heat builds, a steady burn turning into something hotter, more demanding.

In a flash, it's urgent and wild. I grip her hips, lifting her as her legs lock around me, our mouths colliding over and over, chasing the fire that's caught us both.

I walk over to her supply table, pushing paint, brushes, and canvases out of the way as I set her ass on it.

Heat sears inside of me as her nails trace down my back, leaving a trail of tingling pleasure. She whimpers and moans, a chorus of carnal sounds that drive me wild.

One hand cups the back of her neck while I slide my other hand under her shirt, feeling the warmth of her skin. I grope her boob and pinch her nipple, making her gasp.

She meets me with the same eagerness, sliding her hand over my pants to my cock, grasping it as she pulls me down closer. Something about sweat and dirty laundry is being sung in the background, and between the music and her touch, my need for her brews inside of me, ready to tear through us like a tornado.

My pulse is pounding so hard I can feel it in my veins, and my vision blurs, thoughts clouded by how fucking hard I am. Every bit of judgment and spatial awareness is lost to pure need, so without thinking, I shove everything aside, knocking whatever's left to the floor. The crashing and banging only stoke the greedy desire between us. Her breath quickens as I clear the last bit. I need her naked, now. I tear her shirt off, tossing it aside with a roughness that matches the hunger between us. She leans back, and in one swift motion, I hook my fingers around her shorts and yank them off, leaving her bare on the cold table.

Her hands move to my waistband, desperately trying to pull my pants down.

I pull back, standing upright, simultaneously gripping her hips and pulling her to the edge of the table.

Lowering myself, I skim my mouth over her navel, placing kisses and licks as I move down between her legs. Splaying my hands on her thighs, I pin them down to worship her, sending a combination of light and needy flicks of my tongue to her clit, savoring each sensation. Her taste, her scent, everything about her makes it impossible to think clearly. She gasps and arches her back, her hands tangling in my hair as I relish every moment.

She thrashes on the table before me, a slur of curse words and my name being called out savagely, making this all the more intoxicating, and urging me on.

A new song comes on, something I've never heard before, but I keep teasing her, dipping my fingers inside her while maintaining the rhythm of my tongue as she squirms.

She climaxes, her back arching and her fingers gripping my hair. The sounds she makes resonate through me, sending waves of pleasure to my very core. She comes again before I move upward, ready to ravish her whole—one sweeping lick and kiss at a time.

As I move closer, she aggressively tugs at my pants and boxers, pulling them down. I step out of them, kicking them aside.

She pulls my tongue into her mouth, the faint taste of herself mixing with our shared desire, while my hands roam over her, feeling her nipples harden under my touch as she gets more turned on.

Her hands clutch my ass, then slide forward, wrapping around my shaft. She squeezes and strokes with a desperate urgency. "Fuck," I groan into her ear.

She cradles my balls in her hand and whispers, "Fuck me, Leo," and the demanding way she says it is almost enough to make me come right then and there.

She bites my shoulder blade. "God, Vivian," I cry out, possessively taking her mouth into mine. I nip and suck on her bottom lip, and she meets my kisses with the same demanding force. My hand gets lost in her thick hair, and I tug gently, pulling her head back, exposing her neck. I scrape my teeth against her smooth skin, and she purrs, begging me to fuck her.

I yank her close, my arms encircling her tightly. Hoisting her by the ass, I press her against the nearest wall with a rough yet careful touch. I don't have a condom on me, and I know it's careless, but I cannot wait one more second. My legs quiver as I thrust inside her, and *oh my God,* it feels so good on my bare cock as my thirst for her deepens with urgency. She grips her thighs around me, squeezing my sides as she tightens around my cock. I propel myself into her, pressing deeply, banging her carefully up against the wall, over and over, losing track of time.

"God," she cries out, her tongue urgently meeting mine. It becomes too much: the feel of my bare cock inside her, the heat of her pussy, the desperate pleas for me to fuck her. The scorching friction building inside me erupts. I pull out, gripping my cock as I stroke myself to completion. She plants soft kisses along my chest and shoulders, her fingers massaging my scalp. I groan loudly, releasing the most intense orgasm I've ever experienced onto her naked body.

I slowly lower her to the ground and rest my head against the wall, my entire body shaking. She smooths my cheek with her hand and turns my face toward her, bringing her mouth to mine. She kisses me long and deep.

Bringing her other hand up, she cups my face, continuing to kiss me slowly. We thank each other the only way we know how right now, as words escape us, our breathing ragged and shallow. She rests the back of her head against the wall and shuts her eyes, her chest rising and falling with each gasp for breath.

I brush my thumb against her cheek, and she leans into the touch. A lump forms in my throat as I admire her beauty, realizing that I fucking love her with every ounce of my being, despite my efforts to prevent this. My stomach twists in knots as a dreaded fear sinks in.

Unable to voice it, afraid to make it real, I smile, kiss her forehead, and pull her close to me. She tenderly kisses my chest and then leans her ear against it, her damp hair sticking to the sweat formed on my skin. She squeezes tightly, and we catch our breath together, holding each other. *God,* I need her more than I've ever needed anyone.

Chapter 29

VIVIAN

Friday, May 31

Two Weeks Later

I pace in front of the Marionis' house, my stomach in knots, glancing at my watch every few seconds as I wait for Nick's arrival for the final walkthrough. I have our punch list that we created a few weeks ago, and move-in day is a week from today.

Our last encounter had been slightly awkward. I met with Nick a few days after Leo and I arrived home from Paris. I felt I owed it to him to tell him about Leo and me in person.

It was hard for him, but he took it like a champ, as I knew he would because he's a good guy. It turns out his initial fears about Leo and my friendship had been warranted. Turns out, being best friends with the opposite sex can get pretty complicated.

Nick approaches, and a knot of anxiety forms in my stomach. "Hey, Nick," I say as smoothly as I can. He looks good, rugged and handsome as always.

"Hi, Vivian," he glances at me briefly before gesturing toward the house. "Shall we?" he asks, walking toward the home before I can even answer.

Okay...

He's keeping it strictly professional, I guess. It's fine, I get it, and I don't blame him.

We walk through the house, checking off everything on the list, from paint to electrical. We double-check that the few paint issues, the handle on one of the cupboards, and a door have all been fixed since we flagged them a few weeks ago.

I try to make small talk as we go, but Nick's answers are short and to the point, making it very clear that he is here for one purpose. I can't help but notice that he has avoided eye contact the entire time as well.

When we finish our walkthrough, we stand hesitantly at the door, my weight shifting from one foot to the other, my palms growing sweaty.

Shit. Why does this feel so uncomfortable?

"Well, you did a fantastic job on this house, Vivian. I'll see you in a couple of weeks when we meet at the Johnsons," he says, turning to leave, his hand already reaching for the doorknob.

"Wait, Nick," I call out, grabbing his arm.

I stumble for words to convey my feelings. "I'm really so sorry," I say, hesitantly. "I never meant to hurt you. What I felt for you was real, and I need you to know that. Leo and I… it's just… it's complicated, you know?"

"Yes, I know. It's complicated… I figured that much. That's why, back in December, I asked if there was anything between you two. That was your chance to be honest with me about your feelings for him. But you told me it was just a platonic friendship."

"It was, Nick. We were just friends. Sure, I wanted more, but Leo didn't, and I was dating. What was I supposed to do? Just not date anyone in hopes that he might come around?" I shrug, feeling lost.

"We dated for *five* months. Five months of me falling for you. I liked you… a lot, and I thought you liked me too."

"I did, Nick… I really did. I enjoyed our conversations, we had good chemistry, and we had fun together. I liked you a lot." I don't know why I need him to understand this. I know it doesn't matter anymore. I'm grasping at straws here, trying to justify my actions.

He sighs deeply, a look of resignation in his eyes. "Well, the good news is that it just doesn't matter anymore, does it?" He opens the front door. "See you around, Vivian." Without another glance, he walks down the steps and heads to his work truck.

This is going to make work so damn awkward. I blink furiously to avoid crying. I hate making people upset. My chest tightens, guilt swirling in my stomach, I wish I could undo the hurt I've caused Nick. I always liked him, and we did have incredible chemistry, but deep down, I think I knew all along that I wasn't going to fall in love with Nick. I just kept hoping I would start to feel more. I should have at least told him how I felt and let him decide if he wanted to keep seeing me.

I take a deep breath and glance around the house one last time, checking the details we've worked so hard on. The walls, the floors, everything is perfect, but it all feels empty now. Sighing, I walk to my car, the reality of the situation settling in.

Maybe I'll bring this up to Leo later. I don't want this weighing on me this weekend because tomorrow is my birthday, and Leo has something special planned for me. He won't tell me anything about what we're doing, only that I needed a cocktail dress, and I didn't hate having an excuse to go shopping.

* * * * * * * * * *

I'm stuffed.

I open the door to my townhouse, dropping all of my things right there at the door, and bend down to unbuckle the straps on my heels. Shit, my pants are way too tight right now and digging into my stomach.

I went to dinner with Kara tonight at The Purple Pig, one of my absolute favorite places to eat in Chicago. It's tapas style, and the food is seriously so delicious, you have to try everything, so I basically did. I tried it all, and now I'm paying for it.

I drag myself upstairs and slip into my comfiest pajamas. It's only nine, and I have a sexy date with my bed and the television for the rest of the night. A much-needed escape after today's shitshow encounter with Nick at work.

I settle into my bed wearing the coziest pajamas I own, the kind with plenty of give in the pants for post-feast comfort. God, I'm glad that Leo isn't here to witness this spectacle. Overindulging in food is a rare event for me, and when it happens, it definitely shouldn't be in front of the sexy man who shares my bed. Talk about a mood killer.

Leo has poker with the guys tonight, so he won't be over until late. He told me not to wait up for him, but that he'd sneak over when they're all done, giving me plenty of time for my food to settle. We haven't spent a night apart from each other since Paris, switching back and forth between his place and mine. We mostly stay at my place; it's a bit easier for me with all my 'girl stuff,' as Leo likes to call it.

His friends all meet once a month at his place to gamble, smoke cigars, and drink whiskey.

I turn on *Friends,* partly because Leo hates that I miss his references. I like it. The fake laughter grates a bit, but I settle in for the season five finale. It's the episode where they go to Vegas. Ross's doodle on Rachel's face has me laughing so hard I'm gasping for air. I'm at the part where Joey comes into the hotel room and Ross, very drunk, tells him, 'If you need anything, I'm your man,' and then proceeds to sit back into what he thinks is a chair—only to fall straight to the floor. He then asks Joey if he's okay, and I can't help but laugh. The scene is hilarious, but it also reminds me of Sarah saying the same thing to Ben after she fell backward on her birthday—the last night we spent together before he died.

I'm laughing so hard that I'm crying, or maybe I'm crying so hard that I'm laughing. I honestly don't know, but I'm a mess of tears, happy and sad, snot and giggles. Eventually, I gather my wits, blow my nose, and wipe my tears. Yep, it's good that Leo is not here to witness my hot mess tonight. I keep it on play, watching until close to midnight, and eventually fall asleep.

* * * * *   * * * * *

I awaken to strong arms wrapping around me and a warm hand up my shirt, cupping one of my breasts.

"Hey babe," Leo's deep, *sexy* voice resonates in my ear, alerting me to my surroundings as he kisses my jaw, causing me to sleepily smile.

I turn my head enough for his mouth to reach mine and let him kiss me deeply, pulling me into a half-awake awareness while he fondles me under my shirt. He gently squeezes my boob, stroking his thumb back and forth over my nipple. I squeeze my thighs together as a dull throb begins to beat between them.

God, he turns me on.

"What time is it?" I whisper between kisses.

"It's fuck me thirty, love," he says with a chuckle, as his lips brush against mine.

"Oh my God," I say, laughing, "you're drunk." He smells of whiskey and cigars, and I love it. I inhale deeply, taking in the scent of him and his desire for me, turning me on all the more.

"Hmm. Maybe a little… I'm really fucking horny for you." His hand drifts to my stomach. "God, you feel good," he murmurs, his hand falling lower. I gasp as he slips into my underwear, two fingers sliding down my slit. I eagerly lift my top leg to grant access as he glides his fingers along the slick surface.

"Fuck. You're so wet, babe." He slowly drags his fingers up to his mouth, tasting me. "God, and you taste so fucking good."

Sweet Jesus.

I press my ass into him, grinding against his firm dick as he sucks on my ear and kisses my neck. He makes his way back to my mouth, lifting himself atop me as I roll onto my back. I welcome him as he kisses me deeper.

It's the middle of the night, and I'm tired, but we are still in that phase of an early relationship where sex takes precedence over everything else. I could do it six times a day with Leo, anytime, anywhere.

I'm all moans and gasps, entering the euphoric zone that Leo takes me to, when he whispers in my ear, "What does the birthday girl want?" He removes my shirt, taking a nipple into his mouth. He tantalizes and teases, scraping his teeth and flicking his tongue while caressing my other boob, and I'm on my way to my happy place.

"Take your clothes off," I say in desperation, and he obliges, pulling off his shirt and removing his pants, leaving me with all that gloriousness to touch, see, and feel. I welcome his warm body over mine, letting my hands explore every inch of him that I can reach.

He continues to move lower, and I know he wants to go down on me, and Lord knows I want that too because if there was an Academy Award for the best performance down south, Leo would win. Every. Fucking. Time. But it's *my* birthday, and what I really want is to feel sexy and desirable, to pleasure him and savor every moment of him wanting me.

I roll out from underneath him. "Mmm, no babe," I say in a heated whisper, "roll over, on your back." I maneuver my body to roll with his so that I'm straddling him as he lies on his back, gaining control. His body is so solid under mine, so strong.

I wiggle free from my shorts and underwear, lowering myself onto his hard cock, which twitches in response to my warmth. Biting my bottom lip, I bring my mouth inches from his, my eyes locking onto his with intensity. "You wanna know what I want for my birthday?" I ask, and he nods.

"Yeah, babe. Tell me."

I bring my mouth to his ear, scraping my teeth against his earlobe. "I want to tease the shit out of you and make you beg for me," I say as I grind into his cock and flick my tongue against his ear.

"Christ," he groans, desperately wrapping his arms around me before things get really wild.

We become a frenzy of pushing and pulling, tugging and teasing. He wants to be on top, the one in control, driving me crazy, but I won't let him. I have to hold his hands down multiple times, knowing he's strong enough to free himself, to whip me over so he can be on top, but he lets me dominate him. He spanks me and grips my ass. "Fuck. You drive me crazy," he growls, his eyes full of lust with a tinge of savageness.

I do everything possible to tease him, building the fire inside him with the kindling of my touch. Each flick of my tongue, each grind against him is a spark, igniting his desire. As his groans grow louder, I fan the flames, watching the heat rise in his eyes. The fire I've stoked consumes him, and I can feel his need for me burning hotter and hotter.

I position myself between his thighs, running my tongue along the sexy V of his muscles, drawing out each lick as I graze his inner thigh with my fingers, taking my time to work him up. I let the anticipation build as I slowly drag my tongue along the length of his thick, beautiful cock, swirling around the tip, then pulling back, drawing out the torture.

"Fuck, babe," he groans, his voice laced with desperation. I smirk, knowing I've got him exactly where I want him. I look him in the eye as I finally close my lips over the head, scraping my teeth softly against the skin. His hand fists the sheets as I move up and down, gripping the base of his shaft with one hand, kneading his balls with the other. I moan as I take him deeper, seducing him with my mouth.

His body jerks. "Jesus." He's completely unhinged now, the slow build-up driving him insane. I move up and down in perfect rhythm, using every trick I know he loves.

His body trembles beneath me. "Fuck, I'm gonna come," he groans, every muscle tensing. The warm liquid flows into my mouth, and I swallow every last drop like a champ. I savor the way my name falls off his lips as he comes, knowing I've driven him completely wild.

He drags his hands over his face and into his hair. "Goddamn." He breathes heavily, staring at the ceiling. "Best blow job of my life."

He chuckles and looks at me as a wicked grin spreads across his face. "You don't think I'm going to let you get away with that, do you?"

I smile, moving up to his face, hovering above him. I kiss his mouth. "Well, it's my birthday, so I get whatever I want," I say boldly.

"Yeah, that's not going to happen." In one smooth motion, he flips me over, nestles his head between my thighs, and reciprocates until I'm limp as a noodle, sweating, panting, and completely satisfied.

Happy fucking birthday to me.

* * * * * * * * * *

Saturday, June 1

I slip into the metallic Michael Costello dress, its rose gold, gold, and silver tones shimmering under the light. The fabric hugs my curves with a form-fitting stretch that makes me feel like a goddess. A one-inch-wide strap wraps up one side and crosses over to the back, leaving my shoulders bare and cutout. The long sleeves start mid-bicep, giving it an off-the-shoulder look, and cover my arms perfectly. The dress hugs my boobs and then cuts away with a large cutout on one side of my torso, extending around my back and leaving most of my midriff exposed. The side with the cutout has a six-inch fabric panel that transitions into another cutout—a two-inch by six-inch keyhole on my hip, teasing the upper portion of my tattoo.

The dress hits mid-thigh, a mini length that's sexy as hell. I chose it with Leo in mind, knowing how much he loves my stomach. I want to drive him wild tonight, teasing him with one of his favorite parts of my body. Plus, I wanted to feel sexy and youthful as I step into my thirties. Leo had even given me his credit card and told me to buy any dress, shoes, or bag I wanted for my birthday. It felt indulgent but also incredibly sweet. The dress was totally affordable, but the Jimmy Choo clutch and Christian Louboutin shoes? Not so much.

Leo walks into the bathroom wearing a light-gray suit. Frozen except for his eyes, he slowly moves them down, undressing me in his mind.

He chuckles softly, "Jesus, babe. This dress is a weapon. I can't walk around all night with a hard-on. You know I'll have to steal you away for a shag, yeah?"

I stride over to him. "Can't wait," I murmur.

"Where are we going?" I ask Leo in the Uber. His hand rests on my thigh with mine atop his, fingers intertwined.

"It's a surprise."

"Come on, we're almost there. Just tell me, so I know what to expect."

He glances at me. "Fine… We're going to *Aurora Sky Lounge,* a rooftop venue in the heart of downtown. It has incredible views of the city's skyline. Fantastic food too."

I smile. "That wasn't so hard, now, was it?" I say sarcastically, then turn serious. "I'm excited to see it. Thank you for planning something special for me." I give his hand a squeeze, prompting him to kiss me in the back seat.

We arrive ten minutes later and take the elevator to the top floor and step out into a dimly lit room that buzzes with energy. The lounge is packed with people, and one wall is open, revealing the stunning rooftop patio outside. A row of semi-private cabanas lines the patio, each offering an intimate escape with a view of the city skyline.

We weave through the crowd, the sound of laughter and clinking glasses filling the air. I follow Leo as he guides me past the bustling bar and into a quieter hallway behind it. The sounds from the lounge become muffled as we walk further.

Just as I start to wonder where we're headed, we reach a set of doors guarded by bouncers. Leo flashes a wristband, and the bouncers nod, opening the door and letting us through. We step into a spacious event area, and before I can take in my surroundings, a chorus of voices erupts.

"Happy Birthday!" a crowd of people yell.

"Jesus," I laugh, clutching my chest. My heart races as I look around, my eyes wide with surprise. The room is beautifully decorated, with soft lighting casting a warm glow over the elegant setup. There's a DJ booth in one corner, a dance floor ready for action, a small bar along the back wall, and cocktail servers moving gracefully between guests, offering drinks and hors d'oeuvres. The far wall of the event space is open, connecting to the shared rooftop patio, but bouncers are stationed nearby.

As I process the sight of my friends gathered to celebrate, a wide smile spreads across my face. I turn to Leo, who's grinning from ear to ear, and now behind him stand Sarah and Ryan.

"Oh my God!" I cry out, and she runs to me. We embrace tightly, screaming and laughing with joy.

"Ahhhh, when did you get here?" I ask.

"Two days ago. It's been killing me not to see you, but Leo didn't want to ruin the surprise… I didn't either, but I was tempted."

I look to Leo. "How did you arrange this? I'm shocked, truly."

"It wasn't easy," he says. "I had to steal your phone to get Sarah's number, which was not as easy as it sounds because I had to do it while it was still fresh and open from you using it… I don't know your password. We met two days ago when she arrived, and she helped me with some last-minute details of the party."

"I'm impressed, babe. Seriously, come here." I pull him down, kissing him fervently. "Thank you. You scared the bejesus out of me… but thank you."

"This one, by the way," Sarah says, patting Leo's arm, "is a keeper… We like him." She smiles wide with Ryan by her side, and it means the world to me that two of my favorite people have met, and that Sarah has put her stamp of approval on Leo.

Leo's gaze is fixed on me as I glance between him and Sarah. "Yeah… he is… He's a keeper for sure." I'm smiling so hard my cheeks hurt. "I'm gonna make the rounds," I say, looping my finger in a circle in the air as I make my way to say hello to everyone.

I chat with Meredith and Piper, and her friend Johnny, who I've met a few times now. Michael and Stella are here, along with Leo's friend Adam. Carrie and Jill from my work, my boss David and his wife, and Kara and some of her friends that I've gotten to know pretty well. Scarlett and Matt, friends who live in our complex, five of the women from my support group, and a few other people that Leo and Meredith hang out with, part of a larger group that I'm getting to know slowly.

I make my rounds. Guests are enjoying craft cocktails, fine wines, and gourmet bites as cocktail waitresses dressed in black round the room. The floor-to-ceiling windows offer a view of the city lights and the tranquil waters of Lake Michigan. It's perfect, absolutely perfect.

* * * * * * * * * *

I find myself laughing at a story Ryan has told, while the buzz of my third—and final—old fashioned settles into my blood, creating a hazy fog over my vision. Numbness starts to set in around my mouth, and the song *I Can't Feel My Face* starts to play in the back of my mind, as it always does when this feeling settles in.

So far, the night has been great. The DJ's nailing it, the cocktails and food have been out-of-this-world good, and I've been able to talk to everyone for at least a few minutes. Leo even hired a photographer and set up a photo-op backdrop. He really thought of everything, and it makes me feel all the feels for him.

The DJ announces that it's time for dancing and cranks up the volume, starting off with Dua Lipa's *Levitating*. You better believe I'm gonna dance my ass off tonight. It's my dirty-thirty, my best friend is here, and I'm going home with the guy who has an eight-pack, who I love… yeah, it's gonna be a great fucking night.

The girls all head to the dance floor to get the party started, and after four songs, I'm a ball of laughter and giggles as Piper, Sarah, Stella, and I make fools of ourselves. Carrie and Jill are killing me with their 80s dance moves, incorporating the sprinkler and balloon stretch into their routine, causing me to laugh all the more.

I see Leo on the sideline chatting with Michael. I catch his eye and gesture for him to come out here. He flashes me a grin, holding up his index finger, indicating he'll come in a minute.

In da Club by 50 Cent plays, and slowly the men start making their way onto the dance floor. The group of girls in the center of the floor goes crazy, forming a circle around me because you know, *"Go shawty, it's your birthday,"* and well… it's my birthday. We are out of hand, a wild mess of dancing, singing, and grinding on each other—the way us girls do on a dance floor.

Leo and Michael approach us with a tray, grinning mischievously. 'Birthday shots!' Leo announces. I take one, laughing as I clink glasses with everyone and down the shot. The alcohol burns its way down, and I feel my buzz intensify, my plan to avoid getting wasted tonight going out the window.

Leo stays in the center of the circle with me, dancing with moves I didn't know he had. I've got to hand it to him—he's got rhythm, and he's mouthing every lyric. Of course he is, *fuckin' millennial.* Michael and Adam join Stella, Mer, and Piper, adding to the craziness and fun of the dance party.

Leo takes a spot on the floor behind me, and I slowly back up into him as the chorus plays. I grind my ass into him, my hands on my thighs, rounding my booty against him. As I stand, his hands grip my waist. My hands go into the air, and I lean back, dancing to the music.

We dance to a few more songs, all having a great time, and then the DJ plays Ginuwine's *Pony.* The dance floor transforms into a sexy, gyrating mass, complete with friends twirling invisible lassos in the air. I can't help but laugh at the wild scene.

I face Leo, my arms wrapped around his neck, leaving no space between our bodies. I can feel his dick digging into my hip. His hands rest on my waist, his gaze downward, stroking my bare skin with his thumb. A wicked smile spreads across his face.

"How many times have you undressed me with your eyes tonight?" I teasingly ask.

"Oh, are you wearing clothing? Because in my mind, you have been naked all night," he says, chuckling.

Cupping the back of his neck with one hand, I gently slap his chest with the other. "You're so naughty."

He leans down, whispering in my ear, "Oh, I do love it when you talk dirty to me, babe."

I tip my head back, laughing.

"Should we get out of here? Find somewhere for a quick shag?" He pulls back and waggles his brows. "Yeah?"

Grinning, I nod.

Grabbing my hand, Leo pulls me off the dance floor. We snag another shot from a cocktail waitress before slipping out of the event room.

"Where are we going?" I ask, laughing and trailing behind him.

"I don't know yet. I'm just being spontaneous," he calls out.

We find ourselves in a single bathroom, separate from the men's and women's restrooms, with multiple stalls.

We lock the handle behind us quickly, pressing the push button frantically, and start making out. Leo shoves me up against the door as I untuck his shirt and fumble with his buttons, his lips never leaving mine. His hands roam over my body, gripping my hips through the thin fabric and cutouts of my dress.

"God, you look incredible," he mutters against my mouth, his breath hot and ragged.

"So do you," I whisper back, my voice filled with passion. "You're so fucking hot."

I feel the hard press of his cock against my hip, and it sends a thrill through me. An aching, hot pulse builds between my thighs. My fingers work his belt, the need to feel him consuming me entirely. He catches my hand, guiding it to his zipper, and I pull it down with a sharp tug.

"Someone's eager," he teases, his voice low and rough, but there's no mistaking the urgency in his movements as he lifts the hem of my dress.

I laugh into his mouth, "You got that right, babe."

The cold air against my skin contrasts sharply with the warmth of his touch as his hand slips between my thighs. I bite back a moan, not wanting to draw attention to our little escapade, but it's difficult to stay quiet when he knows exactly how to drive me crazy.

"Do you have a condom?" I manage to ask between gasps and kisses.

"I *always* have a condom," Leo replies, taking one out of his pocket and ripping the corner.

He lets out a low growl as he frees himself, the tip of his cock brushing against my entrance over my underwear. He pauses for a moment, his eyes locking onto mine. The intensity in his eyes sends a rush of anticipation through me.

Just as he takes the condom out, the door rattles against us as someone tries to come in.

The lock isn't holding, and Leo quickly reacts, dropping the condom wrapper as he pushes the door closed. "Shit," he mutters under his breath before locking it again. The buzz from the drinks we've had only adds to the chaos. We silently gasp for breath, staring at each other and trying not to laugh. My heart beats wildly, and I can hear it in my ears.

"Hurry," I gasp, the words barely coherent as he finds the edge of my panties and pulls them aside.

He lifts me up, and I wrap my legs around his waist as he thrusts into me, filling me completely. His hands grip my hips tightly, the sensation electric, making my breath hitch. He moves with a rhythm that's both desperate and controlled, each thrust pushing me closer to the edge.

I cling to him, my nails digging into his back as he drives deeper, the sound of our panting breaths and the faint echo of the party outside filling the bathroom.

"Leo," I whisper, my voice trembling with need. He leans in, capturing my lips in a searing kiss, his pace quickening.

The tension coils tighter within me, each movement bringing me closer to release. When it finally hits, it's like an explosion. My body shudders as a surge of ecstasy courses through my veins, a breathy moan escaping my lips. He follows moments later, his grip on me tightening as he finds his own release.

We stay there for a few moments, breathing heavily. Slowly, he lowers me back to the floor, smoothing down my dress as he pulls out. I catch my breath.

"That was… so intense," I say, laughing breathlessly.

He grins, then his eyes widen as he looks down. "Viv, the condom," he gestures toward the floor where the unused condom lies next to its wrapper.

He squeezes his eyes shut, pressing a fist against the door and resting his head on it. "Fuck, I dropped it when someone tried to come in." he mutters, his voice filled with regret. "I must've thought I put it on."

Liquid pools in my underwear as I let the reality of what just happened sink in. I can see the worry etched on Leo's face, the tension in his shoulders. "Don't worry, babe," I say, trying to sound reassuring. "It took Ben and me forever to get pregnant, even with tracking my cycle and everything. It's unlikely that I'd get pregnant from this one time. And you were just tested, so we really don't have anything to worry about."

I'm not overly concerned but still try to calculate where I am in my cycle, but the shots are hitting me and the room is starting to spin.

Damn, I can't think.

I haven't tracked my fertility since I was trying to get pregnant with Ben; there's been no need. Honestly, I don't even remember when I'm fertile, or if I ever figured it out because my cycle can be sporadic. The stress of the situation mixed with the alcohol I've had is making everything a blur.

Leo rubs his forehead, pinching and smoothing the skin between his thumb and index finger. He's squinting, trying to focus, the shots are hitting him as well.

"I've never seen you take the pill. You're not on birth control, right? If not, we'll have to grab a Plan B in the morning," he pleads, more to himself than to me, his words slightly slurred.

"I don't take birth control," I say, my voice steady.

I'm a product of my mom, who's a health nut. I rarely eat junk food, let alone take a prescription that I haven't ever needed. I haven't been sexually active in two years, and we've been using condoms. I didn't feel it necessary to go on the pill. Embarrassingly, I didn't even think about it because it's not something I've had to think about since I was a teenager. Even with Ben, if I had gotten pregnant before we planned, it would have been fine—I was in a stable relationship, and then we got married.

He sighs and kisses my forehead. "Well, we can swing by a pharmacy in the morning then. Let's get back before anyone notices we're missing."

I nod. "Okay, you go first, I need to clean up."

We share one last, lingering kiss before Leo unlocks the door. "Hey, Viv," he says, looking back with a cheeky grin, "You're a fantastic shag. Happy fucking birthday!" He gives me a wink before slipping out the door and back into the party.

I smile to myself.

Hell yeah! I am a great shag.

I toss the condom and its wrapper in the trash, pee, and reflect on what just happened. It was wild and fun. And Leo's right, we'll deal with the condom situation in the morning. I'm not going to let anything spoil my birthday buzz. This is a tomorrow-Vivian problem.

Trying to look as composed as possible after such a wild encounter and our moment of stupidity, I step into the hallway and make my way back to the dance floor. I'm greeted by friends, laughter, and a Nelly song.

The rest of the night is a blur of laughter, shots, and dancing. The music pulses in the background, and I let myself get completely lost in the rhythm, laughing with friends who are just as caught up in the evening. Each shot adds to the buzz, and the worries from earlier seem like a distant memory. When it's time to leave, I'm on a high, feeling euphoric and satisfied. The night was a whirlwind of pure, unfiltered fun—a perfect way to enter my thirties.

Chapter 30

LEO

Three Weeks Later

Wrapping up my lecture, I drum my fingers on the podium, glancing at the clock for what feels like the hundredth time. Fridays always seem to drag, with my last class ending around seven. Normally, I savor these moments, engaging with students and diving into the intricacies of psychology. But tonight is different. Vivian and I have plans to meet at Craft's, our usual Friday evening spot, a tradition that's grown into something I genuinely cherish.

"Alright, everyone," I say, closing my laptop with a sense of finality. "That's all for today. Have a great weekend, and don't forget to review chapter six for Monday." I try to sound casual, but my mind is already on the evening ahead.

As students start packing up, I silently pray no one approaches me with last-minute questions.

I've settled into a new routine over the last few months, and honestly, I've never been happier.

I'm on autopilot as I drive home, change my clothes, and walk to Craft's. I'm meeting Vivian here at eight, and I arrive a few minutes early. She planned to work late tonight, as she's been swamped with new clients lately. The stress has been getting to her.

Lucky for me, a naked massage always helps her unwind, and it usually leads to some incredible sex. It's a win-win for both of us.

I slide into our usual spot at the end of the bar, where Noah has already set out an old fashioned and a Manhattan, just as we like them. Vivian texted me while I was on my way here, saying she'd be running a few minutes late.

At 8:15, Hurricane Vivian sweeps in, sliding into the seat next to me. "Oh my God," she says, exasperated, tossing her purse onto the bar, taking a hefty sip of her drink. "Sorry I'm late." She leans in, pressing her lips to mine, the taste of whiskey lingering on her lips, and it's bloody delicious. She takes a deep breath, exhaling audibly, "What are we having tonight?" she asks, glancing at the menu before looking back at me, taking another large sip.

"Whoa, Viv… babe, slow down, yeah? You alright?" I squeeze her thigh gently and offer a reassuring smile.

"Yeah, I'm fine," she begins, her voice tight with frustration. "I just had a real shitty day at work. I'm super stressed, babe. I've taken on too many clients at once, and I feel like I can't catch up." She tucks a loose strand of hair behind her ear, her fingers trembling slightly as they linger at her temple. "Then today, I had to go on site for my final walk-through at the Johnsons' house—you know, the one I mentioned," she says, her brow furrowing deeply. "And Nick was just making it so fucking awkward. Then we discovered this issue with one of the cabinets—it was made incorrectly. Now we have to rip it out and have it remade. Ugh, it's going to push their move-in date back by a week because our cabinet guy is backed up." She runs her hand through her hair, pausing to pick at the ends, a nervous habit of hers. "This delays the maximum time allotted for the home's completion, which is going to cost the company money… I'm going to have to work all weekend." She lets out a frustrated sigh, her fingers still fidgeting with her hair. "I just feel like I'm drowning, you know?"

She takes another large sip of her drink, her eyes glassy, hinting at tears she's struggling to hold back.

"Babe," I say gently, reaching for her hand and giving it a reassuring squeeze, "I'm really sorry. That sounds like a shit day, and Nick making it awkward doesn't help. But you'll sort it out—I know you will. You're amazing at your job, and sometimes shit just happens."

Vivian nods, her gaze distant. "I know… it just sucks."

"It does suck," I agree, my voice steady. "What do you need right now to unwind, love, so we can make the most of tonight?"

She smiles warmly. "This right here is all I need," she says, squeezing my hand. "Just you." She finishes her drink with a long sip and then waves to Noah for a refill, which makes me chuckle.

Something I love about Vivian is that she is really fucking fun. Despite starting the evening stressed and frustrated, here we are, laughing our asses off and having a fantastic time.

"Okay, quick! You've got ten seconds to find someone in this room to sleep with. Who are you taking home?" Vivian challenges, her eyes twinkling with mischief. "Ten, nine, eight," she counts down as I scan the room, trying to catch sight of someone appealing. "Five, four…" She starts tapping the counter, making it more urgent. I struggle to find a woman I'm attracted to. "Three, come on, Leo! Two," she's practically shouting now.

"I guess the blonde woman over there, the one in the black shirt," I say, pointing toward a woman who seems vaguely attractive.

"You mean the sixty-something-year-old who might be a grandma?" Vivian laughs heartily, tipping her head back. "Come on! What about that girl in the red shirt?" She gestures toward a younger brunette who's definitely a better choice.

"Hey, in my defense, she's a good-looking older woman. I'm not opposed to a hot grandmother," I retort with a grin. "She's probably great in the sack, loads of experience." I chuckle. This is the game Vivian came up with after downing two Manhattans in less than thirty minutes.

"Okay, your turn," I say. "Ten, nine…"

She frantically scans the room, grimacing.

"Eight, seven…"

She makes a face that says, *maybe*.

"Six, five..." Her mannerisms are killing me.

"Umm... I don't know, probably Noah," she says casually, gesturing toward the bartender.

"Oh my God!" I exclaim. "All this time we've been coming here, and you're secretly jonesing for the young bartender?" I laugh and lean in closer. "Should I tell him? Hey, mate!" I call out, not loud enough for Noah to hear, but enough to get a rise out of her.

"No! GOD, don't you dare!" she says, grabbing my arm and pointing a finger at me, her eyes wide and scolding.

"You like robbing the cradle, yeah? Is he even old enough to work here?" I tease with a grin.

"Well, I should hope so, didn't you hire him?" she rebuts, crossing her arms. "Sure, he's a few years younger than me and has a bit of a baby face, but he's a good-looking man... boy... man-boy," she stutters, flustered. "And I had to pick someone... he was the best choice with the ten seconds I had. I bet Noah's a fantastic lay," she adds with a smile, clearly trying to convince herself more than me.

"Oh, I bet," I say, nodding in fake agreement. "Super experienced, that one, with all his twenty-four years of life." I lean closer, my hand resting on her thigh. "I bet he can't make you come like I do," I whisper in her ear, "you know that thing I do with my tongue that you like so much?" I pull back, giving her a pointed look. "I'm just sayin'..." I shrug and grin, challenging her.

I see her eyes light up, a spark of mischief igniting, just as I knew it would. I love this part—whatever comes next is what I love about Vivian. I've just turned her on, and now she's going to try to one-up me. That's how this goes.

Noah sets another round of drinks down for us, and I can't help but smirk. Vivian just smiles confidently, raising an eyebrow at me.

She's still in her work clothes—wearing all white and looking sexy as hell, like always. Her top is one of those suit vests that's appropriate for work but low-cut enough that I've glanced at her tits more times than I can count—waiting for the moment I can rip it off her and take one into my mouth.

Vivian undoes the top button of her vest, giving me an unobstructed view of her cleavage. She then casually slides off her stool and stands between my legs, facing me. Her hand glides up my chest as she bites her bottom lip, eyes locked on mine. She cups the back of my neck and pulls me forward.

I chuckle softly, aware that people might be watching our little seductive show.

She leans in close to my ear. "You know that thing you do with your tongue?" she whispers, her breath hot against my ear.

I nod, savoring every tantalizing word.

"That's what I think about when my hand is between my thighs… imagining it's your tongue. The way you slowly drag it up the center, making me want more. How you tease me with flicks until I'm aching, begging for you to taste me. That's what I crave when you're not with me." She leans back slightly, her eyes drifting down to my hardening cock, undeniably straining against the inseam of my pants. A sly smile curls on her lips, and she lifts her brows, fully satisfied with the reaction she's provoked. She settles back into her chair and casually buttons her vest, her movements slow and deliberate. She plucks a grape from the charcuterie board and pops it into her mouth with a knowing grin.

We *always* have to get the charcuterie.

"You lose," she says arrogantly.

"You don't play very fair," I reply.

"What's not fair about it? There aren't any ground rules."

"Well, there should be." I sip my old fashioned, unable to shake the image of her. It's pathetic how easily she can turn me on. "Do you really think about that… when you touch yourself?" I ask, needing to know, lowering my voice.

Her eyes lock onto mine, and she leans in closer, her voice a sultry whisper. "Every. Single. Time." She bites her lip, letting the silence hang, her gaze never wavering. My pulse quickens, the room suddenly feeling too small, too hot.

"Damn," I murmur, my mind racing. "You're going to be the death of me, you know that?"

She laughs softly, a mischievous sparkle in her eyes. "Only if you're lucky."

I let out a laugh. She's good, but so am I. "I know you think you've won, but after that confession, I think I'm the real winner tonight," I say, a smug grin spreading across my face. "Knowing you think of me while you touch yourself." I relax into my chair, getting comfortable, ready to drag this on all night as she gives me the evil eye. "God, I must be really good if that's what you envision when you get yourself off," I joke, pausing to let the words sink in. "Will you let me watch?"

She cocks a brow. "Maybe," she says, taking a sip of her drink. "Do you think about me?"

"Do I think about you?" I rub my thumb and index finger on my chin, pretending to ponder.

She folds her arms and purses her lips, clearly unamused. "We are not leaving here until you admit it," she says confidently.

"Admit what?" I ask, feigning innocence.

"Oh, you know what."

"I really don't," I say, shaking my head. "You'll have to be more specific."

She lets out a sigh of frustration. She's desperate to know the truth, and I've never seen her so flustered. It's fucking adorable, honestly.

"Yes," I say. Yes, I think about you, all the goddamn time."

I lean in closer, my voice low and intimate. "But I don't just think about you. I imagine every detail—how you'd feel, how you'd taste, the sounds you'd make." I let my words hang in the air, watching the flush spread across her cheeks. "And now, I'm going to think about how you look when you're flustered and biting your lip like that."

"Mmm. I love that," she murmurs, her eyes gleaming with satisfaction. "Thinking about you thinking about me… that's hot." She leans closer, her voice dropping to a whisper. "Maybe next time, I'll let you watch." She smiles deviously, as if there's more where that came from.

The intensity in her look sends a heat coursing through my veins. I lean back, taking a slow sip of my drink, chuckling to myself.

This game is far from over.

* * * * * * * * * *

It's a perfect summer night. The breeze from Lake Michigan cools the warm air, making our walk home pleasant.

As we pass the outdoor patio of a popular bar, our conversation is interrupted.

"Leo?" a familiar female voice calls out.

I turn to see Ashley slide out of her bar-top seat and walk toward me. *Fuck me, sideways.*

This is the last thing I need right now. My grip on Vivian's hand tightens involuntarily as Ashley approaches, and I feel a bead of sweat form at my temple.

"Oh, hey, Ashley," I say awkwardly. Awkward is not a word I'd ever use to describe myself.

Vivian tenses beside me, her hand going limp in mine. Great, just great.

Ashley is beautiful, a very successful Instagram influencer, and she's wearing a shirt, if that's what you'd call it, that leaves very little to the imagination. She doesn't compare to Vivian, in my opinion, but all of that aside, this is not an encounter I want to have right now.

"Who's your friend?" Ashley asks, staring Vivian down.

"Oh, sorry. Ashley, this is my friend, Vivian. Vivian, this is Ashley," I say, immediately regretting the use of friend. Vivian is so much more to me than a friend. But *friend…* it would have been better to say nothing at all, just '*this is Vivian*'.

Ashley smiles, satisfied with my fucking stupidity.

She barely glances at Vivian, giving her a little wave. "Hi," she says, dismissing her just as quickly. She reaches out to touch my arm. "You look good. Give me a call later if you're free," she adds coyly.

"I'm actually tied up all night," I reply, looking at Vivian and silently pleading with her not to hold this against me.

"Well, some other time then," she says confidently. "See you later." She turns and walks back to her seat, completely ignoring Vivian.

"God, I'm sorry, Viv." I don't know what else to say.

"It's fine," she says, but I know from her tone that it most definitely is not.

A stifling discomfort settles between us, making the clean Chicago air feel suffocating.

"That was Ashley."

"She said that," Vivian replies sarcastically.

"She's Johnny's friend… We've… you know, um," I stammer, struggling to find the right words, knowing whatever I say won't help.

"I gathered as much. Honestly, I assume that half the women we pass have fucked you at one point or another. It's fine, I wouldn't expect anything less."

Oh wow, ouch. The claws are coming out, but not in the witty, fun way that I love. I know I should apologize for using the term friend, but that would lead to a conversation I'm purposely avoiding.

We walk the rest of the way home hand in hand, silent except for my occasional attempts to fill the void with surface-level chatter.

When we reach her townhouse, she doesn't stop me from following her inside, which I take as a good sign. She kicks off her shoes and immediately heads upstairs.

"Can you please lock up and make sure all the lights are turned off?" she calls down to me without looking back.

After securing the house and shutting everything off for the night, I find Vivian in the bathroom, washing her face in nothing but an oversized T-shirt and her underwear.

I stand behind her, wrapping my arms around her waist and pulling her close, kissing the top of her head.

"Hey," I say gently, "are you okay?" I pause, noticing her hesitation. "I'm sorry."

She turns toward me and places her hands on my chest, looking up at me with a fleeting fear in her eyes. I hate seeing her like this. Why can't I just call her my girlfriend? Because I'm terrified. The label, the commitment—it ties someone to something more, something deeper. And that scares the hell out of me. I hate myself for it. She deserves more, and I can't even call her what she clearly is.

"Are you?" she asks pointedly. "What are you sorry for?"

"For that awkward encounter." I know it's the wrong answer and that I should apologize for calling her my friend, but I don't. I'm putting up shields, protecting myself.

She sighs softly, rubbing her thumb against my chest. "Okay," she says somberly. "Thanks for the apology."

She offers her lips to mine, a silent truce, and we end up making love because that's what it's become with Vivian. A goddamn connection mixed with incredible sex, making me feel phenomenal things, all while feeling terrified at the same time.

Her heart's not in it, though. She's reserved and quiet, silently pulling away, closing herself off, going through the motions. Her touch lacks the usual fervor. I feel the distance she's putting between us, even in this intimate moment.

When we finish, she turns her back to me, not bothering to get up and use the restroom like usual. I get up and splash my face with cold water in the bathroom sink, gripping the back of my neck in frustration. My stomach churns with a knot of nerves entangling, twisting, and pulling.

I lay back down beside her, scooting closer to close the gap between us. I slide an arm around her, feeling her body tense at my touch. She's building a wall again—maybe not a ten-foot wall, possibly just a fence—but a barrier nonetheless. I don't know how to break it down, I can't lose her.

I lay awake an hour later, watching her, knowing she's wide awake too. She rolls out of my arms, and sleep eludes us both as she tosses and turns for the next couple of hours. Her mind is obviously racing in a million different directions, while mine fixates only on her. Somewhere in the midst of the uncomfortable avoidance, I eventually fall asleep, my arm stretched out across the bed, reaching for Vivian.

280

Chapter 31

VIVIAN

I feel Leo settle into a deep sleep after hours of watching me toss and turn. Turning to face him, I watch the steady rise and fall of his chest. The way his hair falls messily over his forehead, his peaceful expression—it all makes my heart ache. My mind races to places I don't want it to go, replaying the run-in encounter repeatedly. I think about everything we've shared over the past ten months, wondering where I miscalculated our relationship and Leo's intentions.

This is my friend, Vivian, he said. *What*? Where did I go wrong in thinking that we were so much more than that? I mean, I'm looking at him right now, in *my* bed. He's been in *my* bed every night for months. We've got to be more than friends. I love him. I love him so damn much, and right now, I hate that I love him. But I've been so sure that he loves me too. He not only won't say it, he won't even admit we are more than friends.

Good God! Am I just a friend with benefits to him?

From the beginning, I promised myself I wouldn't be the one to say "I love you" first. He has to cross that barrier and get there on his own. He's the one who's scared to love. He's the one who said he was working on things, wanting to try this… whatever *this* is. I didn't want Paris to be a one-time thing, but I was prepared for that to be the reality.

Am I crazy? Did I make this up?

No… *he* moved us forward. *He* wanted this.

I roll onto my back and stare at the ceiling, my mind racing and my body too wired for sleep. My fingers twist in the sheets, every muscle tense as I replay our encounters, especially those leading up to New Year's Eve and our break in January. Every sign tells me that Leo loves me. I know in my gut he feels the same way, and it hurts that he won't admit his feelings. I'm scared this is going nowhere. I'm not getting any younger, and at the end of the day, I want marriage and kids someday.

Ashley… fuck her. A gorgeous five-foot-ten blonde with long, thick hair and legs that go on for miles. She had at least two to three inches on me, even without the stilettos that made her look like a supermodel. Leo is tall, six-foot-two. With her heels, the gap was only a couple of inches.

God, she was a bitch!

I'm so annoyed that I've let some girl I don't even know get under my skin, making me second guess myself and what I have with Leo.

Are all the girls Leo brings home like her? A pretty face with a shit personality? God, it makes me question so many things… about him, about me.

But Leo has a great personality, and I believe he is a good judge of character. He's a solid, well-rounded human, aside from his many bedroom conquests, which are a result of his decision to stay single because of his fucked-up past. I can't judge him for that.

I press the palms of my hands against my forehead, gripping my hair with my fingers. Agh! I can't even judge this Ashley girl. Clearly, she was trying to get under my skin, but she's under the Leo spell. And goddamn, I can't blame her because I'm going insane from the very same man.

Giving up on sleep, I quietly slip downstairs to watch TV, hoping the mindless activity will help me relax and take my mind off things. Regardless, I have to talk to Leo tomorrow about the friend comment. I need to know what I am to him, that this is going somewhere. I can't waste my time with someone who doesn't want more. I want so much more, marriage, a family someday, and if Leo doesn't want that, then I can't be with him.

I really hope he does want that because I don't want a life without Leo. I already lost Ben, and the thought of facing another heartbreak feels unbearable. And **if it can't be us,** I think a part of me will die all over again.

I think I slept from 2:30 to 4:00 on the couch. After waking to pee, I did some yoga on the rooftop, trying to stretch away the tension, but it didn't help. I showered and got partially ready for the day.

It's 5:30 now. Leo's usually up by this time, but he fell asleep late too. Normally, I'd be up on the rooftop with my coffee, excited to sit with him as the sun rises. Instead, I sit at the dining room table, my leg bouncing, fingers tapping my Yeti mug, my stomach a nauseated mess. I stare out the window at the river. The morning sun has already risen and reflects off the water, creating a blinding effect that pours into my front window.

I take a sip of my coffee, hoping it will settle my nerves. What if he doesn't want more? What if this is all we'll ever be?

I hear Leo's footsteps as they make their way down the two flights of stairs. My ears perk like a coyote on the prowl as he pads into the kitchen. The familiar jumbling and clanking of the espresso machine, the whistling of milk being steamed—all familiar noises of our morning routine.

I debate going into the kitchen or waiting for him here. Where do I want to have this conversation that I don't want to have?

Finally, I muster the courage and head to the kitchen, my heart pounding in my chest. Leo is standing with his back to me as he prepares his coffee. The kitchen island stands between us, a barrier both physical and emotional.

"Hey," I say, my voice monotone and barely above a whisper as I step into the room.

"Hey, babe, why aren't you on the patio?" Leo kisses my cheek and settles into a stance across the kitchen island from me. "I was going to come join you up there." He studies me for a moment. "Are you upset about something?"

I sigh, resting my head in my hand, my elbow propped on the countertop.

"Come on then. Out with it."

I force my head up, meeting his gaze even though it's so damn tough right now.

"We need to talk about last night," I say. "And before you say anything, can you please do me a favor and not play dumb? I know that you know why I'm upset, and it's not because of that Ashley girl." I give him a pointed look. "Even though she was a real bitch, by the way. Great job with that one," I add snarkily.

He lets my comment hang in the air, the tension thick between us. Neither of us knowing how to start.

Finally, he breaks the silence.

"You want to discuss how I introduced you, yeah?" he asks.

I fold my arms across my chest, giving a slight nod, trying to steady myself.

"You introduced me as your friend." I elevate my voice a notch. "Your *fucking* friend. What was that? Is that all I am to you? Just another one of your friends?"

"You want to define what we are… put a label on us?" he asks cautiously.

"God, could you not patronize me with your bullshit therapist questions? I can't do that right now. I just need you to have a normal conversation with me, without the psychoanalysis. I need to know why you called me your friend. And I need to know what I am to you. Right now… just say it." I let out an audible breath of annoyance.

"Okay." He rakes a hand through his hair, his voice edged with frustration. "You want to know why I called you my friend? Because you are my goddamn friend. My *best* fucking friend, and we haven't had a discussion about what we are." He pauses, locking eyes with me. "Did you want me to introduce you as my girlfriend? Is that it? Well, we haven't talked about that, Vivian. I'm not going to assume anything. Could you imagine if you thought of me as a friend with benefits and I introduced you as my

284

girlfriend? That would put you in a really uncomfortable, awkward position."

I sigh. "Okay…" I say slowly. "That's fair." It really is. I stand there, arms folded, as if they alone can protect my feelings. "Let's have that conversation now, then." I say calmly but with intensity.

"This isn't exactly the tone I'd like for that conversation," he says.

"What's wrong with the tone? We're just talking."

"You're upset, Vivian. Let's talk about this when we're both calmer."

The way he keeps saying my full name irks me.

"I'm calm," I say, keeping my voice steady. "I feel you're trying to avoid this conversation."

"Why would I be avoiding this conversation, Vivian?"

There it is again. Not Viv, not love, not babe. Just Vivian, over and over.

"Geez, I don't know, maybe because you're too goddamn stubborn to accept that your plans might change. You're too scared to feel things and to tell me how you feel. God! Why won't you just tell me how you feel?"

"It's not that…" He pauses. "I just like things the way they are. I don't want things to change."

I scoff, my eyes flicking down to the counter. I force myself to make eye contact, feeling like I might throw-up.

"Oh, okay. We'll just keep things exactly as they are for the rest of our lives… until you get bored with me. You want me to live next door, and be your neighbor who you sleep with. Maybe we'll crash at your place sometimes, and when people ask what we are, we'll just shrug and say, 'Oh, I don't know. We're more than friends, but not boyfriend and girlfriend.' There will be no progress, no future… we'll just stay stuck in this stagnant limbo. No marriage, no kids, just this half-baked relationship with two separate homes and no real direction."

Shaking my head, I blink back the tears trying to escape. I can't believe this is what he wants—to keep me at arm's length. "That sounds like a really great fucking plan. I'm glad you have that all figured out," I say sarcastically.

He looks as if he's getting choked up, but he stays silent, which frustrates me even more.

"God, why won't you just tell me how you feel? Why can't you fucking commit to me!" I shout, my voice cracking.

Leo stands there, his shoulders slumped, eyes darting away from mine. He opens his mouth but then closes it, his silence pissing me off even more, cutting deeper than any words.

The tears come. They stream down my face, and I feel like my heart is being ripped out and stomped on.

Just when I finally let myself feel happy, when I choose to love again, the universe picks me up and fucks me with a cactus. Just like it did with Ben and Evie.

"You know," I say softly, my voice shaky. "For so long, I felt like I couldn't breathe." I pause, trying to gain my composure as the sobs come stronger. "I was gasping for breath every day… until I met you." I look at him, and he meets my eyes with a soft, loving expression. "You put the air back into my lungs, Leo. And I will forever be grateful to you for that. But right now, it feels like I'm being put in a chokehold."

"If you want to be boyfriend and girlfriend, then let's do it. Be my girlfriend, okay?"

I laugh-cry. "I don't want to be your girlfriend out of pity. I want you to *want* me to be your girlfriend."

This hurts like hell. Loving Ben, and then losing him and my daughter without a say, changed me forever. Time will never heal that wound. But with Leo, I thought maybe I could be happy again, that I could love, even with the pain of loss constantly stabbing me in the heart.

At least Ben didn't choose to leave me. I know he would have fought if he could have. But Leo? Leo's choosing this, to not let me in, to be scared… and to let me go.

"Can you please say something? This isn't like you not to communicate," I plead.

"I don't know what to say, Vivian. I tell you I like the way things are, and that's not good enough. I tell you to be my bloody girlfriend, but you want me to *want* that, and I don't know that I do. So *that's* not good enough for you either. This is all still new to me, and I'm doing my best. I don't know if I ever want to get married or have kids, and I don't know how to tell you that because I don't want to lose you. But I know you want those things. So I just don't fucking know what to say."

I take a deep breath, trying to steady myself. "God, your mother really fucked you up," I say, knowing it's too far, hitting below the belt. He flinches, his face contorting in pain, but I need to get through to him. I grip the edge of the counter, my knuckles turning white. "You know that I would rather live one life with the love that I've had and lost, than live a thousand lives with no one to love. That's not living at all." I release the counter and step back, my voice trembling with anger. "You're being a fucking coward. And I hope you figure out what the hell you want one day." I turn sharply and head for the door.

"Vivian," he calls out, moving to follow me.

I stop, my back to him as I face the door, silently pleading for him to fight for me.

He rushes to me. "Don't leave like this, babe, please."

I turn around, and he kisses me with a desperation that rips my heart in two. I pull away, tearing our lips apart, and when he doesn't say anything, I look at him with all the sadness I've buried deep over the past couple of years.

"You're so worried about losing me, Leo, but what you don't understand is that by not defining this—what we have… you just lost me." I search his eyes, my heart pounding. "People don't date a fuck buddy forever. They don't stick around for just that. Please be gone when I come back." I grab the doorknob, my hand trembling, and run toward the Riverwalk, tears blurring my vision.

In the distance, I hear Leo calling my name, his voice filled with desperation, but I keep running.

* * * * * * * * * *

I come home two hours later to find Leo gone, with a note on the table.

Viv,

Please come over when you get home so we can talk. I don't like the way things were left. I do not want to lose you.

-Leo-

Well, unfortunately, I don't see the words "I love you" on that note, or anything about him making this work, so to hell with that.

I crumple the note in my hand as a fresh wave of anger and disappointment washes over me. Tossing it in the trash, I sink into the couch, my mind racing. I need more than words on a piece of paper.

I pace the room, trying to shake off the frustration. I glance out the window toward Leo's place, hoping he'll come to his senses and come over to confess his love for me. But the street is empty.

Frantically, I start packing a bag. I have to get out of here. I stop only for a moment to find myself a flight to Salt Lake City, sobbing uncontrollably, even though I just sobbed for two hours outside. I find a flight that leaves in five hours and book it… a one-way only. I'll have to talk to Seth and my boss about working remotely for a few weeks, and I'll need to fly in at least twice over the next month to be on-site. Shit, I hope I can make this work.

I throw some clothes into the bag, my hands shaking. I don't know when I'll be back. My one-year contract is up in five weeks, and I was hoping, albeit stupidly, that Leo would ask me to move in with him, so I could let Seth have the condo back. I know he won't mind if I stay, but I'll have to start paying rent, and it's expensive. But if Leo and I are through, I can't live here. Ugh! I don't know what I'm doing. I need to get out of here and get some fresh air. I pack quickly and head to the airport three hours early.

I don't even know where I'm going to stay. I don't want to stay with my parents because my mom will be all positive, and I can't handle that shit right now.

I text Melissa.

Vivian: Hey, I have a random question… do you know if the park city home we did together is available right now or being rented? I need a place to crash for a couple of days. If you think your dad would be okay with it.

Worst-case scenario, I can go to my parents in a few days, but right now, I need to be alone.

Melissa: Hey! It's totally available! Everything ok?

Vivian: Yeah, everything is good. Just needing a Utah visit… don't want to stay at my parents. I arrive tonight.

Melissa: Do you want me to stock the fridge with some of your faves?

Vivian: No, please do not go to any trouble. Girl's night this weekend tho? Watch movies? Can you send me the entrance code and anything else I need to know?

Melissa: Yes to girls night, and incoming. Give me 5.

She sends me all the info I need to get into the house, and I feel a wave of relief. Normally, I'd be thrilled to stay at such an incredible place, but right now, it's challenging to muster any excitement. I debate whether to tell my parents I'm coming. I have to settle my emotions before I see them. I text Sarah to let her know that I'm headed her way.

* * * * *   * * * * *

The Uber driver drops me in front of the 7000 square foot home. The meticulously manicured landscape and accent lighting highlight the home beautifully. I enter the key code. The lock hums and clicks, and I step inside this stunning retreat that I helped create. I gasp, momentarily forgetting how majestic the entrance is. The furniture is fit for royalty, modern and elegant. I walk into the kitchen and fill up my water bottle from the reverse osmosis tap, savoring the brief moment of serenity.

There's a handwritten note on the counter from Melissa.

Hey, I stocked the fridge for you so you wouldn't have to go to the store tonight. I knew you'd at least need cream for your coffee in the morning.

XoXo, Melissa

It's such a simple gesture, but it brings tears to my eyes. Maybe I'm just extra emotional from the day. I think back to my argument with Leo this morning—can I even call it that? It was more me getting upset and talking too much. A wave of nausea hits me, and I feel as if I'm going to be sick. I run to the bathroom, barely making it in time, as I hurl up the dinner I ate at the airport.

I rinse my mouth and gargle some water. Needing my toothbrush, I carry my suitcase upstairs to the master suite. Opening it, I pull out my toiletries.

* * * * *   * * * * *

I slept like shit, again. I feel exhausted and foresee a long nap in my near future.

I open the fridge to grab the creamer Melissa bought, scanning it to see what options I'll have later for breakfast. I take my coffee onto the master suite balcony and sit on the luxurious outdoor patio couch. The view of pine trees and the valley below, with the sun rising, is breathtakingly beautiful. The temperature is perfect, and the only sounds are the array of birds singing, echoing through the mountains. Closing my eyes, I inhale the mountain air. I can almost taste the sap from the trees, and the scent of wildflowers singes my nose hairs.

There is *nothing* like this. The tranquility and peace of the mountains is the most healing thing for my soul.

God, this is just the escape I needed.

I contemplate my last thought, and the word escape stands out in my mind. *Escape*—the act of avoiding something unpleasant. A sudden realization hits me: although I moved to Chicago for what I believed to be the right reasons, I was actually escaping the difficulties I faced every day. And now, I'm doing the same thing again. I'm escaping the problem, the very thing I don't want to deal with.

Maybe the problem isn't all Leo. Maybe it's me too. I keep escaping from the hard things instead of facing them head-on.

Fuuuccckk. I moved to Chicago when things got too hard with Ben. I didn't talk to Leo over my Christmas break, and then again in January and February. Now I'm avoiding him again. But isn't it healthy to avoid getting hurt even more? I need to figure out how to balance protecting myself and confronting the issues at hand. I either need to rip the bandaid off and be done with Leo completely, or be okay with this nameless relationship. I can't change him; I can only do things differently.

At least I recognize my pattern of escaping now. It's not the healthiest, but I am planning to go back. I just need a minute... or a few weeks, to ground myself and come up with a plan.

I pick up my phone and look at my message notifications. I have six new text messages, all from late last night. The only ones I've opened and responded to since I left have been from Melissa and Sarah. There are three texts from Leo, one from Meredith, and two more from Melissa.

Melissa: Did you get in the house ok?

Melissa: Lmk if you need anything... girls night tonight?

I send a quick response, kicking myself for not checking in once I arrived.

Vivian: Yes! Thank you so much for stocking the fridge. You know I can't live without my cream! You're the best... tonight works for girls night. Should we get Thai?

I open Meredith's text.

Meredith: Hey—checking in on you. I spoke with Leo briefly last night... if you need to talk, I'm here.

That's sweet of Mer.

Vivian: Thanks Meredith. I'm ok. I may take you up on that in a few days.

I stare at Leo's messages, nervous to open them, knowing the effect they will have on me. I tap on them.

Leo: Viv... please come over and talk to me.

Leo: Please answer your phone... We need to talk.

He called twice last night, and I sent them to voicemail.

Leo: Babe—please talk to me. I care about you more than anything. Don't push me away.

Don't push him away? Give me a break, I can't push anyone away who won't let me in to begin with. I ponder what to say. I don't want to ignore him completely. I can't run from my problems more than I already have. I have to face them eventually.

Vivian: Hey... I got your messages. I just need some time to think.

I hesitate before pressing send, my thumb hovering over the keyboard. I want to be honest with him, but is this too vague? I delete it and start typing again.

> **Vivian:** I care about you too, but I need to know you're willing to let me in Completely. I need to know that you're open to moving forward with me—not just staying where we are. I'm in Utah for now. I don't know when I'm coming back.

I take a deep breath and press send. The little dots indicating he's typing appear almost immediately. My heart races as I wait for his response.

> **Leo:** I know. I want you to have the clarity you need … I wish you wouldn't have taken off before talking to me. When do you come home?

Jesus.

He wants me to have clarity, but obviously can't give it to me. We keep hitting the same nail on the head over and over—he wants me to understand, but he won't give me what I need to get there. I ignore that, only answering his question.

> **Vivian:** Don't know when I'm coming back, could be a few weeks, or a few months. I may not come back at all… Utah is my home. Chicago was only ever a temporary move.

The dots appear again as he continues to type.

> **Leo:** I wish I could promise you everything you deserve right now. Please don't run away… Come back, you have a life here.

> **Vivian:** People don't make major life decisions and permanent moves for a fuck-buddy, Leo. That's clearly all I am to you when it comes down to it.

Shit. I know that was an immature comment, but I sent it anyway.

> **Leo:** God, you are so much more than that to me. I know I've been an idiot, and I've made mistakes, but I need you to understand that my feelings for you are real. You're not just a 'fuck-buddy' to me. You're everything. You were right when you said what you did about my mum. I've built walls to protect myself, and they're keeping me from fully being with you. I don't know how to break them down… But I'm trying.

Gah! I'm exasperated. I like his message, acknowledging it without engaging further. I switch my phone to airplane mode and slam it down on the table, my fingers trembling with frustration. I don't have the mental capacity to deal with this right now.

I'm not asking for a ring, for crying out loud. Just some sign that there's a future for us. A glimpse of stability in this venture of ours. I take a sip of my coffee, mulling over these texts. The coffee tastes bitter, sending a wave of nausea through me. Ugh. Shutting my eyes, I breathe in deeply and slowly until it passes. My coffee no longer seems appealing, which is not normal for me. Never have I not wanted coffee in the morning, except for when I was first pregnant with Evie.

Oh my God.

Oh my God, oh my God, oh my God.

A wave of anxiety crashes over me as I remember my birthday and the unused condom. I remember Leo and me talking about getting Plan B, but we were so drunk we completely forgot. I pull up my calendar on my phone, checking the start date of my last period and counting twenty-six days from then. My period should have arrived six days ago, but my cycle can be unpredictable, sometimes coming at twenty-one days or thirty-six days.

A knot tightens in my stomach as the nausea intensifies.

* * * * * * * * * *

Thirty minutes later, I sit on the toilet, staring at the plus symbol on the pregnancy test. My hands shake, nearly dropping the stick. I clutch it tighter as my mind races. The emotions hit me all at once, and I start ugly crying, sobbing uncontrollably for the next twenty minutes. I cradle my head in my hands, my nose runny and stuffy at the same time, while the heavy pressure on my chest makes it feel impossible to breathe. Guilt washes over me. I would never not want a baby. After all the loss I've experienced, a baby is something I could only hope for, could only dream of. I'm not crying because I'm pregnant—I'm crying because of the unpredictability of the future. I don't want my child to have a baby-daddy. That's not what I would choose.

I know I have to tell Leo, but knowing him, he'll be all stoic, doing the right thing, which is great, except I don't want him to try to love me out of obligation. I want him to choose me, to want this life with me and our child.

Fuck. Fuck. Fuck.

Chapter 32

LEO

Thursday, June 27

Five Days Later

I sit on my couch, whiskey in one hand, phone in the other, staring at the screen. Five days ago, I sent the most vulnerable text of my life, and it still sits there, liked and read but unanswered.

I can't believe she went to Utah. She just up and left without a word, and now she won't respond to my message.

I'm fucking miserable without her, and it hurts that she won't respond to my texts or answer my calls. But what really kills me is knowing it's my fault. The pain festers like salt in an open wound, feeding all my life-long fears and fueling them with validation. She left me, just like everyone else I've cared for more than a friend.

I'm angry for thinking I could have what my brother Andrew has. I'm angry for trusting myself enough to let Vivian believe I'd changed enough to make her happy, only to cause her pain and suffering—two things I'd never want to inflict on anyone, especially her.

I debate texting again, but what's the point if she won't answer?

I finish my drink and head to the kitchen for more.

What the fuck am I doing?

It's a Thursday, and I don't drink on Thursdays. I run my hands through my hair, groaning. Alcohol never solved anyone's problems. I put my glass in the sink and the whiskey in the cupboard, knowing I won't find the answers in a bottle.

* * * * * * * * * *

Saturday, July 9

One Week Later

The Fourth of July came and went. Mer invited me to join her and Piper, but I wasn't up for it. I stayed home, thinking about Vivian—like I always do—and how fucking miserable I am without her. I ended the night jerking off to thoughts of her, then pathetically fell asleep watching *Love Island* because it makes me happily depressed to watch something Vivian loves.

It's 10:00 PM, and I can't sit here and wallow anymore. It's stifling in my house, and all I want is to be in Vivian's house, in her bed… with her.

Fuck, I need some fresh air. I put on my shoes and head outside, walking off the claustrophobia.

I wind up at a bar. A drink and some fresh air will do me good. I'm on the patio with a Guinness on tap, leaning my arms against the railing when Ashley stands next to me.

God, I really do run into her everywhere.

It's no surprise, though; we frequent the same places, living the same type of lifestyle. We've been together more times than I can count, falling into bed when no one else catches our eye.

"Hey," she says, nudging me. "You here alone?" She turns to lean her back against the rail, crossing her arms—pushing her tits together. My eyes wander to them out of habit, sending a spark of lust through me as my dick starts to harden.

"Yeah, I'm here alone," I say somberly, my throat dry.

"You seem off," she says, pursing her lips. "You okay?"

I half-heartedly smile and scoff. "I'm fine… I will be, anyway." I take a sip of my beer, savoring the cold, bitter taste as it slides down my throat, momentarily distracting me from the chaos in my mind.

"You know I can help with that, right?" she says flirtatiously, eyeing me up and down as she strokes my arm.

It feels good… Ashley touching me. For a moment, it takes the pain away. She looks hot, and I know that taking her back to my place, kissing her, touching her, and feeling her body against mine would feel incredible right now. It would be so easy to revert to my old ways, to take her home and fuck her.

She hesitates, calculating her next move as I stay silent. I stare at her, and she leans in to kiss me. Her lips press against mine, and her touch sends a jolt through me. The warmth of her hand on my skin, her soft lips on mine, ignite a familiar, almost automatic response as my dick starts to harden. Jesus, it feels so good. Ashley's always been a great kisser.

But as soon as I start to kiss her back, Vivian's face flashes in my mind—the way she laughs, her sweet smile, the way she makes me feel. A wave of guilt crashes over me, and I pull away abruptly.

Ashley looks at me, confused and slightly breathless. "What's wrong?"

I take a step back, running a hand through my hair. "I can't do this," I say, my voice shaky. "There's someone else. Someone I care about too much to mess it up." It's a sentence I've never said in my life, and it shocks even me as I say it.

She scowls. "Come on, we're just kissing. There's no one else here tonight—she'll never know."

"But I'll know." I hold her stare.

Ashley rolls her eyes. "It's not that big of a deal." She strokes my arm. "You really want to be with someone who's going to take away your freedom? You're not the monogamous type, Leo, even you know that. You're too sexy and too good in bed to be tied down to one person." She grins, her hands finding their way behind my neck, playing with the short waves at the back of my hair, just as Vivian does. "Are you sure? Because you look rather lonely to me."

"I'm sure. I'm definitely sure," I repeat, trying to convince myself. Because holy shit, I'm turned on, and I'm so fucking lonely.

"It's that girl you were with a few weeks ago, isn't it?" she asks pointedly.

I sigh. "Yes… her name is Vivian. I'm sorry, Ashley, I shouldn't have kissed you." I gently remove her hands from around my neck and step back, folding my arms.

"It's fine." She frowns, a mix of annoyance and resignation in her expression. "I'm just surprised is all. Never thought anyone would be able to take *you* off the market." She scoffs. "I guess I've gotta give props to the girl who has." She pats my arm, then rolls her eyes and adds with a smirk, "Looks like someone's getting pussy whipped."

Without another word, she turns and walks away, leaving me dumbfounded by the entire encounter.

I just turned down sex with a gorgeous woman who I already know is a good lay. I felt guilty when I kissed her, a feeling I never experience when it comes to sex. Goddammit, I *am* pussy-whipped, I don't even know what to do with myself, and over a woman who won't return my texts. A woman who wants to get married and have babies. I need to find a way to get over her. Maybe I should fuck Ashley; that might help. But I can't until I've talked to Vivian, not until I've closed that door. And who knows when that will be? I guess I'm to remain celibate until she decides to pick up her damn phone.

* * * * * * * * * *

Wednesday, July 17

Eleven Days Later

My last couple of the evening walk out, leaving me in the silence of my office, the white noise from the sound machines in the hallways trickling in.

I check my phone and see I have a text from Sarah.

I texted Vivian again a week ago, asking how she was doing, and she responded with *I'm ok*. She didn't proceed to ask me how I was or give me anything else. I felt it was best to leave it be and let her have her space, so I decided to text Sarah earlier, and ask about her.

Sarah: Hey Leo, I'm not gonna lie, I've seen her worse… but I've also seen her better. It's not my place to really talk to you about her, but I will say that I know she misses you. I'm glad you reached out to me. Hope you're doing ok too.

I take a deep breath and rub my forehead. When is she going to come back? I need her in my life, and if I can't have her in the capacity I want her, then I need to at least have closure.

Leo: Thanks Sarah. Please tell her that I miss her.

Sarah: I will.

Meredith walks into my office and stands before me.

"Hey Mer, what's up?"

"Stand up," she demands.

"Why?"

"Just do it," she says impatiently.

I stand, and she directs me to the couch, pushing me to sit down.

"What are you doing?" I ask, confused.

She sits in my chair, pulling it closer in front of me, and places her drink on the coffee table.

"Okay… so since I'm your friend, I'm not going to charge you for this therapy session," she states matter-of-factly, "but you will owe me for helping you clean up the mess that is your life," she says seriously, with a smile.

"Meeerrr," I groan, "not this again." I begin to stand.

"Sit your ass down, Leo Weston. You can get up when I tell you to; we're not even close to being finished here." She shakes her head at me, disappointment evident in her eyes.

I slump back onto the couch, running a hand through my hair in frustration. "What do you want from me? Do you want me to admit that I fucked up? Fine, I fucked up. I fucked up big! It's too late; I tried the therapy thing. We did EMDR, it didn't work, okay? I tried. It turns out that I'm not meant for lifelong monogamous relationships."

"That's such bullshit. How did you try?"

"What do you mean, how did I try?" I snap, feeling my irritation rise. She knows how to get under my skin, and it's working. "I tried my damndest. I stopped seeing other women. I spent every night with Vivian for two months. I devoted all my spare time to her, and in the end, it wasn't good enough."

Meredith crosses a leg, her eyes boring into mine with a mix of frustration and determination. "Oh, I see. That clarifies everything for me. So let me get this straight. You fell in love with Vivian, but you did everything you could to keep her at arm's length. You had your cake and ate it too, stroking your ego, getting all the sex you wanted with the woman you wanted to be with. All while filling your cup by spending time with your best friend because that's how you wanted to spend your time."

She takes a deep breath, her voice rising with each word. "And then, when it came down to giving Vivian something, just a simple label, a definition of what you already were, giving her hope for a future, you pulled away because you're a fucking pussy."

I flinch, letting that sink in as she continues her lecture.

"You let your fear of losing her overtake any hope of things working out, and you lost her anyway because of your cowardice. Did I miss anything?" She shakes her head, her expression a mix of disappointment and sadness. "You didn't just lose her. You pushed her away, and now you're here, wondering why she won't let you back in. For God's sake, figure out what you really want and stop hiding behind your fears. Otherwise, you'll lose the best thing that ever happened to you."

Her tone softens as she stands to move closer, sitting on the coffee table in front of me, and placing a hand on my arm. "Look, I know things from your past make it hard. It's difficult to let go of what you think you wanted. But Leo, I truly believe that's not what's holding you back anymore. You're standing in your own way because you haven't allowed yourself the time or grace to reevaluate what you want. You're stubborn, and it's okay to want something different now."

She pauses, searching my eyes. "Everyone can see how much you've loved Vivian for months. From the moment you met her, something changed. You need to think about your future… what it could look like with Vivian in it. What if it actually worked? What if you were happy? What if taking the risk led to something amazing? If you believe it's worth it, go after her. Fight for her. Show her how much you love her. Prove to her that she can trust you."

Meredith's words hit me like a punch to the gut, leaving me reeling. I look down, unable to make eye contact, knowing she's right.

I do love Vivian. I've known that for a while now. What the hell am I doing?

"What is it that you're *actually* afraid of?" Meredith asks.

I try to pinpoint the answer to her question and realize it's not what I thought it was.

"I've always believed I'm afraid to lose someone I love again." I shake my head, leaning forward with my elbows on my knees. "But that's not it anymore." I look at her, feeling the weight of my words. "I'm afraid I'll fail at loving her the way she needs to be loved, the way she deserves to be loved… the way Ben loved her." I sit up, my voice heavy with exhaustion. "What if I can't make her happy? What if I fuck it all up five years down the road? What if…" I trail off, slouching down and resting my head on the back of the couch.

"What if you don't?" she asks, her eyes wide. "What if you don't fail?"

"I don't know." I shift in my seat. "I've never really considered that as a possibility. When I look to the future, I can't see myself being happy with Vivian; my thoughts always show me failing, hurting her, and ruining everything."

Meredith pats my leg, her expression softening. She leans forward slightly, her eyes locking onto mine with an intensity that makes it impossible to look away. "Leo, you're a psychologist. What would you tell your clients in this situation?"

I pause, her question hanging in the air. What would I tell my clients? I'd ask them to confront their fears, to challenge their negative beliefs. I'd tell them that self-sabotage is a cycle that can be broken. I'd tell them they deserve to be happy. Why can't I follow my own advice?

She takes a deep breath. "Look, I don't want to lecture you all night. You've succeeded in every other aspect of your life. Why not this? If you want something bad enough, you'll find a way to get it." She moves to stand, pausing at the door. "And Leo, if you decide to bet on yourself, don't take no for an answer. I like Vivian." She smiles wide. "By the way, are we still on for dinner Friday night?"

"Yeah, of course," I reply, managing a small smile.

"Great. I'll see you then," she says, and walks out.

As the door closes behind her, her words echo in my mind. What would I tell my clients? Maybe it's time I start taking my own advice.

When I get home, I decide to go for a run to clear my head. The pounding of the pavement and the warm summer breeze melt away some of the stress built up over the past week.

Running along the Riverwalk, I pass the spot where I scared the living hell out of Vivian. I laugh to myself as I think of her yelling at me and shoving me, the fear in her eyes, and how they softened as she melted into me when she realized it was me.

God, my life wasn't as great as I thought it was before she came into it. Everything has been more exciting, more fun, and full of laughs since I met her.

I think of the first night we met, the witty banter we shared. I think of her beautiful smile and contagious laugh, and the way she playfully nudges me when she's teasing. I think of the way my body responds when she looks at me or touches me. I think of her confessions and her tears, the way she's clung to me when she's sad, and how she's trusted me with the most vulnerable parts of herself.

I think of our morning coffee dates, our nights spent at Craft's. I think of her dedication to her job and the way she challenges me, making me want to be a better man. I think of Paris… and the first time we had sex.

Jesus Christ, I love this woman so bloody much.

For the first time in my life, my fear of not having her is greater than any other fear I've ever had—the realization hits me like a ton of bricks—and what I want more than anything is her. I want her more than any one-night stand. I want her more than the freedom I've always enjoyed as a bachelor. I want her more than the safety and predictability of being single.

I imagine my life with Vivian, and it's a stark contrast to the single-bachelor existence I've always envisioned. Instead, I picture Vivian in my home, in my bed. I envision her greeting me with a kiss after a long day, our vacations together, family dinners… maybe even starting a family of our own. The cool air stings my eyes, and they begin to glisten. My vision blurs as a profound sense of calm washes over me.

What I need to do is show her that I'm committed to being there, supporting her, and growing together, one day at a time. It's not just about her trusting me to move forward; I need to trust her too.

I slow to a walk, catching my breath as my heart races. I pull up my Delta app and check flights to Salt Lake City. There are no flights after 7:30 PM on Friday, and my last lecture ends at 7:00. I check Saturday and find an early flight that arrives around 10:30 AM. I book it, not having a solid plan yet but hoping I can come up with one in the next few days.

I'm unsure about what the future holds or if I can ever commit to marriage, but I can commit to being with Vivian, to staying loyal to her. I hope that will be enough because I fucking miss her. I'll do anything to get her back. She makes me happy… I love her.

I text Sarah again, knowing I'll need her help if I have any hope of another chance with Vivian.

Chapter 33

VIVIAN

Two Days Later

My watch vibrates, drawing my attention to the message from Leo that flashes on the screen. I press the side button to clear it, then pick up my phone.

"Sorry," I apologize, distracted. "Leo just texted me again." He's been sending these sweet, persistent texts over the past few days, and they're making it really hard for me to stay mad at him.

"Well, what does it say?" Sarah asks.

We're on the patio of *The Spur Bar and Grill*, enjoying drinks and live music. Sarah is sipping on margaritas while I'm sticking to sparkling water.

> **Leo:** Do you remember how Jacob falls for the girl from the bar, at the end of "Crazy, Stupid, Love"? And how I said that would never be me?... It turns out I was wrong.

A smile tugs at my lips as I read his message. I turn my phone toward Sarah so she can see.

"Ahhh, that's sweet," she says, taking a thoughtful sip of her margarita. "What are you going to say back?"

I sigh. "I don't know. It's not like a few text messages mean he's going to commit to me," I say, resting my elbow on the tabletop and propping my chin on my fist.

"What do you want to say?"

"I want to tell him to either go to hell or fuck off," I say with a quiet laugh. "But I also want to tell him that I love him and that I miss him…" I trail off, my mood turning somber.

"Well," she says laughing, "I guess you could say all of those things. Nothing wrong with being honest."

"I know. I just don't want to give him anything until I'm clear on his intentions."

"What do you think they are?"

"I'm not sure. It feels like he wants me to come back so we can fall into the same dysfunctional pattern we've had for months—the endless push and pull of Vivian and Leo." I shake my head, leaning back and crossing my arms. "I think he wants more, but will struggle to commit. I feel he loves me, but I don't know if leaving Utah to go back to Chicago will change anything," I say quietly. "And that terrifies me."

She looks at me with concern. "That's tough… especially given your current situation."

I put my phone away. "I'll figure out what to say later," I say with a smile. "I don't want to be distracted while I'm with you."

The music drifts onto the balcony from inside, and the lights on Main Street shimmer in the night. "I don't mind talking about it." Sarah reaches across the table and takes my hand in hers, giving it a reassuring squeeze. "It's going to work out. Everything's going to be okay."

Right… because that's how my life usually goes.

I say goodnight to Sarah as she heads into one of the guest suites. The house, a luxury ski home, has four large master suites, two with balconies and hot tubs. Since Sarah had been drinking, she's staying over. I wouldn't feel right sending her down the canyon late at night, for obvious reasons.

I sit cross-legged on my bed and open my phone, staring at the message from Leo. It's almost midnight in Chicago, and I debate waiting until morning to respond, but I don't want to.

Vivian: Really? Who's the lucky girl… do I know her?

Smiling, I send the message, not expecting a reply until morning. I leave my phone on the bed and brush my teeth.

I climb into bed and turn off the lights with the remote on the nightstand. As I reach for my phone to plug it in, it lights up.

Leo: Hmm. I don't think you do. You'd like her though, she's about your height, dark brown hair… come to think of it, she reminds me of you. She's witty, cool as can be, and sexy as hell.

Vivian: Is that right? Well I know how things end in the movie… what's your ending look like?

Leo: They live happily ever after, love. :-)

I shake my head, a smile tugging at my lips as my heart skips a beat. Damn him.

Vivian: Good night Leo.

I set my phone on the charger and roll over, nestling my head into the pillow. Tonight feels better than it has in a while. For the first time in weeks, I allow myself to feel hopeful, imagining a future where maybe, just maybe, Leo and I could find that happy ending.

* * * * *　* * * * *

The next morning

"Do you think you'll move back? Raise the baby here?" Sarah asks, sipping her coffee.

We're on the balcony of her room, which faces the back of the mountain, making it feel like you're in the woods. I watch a doe and her two fawns grazing a short distance away, their ears twitching occasionally.

"I don't know. I'd like to be near my mom and dad, but I do like Chicago. Honestly, it depends on Leo. I wouldn't move away if he wanted to be actively involved." As I say it, I realize he will want to be, based on our conversation during that walk. "I feel stuck."

"Do you think he'd ever move here?"

I consider the question for a moment. "I'm not sure; I haven't really thought about that as an option," I admit honestly. I purse my lips, a scowl forming. Maybe he *could* move here.

I start to envision what my life might look like, and a pang of sadness washes over me as I realize that my future might not include a husband to share it with. I'm in love with someone who won't commit, and I can't fully separate from him because we're now connected through my pregnancy. I thought things were complicated enough before, being a widow, but now it feels like an absolute clusterfuck.

For a moment, I allow myself to picture us in the same home, raising kids together, and a warm happiness washes over me. I find myself teary-eyed as I sip my coffee, forcing it down despite its bitter taste. It still doesn't taste great, but I don't want to face the caffeine headache that comes with cutting it out entirely. I stick to a small cup each morning, mindful not to overdo it for the baby's sake.

A wave of nausea hits me, and I rush inside to the bathroom in Sarah's suite—I know I won't make it to mine. I vomit into the toilet, the tears that had already pooled now streaming down my cheeks. I hate throwing up with a passion and definitely don't do it gracefully. Hoping the nausea subsides soon, I rinse my face with cold water, swish and gargle some mouth rinse, and pat my face dry before rejoining Sarah outside.

"Have you told your mom yet?" Sarah asks as I sit down. The sun is starting to reach the corners of the deck, and I know the sweatshirt I'm wearing will be too warm in the next twenty minutes.

"No, not yet. I want to wait until I have a bit more clarity," I say.

Sarah is the only one who knows about the pregnancy right now. I have my first appointment in a week and a half, and I'd like my mom to be there, so I might have to tell her by then. I could bring Sarah, and I'd love for her to be there with me, but I might really need my mom's support.

"When do you plan to tell Leo?" Sarah asks, her brow furrowed in concern.

"Ugh, I don't know," I reply, rubbing my temples. "Soon? I have to go to Chicago in a week for work, and I'd rather do it in person. I could tell him over lunch."

Sarah nods thoughtfully. "That sounds like a good plan."

I take a deep breath and shift my gaze, then ask, "Are you and Ryan trying yet?" I remember her mentioning at my birthday party that they were considering starting a family soon, which makes sense given Ryan's age.

"Yes!" Sarah says, her eyes sparkling. "We're officially trying, as of two weeks ago. Wouldn't it be amazing if we both had babies within a few months of each other?"

"Yeah, that would be really great," I agree, smiling at the thought.

We chat more, but as the sun rises and warms the deck, the brisk mountain morning air starts to fade, leaving me feeling uncomfortably hot, and killing the vibe.

* * * * *   * * * * *

After breakfast, Sarah gathers her things into her overnight bag. I walk her outside, where the sun is blazing hot now. We share a hug goodbye, and I remind her to text me when she gets home, as I'm always worried about her drive.

Once Sarah leaves, I decide to start my day with a Peloton ride. I push through a challenging workout, the sweat and endorphins clearing my mind. Feeling energized, I head to the shower and dry my hair while pondering how to spend my Saturday. I know I have a few hours of work to catch up on, so I grab my laptop and head to the office. The room has a floor-to-ceiling window that offers stunning views and floods the space with natural light. I could get used to living here, but I remind myself that this is only a temporary escape.

Fifteen minutes into my work, the familiar buzz of my phone breaks my concentration. It's a text from Leo.

Leo: Good morning, love. What are you up to today?

I scowl at the phone, unsure of what to do with this. This text is different from the cutesy messages he's been sending lately; it feels normal, like we're just good friends and no time has passed.

Does he think we can simply pick up where we left off or become more by exchanging texts?

I guess it's technically my fault for the lack of communication since I left and haven't answered his calls. That realization stings a bit.

Vivian: Just getting some work done.

There. Simple and to the point.

Leo: Are you home?

Vivian: Yes.

Leo: Could you do me a favor?

Is there a more vague question?

Vivian: I don't know… I guess it depends on what it is.

I type it irritably.

Leo: Can you take a few minutes to listen to a song? I picked it carefully for you from one of your favorite artists. I know music speaks to you and can define moments in your life. I want you to have a defining moment right now, a memory that's sparked every time you hear this song. It conveys what I want to say to you. I'd sing it for you, but that would ruin the effect I want it to have.

He adds a grimacing face emoji at the end, which makes me smile slightly.

I sigh. Is there any harm in agreeing to do this? It's three minutes of my time, and it seems important to him.

Vivian: Okay…

He sends a link to a James Arthur song, one of my favorites. I click on it because I agreed to listen right now, even though I already know the song by heart.

I push play on "Say You Won't Let Go," and by the first chorus, I'm in tears. Waves of emotion rush over me as he sings about knowing his love but hiding it out of fear, needing someone but never showing it, and wanting to stay together until we're old.

As the song continues, I'm hit with a mix of emotions as he sings about waking up to breakfast in bed, bringing coffee with a kiss, and the simple joy of taking the kids to school.

I imagine a life filled with love and gratitude, even in the small, everyday moments. A lump forms in my throat as I picture us growing old side by side, supporting each other through everything. Tears stream down my face as I imagine that kind of love, hoping against hope that it's not just a dream or something that was once had, but is now gone forever.

The song ends, and I stare at the lyrics on my phone, reading them over and over, trying to comprehend what this means. Is this Leo's way of telling me he loves me? Is he promising me these things? Or is it just a song that reminded him of us, without him being able to say these things or commit? My phone vibrates.

Leo: Did you listen to the song?

Vivian: Yes. It's a beautiful song… one of my favorites.

Leo: Good…

Good? What the hell?

Leo: Now will you come and answer the door so I can show you what those lyrics truly mean?

A laugh escapes my lips as I practically run out of the office and down the stairs, wiping at my tears as I go. Swinging the door open, I find Leo standing there, looking incredible as he always does.

A soft smile lies on his face. "Hey, Viv," he says coolly, with a hand in his pocket.

I let out a breathy "hi", trying to hide the new wave of emotion hitting me all at once. Pregnancy making everything more difficult.

"God, I've missed you," he sighs, his voice thick with emotion. "I've been so bloody stupid. This past month without you has been torture." He looks down, shifting his weight, trying to pull himself together. When he meets my eyes again, they're glassy with unshed tears. "I missed your smile… and your laugh… the way your eyes light up when you're excited."

He takes a shaky breath, his gaze locking onto mine. "I love you, Vivian. I love the way you're always thinking of others, how you come up with your own words or phrases, your obsessive organization, and how you take over my kitchen like it's yours. I love your wit, your humor, your stubborn determination… you're fucking incredible. I love everything about you. And I've felt this way for a long time."

He laughs softly, a hint of vulnerability in his eyes. "I'm not even sure when I fell in love with you. I just did. Somewhere between you giving me shit, our morning coffee chats, hearing you laugh, watching you sleep…"

He pauses, taking a step closer. "And making love to you," he takes another step, closing the gap between us until I feel the heat of his body merge with mine. "Because that's what it's been. In Paris… that wasn't just sex for me. That was the first time I've ever really made love to someone, and I'll never forget that night as long as I live."

Tears of joy stream down my cheeks. He takes my hands in his, looking deeply into my eyes.

"I love you, Vivian Walker. This past month has shown me just how much you mean to me. I can't promise I'll be the perfect partner or that I'll want to get married."

My heart sinks at those words.

"But I can promise I'll be here for you, that I'll love you every step of the way, that I'll try, and that I'm committed to you. Whether you're my girlfriend, my life partner, or someday, my wife—none of those labels matter to me. What matters is that you're beside me in life until I take my last fucking breath."

He searches my eyes as he waits for me to respond, toying with my fingers, stroking them gently. I'm so overwhelmed that I can't find the words. He said he loves me. I knew he did, but hearing him say it changes everything. He's confronting his past, moving forward, and he's ready to commit to being with me.

He waits, patient and hopeful, looking for anything, an answer, a confession, a nod… something.

The words are stuck in my throat, so I answer him the only way I can right now. I lean in and kiss him, pouring all my feelings into it. His lips are warm and soft, responding with a gentle intensity that speaks volumes. And it feels so damn good. The kiss deepens, and I wrap my arms around his neck, giving him everything I have. The connection between us solidifies, a silent promise that we we'll face whatever comes together.

I pull back, cupping his face in my hands. "I love you too. God, I love you so much!"

We kiss for several minutes, lost in the moment and each other's tender touches. His hands slide up my back as I thread my fingers through his hair, the silky strands slipping between them. He pulls back just enough to press a kiss to my forehead before resting his forehead against mine, sharing breath like we've done dozens of times before. I close my eyes, savoring the moment—the rhythm of his breathing, the lingering scent of his cologne, the soft stroke of his thumb against my cheek. I never want to forget this.

"Viv," he says softly, "will you move in with me?"

I simply nod. I don't open my eyes, I don't speak, I don't look at him, afraid to find this is all a dream. All I can do is just be in this moment, and there is nothing I want more than to move in with him.

I nod again, more urgently, as my lips search for his, my eyes still closed. They find them, and his tongue teases mine as I welcome it into my mouth.

I break our kiss, grabbing his hand to lead him to my bedroom, where I want to give myself to him completely.

"Come here." I say, my voice soft and raw.

I lead him up the stairs and down the hallway. Once inside, I turn to face him, my heart pounding with anticipation.

Damn, it's been way too long.

Leo gently brushes a lock of hair from my face, his fingers trailing softly along my cheek. "You're so beautiful," he whispers, his eyes filled with adoration.

I smile, feeling a warmth spread through me. "I love you," I say, my voice barely a whisper.

"I love you too."

"Show me," I challenge.

His hands move to my waist, sliding under the hem of my shirt, pulling me closer. Our bodies press together, and I melt into him. His lips find mine again, and I fist his shirt in my hands to steady myself.

Leo's hands glide lower, caressing my ass as he pulls me even closer. My stomach does flips, and I can already feel that tingling numbness building between my thighs. I raise my arms, and he pulls my shirt over my head, slowly undressing me. He presses tender kisses all over my body between each article of clothing that's shed, his eyes never leaving mine, as if he's committing every moment to memory. I do the same, pulling his shirt over his head and feeling the smooth skin beneath my fingertips, appreciating every detail of him.

We move to the bed and he lays me down gently, his lips never straying far from mine. His kisses travel down my neck, each one lingering and sweet. His hands explore every curve of my body with a reverence that makes me feel cherished and loved.

As his hands slide lower, his breath hovers hot against my ear. "Missed feeling you like this," he murmurs, his voice rough with desire. His fingers trail down my stomach, a slow, deliberate glide that has my breath catching.

When he reaches my thighs, he doesn't rush. Instead, he lingers, brushing just close enough to drive me crazy—the pulsing between my legs intensifying. His movements are deliberate and teasing, his fingertips ghosting over my skin until I'm aching for him. I gasp, subconsciously arching toward him, silently begging for more.

Leo leans into my ear. "Are you wet, love?" His voice carries a hint of cockiness.

I nod, squeezing my eyes shut, the throbbing ache too strong for words.

"Tell me how wet you are," he says, his tone dark and commanding. That *sexy fucking voice* alone is enough to make me lose all control.

"I'm wet. I'm so wet for you, babe," I manage, breathless.

He continues to tease, drawing it out. His fingers glide close to where I need them, only to pull away as he plants slow, sensual kisses on my skin.

"How bad do you want it?" he murmurs.

I can't take the torture anymore. I grab his hand and guide it toward the dull throb. His fingers brush the top of my slit and stop.

I let out a frustrated groan.

"Tell me how bad you want it." My eyes are closed, but I know he's smirking—enjoying this slow torture while I squirm—building my desire until I'm desperate and begging for him.

"I want it so bad. I want you, babe. Please, touch me. Give it to me." I'm a mess of submissiveness, my voice barely more than a whisper.

I slide my thighs together, desperate for some friction. He chuckles softly, a deep, wicked sound, before his fingers slip exactly where I need them, pressing into me with just the right amount of pressure.

"God," I hiss.

"Fuck, you're soaked." he whispers, his lips grazing my neck as his fingers begin a rhythm that has my body instantly responding, pulsing with need.

Every movement is steady and skilled, designed to keep me trembling beneath him, desperate for release. His muscles tense against me as he takes his time, stretching the moment out until all I can think about is him and the pleasure he's pulling from my body.

"Fuck me," I say, with a raw urgency in my voice, pulling him closer. "Leo, I want you inside of me."

I open my legs wide for him as he nestles between them. His tanned, muscular build presses against me, every ridge and contour of his body ignites a fire within me. I surrender completely to him, losing myself in the moment.

When he finally slides into me, our bodies align perfectly. He takes his time, each thrust slow and purposeful, every kiss sending a delicious burn to my core. His eyes lock on mine, filled with so much emotion that my heart swells.

I can't resist rolling us over, needing to take control, to feel the intensity build under my lead. As I ride him, the rhythm is slow, every motion driving us deeper into that sweet, intimate connection. He sits up, leaning against the bed, angling himself just how I need. The pleasure coils tighter as I control the pace, speeding up as our bodies moves in perfect sync. His hands grip my hips, guiding me faster, pushing us closer to the edge.

When we finally reach that peak together, it's not just a physical release but an emotional surrender. I dig my nails into his back. "God," I moan as Leo curses. Our bodies tremble and lock together, holding on as if it's the only thing that matters.

We cling to each other, the pleasure crashing over us in waves, leaving us panting and intertwined—my love deepening for him with every heartbeat.

Afterward, he holds me close, our bodies still entwined. He kisses the top of my head, and I look up at him, my heart full.

"I've never felt this way before," he whispers. "I know you have with Ben, but for me... this... I've never felt this, Viv."

Damn.

"It's feels so good to hear that," I say, pressing my lips to his. "It's different, though," I say with unwavering certainty. "I love both of you... in distinct and unique ways. What I feel for you is its own kind of special, and I never want you to think I love you any less than I loved Ben. It's different, but just as real."

I loved Ben wholeheartedly. We had passion and chemistry and were best friends, just like me and Leo. I needed to know this was possible, that I could have both... just as Leo told me months ago. He told me that I didn't have to let go of my past to embrace my future. And now, lying here with him, I believe it. I feel the love I have for Ben in the back of my mind, and I feel this incredibly intense love for Leo at the forefront, and I'm overwhelmed with a bittersweet joy.

As I lie in Leo's arms, his skin against mine, I know that we're starting a new chapter together. One filled with hope, love, and endless possibilities.

Chapter 34

LEO

Her words strike deep, resonating with an intensity that leaves me overwhelmed. We lie in silence for several minutes as I stroke my fingers along her back, drawing lines and tracing circles over her skin.

She breaks the quiet, "Tell me something," she murmurs into the stillness.

"What kind of something?" I ask, my voice reverberating through my chest where her head rests.

"What took you so long?" she asks, shifting her weight, pushing up on her elbow, and turning her body to look at me.

My breathing becomes shallow as I become fixated on her. She now lies on her stomach, leaning on her elbows, her tits pressed together. Her hair's a beautiful mess that screams *I just got fucked.* Her bright-green eyes shine intensely as they stare into mine. Her lips are slightly swollen, making them even more desirable.

Damn. I can't believe she agreed to move in with me, that she's allowing me to love her.

She furrows her brows. "What are you thinking? Why are you staring at me like that?" A smile forms as she lets her head hang for a moment, laughing softly before looking back at me.

"I'm thinking I'm the luckiest fucking guy in the world," I say, "and I can't believe you love me."

"Of course I love you, Leo. I've loved you for so long," she says, leaning in to kiss me gently on the lips.

"Because I'm a jackass," I admit when she pulls back.

She gives me a confused look.

"That's why it took me so long, Viv. Because I'm a jackass. But I became so afraid to not have you in my life that nothing else mattered. The moment I realized how much I loved you, I booked a flight immediately."

She smiles, combing her fingers through the ends of her hair.

"Now, you tell me something," I say.

"Hmmm," she hums as she lowers onto her side. Her head rests on her pillow, and I turn so that we're face to face.

"Remember my birthday party?" she asks.

"Of course."

"Remember when we did it in the bathroom?"

"How could I forget?

She purses her lips. "But do you really remember? Because we were both pretty drunk…"

"Yeah, I have a pretty clear memory of what took place. You were looking sexy as fuck, and I took you up against the bathroom door," I say with a smirk, recalling the heated moment.

One of her hands rests underneath the pillow while the other takes mine and moves it toward her stomach. She splays my hand flat on her belly and rests her hand on top of mine.

"Well, you dropped the condom, and we were going to get the morning after pill, but we forgot." She looks down at our hands and then into my eyes. "I'm pregnant," she whispers, a tiny smile forming on her lips.

Whoa.

I stare at her, my mind racing. A thousand thoughts collide, but one stands out—I'm going to be a father.

I take a deep breath, my eyes never leaving hers. "Pregnant," I say, tasting the word, trying to wrap my head around it. "We're having a baby?"

She nods, her smile widening, a mixture of hope and fear in her eyes.

A laugh bursts out of me. "Holy shit. Are you serious?" I ask, grinning, unable to contain this weird sense of happiness.

She nods again. "I don't want you to stay with me just for the baby, Leo. And if this isn't what you want, I completely understand. I know you've never wanted kids… this wasn't in the plans…" she trails off.

"God, no." I grab her face and kiss her. "Don't ever think that. I'm with you, babe. It's not that I've not wanted kids, I've never had anyone to have kids with. And I know this is a surprise, and holy hell, I'm in shock! But we're in this together… I've got you. I'm scared to death, but I'm strangely fucking excited, I think." My hand presses against my forehead as I roll onto my back. "I'm going to be a dad. This is crazy." I laugh at the ceiling, feeling a mix of fear and exhilaration.

She grins, and I kiss her again, neither of us able to stop smiling.

"Are you serious? You're sure? Don't joke with me on this," she exclaims.

"I would never. I'm sure. Let's fucking do this, yeah?" I say, looking into her eyes, feeling more certain than ever.

Her eyes glisten as she squeezes my hand. "Yeah. We're in this together… All the way."

I pull her into my arms, holding her close, letting this new reality settle in.

At this moment, everything changes, it feels right. And I'm fucking ready.

"How far along are you?" I ask.

"About eight weeks."

"And how are you feeling about it all—emotionally and physically?" I stroke her hair, my fingers tracing soothing patterns down her back, offering comfort as she speaks.

"Hmm, I've been a little nauseous, throwing up occasionally, which is never fun. I'm nervous… but I'm excited too. I've had a few weeks to process it all, and I'm really happy about it." She takes a deep breath, exhaling slowly. "Knowing that you're in this with me—that we can do this together—makes it feel a little less scary."

I tilt her jaw up with my thumb and kiss her deeply, a surge of gratitude coursing through me.

She's the best fucking thing that ever happened to me.

I step into the shower's steam, the hot water pelting my skin. *God* it feels good after a day of travel—though I'd be fine never washing Vivian's scent off me. The shower is massive, easily fifteen feet long, with seven shower heads and benches lining two of the walls. I stand under the large waterfall shower head, closing my eyes as the water runs over my face. The door opens, and I turn to see Vivian turning on a shower head at the other end.

I swipe water from my eyes and start toward her, but she shakes her head, lips curving into a smirk.

"No, no," she says. "You stay put. This is my shower area. You're in a watch-only zone."

Intrigued, I do as she says. She bites her bottom lip, her hand drifting to her stomach. Slowly, she glides it up, inching toward her breasts. She squeezes one, her moan echoing off the tiles as she tips her head back under the water. Her other hand pushes her hair back, water cascading down her face. When she tilts her head back down, her eyes lock on mine. She drags a hand to the back of her neck, gripping it as she pulls her hair forward and slides her hand across her tits, pinching a nipple.

I'm entranced. I feel like I'm fourteen again, watching a porno for the first time. Where's the damn popcorn? My cock stands at attention, throbbing and aching.

Seeing her like this does things to me. Her slick, wet skin, the sounds she's making, the way she touches herself... *good God, the touching.* Her hand slides lower, finding her wet, delicious pussy. It's my undoing as I watch her fingers glide over her slit and circle her clit. She lets out a throaty moan, and I can't take it anymore. I grab my cock, stroking hard, but I don't want to jerk off. I want her—want her to touch me and, *fuck,* I want to touch her.

Before she can protest, I move, pressing her up against the wall, crushing my lips to hers.

"You fucking tease," I rasp in her ear.

She laughs, low and wicked, "You're supposed to be watching."

"No more watching," I say, slipping a finger inside her, curling deep. She cries out.

"Shit," she breathes.

She takes my tongue into her mouth, her hand gripping the base of my cock, stroking it hard. My fingers work her while she strokes me, and we're a rough tangle of tongues, moans and groping. She rakes her nails down my back, sending a shiver straight to my dick. I spank her ass, and she tugs my cock, making me groan deeply.

She trails kisses down my pecs, her mouth moving lower until she takes me in. I hiss through my teeth. The sight of her kneeling, water pouring over her, my cock in her mouth—it's enough to push me over the edge.

"Fuck, babe, I'm gonna come if you keep doing that."

She takes me deeper, and I steady myself against the wall with one hand. But I don't want to come yet. I pull back, yank her up, and spin her around. Wrapping an arm around her waist, I kiss her neck, scraping my teeth against her skin while my fingers find her clit again, circling it. She arches into me, gasping, backing her ass up against me, positioning me at her entrance. I oblige. She bends over, bracing herself on the bench as I drive into her hard. Her moans ricocheting off the shower walls, combined with the hot spray against my skin, and the tight grip of her pussy around me—it's all a sensory overload. *Feels so fucking good.* She braces one hand against the wall while the other moves to her clit, rubbing herself fast and desperate.

She cries out, "Fuck. Oh God," as she clenches around me, and I come with her. My legs quiver, about to pull out, but then I remember—she's pregnant, and I can come inside her. It feels way too good to leave her pussy.

When we finish, I pull out, my legs weak, and she collapses to the bench, spent.

"Holy fuck," I exhale, trying to catch my breath.

We make eye contact, both breathless and grinning, and Vivian starts laughing, which makes me laugh too. She stands, wraps her arms around my neck, and kisses me softly. "I love you," she whispers.

I let out a deep breath, "I love you, too."

We stand there like naked fools in love, holding each other close and kissing for what feels like forever, the water pouring down around us. I fucking love this day. And I love her even more.

* * * * * * * * * *

We're able to pull ourselves from each other long enough to get dressed and meet in the kitchen for dinner.

Vivian whips up some chicken tacos. I'm famished from my long morning of travel and all the calories burned from our afternoon of sex. I mash some avocados for fresh guac while Viv chops the fixings.

"I have an appointment in ten days, if you want to come to that," she says, scraping tomatoes from the cutting board into a bowl. "I don't know how long you're planning to stay."

"I'll be there. I'll be at every appointment," I say, shaking some salt and garlic into the mashed avocados. The chicken sizzles in the background on the stove, its savory aroma mixing with the fresh scent of cilantro and lime. "But how long are you planning to stay here? Wouldn't it be best to establish a doctor in Chicago?" I ask, genuinely curious.

"Yeah… you're probably right. I hadn't really thought about that because I've just been here. I didn't know you'd come out, and obviously, now things have changed." She scowls at the cutting board. "I might not be able to get in at ten weeks if I change things now. I'll get some referrals and research doctors in Chicago this weekend, and call first thing Monday morning."

"Have you told your mum?"

"No, I haven't told anyone but you and Sarah. It's still early on; I'd want to wait a few more weeks." She stops chopping and turns to me, hesitant. "I'm supposed to have family dinner tomorrow night at my parents'… will you come? My mom's practically in love with you herself; she'll be dying to meet you."

I laugh. "Your mum's in love with me?"

"Oh my God, yes," she says, dramatically rolling her eyes. "Not how I love you, obviously, but it's annoying. She's had this *feeling* that you were going to come around someday. You should have seen her at Christmas, asking if I'd called or texted you. She's been obsessed with the idea of us since I met you."

"I like her already," I say, giving her a playful nudge. "What about your dad?"

"Oh, my dad's another story," she says, cocking an eyebrow. "You'll have to convince him to like you for sure."

"Challenge accepted," I say, chuckling.

I move to heat the tortillas, crisping them just a bit in some butter on the stove. When everything is ready, I take a look in the fridge and grab the two items I'm looking for. I start squeezing them into one of the small bowls Vivian has out for the toppings.

"What are you doing?" Vivian asks, her brows furrowed.

"I'm making my special taco sauce. You're going to love it."

"That's not taco sauce; that's fry sauce. And fry sauce doesn't belong on a taco."

"I don't know what the hell fry sauce is, babe, but this is taco sauce, and it will elevate the experience of the taco."

She laughs. "I'm not putting fry sauce on my taco. That's a Utah thing—ketchup and mayonnaise. It's been used and served as fry sauce forever here."

"No," I rebut, "this is the Weston taco sauce. It's been made for generations for tacos. I'm serious, it's so good. Once you go Weston taco sauce, you'll never go back."

Needing to prove it to her, I fix up a taco, holding it to her mouth. "Take a bite, babe."

She backs away. "No, I'm not eating fry sauce on a taco. It's an abomination!"

I keep my taco steady in front of her mouth as she maneuvers away, laughing. She gets backed up against a wall, and I playfully shove a corner of the taco into her mouth. She takes a bite, chews thoughtfully, and curses under her breath, trying to hold back a smile.

"Ha! I knew you'd like it! How's that humble pie taste? You want some more?"

She just laughs, takes a drink of her water and proceeds to make her taco, using the sauce. "I feel like I'm cheating on fry sauce," she says, glancing in my direction. "Remind me, by the way, never to marry you. After that spectacle, you'll be the guy who smashes the cake in the bride's face."

We're quiet for a moment while we meticulously put together our tacos.

"No." I stop what I'm doing. "I would never do that."

She looks at me confused.

"I would never smash the cake in your face, babe." Turning back to my taco, I add, "I just thought you should know that."

She pauses, her expression softening. "Good to know," she says, a hint of a smile playing on her lips. "But I'm still keeping an eye on you."

I grin, "Fair enough."

As we finish making our tacos, I can't help but think that moments like this are what make life so damn great.

The next day

"I'm just warning you, my dad can be a lot," she says nervously as we walk up the porch steps to her parents' home.

It's a beautiful house, backed up against a mountainside with a gorgeous view of trees and mountain peaks.

"His job can be really stressful. When he's home, he becomes completely unhinged."

I laugh. "What do you mean?"

"I don't know. I can't explain it. He just gets weird. He'll belt out songs and make inappropriate jokes or comments. It drives my mom nuts, but I think she loves it at the same time." She pauses to laugh. "You'll see what I mean."

She reaches for the door handle, opening the oversized oak door. Stepping inside, we're immediately greeted by Vivian's mom as she sweeps Vivian into a hug, then turns to me with her arm extended.

"Hi Leo, I'm Jackie. I've heard so much about you," she says, giving a side glance to Vivian. "It's nice to finally meet you."

"Likewise, it's great to be here. Thank you for having me."

"Wow, you really are as handsome as Vivian has made you out to be," Jackie says, looking back and forth between the two of us.

"You hear that, Viv? Apparently, I'm handsome," I tease, nudging her.

She rolls her eyes. "God, Mom, don't stroke his ego. It'll go to his head."

"Keep it in your pants, Jackie!" Vivian's dad yells from the couch.

Jackie sighs. "Excuse him," she says, rolling her eyes.

"See what I mean?" Vivian whispers to me, laughing softly and shaking her head at her dad.

She leads us into the kitchen. Vivian's dad is on the couch, intently watching golf. The final match of The Open is on today. I catch a glimpse of Justin Rose on the leaderboard, a fellow Englishman, and I can't help but look longingly at the game.

Vivian notices. "You can watch, babe," she offers with a smile. "I'm out. I only watch if Rory's playing."

"Oh, I know how you've got a thing for Rory, babe," I tease, nudging her playfully.

She laughs. "Well, I wouldn't *not* put him on my list."

"Paul!" Jackie calls from across the kitchen. "Get your butt off the couch, and come meet Leo."

Paul gets up, casting a longing glance at the TV before making his way toward us. He enters the kitchen, his expression shifting from reluctant to welcoming as he greets us.

He comes to me first, and I extend my hand. "Mr. Stone, I'm Leo. It's a pleasure to meet you."

He shakes my hand firmly, nodding. "Please, call me Paul." He then turns to Vivian, opening his arms. "Viv, my little star," he says warmly. She folds into her dad's arms, and he kisses the top of her head. It's sweet and touching to see her dad embrace her with such affection.

"Mom, do you need any help?" Vivian asks.

"No, honey, you and Leo go enjoy yourselves. Dinner will be ready in about twenty minutes."

"You sure?" she insists.

Her mom gives her a pointed look, and Vivian shrugs. "Okay, thanks, Mom."

"Do you want to watch golf?" she asks me, gesturing to where her dad is settled back on the couch, the low hum of the game filling the room.

"Yeah, in a bit," I say, glancing around. "Give me a tour. Is this the house you grew up in?"

Vivian nods, her eyes bright with a mix of nostalgia and pride. "Yep." She takes my hand and guides me through the house. The home, while older, has modern updates—sleek lines and minimalist décor. Family photos and expensive-looking artwork hang on the walls, and the smell of a delicious meal fills the air. I notice the photos of Vivian growing up, each one capturing her beauty, even as a teenager.

We take the stairs to the second floor, where the railing opens up to the airy living room below. We navigate down another hall, arriving at a room at the end.

Vivian pauses, "This is my room," she says, opening the door as we step inside. The room features hardwood floors like the rest of the house, a large gray and white rug, and a queen-sized bed. An oversized modern light fixture hangs in the center of the room, and framed artwork decorates the wall above the headboard. In one corner, a plant stands tall, and two nightstands, each with a lamp, sit beside the bed.

I smile. "I take it you've had a hand in decorating this room?"

Her arms are crossed as she smiles smugly, nodding with pride.

"Please tell me it hasn't always been this pretty and that you had a normal kid's room," I tease.

She laughs. "I did. We redid the room entirely about twelve years ago, and then I redecorated it a few years back."

"When can we christen it?" I joke.

She wraps her arms around my neck. "How about now?" she says seductively, pressing her lips to mine and pulling away with a soft tug on my bottom lip.

"Babe, we can't. Your parents are downstairs."

"Yes, they are," she says, kissing me again, more fervently this time.

I laugh, unable to tell if she's serious. "Babe, you better back away, or I'm going to take you right here, right now."

She presses her body against me, toying with the hair at the nape of my neck, and kisses me seductively, egging me on.

I match her intensity, and we make out heatedly in her bedroom for several minutes.

Remembering that we are in her parent's home, and this is my first time meeting them, I pull back.

"Damn, you drive me crazy, you know that?" I say, smirking. "We should get back to your parents before they come looking for us."

"You might want to give it a few minutes," she says with a mischievous grin, eyeing my boner. "Better think of a turn off real quick," she says, laughing. "How about Gary and Brenda naked… or my parents having sex?" she offers up freely.

"Jesus, now I won't be able to look them in the eye at dinner," I say chuckling.

"Come on, let's go." She gestures to the door, and we join her parents at the dinner table, where Vivian and her mom talk about all the latest Park City gossip, and her dad and I chat about The Open, keeping one eye on the TV throughout the meal.

Her dad is hilarious and has me laughing on multiple occasions.

After dinner and clean-up, we play a game of *Cards Against Human-ity*, which has me rolling on the floor with laughter. These people are so cool, and when Vivian's mom wins by playing a card that reads *My mother's double-sided dildo*, we die laughing.

We stay until late in the evening, chatting around the dining room ta-ble. When we say our farewells, Vivian's mom pulls me into a hug as if I'm her own son. It triggers a pang of sadness in me, knowing my own mother never hugged me like this.

As we leave, I can't help but feel a sense of belonging that I've rarely experienced. I squeeze Vivian's hand a little tighter, grateful for her and for the life we're about to build together.

* * * * * * * * * *

"My parents loved you," Vivian remarks, as I navigate us home in the rental car.

"They're really great," I reply, my eyes flicking to her briefly before returning to the road. "Glad I managed to win them over."

"Well, it's not difficult to like you."

I reach over and take her hand, letting it rest in mine on the middle console. Her skin feels smooth and soft against mine. "Your dad is seri-ously hilarious. I can see where you get your humor," I say, stealing an-other glance at her.

She laughs. "Isn't he the best?"

"Yeah, he really is, and your mum's incredibly kind and fun too. You're really lucky. You've hit the bloody jackpot with your parents."

I feel her gaze on me, a steady warmth that I catch in my peripheral vision.

"You're going to be a really great dad," she says, giving my hand a reassuring squeeze. "I have no doubt about it."

A great dad. The thought hits me with a mix of excitement and sheer bloody terror. What if I fail? What if I fuck it all up?

But then I look at Viv, her eyes brimming with trust and certainty. She believes in me. With her by my side, maybe I can become the dad I want to be.

"Thanks, babe," I murmur, squeezing her hand. "I have no doubt you'll be an incredible mum."

"Ahh, can we move to London, so our kids will call me '*Mum*' and have an adorable British accent?" she teases, grinning at me.

Chuckling, I pull into the driveway and shift the car into park. Bringing her hand to my lips, I kiss it softly, feeling the warmth of her skin, then look at her adoringly. "Babe, you're so close to your parents. Are you thinking about raising the baby here, near them? You know, for their support and everything?" The faint smell of Vivian's perfume mixed with something uniquely her hangs in the air, and the distant chirping of crickets sounds in the background.

"I don't know," she says, leaning back in her seat and resting her head. She turns to look at me. "I think about it a lot, but I haven't really focused on being here because you were always in the picture. Your life is in Chicago, and part of mine is there too. I'd never want to uproot your life just for me."

I squeeze her hand gently. "I know you wouldn't, but I'd move for you… for our family," I reply, my voice steady and sincere.

"I know, and that's why I love you, but I can't ask that. You have your work, your clients, Meredith, and all your other friends—they're your family."

"But I'm not starting a family with them, babe. They're not my future. You are, and this baby is." I pause, feeling the weight of my words as I say things I never thought I'd say, and consider the possibility of living here. "Do you think your father-in-law would sell this house?"

Her eyes widen with surprise. "You'd want to buy it?"

I nod. "I'd do anything for you. I know how much you love this house. As you should—it's incredible, and you designed it. You did an amazing job."

She hesitates, "I don't know. It's possible he would sell it to me, but it would be very pricey."

"I'm not worried about the price. It's worth looking into. Even if it means splitting time between here and Chicago."

Her eyes search mine. "You really mean that, don't you?"

"Of course I do. This house or my place in Chicago… they're just details. What matters is us and our future family."

A smile slowly spreads across her face. "I love you. I wouldn't want to do this with anyone else."

"I love you too, babe," I say, pulling her into a kiss. Her lips part, and my tongue strokes gently against hers.

We pull apart but our faces stay close, her eyes searching mine. The weight of our future presses gently against us, and for the first time, it feels less daunting and more like a promise.

"We've got this," I whisper, my heart swelling with hope. She nods, her eyes shining with a mix of determination and love that makes my own resolve stronger. I'm not just stepping into this unknown with her; I'm stepping into it with a clear sense of purpose and a deep, unshakeable connection.

We step out of the car, hand in hand, walking towards the house that might just be our future home. The night air feels crisp and promising, and every step feels like a step towards something real and lasting. Together, we are ready to build something truly beautiful, and this is just the beginning of our next adventure.

Epilogue

VIVIAN

Saturday, November 2

I stare blankly out the window of my office, my eyes drifting over the vibrant colors of the changing leaves on the trees below. Fall in Park City brings a comforting sense of tranquility. A hot cappuccino sits on my desk beside a sheet of paper and a pen, with a tissue box nearby for the tears I occasionally dab from my eyes.

It's mine and Ben's wedding anniversary, and as I write him my letter this year, I can't help but look back on the past year with gratitude. This day will always be hard, filled with bittersweet memories. But this year, I have Leo to love me through it.

I place a hand on my growing belly, feeling the gentle flutter of the baby girl inside, and look down at the paper to see what I have written so far.

Dear Ben,

It's been a year since I last wrote to you, and still, not a day goes by that I don't miss you and the dreams we once shared.

The past few years have been incredibly tough. There were moments I doubted if I would ever find happiness again or if I could ever love someone as deeply as I loved you.

So much has changed since you left. Leo and I are building a beautiful life together, and soon we'll welcome our baby into this world. Our days are filled with so much love and joy. I wish you could see it.

I believe you'd like Leo. Sometimes I picture the two of you golfing together with my dad, shooting the shit like old friends. It's a comforting thought.

I glance at the ring on my finger, a symbol of Leo's love and our future together. He gave it to me last month in Hawaii, taking me to a secluded beach where a blanket was spread out on the sand with a bottle of champagne. The setting was beautiful and perfect, just like the moment. Leo wanted to make me a promise—it wasn't a proposal, but he wanted to show me he was committed to our little family and the future we're building together.

I miss you. This time of year brings so much nostalgia with our anniversary and the holidays. I always think of our first kiss on Halloween. We went to Rachel Hansen's Halloween party up by Deer Valley as Barbie and Ken—pretty sure that was all my idea, and you went along with it to appease me. You wore a perfect Ken outfit and kept a straight face all night. I couldn't stop laughing. Several of the senior kids were stripping down to their underwear and jumping into the heated pool. We went outside to watch. It was freezing that night, and you offered me your coat. I snuggled into its warmth, I distinctly remember it smelling like you. You told me I was beautiful and brought your hand up to my cheek. I remember holding my breath.

Then you looked into my eyes and kissed me. The cold air disappeared, and all I could think about was that you were it for me, Ben. The only one I ever wanted to love.

Obviously, things are different now. You're no longer here, and I had to move forward in life without you. I used to be so angry with you for leaving me, for abandoning our dreams. The pain of missing you was unbearable, like a constant ache that never went away.

I move forward, but I will not move on. You will always have a place in my heart, my past, and my memories.

I have grown so much over the past year. I have learned to love you, to make room for loving others, and to be loved in return. Just as you don't run out of tears, you don't run out of room for love—you just make more space for it, and it grows with you. You hold my heart in the past, and Leo holds my heart for the future. I love you both more than I ever knew I could.

I have no regrets, Ben. We had a beautiful life together, you were my best friend and my first love. I will never forget you.

Love always, Vivian.

Happy, sad, and bittersweet tears stream down my face as I hear Leo come into the room. "Hey babe," he says, pausing for a moment to take in the scene. He quietly walks over and stands behind me, placing a kiss on my cheek. He gently places his hands on my shoulders, rubbing them softly. "Writing to Ben?" he asks, glancing at the letter.

I nod, wiping my eyes. "Yeah, just reminiscing about old times."

Leo gives my shoulders a gentle squeeze. "He was lucky to have you, babe. Can I read it?"

I smile through my tears, nodding, feeling the comfort of his presence.

He picks up the letter and reads it. "This is really great, love," he says, setting the letter down and pulling me up to him. He wraps his arms around me, holding me tight.

"You always know how to make me feel better, especially when I'm a mess," I sigh out.

He leans down and kisses the top of my head. "That's because I love you, mess and all." Then he gently takes my chin, tipping my face toward him, and locks our lips in a deep, meaningful kiss that sends a flood of warmth to my core, swirling around its center.

He looks at me with a soft smile. "How about we take a walk, Walker? Get some fresh air?" he suggests with a playful tone, rubbing my back gently.

A slow smile spreads across my face, and I laugh softly. Pulling back, I place my hand in his, interlocking our fingers. He gives it a reassuring squeeze, and I squeeze it back, feeling so much gratitude for the two men who taught me how to love.

Vivian's Playlists

2012 Senior Year:

1. "Somebody That I Used To Know" – Gotye
2. "Call Me Maybe" – Carly Rae Jepsen
3. "Wild Ones" – Flo Rida
4. "Payphone" – Maroon 5
5. "Titanium" – David Guetta & Sia
6. "Beez In The Trap" – Nicki Minaj
7. "Diamonds" – Rihanna
8. "Just Give Me A Reason" – Pink
9. "Burn It Down" – Linkin Park
10. "Whistle" – Flo Rida

Between The Sheets:

1. "I Don't Wanna Live Forever" – ZAYN & Taylor Swift
2. "Slow Hands" – Niall Horan
3. "Love U Like That" – Lauv
4. "Bloodstream" – Ed Sheeran
5. "Bom Bidi Bom" – Nick Jonas & Nicki Minaj
6. "Sacrifice" – Black Atlass & Jessie Reyez
7. "Unsteady" – X Ambassadors
8. "Talking Body" – Tove Lo
9. "Fortnight" – Taylor Swift & Post Malone
10. "South Of The Border" – Ed Sheeran

Pre-Party:

1. "Best Friend" – Saweetie
2. "Super Freaky Girl" – Nicki Minaj
3. "The Way I Are" – Timbaland
4. "Body" – Megan Thee Stallion
5. "Up" – Cardi B
6. "Yeah!" – Usher, Lil. Jon & Ludacris
7. "Go Girl" – Pitbull
8. "Got Money" – Lil Wayne & T-Pain
9. "Low" – Flo Rida
10. "Downtown" – Macklemore & Ryan Lewis

Cold & Gray:

1. "Glycerine" – Bush
2. 'Scar Tissue" – Red Hot Chili Peppers
3. "The Difference" – Matchbox Twenty
4. "Makes Me Wonder" – Maroon 5
5. "Longview" – Green Day
6. "In The End" – Linkin Park
7. "Snow (Hey Oh)" – Red Hot Chili Peppers
8. "Bring Me To Life" – Evanescence
9. "One Headlight" – The Wallflowers
10. "December" – Collective Soul

Big Lift Energy:

1. "Till I Collapse" – Eminem
2. "Lovin On Me" – Jack Harlow
3. "Wow." – Post Malone
4. "Industry Baby" – Lil Nas X & Jack Harlow
5. "Gas Pedal" – Sage The Gemini
6. "Killer (Remix)" – Eminem, Jack Harlow & Cordae
7. "Hot Revolver" – Lil Wayne
8. "GHOST" – Jack Harlow
9. "I'm Good (Blue)" – David Guetta & Bebe Rexha
10. "River" – Eminem & Ed Sheeran

Paris – Curated By Leo:

1. "Say You Won't Let Go" – James Arthur
2. "Falling Like The Stars" – James Arthur
3. "Something To Remember" – Matt Hansen
4. "Someone You Loved" – Lewis Capaldi
5. "Love The Hell Out Of You" – Lewis Capaldi
6. "Perfect" – Ed Sheeran
7. "Can I Be Him" – James Arthur
8. "Shallow" – Lady Gaga & Bradley Cooper
9. "Beautiful Things" - Benson Boone
10. "Eyes Closed" – Ed Sheeran

Acknowledgments

First and foremost, my deepest thanks go to my husband, who made all of this possible. Not only did you believe in and support this wild dream of mine, but you also picked up the slack when I was so deeply immersed in writing that my duties as a mother and wife sometimes fell short. Babe, I love you more than you know.

To my beta readers and best friends, thank you for your unwavering support and enthusiasm for this journey. In no particular order: Sydney Lambert, Alycia Haslam, Nikole Allred, Natalie Peacock, Danielle Knox, Ashleigh Johnstun, Kelli Hamilton, Kara Olson, and Alley Carsey. And to Kyle Carsey, Tyler Allred, and Luke Hamilton for providing valuable feedback from a male perspective.

A special thank you to my editor, Celia Killen, who not only provided me with the most valuable feedback and helped shape this book into what it is today, but also offered the kindest and most encouraging words about this story. I couldn't have done it without you.

To my beautiful children, thank you for your patience as I holed up with my laptop for hours on end. I love you with all of my heart.

To my sister, who became a young widow while I was in the middle of writing this book—you are one of the strongest people I know.

To my friend Natalie, a young widow and therapist, thank you for offering such valuable insight into the raw vulnerabilities young widows face every day, as well as your perspective on crafting Leo as a therapist. While his portrayal doesn't fit perfectly within the traditional scope of a psychologist, I've done my best to create a believable therapist with a deeply emotional past, all while maintaining an engaging story. You are one of the wittiest and most resilient people I know. And thank you for gifting me those perfect lines for Vivian to use in this story. You know which ones they were.

To the person who lent me *It Ends With Us*—you know who you are. Thank you for helping me rediscover my love for books. And to Colleen Hoover, for writing stories I fell in love with.

Thank you to Meghan Quinn. Your book *A Not So Meet Cute* inspired and gave me the courage to write my own story.

And to James Arthur—your music wasn't just a source of inspiration, it was the perfect backdrop to Leo and Vivian's story. There were moments when I could almost hear your songs playing during their scenes, especially "Say You Won't Let Go," and "Falling Like The Stars," which was all I could hear during their Paris yacht scene.

And finally, to you, the reader—thank you for believing in me and giving this book a chance. I hope these characters have found a place in your heart as they have in mine.

About The Author

Erin Cornia lives in Austin with her husband, two children, and two mini golden doodles. She rediscovered her passion for reading after a long break when *It Ends With Us* by Colleen Hoover fell into her hands. Now, she has a deep love for romance novels—contemporary, fantasy, and historical alike.

Some of her favorite authors include Sarah J. Maas, Colleen Hoover, Meghan Quinn, Tessa Bailey, Judith McNaught, and Elle Kennedy, with *Throne of Glass* by Sarah J. Maas holding the spot as her favorite series of all time.

When she's not reading or writing, she enjoys traveling, playing pickleball, and spending time outdoors. You can often find her watching *Schitt's Creek*, *Sex and the City*, or *Emily in Paris*—with a bowl of home-made popcorn.

Instagram: @erincornia_author

Facebook Reader Group: Erin Cornia: Romance, Heartbreak, Healing & Hard Earned HEAs

TikTok: @erincornia_author